UNWELCOME VISITOR

Out of the corner of his eye, Han could see the ventral laser cannon pop out of its recess and blaze away. The cannon swept along the cases from starboard to port, herding their visitor toward Han. The cases blew apart under the withering fire.

And suddenly, in the flashing strobelike bursts of the laser cannon, it was bright enough for Han to see the thing he was chasing.

A probe droid, an old-style Imperial probot, floated in midair not ten meters from him, its eight cruel-looking sensor arms hanging down from its rounded central body. The laser cannon stopped firing and darkness returned. No doubt Chewie didn't want to risk shooting Han. Thoughtful of him.

Even without the laser fire, the packing cases were burning bright enough for Han to see his adversary. But if Han could see the probe droid, the probe droid could see him. One of its arms swung around, aiming a built-in blaster dead at him.

AMBUSH AT CORELLIA

Book One of the Corellian Trilogy

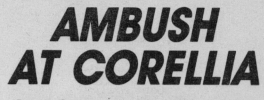

Roger MacBride Allen

BANTAM BOOKS

New York   Toronto   London   Sydney   Auckland

AMBUSH AT CORELLIA

A Bantam Spectra Book / March 1995

ISBN 0-553-29803-8

Published simultaneously in the United States and Canada

Bantam Books are published by Bantam Books, a division of Bantam Doubleday
Dell Publishing Group, Inc. Its trademark, consisting of the words ''Bantam Books''
and the portrayal of a rooster, is Registered in U.S. Patent and Trademark Office
and in other countries. Marca Registrada. Bantam Books, 1540 Broadway, New
York, New York 10036.

PRINTED IN THE UNITED STATES OF AMERICA

OPM 0 9 8 7 6 5 4 3

To Kathei and Taylor,
as they start their own adventure

Author's Note

I would like to thank Betsy Mitchell for thinking of me for this project, and I'd like to thank Tom Dupree for sticking with me. I would also like to thank all the good people of Lucasfilm, but most especially Sue Rostoni, who inundated me with helpful information. I would also like to thank *Star Wars* colleagues Kevin Anderson, Kathy Tyers, Dave Wolverton, Vonda McIntyre, and Tim Zahn severally and individually. I received much sage advice, and borrowed a character or two. Likewise a nod to Heather McConnell, whose suggestions led me straight to Q9-X2.

On a more personal level, I would like to thank my wife, Eleanore Maury Fox, for putting up with a great deal of writing in the midst of a spring and summer that were already rather crowded with events. For example, somewhere in the middle of our travels through the list of places below, we got married. Her notes on the manuscript vastly improved the book you hold in your hands. In a similar vein, I would like to thank my parents, Tom and Scottie Allen, and my brand-new in-laws, David Fox and Elizabeth Maury, for incredible generosity and tolerance above and beyond the call of duty.

Just for the record, this book was written, somehow, between April 1, 1994, and September 20, 1994, and it was written in the following places, in this approximate order: Lisbon, Portugal; the train from Lisbon to Coimbra; in flight, Lisbon to London; in London; in the London Underground; in flight, Washington, D.C. to London; in flight, London to Washington, D.C.; New York City; Washington, D.C.; Tyson's Corner, Virginia; Arlington, Virginia; Bethesda, Maryland; Border's Bookshop, McLean, Virginia; Fresno, California; Ashland, Oregon; Nordstrom Department Store, Portland, Oregon; Winnipeg, Canada; the National Foreign Affairs Training Center, Arlington, Virginia; and Charlottesville, Virginia.

As the song says: "What a long strange trip it's been."

ROGER MACBRIDE ALLEN
September 1994
Arlington, Virginia

AMBUSH AT CORELLIA

CHAPTER ONE

Visible Secrets

All right, Chewie, try it now.'' Han Solo stuffed the comlink back in his pocket and stepped back a bit from the *Millennium Falcon*, an anxious look on his face. It *ought* to work this time. But that was what they had figured the time before, and the time before that. He could see into the *Falcon*'s cockpit viewports from where he stood, and Chewbacca didn't look all that confident, either. He saw Chewbacca reach for the lift controls. Han realized that he had been holding his breath, and forced himself to exhale.

The *Millennium Falcon* shifted slightly on her hard stand, then rose slowly into the evening air. Chewie took her up until the landing pads were at Han's eye level, and held her there.

Han pulled out the comlink again and spoke into it. ''That's good,'' he said. ''Good. Now engage the shields.'' The air all around the *Falcon* seemed to shimmer a bit, and then steadied down.

Han stepped back just a bit farther, not wishing to be all *that* close when Chewie cut the repulsors. ''All right, Chewie, repulsors—off!''

The glow of the repulsors dimmed, and the *Falcon* dropped abruptly—and stopped, suspended in midair, with the landing pads waist-high off the ground. Sparks and scintillations flared and flickered here and there on the hard stand as the shields' energy webs shifted under stress.

"Good," Han said. "Very good." Short of firing a turbo-laser at the ship from point-blank range, it was about as good a field test of overall shield strength as you could ask for. If the shields could support the weight of the ship, then they could—

Suddenly the sparking grew brighter, fiercer, just under the number-two landing pad. "Chewie! Repulsors on! It's going to—"

With a shuddering flash of light, the rear shields blew out. The aft landing pads slammed into the hard stand with a bone-rattling impact that sent Han sprawling. The forward end of the ship hung in midair as the rear half bounced on its jacks, back up into the air.

Just as the rear of the ship was at the peak of its travel, the forward shields died. In the same instant the forward repulsors flared to life. The rear repulsors came on, lighting a split second after the forward units, and flickering a bit. Getting slammed into the pavement like that hadn't done the rear repulsor coils any good, that was for sure. Still, Chewie had timed the recovery nicely. Han had seen ships flipped onto their backs trying to recover from a failed shield hover.

Chewie brought the *Falcon* back down to a gentle landing and cut the repulsors. A moment later the gangway lowered itself and Chewie came out, clearly none too happy with the situation. He made a loud bugling noise, turned back up the gangway, and returned a moment later carrying a shield-tuning set.

That was not good. After all the years Han had spent with Chewie, he knew better than to let a frustrated Wookiee vent his feelings on a repair job. He was just as likely to tear the shield generator out by the roots as he was to retune it. "Ah, maybe that's not such a good idea, Chewie. Leave it for now. We'll come back to it tomorrow."

Chewbacca roared and threw the tool kit down.

"I know, I know, I know," Han said. "It's taking longer than it should, and you're tired of tweaking up subsystems that we optimized last week. But that's the way it is on a ship like the *Falcon*. She's a finely tuned instrument. Everything affects everything else. Adjust one system and everything else reacts. The only way not to go through this would be to scrap her and start over—and you don't want to scrap the *Falcon*, do you?"

Chewie looked back toward the ship with an expression that told Han not to press his luck on that point. The Wookiee had never felt as deeply for the *Falcon* as Han had, and even Han knew the old girl would have to be retired someday. Sooner or later it would be the scrap heap for her—or a museum, more likely. *That* was an odd thought, but after all, the *Falcon* had made more than her share of history.

But just now the key thing was to get Chewbacca calmed down, or away from the shield system—or, preferably, both.

"Tomorrow," Han said. "Back at it tomorrow. For now, let's leave it, all right? Leia's probably waiting dinner on us, anyway."

The mention of food seemed to brighten Chewbacca up—as Han had intended that it do. Wookiee management was a full-time chore, and then some. Now and then Han wondered just how much effort Chewbacca put into Han management. But that was another point to consider later. It was time to knock off for the day.

Amazing, how times changed, how time changed life. After all the close calls, all the battles, all the captures and rescues and risks and victories Han had been through, now it came down to getting home to dinner. I'm a family man now, Han told himself, still a bit amazed by the fact. And perhaps the most amazing thing of all was how much he *liked* being one.

Han Solo looked up into the evening sky of Coruscant. What was it now? Eighteen years? Eighteen years since he had hired on to fly a crazy old man named Ben Kenobi and a kid named Luke Skywalker out of Tatooine. Taking on that job had changed his life forever—and changed the course of galactic history, if you wanted to get grandiose about it.

It was nine years since the defeat of Grand Admiral Thrawn and the Dark Jedi Master. Nine years since the birth of the twins, and just over seven since Anakin was born.

"Captain Solo?"

It was a female voice that pulled him out of his reverie. The voice was low and throaty, and came from behind him. Han did not recognize it. The unknown voice sounded *dangerous*, somehow. It was a little too quiet, too calm, too cool.

"Yeah," Han replied, turning around slowly. "My name is Solo." A small, slight, dark-skinned human, a woman, stepped out of the shadows by the hangar entrance. She wore a dark blue uniform that might be one of the Republic Navy branches, but then it might not. Han was not up-to-date on what the navy was wearing these days. "Who might you be?" he asked.

She came toward him, smiling calmly. He could see her a bit better now. She was young, maybe twenty-five standard years at most. Her eyes were set a bit wide apart, and a trifle glassy. Her gaze seemed to be a bit off-kilter, as if she were almost, but not quite, cross-eyed. She was looking right at Han, and yet he had the distinct impression that she was looking over his shoulder, into the middle distance—or into the next galaxy over. Her jet-black hair was done up in an elaborate braid that was coiled on top of her head.

She walked toward him with an easy confidence that seemed to brook no discussion. "Glad to meet you," she said. "You can call me Kalenda."

"All right," Han said. "I can call you Kalenda. So what?"

"So I have a job for you," she said.

That brought Han up short. A job? He was about to reply with some sort of flip remark, but then he stopped. That didn't make sense. She obviously knew who Han was—

which was not much of an accomplishment, as Han and Leia and Luke were famous throughout the Republic. But if she knew who he was, she would *have* to know he was no longer available for casual hire. Something wasn't right. "Go on," Han said, careful to keep his voice neutral.

Kalenda shifted that strange gaze of hers so she was looking almost, but not quite, in the direction of Chewbacca. "Perhaps we should talk alone," she said quietly.

There was a low growl from Chewie, and Han did not even bother to glance over his shoulder at the Wookiee. He knew what he would see. Let Kalenda get a look at Chewie's fangs. "Perhaps we shouldn't," he said. "I don't want to hear anything you have to say that Chewbacca can't hear."

"Very well," she said. "But perhaps, at least, the *three* of us could talk in private?"

"Fine," Han said. "Come on aboard the *Falcon*."

Kalenda frowned. Clearly, she didn't like that idea either. The *Falcon* was Han's turf. "Very well," she said.

Han gestured toward the ship with a sweep of his arm, and bowed very slightly, just enough to make it clear the gesture was sarcastic. "Right this way," he said.

* * *

The probe droid hovered silently up into position, coming up over the wall of the hard stand area, then dropping in behind packing cases to keep out of sight. It was painted matte black, and was all but invisible in the deepening shadows. It watched the two humans and the Wookiee head up into the ship.

It extended an audio monitor probe and aimed it at the *Millennium Falcon*. After a moment's hesitation, it moved in closer to the ship. Doing so exposed it to a greater risk of detection, but the probe droid's masters had programmed it to place a high priority on eavesdropping on just this sort of meeting. The droid decided it would be worth the risk if its masters were able to get a good recording of the conversation that was about to happen.

*   *   *

Kalenda walked up the ramp and into the ship, Han and Chewie following. It might have been more polite to lead her aboard, but Han wanted to annoy her and he had the hunch she wasn't the sort who liked people behind her. Han could not pass up the chance to make her a bit edgy. She reached the top of the ramp and walked smoothly and confidently toward the lounge.

It took Han a moment or two to realize that she had never been aboard the ship before. She should have stopped at the top of the ramp, uncertain of where to go next. Instead she was sitting back in the cushiest seat in the lounge almost before Han and Chewie got to the compartment. She must have pulled up some set of plans from somewhere and memorized the ship's layout. She had just demonstrated how much research she had done on him, how much she knew.

All right then, fair was fair. If Han wanted to play games with her, it was only to be expected that she would play a few right back at him. "Fine," Han said as he sat down. Chewie remained standing, and just happened to be blocking the exit to the compartment. "You know everything about me, down to the blueprints of my ship," Han went on. "You have resources. You did your homework. It doesn't impress me."

"No, I suppose not," Kalenda said. "You're probably pretty hard to impress."

"I try to be," Han said. "And right now, I'd like to get home to my wife and family. What is it you wanted to see me about?"

"Your wife and family," Kalenda replied, not so much as batting an eye. Now her odd, near-off-kilter gaze seemed to lock and track perfectly, and she looked right at Han, her expression flat and hard.

Han stiffened and leaned in toward her, and Chewie

bared his fangs. His family had been exposed to too many dangers, too many times, for him to take even the hint of threat less than seriously. "Threats don't impress me either," Han said, his voice as hard as her face. "With Chewbacca around, the people who make them don't live very long. So you just pick your next words very, very carefully."

The compartment was silent for a moment, and Kalenda stared hard at Han. Their eyes locked. "I am not threatening your family," she said, her voice still expressionless. "But New Republic Intelligence would like to—make use—of them. And you."

New Republic Intelligence? What the devil was NRI doing coming to *him*? If Han was too well-known a person to do smuggling work, he was definitely too well-known to be much use as a spy. Beyond which, he didn't much like government spies, no matter who the government was. "You're not improving your survival odds," Han said. "Just how are you going to 'use' us?"

"We know you're going to Corellia," Kalenda said.

"Nice work," Han said. "You must have a crack team of researchers that check the news every single day. Our trip to Corellia is not exactly top secret." If anything, it was what passed for headline news in these quiet times. Leia was part of the Coruscant delegation to a major trade conference on the planet Corellia.

It was supposed to be the first step in reopening the whole Corellian Sector. The sector had always been an inward-looking part of the Empire, and of the Old Republic before that. By the time Han had left, Corellia had gone past inward looking to downright secretive and hermetic.

By all accounts, things hadn't improved much since the New Republic had taken over. It was rare indeed to see a mention of the Corellian Sector without words like "insular" or "paranoid" or "distrustful" popping up as well. Leia had counted it as a triumph just to get the Corellians to host the conference in the first place.

"Your wife's attendance has been reported, yes," Kalenda said. "But there has been little or no mention of *your* going along, or your children."

"What is all this about?" Han demanded. "My wife is going to a conference on my homeworld. So what? I'm going, and we're taking the kids. Be nice to show them where the old man came from. Is that a crime? Is there something suspicious about that?"

"No," Kalenda said. "Not yet. But we'd like to *make* it suspicious."

"Now you've lost me. Chewie, if the next thing she says doesn't clear things up, you get to throw her off the ship."

Chewie let out a half yelp, half howl that had the intended effect of unnerving their visitor. "That means he's looking forward to it," Han said. "So. This is your big chance to tell me, clearly and concisely, what this is all about. No more riddles."

Kalenda had lost some—but not all—of her poise. Han had to hand it to her. Even the vague notion of tangling with Chewie was enough to make most people snap. "Something's going on in the Corellian Sector," she said. "Something big, and something bad. We don't know what. All we do know is that we've sent in a half-dozen agents— and none of them have come back. None of them have even managed to report."

Han *was* impressed by that news. The NRI was, by all accounts, very, very good at what it did. It was the successor to the old networks of Rebel spies, back during the war against the Empire. Anyone or anything that could kill or capture NRI agents at will was a force to be reckoned with. "I'm sorry to hear that," he said. "But what does it have to do with my family?"

"We want to send in another team. And we want to provide cover for them. That's you."

"Look, Kalenda, or whatever your name really is. If the Corellians are as paranoid as you're saying they are, they probably suspect me already. I'm not the espionage type. I wouldn't even make a good amateur. I'm not a very subtle person. Your files aren't so good if they didn't tell you that.''

"Oh, but they did tell us that," Kalenda said. "And we didn't *need* them to tell us that, because everyone knows it already. The Corellians will be watching you like a hawk. We don't want you to *do* anything except act suspiciously.''

"I don't get it," Han said.

"We want you to act as suspiciously as possible," Kalenda said. "Give yourself a high profile. Be visible. Ask nosy, awkward questions. Offer bribes to the wrong people at the wrong time. Act like a bad amateur. We want you to draw their attention, distract them while we insert our real teams.''

"What about my family?" Han asked. "What about my children?''

"To be frank, your children have a reputation all their own. I doubt we'd even be approaching you if they weren't in the picture. We're assuming they'll cause the opposition headaches all by themselves.''

"I meant, will my children be *safe*?" Han asked. "I'm not so sure I should even be taking them if things are as bad as you say.''

Kalenda hesitated a moment. "The situation on Corellia is unsettled. There is no question about that. However, if our understanding of the situation is correct, the role we are asking you to perform will not expose them to any additional risk. Family is still held in high respect on Corellia. It is considered most dishonorable to involve innocent family members in a quarrel. You should know that.''

There was something in her tone of voice in that last answer that gave Han pause. As if she were talking about something more than planetary tradition, and something a lot closer to home. The trouble was, he had no idea what. Did the NRI know things about Han's own past that Han did not? Han looked her straight in those strange eyes of hers, and decided that he did not want to ask. "If I understand what you're saying," he said, "you believe the job you are asking me to do will not make Corellia any *more* dangerous for my children. Is that correct?''

"Yes," Kalenda said.

That didn't satisfy Han. He had the feeling that ''yes'' was a true answer, if not a complete one.

"All right, then," he said. "Now, this next question I am asking as a father, as a Corellian who believes it is dishonorable to involve the innocent. Would it be dangerous to take my children to Corellia?"

Kalenda slumped back and sighed. All the surface smugness went out of her, and Han could see doubt and uncertainty. It was as if the NRI agent had suddenly vanished and the person behind was appearing. "I give up being careful. Not when you put it that way. But I wish to the dark suns you hadn't asked me that," she said. "I honestly don't know. We simply don't *know* what's going on out there. That's why we need to do anything we can to get agents in place so we can find out. But there are children on Corellia right now. Are they in danger? Is Corellia a riskier place than Coruscant? Almost certainly, though by how much I couldn't say. On the other hand, travel all by itself is more dangerous than staying home. Maybe you should never travel at all. If avoiding all risk is your only concern, take your children and hide them away in a cave, just to be sure. But is that the way you want to live?"

Han looked deep into those strange eyes that seemed to see things that were not there. In his old days, his reckless days, he wouldn't even have thought twice about flying straight into the worst sort of danger. But fatherhood did things to a fellow. It wasn't just that he didn't want to endanger his kids. It went beyond that. He didn't want to endanger himself needlessly either. Not for fear of death on his own part—but the thought of leaving his children without a father—it was something he had to work into the equation.

But suppose he *did* put his children in a cave, and put a

round-the-clock guard on them. And suppose there was an underground rock slide? Or what if he *did* manage to protect them from all danger? What sort of life would they have? And how could they be expected to deal with a world full of risk and danger as adults if they had never faced them growing up?

There were no good answers, no certainties. Risk was a part of life, and you had to take a slice of it along with everything else. But there were questions of honor, and duty, as well. If there was trouble back home, in the sector that had given him birth, what sort of man would he be if he could help and did not?

There was yet another factor. Leia was, after all, the Chief of State. She had been getting intelligence reports about Corellia. She had to know about the situation. Very probably she even knew the specific fact that the NRI had agents gone missing. Yet she was willing to bring her children along. And that was good enough for Han.

"Thank you," Han said. "I always appreciate a straight answer. But we'll be going to Corellia—and I'll do what I can to act suspiciously. I have a feeling it will fit in with my natural talents."

"Officially, I'm glad to hear that," Kalenda said. "But unofficially—very unofficially—I wouldn't blame you if you decided not to go at all."

"We go," Han said. "We're not going to be scared away from living our life."

"Just like that?" Kalenda asked. "Without even asking any questions? The NRI doesn't have much information, but shouldn't you know what we do?"

Chewie let out a low, throaty rumble, the Wookiee equivalent of a chuckle, and then growled a retort.

"What?" Kalenda asked. "What's funny? What did he say?"

Han smiled, even if the joke was more or less at his expense. "Something to the effect that I've never been one to let facts or information interfere with my decisions. But in all seriousness, it might just be that the less I know the better. If you want me to blunder around like an ignorant fool, maybe I'd do better if I *was* ignorant.''

"We half expected you to say that," Kalenda said.

"If you know me that well, then the next thing you should be expecting me to say is that it's dinnertime and the family's waiting.''

Kalenda stood up. "Very well." She turned toward Chewbacca, who was still blocking the exit. "If your friend will excuse me?'' she asked, staring straight at Chewie. The Wookiee gave a sort of snort and let her by.

After she was gone, Chewie looked toward Han. "I know, I know," he said. "You're going to say it's none of my business. But our agents are vanishing on my turf. Is that *my* people doing that? She said something is going wrong in the Corellian Sector, my home sector. Should I just turn my back? You tell me. What should I have said?''

Chewie didn't have an answer for that one. Instead he grunted and turned back toward the cockpit. Han followed behind him to help him power down the ship.

But the Wookiee stopped dead just inside the entrance to the cockpit, and Han nearly walked up his back. "Hey!'' he cried out. "What are you—''

Chewie moved his left arm slowly back until it was behind his back. He gestured for silence with a wave of his left hand as he stared straight ahead, out the cockpit's viewport. Han froze, and tried to see around Chewbacca's looming bulk. He saw nothing, but that told him as much as he needed to know. A probe droid or a living snooper. Chewie had spotted something, some tiny movement or other. Nothing else would explain his reaction.

"What—what are we going to do about the shields?'' Han asked, trying to make it sound smooth and convincing. Chewbacca took the cue, and growled a casual-sounding answer as he plopped down into the copilot's seat. Han followed Chewie's gaze as the Wookiee scanned his panels. Han saw Chewie's eyes flicker toward the packing cases at the edge of the hard stand for just a moment. All right, then.

Han sat down in the pilot's seat and tried to think fast. Someone or something had been listening in on their little chat with Kalenda. The fact that the snooper was still out there could only mean they were hoping to hear more. Otherwise, the snooper would have pulled back the moment Kalenda was gone.

And that meant the only chance of catching the snooper would be to keep him or her or it busy until Chewie and he had managed to set something up. Better do something to sound interesting. "That sounds good on the repulsor," Han said. "But if our visitor was right, hardware glitches are going to be the least of our troubles."

Chewbacca looked toward Han in some surprise. "Oh, yeah," Han said, improvising as best he could. "With what she was saying, we're going to have a *lot* to talk about on the way home. *Lots* of profits in it for us if we play it right." That ought to be intriguing enough to keep their friends interested. Han gestured with his hands, being careful to keep them well out of view of the cockpit ports. He pointed toward himself, and waggled his first two fingers back and forth in a pantomime of walking. He pointed toward the outside of the ship, and then pantomimed pulling a trigger.

Chewie nodded very slightly, then pointed at himself, pointed down, indicating he would stay where he was, and then tapped the controls for the ventral laser cannon. Chewbacca burbled his agreement on the subject of profit and nodded a bit more emphatically for the benefit of whoever was outside.

"Listen," Han said. "You finish up the power-down, all right? I want to go take a look at the rear landing pads and see if they took any damage."

Chewie nodded. Han slipped his left hand under the pilot's chair and pulled out the small holdout blaster that he kept there. It wasn't the most powerful bit of armament, but it was small enough to hide in the palm of his hand.

Han got up and headed toward the hatch. He made his way toward the open gangway, moving at what he hoped was a nice, casual pace. If he and Chewie were better actors than he thought they were, or if their snooper was a bit more gullible than average, they would still have company.

He walked down the gangway, whistling tunelessly to himself, and paused at the bottom. He yawned and stretched in what he hoped was a convincing sort of way. He wandered over toward the port side of the ship, as if he was about to head around and look at the aft landing pad.

By doing so, he came around the side of the heap of packing cases. Anything or anyone hiding behind them would have to drift back a bit, back into the corner, in order to stay out of sight. Han swung his left hand around so his body hid it from view, and got the holdout blaster into position. He continued his leisurely walk toward the rear of the ship—and then suddenly shifted direction, started running straight toward the packing cases, moving as fast as he could, blaster at the ready.

Out of the corner of his eye, he could see the ventral laser cannon pop out of its recess and blaze away. The cannon swept along the cases from starboard to port, herding their visitor toward Han. The cases blew apart under the withering fire, lighting up the hard stand.

And suddenly, in the flashing strobelike bursts of the laser cannon, it was bright enough for Han to see the thing he was chasing.

A probe droid, an old-style Imperial probot, floated in midair not ten meters from him, its eight cruel-looking sensor arms hanging down from its rounded central body. The laser cannon stopped firing and darkness returned. No doubt Chewie didn't want to risk shooting Han. Thoughtful of him.

Even without the laser fire, the packing cases were burning bright enough for Han to see his adversary. But if Han could see the probe droid, the probe droid could see him. One of its arms swung around, aiming a built-in blaster dead at him.

Han fired without taking the time for conscious thought, and thanks either to luck or marksmanship he shot the blaster off the droid.

But the loss of its blaster didn't even slow the droid down. It brought another arm to bear, one with a cruel, needle-sharp end, and moved toward Han at speed. Han dove for the ground and rolled over on his back as it bore down on him, that needle arm reaching to skewer him through the chest. The arm jabbed down, and Han rolled out of the way just barely in time. The needle arm spiked into the permacrete and jammed there for a moment.

Han fired up at the droid, but it must have been luck on the first shot, because this time he missed completely. He squeezed the trigger again and nothing happened. The hold-out blaster's tiny energy cell had been depleted with only two shots. Han scrambled to his feet and realized he was boxed in by the sound barrier wall of the hard stand. The droid pulled its needle arm up out of the permacrete, and then turned back toward Han, ready to move in for the kill.

A single shot from the *Falcon*'s laser cannon flared out, and caught the droid square in the body. The ghastly thing crashed to the ground, and Han started breathing again.

Chewie came running up a moment later, carrying a glow rod. He pointed it at the droid as he looked at Han and let out a complicated series of snarls and burbling roars.

"I can see that," Han said. "Imperial probe droid. Twenty years old at least. Someone dug it up from somewhere and reprogrammed it."

Chewie knelt down by the droid and shone the light on it. He glanced up toward Han and yelped a question.

"Because that's not the way the Imperials programmed the things. They weren't supposed to fight, they were supposed to spy. If they got caught and couldn't run, they transmitted their data on a tight beam and self-destructed. This one tried to shoot its way out. And don't ask me what that tells us, because I don't know."

Except he did know, at least in part. It told him that someone out there was playing for keeps. What the game was, or who the players were, Han had not the slightest idea. But it had to be Corellia. It had to be.

Han stared at the dead machine by the light of the burning packing cases, and wondered what to do about the probe's carcass. The fact that it had been here at this particular time and place had some unpleasant connotations. If the NRI's agents were being followed, he certainly wasn't going to rush to them and report this little incident. No. Best keep it as quiet as possible. "No one hears about this," Han said. "Not the NRI, not Luke, not Leia. Nothing they could do about it except get upset, and there might be other listeners out there. We get rid of this thing, *fast*, clean up the mess, and that's that."

Chewbacca looked at Han and nodded his agreement.

Han knelt down next to the Wookiee and started trying to figure out *how* to get rid of the probe. Later he could worry about the other trifling problems, such as the question of who had sent the thing and why.

It occurred to Han that he really only knew two things for certain.

First, he knew that if someone out there was trying to make him not want to head for Corellia, they were going about it the wrong way. Spies and vague threats and probe droids might intimidate other men, but Han never had been much for responding to intimidation.

And second, he knew it was going to be an interesting trip.

CHAPTER TWO

Breakage and Repairs

Jaina Solo squatted down next to her younger brother and handed him one of the circuit boards. "Come on, Anakin. You can figure it out. You can make it work."

Anakin Solo, all of seven and a half years old, sat on the floor of the playroom, surrounded by broken bits of droid and rather worn-looking circuit units.

Jacen, Jaina's twin brother, had done most of the scavenging for parts, digging through the discard bins and refuse parts of all the droid repair shops and part suppliers. Jaina had done most of the mechanical assembly work, but now it was up to Anakin. All three of them were good with their hands, gifted in mechanical things—but Anakin went beyond merely being gifted.

He could fix things so they worked—even if he didn't know what they did, or what they were. It was almost as if he could see *inside* machines, read the circuit patterns of even the tiniest microscopic components—and even tempt the broken circuits to heal themselves. Outsiders would have thought it all very remarkable, and perhaps even impossible. But the twins were used to it. To them, all it meant was that Anakin could tap into a different aspect of the Force than most people. Or maybe he didn't know yet that what he did was impossible. If and when the grown-ups found out and convinced him that he could not do what he did, then perhaps the game would be over.

For now, a little brother who could make machinery and

computers sit up and beg was a most useful asset. In the past, the twins had set him to work on all sorts of jobs when they went exploring the parts of the Imperial Palace they weren't supposed to see. He had opened foolproof locks for them, made security cameras shut down at just the right moments so no one would catch them, powered up lift tubes that were supposed to be inert, and generally come in most handy in the service of his older siblings.

But that had just been wandering around the old palace. This ought to be better. This ought to be the best of all. Now they were going to have their own secret droid, with no grown-ups able to force overrides or countermand instructions, or take it away as a punishment.

Anakin stared at a bit of circuit board, and turned it over slowly in his hands. "*This* goes over *that* part," he muttered to himself. "It goes sideward."

Anakin could make himself understood when he was talking to the twins, or to the grown-ups, but not even Jaina or Jacen could make much sense of him when he talked to himself. It didn't much matter, of course. Not so long as the job got done.

Jacen watched intently as his little brother went to work. He was better with plants and animals, living things, than he was with machinery. Jaina was the twin who knew machines, the way their father did. She was forever fiddling with this bit of hardware or that, seeing what she could get her multitool to do. She and Jacen closely resembled each other, with dark brown hair and pale brown eyes. They were solid, healthy children, if not especially tall or strong for their age. Anakin was something a little different. He was small for his age, but distinctly brawny and strong. His hair was darker, and his eyes a disconcertingly cold ice-blue. It was easy to spot the family resemblance to both parents in all three children, but Anakin was the one least like anyone else in the family. And the least like anyone else, for that matter. Anakin marched to the beat of a drum that no one at all was playing.

Anakin plugged the board into the innards of the droid

and pressed a button. The droid's black, boxy body shuddered awake, it drew in its wheels to stand up a bit taller, its status lights lit, and it made a sort of triple beep. "That's good," he said, and pushed the button again. The droid's status lights went out, and its body slumped down again. Anakin picked up the next piece, a motivation actuator. He frowned at it as he turned it over in his hands. He shook his head. "That's *not* good," he announced.

"What's not good?" Jaina asked.

"This thing," Anakin said, handing her the actuator. "Can't you *tell*? The insides part is all melty."

Jaina and Jacen exchanged a look. "The outside looks okay," Jaina said, giving the part to her brother. "How can he tell what the *inside* of it looks like? It's sealed shut when they make it."

Jacen shrugged. "How can he do any of this stuff? But we need that actuator. That was the toughest part to dig up. I must have gone around half the city looking for one that would fit this droid." He turned toward his little brother. "Anakin, we don't have another one of these. Can you make it better? Can you make the insides less melty?"

Anakin frowned. "I can make it *some* better. Not all the way better. A *little* less melty. *Maybe* it'll be okay."

Jacen handed the actuator back to Anakin. "Okay, try it."

Anakin, still sitting on the floor, took the device from his brother and frowned at it again. He turned it over and over in his hands, and then held it over his head and looked at it as if he were holding it up to the light. "There," he said, pointing a chubby finger at one point on the unmarked surface. "In there is the bad part." He rearranged himself to sit cross-legged, put the actuator in his lap, and put his right index finger over the "bad" part. "Fix," he said. "Fix." The dark brown outer case of the actuator seemed to glow for a second with an odd blue-red light, but then the glow sputtered out and Anakin pulled his finger away quickly and stuck it in his mouth, as if he had burned it on something.

"Better now?" Jaina asked.

"*Some* better," Anakin said, pulling his finger out of his mouth. "Not *all* better." He took the actuator in his hand and stood up. He opened the access panel on the broken droid and plugged in the actuator. He closed the door and looked expectantly at his older brother and sister.

"Done?" Jaina asked.

"Done," Anakin agreed. "But *I'm* not going to push the button." He backed well away from the droid, sat down on the floor, and folded his arms.

Jacen looked at his sister.

"Not me," she said. "This was your idea."

Jacen stepped forward to the droid, reached out to push the power button from as far away as he could, and then stepped hurriedly back.

Once again, the droid shuddered awake, rattling a bit this time as it did so. It pulled its wheels in, lit its panel lights, and made the same triple beep. But then its camera eye viewlens wobbled back and forth, and its panel lights dimmed and flared. It rolled backward just a bit, and then recovered itself.

"Good morning, young mistress and masters," it said. "How may I surge you?"

Well, one word wrong, but so what? Jacen grinned and clapped his hands and rubbed them together eagerly. "Good day, droid," he said. They had done it! But what to ask for first? "First tidy up this room," he said. A simple task, and one that ought to serve as a good test of what this droid could do.

"Certainly, young master." The droid rolled toward a bit of junk on the floor. It extended a work arm to pick it up—and then stopped dead. Its body seemed frozen, its arm locked in place halfway toward the bit of debris.

The one thing it seemed to be able to move was its viewlens. The lens swiveled from one child to the next, and then stopped on Jacen. "Oh, dear," the droid said. "I seem to have thrun. I am afraid I yam goinn—"

The droid's voice cut out abruptly and it started rocking back and forth on its wheels.

"Uh-oh," Anakin said, scrambling to his feet.

Suddenly the droid's overhead access door blew off and there was a flash of light from its interior. A thin plume of smoke drifted out of the droid. Its panel lights flared again, and then the work arm sagged downward. The droid's body, softened by heat, sagged in on itself and drooped to the floor. The floor and walls and ceiling of the playroom were supposed to be fireproof, but nonetheless the floor under the droid darkened a bit, and the ceiling turned black. The ventilators kicked on high automatically, and drew the smoke out of the room. After a moment they shut themselves off, and the room was silent.

The three children stood, every bit as frozen to the spot as the droid was, absolutely stunned. It was Anakin who recovered first. He walked cautiously toward the droid and looked at it carefully, being sure not to get too close or touch it. "*Really* melty now," he announced, and then wandered off to the other side of the room to play with his blocks.

The twins looked at the droid, and then at each other.

"We're dead," Jacen announced, surveying the wreckage.

"We didn't *mean* to break anything," Jaina protested.

"If we only got in trouble for things we meant to do, we'd never get in trouble," her brother pointed out. "Well, hardly ever," he conceded after a moment. Uncle Luke was very insistent on the subject of honesty, and doubly so on the subject of being honest with yourself.

"Maybe we can blame it on Anakin," Jaina said. "We could tell them he did it. After all, he *is* the one that did it. Sort of."

Their little brother, already having made a nice stack of blocks, looked up at the two of them, a little bit worried, a tiny bit startled, yet still a lot calmer than he should have been, under the circumstances. But then, even the twins didn't pretend to understand Anakin completely.

"No," Jacen said. "We can't tell them. If they knew the kind of stuff Anakin can do, that would spoil everything." So far as Jacen and Jaina were concerned, "they" and "them" meant the grown-ups, the opposing team. It was the grown-ups' job to stop Jacen and Jaina, and the twins' job to outwit the grown-ups. Jacen was enough of a strategist to know that sometimes you had to lose a battle in order to win the war. If they revealed Anakin's abilities, that might protect them for the moment, but the grown-ups would be sure to *do* something about Anakin, and *then* where would the twins be? "We can't let them know about Anakin. Besides, it wasn't his fault. We *did* make him do it. It'd be no fair getting *him* in trouble."

"Yeah," Jaina said, agreeing reluctantly. "I guess you're right. But how do we explain a melted droid?"

Jacen shrugged and prodded the ruined machine with the toe of his shoe. "I don't think we can," he said.

"I'd sure like to hear you try," someone said from behind them.

There were very few people who could enter a room without Jacen realizing it, and only one of that number was likely to be anywhere near the Imperial Palace. Even if he had not recognized the voice, Jacen would have known who it had to be, and the knowledge both relieved and mortified him. "Hello, Uncle Luke," he said as he turned around. If they were going to be caught, Uncle Luke was probably the best—and worst—grown-up to do the catching.

"Hello, Uncle Luke," said Jaina, her tone no happier than Jacen's.

"Lukie!" Anakin cried out as he jumped up and rushed over to him. At least *someone* didn't feel at all guilty.

Luke Skywalker, Jedi Knight and Master, hero of a hundred battles and a thousand worlds, champion of justice, loved, revered—and feared—throughout the New Republic, knelt down to scoop up a bundle of fast-moving nephew. Uncle Luke stood again, holding Anakin in one arm as he surveyed the damage. "Pretty impressive," he said. "So what *did* happen?"

Jacen Solo looked up at his uncle and swallowed nervously. At least it was Uncle Luke, and not Mom or Dad—or worse, Chewbacca—who had caught them. "Well, it was my idea," he said. There was no sense in pointing at your sister and shouting "She did it! She did it!" when you were talking to an uncle who could sense the truth or falseness of everything you said.

"Uh-huh," Luke said. "Somehow I'm not surprised. But what exactly *was* the idea?"

"We wanted our own droid," Jaina said. "One we could use without bothering the grown-ups."

"And without getting the grown-ups to give you permission," Luke said. It was not a question. "You know you're not allowed to use droids without asking your parents or me or Chewie. And you know why, too. So don't go pretending you were trying to make a droid to make things easy on *us*."

"Well, all right," Jaina conceded. "That's not why."

"You were trying to get away with something," said Uncle Luke. Once again, it was not a question.

"Yes," Jaina said. Jacen wished she hadn't confessed quite that fast, but she knew as well as he did that trying to tell fibs to Uncle Luke was pointless.

"So. You tell me. Why aren't you allowed to use droids for most things?" Luke asked.

"Because we have to learn to do things on our own. Because we shouldn't rely on them to do our work for us. Because they can't do a lot of things as well as we can." Jaina spoke the words in a flat, expressionless voice, reciting what she had learned by rote. Jacen could have done it along with her. He had gotten all the same lectures she had.

"And you've just learned another reason," Luke said. "It's dangerous to fool around with things you don't understand. Suppose one of you had been close to the droid when it went up? Do you want to spend a week in a bacta tank regenerating?"

"No," Jaina agreed.

"I didn't think so," Luke said. "But there's more to it

than that. You're not going to live your whole life on Coruscant. There's a whole galaxy out there—and most of it doesn't much care about people who can't take care of themselves. You're not always going to have droids around to pick up after you."

"But you have R2-D2," Jacen protested. "He follows *you* around nearly all the time."

"He helps me pilot my ship, and to do data access—and to do other *real* jobs that he was *designed* for. Artoo helps me do my work so *I* can do it better—he doesn't do it *for* me, or help me get out of doing it." Luke nodded at the melted hulk in the center of the room. "Back before you repaired him so well, did you really think that droid there was designed to do homework for sneaky children?"

"Well, no."

"Sneaky?" Anakin asked, patting Luke on the shoulder to get his attention. "Not me. *I'm* not sneaky."

Luke smiled and bounced Anakin up and down once more. "No, you aren't," he agreed. "And I want to make sure your brother and sister don't make you that way. They got you to help them do this, didn't they?"

"Help? *I* did it, mostly. They helped *me*."

Luke frowned thoughtfully at that, and Jacen held his breath. If any grown-up were going to figure out just what Anakin could do, it would be Uncle Luke. This was far from the first incident concerning Anakin's abilities.

But the same thing that had saved them before saved them this time as well. Uncle Luke laughed, and it was plain from the look on his face that he couldn't quite imagine seven-and-a-half-year-old Anakin Solo assembling a droid.

"Sure you did," Luke said. "Sure you did. But right now, I think the question is: What are your brother and sister going to do about the little mess here?"

"Clean it up!" Anakin said, shouting gleefully.

Luke laughed. "That's right. They're going to clean it up, right after dinner. And during dinner I'll have to think about the rest of their punishment."

"Yeah!" Anakin said, smiling. "Punishment!"

Jacen sighed. That was the thing about Anakin. He was always ready to help Jaina and Jacen get into trouble. But somehow, he always managed to avoid helping them back *out*. He plainly enjoyed avoiding the punishments his siblings got.

Sometimes, Jacen wondered just how unsneaky Anakin really was.

*   *   *

Leia Organa Solo, onetime princess, senator, ambassador, and minister of state, and present Chief of State to the New Republic, did not like it when her family was late to dinner. She knew it wasn't fair, but there it was. If *she* could juggle her hopelessly complicated schedule to be home for a family meal, why couldn't her husband or brother or children manage?

Deep in her heart of hearts, Leia knew she had little right to complain. After all, nightly family dinners had been her idea—and even she had to admit that she missed more dinners than anyone else in the family. There was a price—and a high price—to being Chief of State.

But there was not much point in struggling to make time for her family if her family never showed up for dinner. Where *was* everyone? Leia was on the verge of ordering the kitchen droids to program another twenty-minute delay into the meal preparation when Han and Chewbacca finally came in the door. She was about to light into them both for being late—but then she got a look at Han's expression, and all her angry words melted away.

She could instantly see how hard he was trying to pretend everything was fine. Maybe that lopsided grin was sincere enough to fool a bunch of smugglers around a sabacc table, but Leia was not buying it.

"Hello, Leia," Han said. "Sorry we're late. Didn't quite get as far with the shield tests as I expected."

"I see," she said, speaking in a cautious voice rather than a hard or accusatory one. Years of diplomatic maneuvering had taught her how to control the tone of her voice. She did not want to push Han. She knew that much at once.

Leia had never really gotten caught up on her Jedi training. By now she was resigned to the knowledge that she was never going to be as strong in the Force as her brother Luke. She might have every bit of the potential he did, but she had never had the time for the training. Even so, there were times when she didn't need the Force to know something was wrong. One look at Han's face told her that much. But in that same moment she knew that she had to pretend right along with him. If she pressed him, demanded to know what was going on, he would tell her. Han might leave a few things out, but he would never lie to her, or let anything harm her if he could prevent it. She knew that. And so if he left things unsaid, he had his reasons.

Leia glanced at Chewbacca, and was even more certain that something was wrong. Wookiees had many fine qualities, but they were decidedly below standard in concealing their emotions. Chewie was clearly unsettled, his eyes nervous and edgy.

She was tempted to speak, to ask, to demand, but then she stopped. No. He had a reason, a good reason, for saying nothing about whatever it was.

"It's all right," Leia said, turning her tone light and casual as she stepped forward and gave him a kiss. "No one else has gotten here yet. You have time to go freshen up." As she got close to him she could not help but notice the slightest scent of smoke and fire, and something that smelled like the ozone after-tang of blaster fire. But she revealed nothing of that in her expression.

"Great," Han said. "I'm feeling a bit grubby at that."

Chewbacca made a low growling noise and headed to the Wookiee-style refresher unit down the hallway. Chewie was a frequent enough visitor that it had made sense to install the unit for his use—but Leia had never seen him quite this eager to get cleaned up. Clearly Chewie wanted to be out of the way—and maybe wash the same scents out of his fur. Something else to ignore.

Leia smiled as warmly as she could and gave Han a kiss on the cheek. "See you in a minute," she said.

* * *

Han breathed a sigh of relief as he crossed through the bedroom to the refresher unit. Either she hadn't noticed something was wrong, or she was pretending she hadn't noticed. It didn't so much matter which it was. He stripped off his clothes, wondering if Leia had noticed the burned smell they had picked up from the roasted packing cases. He took a quick shower and hurried a bit through the drying cycle before dressing in fresh clothes. Somehow, the familiar ritual of getting cleaned up for dinner settled him down, let the worry drain out of him. The old cockiness seemed to flow back into him, and the fretful worries of a husband and father seemed like they belonged to another man. Let NRI chase shadows and play at spies. All they were really asking him to do was behave naturally, do what he would have done anyway. And after all, this was Corellia they were talking about. His home turf. He knew his way around. Let the probe droid lurk about. He didn't know anything anyway. Right now the biggest challenge he faced was in getting the shields on the *Falcon* back up to speed.

Amazing how getting cleaned up could improve your whole outlook. Everything was going to be fine.

Han headed back out to the living room and settled himself down in his favorite chair just as Chewie emerged from the refresher. Chewie gestured at the chair and gave Han a derisive little burbling noise.

"All right, so I'm getting a little soft. Is there some grand crime in liking a comfortable chair?"

Chewie didn't answer—but Han could not help notice that the Wookiee declined to take a seat himself. Han grinned and shook his head. Even after all these years. he was never quite sure what the Wookiee would decide to get competitive about.

Leia came back into the room. "I told the kitchen droids

to go ahead and get dinner on the table. They can reheat it for the kids. Maybe a dinner or two of overcooked food will teach them to get here on time.''

Han was about to reply when he heard the apartment's outer door opening. ''Looks like they're in just under the wire,'' he said. He could hear youthful voices and a bit of giggling and the sound of small feet, but it was not his children who appeared at the living-room entrance, it was his brother-in-law. Han had clean forgotten that Luke was eating with them tonight.

''Sorry we're late,'' Luke said as he came in. ''I walked in on the kids trying to burn down the palace again. We had to have a little talk. I sent them to go wash up.''

''What was it this time? Anything we need to know about?'' Leia asked.

Luke hesitated before he answered. ''We've already sorted out a punishment. If I tell you, you might feel obligated to reopen negotiations—''

''And that might end up getting us all a worse deal,'' Leia said. ''All right. Tell me in a day or two, once the dust has settled.''

Han, sitting back in his favorite chair, couldn't help but smile. Leia and Luke's side of the family might be the high-and-mighty, important one, all strong in the Force and busy in politics, but it was obvious that his children took after him. So what if that did mean the little monsters were a constant source of aggravation?

It seemed as if none of his children were happy unless they were a hairbreadth from some sort of disaster. He had lost count of the times they had ''experimented'' with their uncle Luke's lightsaber. Rules did not set limits for the children of Han Solo—they represented challenges. Han smiled, thinking back on a few moments from his own childhood. It pleased him no end to see so much of himself in his children.

The twins, Jacen and Jaina, were more overt troublemakers than Anakin would ever be. Anakin was a dreamier child, seemingly off in his own little world, but that was deceptive. He was capable of causing at least as much damage as the other two put together. It was just that Anakin never seemed to notice the chaos he caused—while the twins absolutely reveled in it.

At that moment the children came tumbling into the room, the twins just a little ahead of Anakin.

"Come on," Han said as he stood up. "Let's go in to dinner."

CHAPTER THREE

Family

Pharnis Gleasry, agent of the Human League, sat in his hidden bunker, deep in the bowels of Coruscant, and checked his detectors one more time. He came up with nothing once again. The probe droid had vanished utterly, and was not responding to any call codes.

Pharnis fretted to himself, knowing just how costly and difficult it could be to get probe droids, even obsolete ones. Yes, you expected to lose a certain amount of equipment. That was part of the fortunes of war. But he could not imagine the Hidden Leader would be exactly *pleased* to learn the droid had vanished.

But still, the droid's task had been secondary. The real task—of getting to Skywalker—was yet to come. Everything had been carefully timed, the sequence of events worked out most precisely. The Hidden Leader's plan afforded only a narrow window of time for Pharnis. It would have to be after the moment Organa Solo took off for Corellia and before the planned demonstration. If he delivered the message too soon, Organa Solo could elude the trap. If he delivered the message too late, all of the Hidden Leader's other plans might well fall apart.

It was a grave responsibility. And truth to tell, Pharnis had not felt completely up to it even before the loss of the probe droid.

* * *

It was not a happy meal, Jaina thought. There was something in the air, something unsettled and nervous. Jaina was not as good as Jacen at sensing such things, but it seemed to her that, somehow, her father was at the center of it. Something was going on with him, something that got Mom upset, and even had Chewbacca a little edgy.

Jaina wanted to ask what was wrong, but thought better of it. If the grown-ups wanted to pretend everything was fine, she could do the same thing, even if she did not know what the problem was.

Besides, there was another question preying on her mind, one occasioned by the droid they had just blown up. They had built it to get out of doing work they didn't want to do, work that the grown-ups didn't let droids do for the kids. But suppose even the regular droids weren't around? She and Jacen would get stuck doing even more chores. What if the droids weren't coming on the trip?

"Dad? Are we taking R2-D2 and C-3PO to Corellia?" Jaina asked as she stabbed at another bite of food.

Her father sighed, gave her mother a meaningful glance, and got the slightest of nods in return. Jaina knew what *that* meant: Mom was on his side with this one. She instantly regretted having raised the question. Bad tactical error. There was always the chance of getting around Mom or Dad, but she should have known there was no hope at all when they presented a united front.

"We've been through this a dozen times," Han said. "One, you kids are getting way too dependent on the droids to take care of you. Two, there won't really be room for them on the *Falcon*. Three, I don't like having droids around in general. Four, I especially don't like them on my ship. I don't carry them if I don't have to."

"But—"

Han pointed a warning finger at Jaina and cut her off. "And five, I'm your father, and that's final."

"I should think now was not exactly the moment for you kids to be asking for more droid favors," Uncle Luke said, nodding his head almost imperceptibly toward the compartment down the hall with the melted results of their failed experiment in it. "I *was* going to talk about the other matter with your parents later, but now you've raised the subject. Of course, if you *really* want me to discuss it with them here and now—"

"No, no, that's fine," Jacen said in hurried tones. "No need to bother. The droids aren't coming. Fine. Fine."

Jaina gave her twin brother a dirty look. Just like him to retreat like that. But still, what else could he do? The grown-ups had won this round, and no doubt. Even so, there was still a little part of her that couldn't go down without a fight. She was still a little mad and embarrassed about being caught by Uncle Luke. The temptation to stir things up on another front was irresistible. "Maybe there'd be room for the droids if we didn't have to take the dumb old *Falcon*," Jaina half mumbled, glaring at her plate.

There was a moment of utter silence around the table, and Jaina knew, even as the last words were leaving her mouth, just how big a mistake she had just made. She looked up to see everyone, even little Anakin, staring at her. She stole a glance at her twin brother and saw him shaking his head at her in mute exasperation.

"You know how much that ship means to your father," her mother said, using the coldly reasonable tone of voice that was somehow worse than the loudest yelling. "You also know that the *Falcon* has saved the lives of half the people around this table, some of them many times over. And *I* know *you* know that *we* know you know. So I can only assume you said something that spiteful and insulting with the deliberate intent of being disrespectful to your father. Am I correct?"

Jaina opened her mouth to deny it all—but then she caught Uncle Luke's eye, and knew there was no point to it. For that matter, her mother had the same skills in truth sensing as Uncle Luke. That *would* be the one facet of her abilities in the Force that her mother would have practiced. Life would have been a lot easier if she could fib to her parents the way other kids could. But as it was, there really wasn't any point. "You're correct," Jaina said, not quite able to keep a sulky tone out of her voice.

"In that case, I think it is just about time for you to go to your room, young lady."

"But—"

"But nothing," Han said. That did it for Jaina. There was no point in fighting against her father when he used *that* tone of voice. She got up from the table and stalked to the room she shared with her brothers, still pouting and annoyed at them all—even though she knew, deep in her heart of hearts, that it was all her own fault.

That was the other problem with all this Jedi business. You couldn't even tell fibs to yourself.

* * *

The rest of the meal did not go much better after Jaina was sent to bed, Leia thought. There was sort of a chain reaction whenever they punished one of the twins. The other twin would get edgy, and ask to be excused, so as to slip away to commiserate with the prisoner. Then Anakin would notice something was wrong and want to go see what was up. Send one child away, and all three would be gone from the table in ten minutes. Usually the adults managed to have a pleasant meal afterward by themselves, and enjoyed the peace and quiet. Not tonight. Han was relentlessly pretending everything was fine, Chewie was being even less convincing, and Luke was doing his best to go along with the charade.

"Looking forward to the trip to Corellia?" Luke asked, plainly trying to make conversation.

"Hmm? Oh, yeah. Absolutely," Han replied. "It's going to be great. Wish you could come along."

"It's tempting," Luke said. "But I promised Lando that I'd help him with some sort of secret project of his."

"Yeah, he mentioned something about that," Han said. "Any hint about what it might be?"

Luke shook his head. "Not a word. Just that it might take a few weeks."

"Well, I can't wait to see what he's gotten himself into this time."

"Me neither," Luke said. "Oh, Leia, by the way, speaking of secrets, I'm supposed to have a meeting with Mon Mothma tomorrow evening. She wouldn't tell me what she wanted, either. Nothing but classified missions for me, I guess."

Han gave Luke a strange look, and had to force a smile. "Yeah, real hush-hush stuff," he said.

At last Leia couldn't stand it anymore. "Excuse me," she said. "I really have some work I have to do tonight." She got up from the table, not really caring how lame the excuse sounded, and hurried along to her study. She closed the door and slapped the override on the light control before the automatics could brighten the room too much. She edged the lights up just a trifle from minimum. Let it stay dim in here.

Of course, the sad part was that work wasn't actually an excuse. There was always some bottomless pit of work, no matter how much she delegated. Leia let out a sigh and crossed to her desk. The desk light turned itself on, a shaft of light bright and clear, and she left it that way. She sat in the darkness, on the edge of a pool of light, and found that she could not bring herself to deal with even one of the vital documents that covered her desk.

Why should such a tiny dinnertime scuffle upset her so much? She knew that most of it was the underlying tension at the table, but there was more to it than that. There were times, and this was one of them, when, for no clear reason at all, the whole idea of motherhood, of the job of molding her children into civilized humans, seemed suddenly terrifying.

She saw now just how much of her childhood had been spent being told to be quiet and not to fidget during state dinners, being constantly handed off to nannies and guardians when her father was too busy. She had had far more meals with the droids and servants than with Bail Organa. And what childhood she did have had not lasted very long.

She had still been in her teens when she found herself getting pulled deeper and deeper into politics. It had been a real accomplishment to become a senator as young as she had— but the accomplishment was purchased by surrendering the last of her childhood, the last of her innocence. Only now, as she looked at the world through her children's eyes, did she realize just how steep a price that had been.

Han never did say much about his own childhood, or about much of anything concerning his life before leaving Corellia. Luke had come the closest of any of them to having a normal upbringing. He had been raised on Tatooine, thinking a farm couple, Owen and Beru Lars, were his aunt and uncle. But his early life had been just as isolated as Leia's, in its own way. A moisture farm must have been a pretty lonely place for a child to grow up on, even in normal circumstances—and circumstances had been far from normal.

Owen and Beru had posed as Luke's uncle and aunt. As best Leia understood, they had been kind to Luke, but in a distant sort of way. There had never been the closeness, the warmth, Leia wanted for her own children.

It didn't escape Leia's notice that neither she nor her brother had actually been *adopted* by the people who raised them. Circumstances had required a certain degree of subterfuge, of well-intended deception, of careful distance for everyone's protection. Foster daughter and purported nephew were the closest ties Leia and Luke could claim.

There was another piece of knowledge, guilty knowledge, that gnawed at Leia's conscience, and, she had no doubt, at Luke's as well. Each had been the unwitting, unwilling agent of death for the people who had raised them. The planet of Alderaan was chosen as a fit target for destruction by the Death Star in large part because it was Leia's home, and Owen and Beru had been killed by Imperial stormtroopers as they searched for the droids Luke had.

With all that baggage to carry around, it was scarcely surprising that Leia was determined that her family would *be* a family, and not just a collection of strangers who happened to share some ancestors. Nor was it ever far from her mind that the children of powerful or prominent families often found themselves as players—or worse, pawns—in complicated power struggles. Even if her children were not going to inherit her office or her powers, they were still the next generation of what came close to being the Republic's royal family.

Like it or not, intended or not, her children were, in effect, the second generation of a dynasty. It did not take much imagination to see the dangers in that. The temptations of power and wealth could be strong. Suppose that, somehow, they proved stronger than family ties?

Suppose, twenty years from now, Anakin were plotting to gain some advantage over Jacen? Suppose some untrustworthy adviser urged Jacen to push his brother and sister out of the way of some glittering prize? It seemed impossible—but history was littered with such tales.

But there was more, and worse. That her children were strong in the Force was, beyond doubt, a great gift. But it was also a great danger. It was never far from Leia's mind that Darth Vader, her father, her children's grandfather, had likewise been strong in the Force—and had been destroyed by the dark side. The day would dawn, no doubt, when each of her children would have to face the dark side. The very idea terrified Leia. It made her fear that they might someday bicker with each other over money or power seem utterly trivial.

Every little outburst of childhood surliness, every momentary black mood, every childish temptation to tell an obvious fib, scared her to death. It was illogical, irrational, but she could never stop herself from wondering if *this* bit of childish naughtiness or *that* bit of youthful bad judgment was really a child succumbing to some temptation of the dark side of the Force.

In theory, that was not supposed to be possible. Jedi lore held that childish innocence was a bulwark against the dark side. But Jedi lore also held it all but unheard of for any child to display the ability and strength in the Force that her children exhibited.

The dangers were great, but it seemed to her there was but one defense against both dangers, a defense so commonplace that it almost seemed absurd that it could triumph over such mighty forces, but there it was. The best she could do was to raise her children well.

Leia Organa Solo was bound and determined that *her* children would reach adulthood with their characters strong and firm and honest, their family ties solid, with love in their hearts for each other. If that meant being strict with her children, or sending Jaina to bed straight from dinner, or refusing them droid servants, then so be it.

Leia propped her elbows up on the desk and rubbed her eyes. She was just too tired, that was all. A minor dinnertime squabble should not induce this much worry. It would be good to get away, take a rest. It was a fine idea of Han's for them all to go to Corellia for a family vacation before the trade conference.

It would be wonderful to have some peace and quiet.

* * *

"Brilliant move tonight, Jaina," said Jacen as he got into his bed and pulled the covers up.

"I didn't mean to do it," Jaina replied as she got into her own bed on the other side of the room. "Room, lights-to-sleep mode," she said.

The lights lowered, with the only illumination coming from the dim night-light in Anakin's adjoining alcove. The three children could have had their own rooms, of course, and had even tried that arrangement at times, but had soon discovered they were too used to being together. The present arrangement of one big shared room, with Anakin just slightly off to one side, suited everyone best. Besides, they were going to be a bit crowded on the *Falcon*. They might as well get used to it.

Neither of them spoke, and the room was quiet for a moment. The twins could hear Anakin's gentle, rhythmic breathing. Their little brother was already asleep.

Jacen found himself in a thoughtful mood as he stared up at the darkened ceiling. "Aren't you being kind of easy on yourself?"

"What do you mean?" Jaina asked.

"You didn't mean it, so it doesn't count," he said. "It's not what you mean to do that matters. It's what you actually do." That sounded a little preachy, especially considering that he had been tempted to use the didn't-mean-it defense himself a couple of hours before. But it seemed to Jacen that being tempted and not doing whatever it was counted for something. "Anyway, you *did* mean to cause trouble, and you know it."

"Now you're starting to sound like Uncle Luke," Jaina said.

"I could do worse," Jacen said, noting that his sister hadn't denied the charge of deliberate troublemaking. "Uncle Luke is pretty smart. But if it's any help, I don't think it was all your fault tonight. They were already upset before we came in."

"Yeah," Jaina agreed. "They were all worked up over something."

"*And* everyone was making believe there was nothing going on," Jacen said.

"Including us," Jaina pointed out. "We didn't say anything either, and we could tell. The only one who wasn't pretending was Anakin."

"Don't forget, he let Uncle Luke think he didn't have anything to do with the droid," Jaina said. "He's the best actor of all of us. We *knew* Anakin was the one that built the droid, and we still couldn't tell if he was pretending with Uncle Luke. Maybe Anakin was putting us on, or maybe he didn't even know what he did."

"I hadn't thought of that," Jacen said. But Anakin was an old, familiar mystery. They were used to the fact that he was incomprehensible. "So what do you think is wrong?'' Jacen asked as he stared up into the cool, quiet dark. "With the grown-ups, I mean.''

"No idea," Jaina said. Her sheets rustled as she turned over on her side. "But my guess is that Dad knows something he doesn't want to tell Mom or Uncle Luke.''

Jacen turned toward her as well and propped his head up on his hand. He could just make her out in the dim light. She was facing him, mirroring his own pose. "Do you think it's a real big deal?'' he asked her. "Or just some dumb politics thing that doesn't really matter?''

"I don't know. But whatever it is has something to do with *us*. Mom and Dad never act that weird unless they're worried about us three little darlings.''

"That's for sure,'' Jacen agreed. "They sure do worry.''

Jaina chuckled softly as she turned over on her other side to go to sleep. "Come on, Jacen,'' she said, her voice a bit muffled by the pillow. "If you were our parents, wouldn't *you* worry?''

Jacen rolled back onto his back and stared at the ceiling. He had to admit that she had a point.

CHAPTER FOUR

The Dangers of Peace

*I*n deep space, far from any inhabited system, a small, solitary star hung in the firmament. It had no name, but only a code number, a string of digits to identify it on the celestial charts. Star Number TD-10036-EM-1271 had no planets to speak of, only a few debris belts that had never coalesced into worlds of any size. It had no resources that were not available someplace else, and was not of any particular aesthetic or scientific importance. In short, there was no good reason for anyone to bother with it—and no one did.

There were quite literally billions of stars like it in the galaxy, and it was of a size and age and type as well understood as any. Any astrophysicist worth his or her or its salt anywhere in the New Republic would have been able to make several very basic measurements of that star, and report back immediately on its age, the course of its development, and the pattern of its future evolution.

And all of the astrophysicists would have been wrong.

Many light-years away, hidden deep in the Corellian System, a secret team of technicians and researchers was seeing to that. They had been working for a long time, but soon their efforts would bear fruit. Soon the energies of their machines would reach across the stars.

Soon they would change everything.

* * *

Luke drew himself up and took a deep breath before he pressed the door annunciator at Mon Mothma's quarters. He had learned to respect many beings in the galaxy over the years, but Mon Mothma held a special place in his esteem. Perhaps it was because of her seeming ordinariness, her quiet, backstage approach to things.

People who had not been paying attention might easily think that she had played, at best, a rather minor role in recent galactic history. She had commanded no fleets, fought no battles. She had no strange powers, or mysterious past, or remarkable talent.

She was nothing more, and nothing less, than a brave, intelligent, ordinary human being, a human being who had pressed and prodded the Rebel Alliance into being. More than any other single person, she had created the New Republic itself.

If that did not rate respect, even from a Jedi Master, Luke did not know what did. He pressed the annunciator and the door slid silently open. Mon Mothma stood just inside the entrance. She nodded to him and smiled. "Greetings, Jedi Master. Welcome to my home. Please come in."

"Thank you, ma'am," Luke said. It seemed to him that "ma'am" wasn't much of a way to address a person of such importance, but Mon Mothma had never been much for titles or honorifics.

Luke stepped inside, and looked about with interest. He had, of course, known Mon Mothma for years, but he had been in her home only a handful of times.

Mon Mothma's current quarters resembled the woman herself—quiet, unassuming, yet with an air of steady confidence. There was little furniture, but every piece was finely crafted, graceful and yet sturdy, everything perfectly matched to everything else, in muted shades of ivory and white. The room gave the appearance of being larger than it actually was. No doubt that was at least in part an effect of simple contrasts. Most homes of the high-ranking families of Coruscant were cluttered with bric-a-brac, gaudy souvenirs and collectibles from every world of the New Republic.

It was something of a relief to find a home that did not resemble a crowded and badly organized museum.

"I am pleased you could come and visit me, Jedi Master," Mon Mothma said.

Why in space was she, of all people, addressing him by his most formal title? "I am pleased to come," Luke replied.

"I am glad," Mon Mothma said. "Please take a seat."

Luke sat down in a severe-looking stiff-backed chair, and was surprised to find that it was much more comfortable than it looked. He did not speak. His host was capable of speaking her mind without prompting from him.

Mon Mothma took a seat opposite Luke and looked at him with an appraising eye. "Tell me of your current circumstances, Jedi Master."

Luke was taken aback by the question. Then he realized it was no question at all, but a command. After all, why should she ask when she knew the answer as well as he did? She was the former Chief of State. She had access to all sorts of information, and had always followed Luke's career with particular interest. "Well, ma'am, as you know, the Jedi academy is now well established. I still visit from time to time there, but the students are progressing well and the first class has reached the point where they should be learning on their own, and, indeed, some now spend as much time teaching the second and third class as they do learning."

"So you are not needed there."

"Not full-time, no. To be there too much at this stage would be to distract from the process of learning."

"So it goes deeper than your not being needed. You choose to stay away so you will not interfere."

It was not the most diplomatic way of expressing the thought, but it was true enough. "That is one way to put it, yes."

"So what are you doing with yourself?"

Luke shifted in his seat, and found that it now seemed far less comfortable than it had before. He had not expected this sort of interrogation. But even if the questions were awkward, a Jedi spoke the truth. And even if the questions were a bit more intrusive than was polite, even a non-Jedi would find it hard to lie—or even shade the truth—when looking Mon Mothma straight in the eye. "I find that I have not been doing a great deal," Luke said.

"No grand crusades? No desperate battles or heroic missions?"

"No, nothing like that," Luke said, starting to feel a bit annoyed. Revered figure or not, she had no right to be so rude to him.

"Of course not," she said. "We're at peace." She smiled and laughed in a tired sort of way. "That's the problem with peace," she said. "No crisis. No trouble. No adventure. Which means there's not much need for people who are good at dealing with crisis and trouble. There's just no call for adventurers these days. Or for revolutionaries either. Do you know, Jedi Master, that I haven't been doing a great deal myself in recent days?"

There really didn't seem much Luke could say in reply to that, and Mon Mothma didn't seem to be expecting an answer anyway. He kept silent.

"You are wise to say nothing, Jedi Master," Mon Mothma said. "You have no idea why I have called you here, or what the point of all this uncalled-for rudeness could be. Well, I shall tell you." She stood up and crossed the room to the opacified window. She touched the controls and the window turned transparent.

Coruscant's sun was setting in a glory of reds and yellows that lit up the sky. A spacecraft heading for orbit streaked up through the blaze of light, and reached for the night. "Perhaps I had them put my quarters on the wrong side of the building," she said. "Every day I see the sunset, but never the sunrise. The symbolism is a bit too much for me at times. Every day I look out this window and am reminded that my day is over. I know that I have done good, that I have left my mark on the galaxy. I know that it is even possible that I will be of service someday in the future. Yet I cannot imagine that the *future* will offer up any challenges like the ones I confronted in the past. Praise be for that, but it leaves me at loose ends. It is—unsettling—to have my life's work ended before my life is. Do you ever feel that way?''

Luke could think of nothing to say. Mon Mothma turned away from the window and looked toward him.''If you *do* feel that way, it must be harder for you than for me. My day is past,'' she said again, ''but I am an old woman. At my time of life, I find that, at least at times, I *welcome* the prospect of peace, of quiet, of leisure and privacy. The restlessness, the urgency of youth have burned themselves away, and I can enjoy my life as it is.''

Mon Mothma looked directly into his eyes. ''But what of you?'' she asked. ''What of the Jedi Master? I fear I know the answer.''

''And what *is* the answer?'' Luke asked.

''That *your* life's work is indeed done as well,'' Mon Mothma said. ''You have fought your wars. You have saved countless lives, liberated any number of worlds, fought great battles. You have restored the Jedi Knights. Now all that work is done and yet you are a young man still.

''You grew up in wartime, and the wars are over. History tells us that peacetime is often not very easy for warriors. They don't fit in. In plain words, Luke Skywalker, *what will you do now?*''

''I don't know,'' Luke said. ''There are things I *could* do, but—well, maybe the reason I've been at loose ends for a while is just that I've been trying to find things to keep busy. Things I *could* do. Not things that I *wanted* to do, or things that *needed* to be done.'' His protest sounded hollow.

Mon Mothma nodded thoughtfully. ''That all sounds very familiar,'' she said. ''But that is the problem. What could compare with what we have done in the past, you and I?''

''I don't know,'' Luke said. ''It sounds like you might have some ideas, though.''

''Well, it does strike me that another member of your

family has faced the same problem," said Mon Mothma. "That person seems to have dealt with it."

"I'd say that Han is more at loose ends than I am," Luke said. "I don't think I want to look to him for an example."

"It was not Han that I was thinking of. But just in passing, I wouldn't worry about him. He might be having a quiet spell for the moment, but somehow I don't think the universe is likely to leave him alone for long."

"That's true enough, I suppose."

"I was thinking of another member of your family who also faced the same situation, the same transition from war to peace. *She* did rather well for herself."

Luke frowned thoughtfully. "Leia? I hadn't even thought of her."

"My point exactly," Mon Mothma said.

"But it's different for Leia," Luke said. "She was doing the same sort of diplomatic and political work she's doing now even before the war. And after the war, she just kept going on with it until—"

Mon Mothma smiled. "Until she got my job. I was glad to let the work go, of course, but there are times I miss it. And I might add that it's a job that suits Leia."

"I don't know that it's the sort of job that would suit *me*, if that's what you're getting at. I'm just not good at that sort of thing. I don't think I'd like it."

"Leia shows few signs of *enjoying* her work—but she is good at it. Probably better than I was. But tell me—what sort of a Jedi is Leia?" Mon Mothma asked, changing the subject again with startling abruptness.

Luke looked up in surprise. Once again, Mon Mothma surely knew the answer as well as he did. But he could tell she was not looking for a pat answer. She wanted Luke to hear himself answer. "She has the innate skills, the inborn talent," he said carefully. "That much is obvious. But there has always been some other demand on her time, that prevented her from pursuing a course of dedicated instruction. That has cost her part of her potential. Even so, if she applied herself, starting now, and studied full-time, she could, in time, have very close to my degree of ability."

"But at present she has nowhere near your level of skill in the ways of the Force," Mon Mothma said. "She has not made the most of her gifts."

"She has not *yet* made the most of them. She still could," Luke said, with a bit more passion than he had intended. "*If* she gave up all the other demands on her time, and studied the ways of the Force, she could develop her skills tremendously."

"Do you see any chance of that happening?"

Luke shook his head slowly. "No," he said. "She has made her choices already. Her career in politics put too many demands on her. Besides which, she has three children to raise."

"Yet it has always been a regret to her—and to you—that she has not developed her skills more. And if I am not mistaken, the issue has been the cause of gentle and repeated reproaches from you?"

"Well, yes."

"Do you find it upsetting that your sister has great gifts and has not developed them? That she has not made use of them? Do you find it something close to a scandalous waste?"

Luke raised his head and looked Mon Mothma straight in the eyes. The truth. That was what she wanted to get—and, he realized, what he wanted to give. The truth, solid and clear. "Yes," he said in a slow, firm voice. "Yes, I do."

"Then, Luke Skywalker, I suggest you consider the fact that some mirrors reflect both ways." Suddenly there was nothing remotely gentle or subdued about her voice or her manner.

"Excuse me, ma'am?" Luke asked. It occurred to him that he had had difficulty reading Mon Mothma's emotions since he had come in here. Her calm manner had hidden a subject about which she felt great passion. "I don't understand."

"I have heard it time and time again, from all sorts of people," she said, somewhat testily. "How the two of you are twins, how you each inherited the same potential, but only one of you made use of it, while the other chose to do something else, something less. People say what a shame it is. And always it is Leia Organa Solo, the Chief of State of the Republic, that they talk about that way. The Chief of State, and they whisper that she has not done enough with herself!"

"What's your point?" Luke asked, feeling his temper starting to flare.

"My point is that I think it is long past time for you to consider that Luke Skywalker made some choices as well. It is long past time to reflect on the fact that *you* have talents and potential you have never developed."

"For instance?" Luke said.

"If Leia has potential in the Force because *you*, her brother, have shown you do, does it not follow that you have potential in other areas because *Leia*, your sister, has shown she does? She has become a leader, a stateswoman, a politician, a spouse, and a parent. She is building the New Republic even as she is raising a new generation of Jedi.

"Let us look in the mirror again," Mon Mothma said. "The Republic is in need of a new generation of political leadership. I don't know whether you realize it or not, but it is all but inevitable that you will enter politics, whether you like it or not."

"Me?" Luke asked. "But I'm—"

"A hero of the Rebellion. You're famous throughout the Republic, and on hundreds of worlds outside it. The various powers-that-be will not be able to resist someone as well known, or as well liked, or well respected, as yourself. You will be an inevitable focal point of political maneuvering in the years to come."

"But I'm a Jedi Knight," Luke protested. "A Jedi Master. I can't go into politics. Besides, I don't want to."

Mon Mothma smiled. "How much of your life so far has consisted of what you wanted to do? But let's talk about the Jedi, what I most wanted to talk with you about. What are the Jedi to become?''

''I'm sorry,'' Luke said. ''I don't understand what you mean.'' It seemed to him that the whole conversation had been little more than riddles of one sort or another. If the Jedi were the most important thing on her agenda, why had she waited until now to bring them up? As for her question, the Jedi were—Jedi. What else would they be?

''All right,'' Mon Mothma said. ''Let me put it another way. In the years to come, as the Jedi grow from a handful of students into an order of thousands of Knights, will they set themselves up as an elite priesthood or as a band of champions? Are they to be cut off from the people by privilege and mystique, answerable to themselves alone? Or will they act in the service of the people, be intimately *bound* to the people? Will they be *part* of the people, the citizenry, or outside them?''

Luke had never considered the question in quite that way before. ''It's obvious what answer you want,'' he said, ''but I think it's the answer I would choose no matter what. It seems to me that an order of Jedi that isolated itself from the population would be a very dangerous thing indeed. It would be very easy to forget the ways of ordinary folk if you never experienced the things they did.''

''Precisely,'' Mon Mothma said. ''I believe, and believe strongly, that the Republic needs Jedi that get their hands dirty, that are part of the Republic's daily life. Jedi that live in ivory towers might be more dangerous than no Jedi at all. You need look no further than our very recent history to see that it has been the Dark Jedi that have sought isolation. To be a Jedi of the Light, a Jedi must be one with the people. There must be a Jedi on every planet, a Jedi in every city—not a few planets full of Jedi and nothing else. There must be Jedi doing what ordinary folk do, Jedi who *are* ordinary folk. There must be Jedi doctors and judges and soldiers and pilots—and politicians.''

''And you believe that my path will guide me into politics,'' Luke said.

"Yes. If for no other reason than because it is your duty to set an example—and you have always been a slave to duty. If *you* wander off to brood on a hilltop somewhere, your followers will head off to find their own hills to brood on. If you are out in the world, so, too, will they follow that example."

"I see your point," Luke conceded, none too happily. Setting a good example was a laudable reason for most things, but it was not one that made the heart beat fast with excitement. But Mon Mothma had a point—excitement was going to be in short supply for a while—and for the general population, that was, perhaps, no bad thing. "Do you really think I'll get pulled that deeply into politics?"

"*I* certainly have no way to see into the future," she said. "I cannot see your path. But people will look for leaders, and I believe they will look to you."

"I suppose it is possible," Luke conceded.

"It is highly probable. Probable enough that you should consider the situation in advance."

"But I've never been interested in power," Luke said. "I'm not going to wake up one morning and decide to run for office."

"No, of course not. But that is not how it will happen. Someone—I don't know who, or when, or how many, or why—will come to you, seeking not a leader but a champion. Someone who will ask you to take up their cause, speak on their behalf, fight for their rights. You are not interested in *power*—but could you resist a call for help?"

"No," Luke said, something half-regretful in his voice. Mon Mothma was right. It was exactly the sort of approach he would find impossible to resist. "No, if someone put it that way, of course I'd have to say yes."

"And sooner or later someone *will* put it that way. The question then is, will you become a real leader or just a figurehead."

"I beg your pardon?" Luke said.

"Will you be a figurehead?" Mon Mothma asked again. "Will you know the craft of leadership, of negotiating when you should and of making difficult decisions when you must? Or will you be full of good intentions but ill trained and ill prepared to function in the world of politics, so that others must guide and control—and manipulate—you? If you are to be a real leader for the people, you must *prepare* for the job, just as you prepared to be a Jedi. You must undergo the training that Leia underwent while you were learning your Jedi skills.''

There was an unmistakable hint of reproach in her tone, if not in her words. *Leia was learning by doing the boring, necessary drudge work while you were out having exciting adventures.* She did not say it, but Luke got the message. ''There's been a little more to what I've done than fun and games,'' he said.

''Yes, of course. You have, beyond question, served the Republic well, even heroically. But history moves on. Times change. Tomorrow's galaxy will demand new and different things of us. It is time that you found ways to act as a leader, a negotiator, a spokesman for those with no voice. You will be a guide or a commander or a mentor. Now comes the day of the people marching together. Will you be at the head of the parade?''

''I suppose you're right,'' Luke said, though he didn't feel very convinced. ''But even if I wanted to do what you say, there wouldn't be much I could do about it. Not much is going on.''

''Yes,'' Mon Mothma said, smiling again. ''Very few opportunities for dynamic leadership are presenting themselves at the moment. That's what happens in peacetime. In a way, peace is the whole problem.''

''How could peace be a problem?'' Luke asked.

''Please, don't get me wrong,'' Mon Mothma said. ''War is a terrible business, and I hope it never comes again. But there are ways in which war is simple and clear as peace rarely is.

''In war, the enemy is clear, and he is outside your group. All of your friends and allies must come together for survival. In peacetime, there *is* no enemy. There are merely people who vote against you on this issue, and side with you on that proposal.

"We fought the Empire in the name of liberty and justice. But now our task is to make liberty and justice real. We are now seeking to correct wrongs that would have seemed trivial in the old days. There was no time to worry about the fine points of fair legislation when we were about to get our throats cut.

"Peacetime is complicated, murky. We could win the war by blowing up a Death Star or two—but we can only win the peace by building new space stations, new houses, new cities. That is not a question of largess or generosity. If we do not rebuild, there will be new unrest, new disturbances, and new war. In peacetime, you cannot win by destroying, but only by building—and it is always far easier to destroy. That is quite literally a law of nature.

"Rebuilding is slow, painstaking work, unsuited to a warrior's mentality. That is the real problem, for people like you and me. We became addicted to the thrills, the challenges, of war, and now they are gone. There are those who will be tempted to stir up trouble just for the sake of having some excitement."

"I doubt that is so, Mon Mothma," said Luke. "There will always be perils and challenges. The universe is a dangerous place. And I also don't know that I am addicted to such things. I could live the rest of my life quite happily if no one ever tried to kill me again."

"Perhaps you are right, Luke Skywalker. But even if no task now calls out for you to serve as leader—be ready for such a chance when it comes. Seize it, learn by it. Be not just a Jedi, not even just a Jedi Master—but a Jedi leader."

"I will consider your words," Luke said, standing up and preparing to take his leave.

"That is all that I hoped for," she said. "But there is one other matter in which I hope you will indulge an old woman."

"And what might that be?" Luke asked, a bit warily.

"You are to meet with Lando Calrissian," she said. "He is going to ask you to assist in a—project—of his."

"Yes," Luke said, wondering, not for the first time, where she got her information. "That is so. But I do not yet know what the project is."

"Ah," Mon Mothma said, smiling one more time. "I *thought* you might not. It just so happens that I *do* know what he is up to. It is an *unusual* sort of project for Lando to undertake, but it does have that grandiose element to it."

"And you wish me to talk him out of it."

"On the contrary, I would like you to offer him every assistance. That it is grandiose does not make it ill advised. No. Help your friend. I believe that in doing so, you will do *yourself* great good as well."

It was not until sometime later, when he was out the door, that Luke realized that he hadn't quite managed to ask what she had meant by that.

CHAPTER FIVE

Rough Welcome

L ieutenant Belindi Kalenda hesitated a moment before she activated the cargo transport's lightspeed engines. The little ship hung in the dark between the stars, its navigation checks complete, all systems ready for the final stage of the journey to Corellia. Once she fired up the engines, she was committed, with no way back, no way out. That shouldn't have bothered her quite so much, but she knew what was going on in the Corellian System—at least she knew as much as anyone from the outside did.

She was flying a small, nondescript freighter, very carefully chosen by NRI to fit her profile of a slightly down-on-her-luck trader. She carried a varied cargo from a half dozen worlds, and the ship's logs had been expertly manipulated to show that she had indeed been to all those places. Bits of litter in the trash matched her previous ports of call. The air filters even contained stray hairs and bits of shed skin and carapace, all of which matched the various intelligent species of the worlds to which she had allegedly been.

But the thing that got her most nervous was the deliberate flaw in the lightspeed engines. The remodulating buffer heat sink was just about to go. The NRI technicians assured her that it would function for exactly one more start-up, and then be blown by the heatpulse at shutdown. In short, her hyperdrive would die just as she arrived in-system. They would not be able to throw her out of the system, and they would more or less have to allow her to land and get to the central repair facility, where, by all accounts, it took weeks, or even months, to get anything repaired, unless a bribe changed hands. And Kalenda would just barely have enough to pay the standard repair costs—if she managed to sell her cargo.

In short, she was going to be stranded for an indefinite period of time the moment she hit the Corellian System, hoping that the role of a cargo pilot having a run of bad luck would be convincing enough to let her escape detection.

Kalenda sincerely wished that she could wait to go in until after Solo and his family had arrived to serve as a diversion. But that was not to be. No one could make the two operations dovetail like that, for the very simple reason that no one else in NRI even knew about Solo. She had been doing a bit of freelancing there. It would be better for all if no one—and she meant no one—knew about that plan. If one thing was plainly clear from all the things that had gone wrong recently, it was that somehow someone in the Corellian System had done a very good job of penetrating NRI.

If she had cleared the Solo-as-diversion plan with her superiors, the odds would have been strong that the Corellian opposition—whoever that was—would have learned about it already, and the whole plan would have been wrecked before it got started.

Besides which, she had at least managed to give Solo some sort of warning that something was wrong. It would keep him on top of things, make sure he watched out for his children. They needed some sort of protection. Leia Organa Solo had insisted that her family travel together, alone, before the trade summit. Once the official part of the trip got under way, the Chief of State's security detail would have a free hand. Until such time, they were on their own—giving the NRI plenty to sweat about.

Speaking of being on top of things, it was past time to get her own little operation started.

But had *it* been compromised? There was the question. If talking to Solo had been a bit of freelance enterprise, then setting up Kalenda's attempted infiltration had been a one-hundred-percent standard-issue NRI operation. NRI prided itself on meticulous planning and team effort. Normally that was all to the good, but every member added to the prep team increased the odds that the Corellian source would have found something out.

Kalenda wished she could change her coordinates for arrival in-system, but she knew that was impossible. The Corellian Defense Forces Space Service had a well-earned reputation for jumpiness as it was. If she arrived from hyperspace outside the authorized entry coordinates, they would go absolutely wild. At best, she would attract a hell of a lot of unwanted attention for herself. At worst, she would get blown out of the sky.

Maybe, just maybe, the fact that she had dawdled a bit and was going to arrive a few hours late would throw off any hypothetical Space Service border guards. Maybe they would think she wasn't coming after all, and would give up and go home. Or maybe she was just giving them time to get into position for the intercept.

There was nothing more she could do but activate the navicomputer, make the jump to light speed, and hope to luck. Kalenda swallowed hard, flexed her hand a time or two, and pressed the button.

She watched through the freight's forward viewport as the stars flared off into starlines and her ship leaped into the unknown and unknowable darkness of hyperspace. She let off a sigh of relief as the last of the stars winked out of existence behind her. She was safe, at least for the moment.

Unfortunately, her departure point was only a light-year out from the Corellian System, and she was not going to stay safely hidden for long. She spent the short ride worrying about all the things that could go wrong on her mission— or at least some of them. She would have needed a lot more time to get through the whole list.

All too soon the navicomputer beeped its get-ready warning. Kalenda settled herself in the pilot's chair and wrapped her hands around the controls. This was it. The navicomputer finished its countdown and dropped her back into normal space.

The universe flared back into existence around her spacecraft. Kalenda saw Corell, Corellia's sun, right where it ought to be. She checked her navigation displays and confirmed her position. Good. Good. Right in the middle of the authorized approach lane, nicely on course for Corellia itself.

Maybe she was going to pull this off after all. All she had to do was play her assigned role and everything would be fine. Speaking of which, it was time to contact Corellian Traffic Control.

She switched on the com system and punched in the proper frequency. "Corellian Traffic Control, this is Freighter PBY-1457, on approach to Corellia. Requesting landing and berthing instructions and permission—"

Wham! Something slammed her forward in her restraint harness, and her freighter shuddered from a massive impact. Kalenda lunged for the flight controls. It couldn't be the buffer heat sink blowing already. The techs had promised it would be at least half an hour before it went. It had to be—

Wham! Another hit. That was no internal explosion. Someone was shooting at her. Even before she had completed the thought, she had flipped her freighter into a barrel roll and taken it into a dive straight for the planet.

There was a flare of light off her port bow as the next shot went wide. She punched up a view from the rear external camera on her cabin display and risked a peek at it even as she jinked her freighter sideways to dodge the next shot. A Pocket Patrol Boat, just as she had thought. If anything but a PPB had made two hits on this old tub, she wouldn't still be alive. A PPB was a very small single-pilot ship that traded high speed for limited firepower. Of course, even the popgun on a PPB would be more than enough to take out this unshielded, unarmed junk heap if she took enough hits.

She jinked again, just in time to dodge the next shot. Blast it all! It was obvious they had been waiting for her. Her cover had been blown before she even entered the system. She had to think, and think fast. She couldn't outrun a PPB, and she couldn't outmaneuver it for long. She threw another random turn into her flight path as she rushed for the planet. Could she bluff a run back toward hyperspace? No, *think!* They obviously knew everything else about her. They'd have to know her hyperspace motors had been gimmicked. The bluff wouldn't fool anyone. She couldn't enter hyperspace without the whole hyperspace engine blowing out—

Wham! A bigger hit that time, harder. Alarm bells started going off, and Kalenda could smell smoke and burning insulation. Dead. She was dead if she played by the rules. Her freighter lurched suddenly as the number-three engine flared and died.

Kalenda cut the power to number three and diverted it to numbers one and two. No sense worrying about engine overloads now. The PPB would stay on her tail and use her for target practice until it ruptured the hull and got her dead. She couldn't reach the planet and she couldn't enter hyperspace without the buffer heat sink exploding and dropping her right back out—

Yes! That was it. It was a near-suicidal plan, but everything was relative, and staying here would be *utterly* suicidal.

She reached for the hyperspace controls with one hand as she flew the ship with the other. She cut off all the safeties and overrides, cut the selector to manual, and stabbed in the activate button before she could think of what she was doing. An uncalibrated, uncalculated jump into hyperspace this near a planet was nothing more than a fancy way to kill herself, but if she stopped long enough to tell herself that, she would already be dead.

No smooth transition to light speed this time, but a lurching, horrific crash into hyperspace, as graceful as slamming the ship into a brick wall. The freighter started to tumble end over end, but Kalenda didn't even try to stop it. Not when—

Blam! With a horrible, shuddering explosion that sent the ship into new paroxysms, the buffer heat sink blew. The plan had been for it to give out quietly during the cooldown phase. But with the hyperdrive under power, the heat sink failed in far more spectacular fashion, detonating with almost enough energy to tear the ship in two. The hull breached somewhere in the engine compartment, and air thundered aft out into space. The cockpit's hatch slammed shut automatically. Alarms were clanging everywhere, and Kalenda hit the general override button, cutting the alarms off and killing power to all systems.

With the heat sink destroyed, it took less than a half second for the hyperdrive coils to overheat and melt down. With an even more violent lurch, the freighter crashed back into normal space. At least Kalenda *hoped* it was normal space. Plenty of ships had vanished from hyperspace over the millennia and no one knew where they had gone.

But Kalenda had more immediate concerns than what sort of space-time continuum she was in. She had to keep the ship from breaking up or blowing up. She needed to get the tumble under some sort of control. It wasn't easy with half the altitude control system destroyed, but she managed to get rid of about ninety-five percent of the tumble, leaving the ship in a sort of slow, off-kilter barrel roll. She checked her system displays and confirmed what she had already suspected—the hyperdrive system wasn't there anymore. It looked as if the number-one engine was out for good as well. That left her the number-two engine, with a very large question mark behind it. The cockpit displays said it was still there, and Kalenda devoutly hoped they were telling the truth.

At last she had time to look around and figure out where she was—and found that she had finally drawn at least one piece of good luck. There, hanging round and lovely in the firmament, was Corellia, the planet half in daytime and half in night from this angle. At a guess, she had managed to travel all of a few hundred thousand kilometers in hyperspace, and in something roughly like the right direction. At an eyeball estimate, she was on the opposite side of the planet than she had started out from, and perhaps twice as far away from it. She could just as easily have been thrown completely out of the galaxy, or into the dark between the stars.

In theory at least, she ought to be able to get down to Corellia from here. If that one engine really was still in one piece, she still might get out of this thing alive.

If she were *really* lucky, the Corellians would think she was dead. Maybe the PPB pilot would get it wrong and report her ship had blown up instead of jumping into hyperspace. Or maybe everyone would—quite properly—assume the odds against surviving an uncontrolled hyperspace jump were too high to worry about her surviving.

In any event, even on the odd chance that they thought she was alive, they certainly did not know where she was. She hoped to keep it that way.

*   *   *

Part of knowing how to survive was knowing when to rush, and when to take things slowly. Kalenda gave herself a good three hours for the next step. She did a careful checkout of the freighter—or as much of it as she could manage from the cockpit. The only pressure suit on the ship was in its rack, in vacuum, on the other side of the sealed cockpit hatch. A triumph of planning and design, that, but there was no help for it now.

Even on this ship, the cockpit data displays could tell her an awful lot. She concentrated on the surviving main engine, and confirmed, by every means she could, that it was still operational. Not that she was going to trust it at anything like full power, of course. She would have to assume that it was about to fail, and treat it very gently. The cockpit's life support was in moderately good shape, though there seemed to be a few slow microleaks in the hull, and the cooling system was showing signs of failing. She wouldn't want to stay in the cockpit more than a day or two. Not that she could, anyway. There were no food or water or sanitary facilities in the cockpit. The ship's survival pack was stowed in a rack right next to the pressure suit.

Obviously, the only way out of this mess—and, incidentally, the only way she could complete her mission—was to get down to one of the planets in the Corellian star system. Corellia itself was the obvious target, but not the only one.

For a moment she toyed with the idea of trying for another of the habitable planets in the Corellian System. There were certainly enough of them. Besides Corellia, there were Selonia, Drall, and the Double Worlds, Talus and Tralus, two planets that orbited about each other. If there were to be a search for her, it would almost certainly take place on Corellia, making it a good place to avoid.

But there were strong arguments against that line of reasoning. They probably did think she was dead.

Therefore, there probably would not be a search. Besides, a planet was a rather largish place. Even if they were on the lookout for her, she was a trained operative, after all. She ought to be able to stay one step ahead of them.

Them. Who were the "them" in this case? And what were "they" up to that merited the taking of such risks? One didn't attack New Republic operatives lightly. Kalenda realized she had no idea who she was up against. She had not spent any time at all wondering why the Corellians— or some group of Corellians—was so intent on killing NRI agents, or on how they knew her arrival plans. But no time to worry about such things now. They were certainly important points, but they really didn't matter, one way or the other, unless she stayed alive. Best to focus on that small matter first.

She decided not to try for any of the other worlds. Corellia was closest. She had the best odds of reaching it. The risk of detection was only marginally greater there than on the other worlds. Besides, Corellia itself was where the action was. Whatever was going on, was going on *there*.

The question then became one of how to get there. It was all very well to look out the port and see the planet, but she couldn't simply point the freighter at Corellia and switch on the engine. She needed to do a great deal more navigation work first. One bit of good luck was that she seemed to have retained more or less the same initial velocity as she had started out with before her abortive jump to light speed. The only difference was that she was on the other side of the planet, moving away rather than toward it. The planet's gravity was slowing her, of course, and sooner or later would start pulling her back.

In plain point of fact, she was going to fall straight in on the planet and land about as lightly and gently as a meteorite unless she did something.

And, of course, she did not dare make anything like a normal landing. A daylight landing of any kind was out of the question. The risk of detection was too great.

A few minutes' careful work with the navicomputer let Kalenda work out a slow and careful approach to the planet that met the conditions she had chosen: a water landing, at night. She managed to find a trajectory that would allow her to come in just off the east coast of the main continent.

Not that she was especially pleased to find it was possible to do that sort of landing, but the risks of touching down on land at night were just too great. Kalenda did not know the lay of the land well enough to look out the window in the dark and judge whether she was coming down in a nice, empty glade or a village square, a soft canopy of trees or a patch of low scrubby bushes that hid solid rock just below. Water was water no matter how you landed on it, and was more likely to be private. The odds on being heard or seen were much lower over water. Of course the odds on *drowning* were nil over land, but that could not be helped.

Kalenda laid in her course and powered up that one remaining main engine as slowly and gently as she could, taking a good ten minutes to bring it up to one-quarter power, to the accompaniment of a number of disturbing bumps and thuds and bangs as the ship's structural members strained against the unbalanced thrust and bits of debris knocked themselves loose and clattered around in the compartments behind the cockpit door.

Kalenda watched her displays carefully, and it did not take long for her to be inspired to curse a blue streak. Even at one-quarter power, she was getting a whole series of rather alarming readouts. The engine seemed to want to overheat. Its cooling system must have been damaged. She backed off to one-eighth power and tried to divert cooling power from the dead engines, to little or no effect. More than likely she was sending commands to systems that weren't even there anymore. Lowered thrust required a longer engine burn, of course, but that beat having her last engine melt down. She adjusted her course to compensate and watched Corellia grow bigger in the viewport.

Now she *did* have the leisure to worry over how they had known to jump her, and over what the devil was going on down there on the planet. The Corellians seemed to be zeroing right in on NRI's objectives, such as herself, without any need to bother searching through civilians to find them. There *had* to be some sort of leak back at HQ.

Kalenda had a hunch that the higher-ups in NRI were starting to figure that out for themselves. That meant they were working on some more carefully compartmentalized operations against Corellia, wherein the left hand would not have the least idea what the right was doing. She had suspicions that there were a few NRI agents placed among the trade delegations.

For all she knew, the attempt to insert her was at least in part meant as a diversion, to get the opposition looking the other way from someone *else's* arrival. It occurred to her that she should have been bothered at the thought of being someone else's diversion, but that was the way of the world—at least the espionage world. If you did not wish to risk the chance of being a piece on someone else's game board, it was best not to volunteer for the service.

But there was at least the hope that, even if she did not get through, did not find out what was going on in this madhouse of a system, *someone* would. Maybe that was why the thought of being a diversion did not upset her. If she was a diversion, and she did die, and managed to get the Corellians looking in the wrong direction at the proper moment, then at least her death would not be in vain.

Not much of a comfort, but with the Corellians gunning for her, and her life staked on an engine that wanted to give up and a night water landing, Lieutenant Kalenda needed all the comforts she could imagine.

*   *   *

Kalenda woke with a start as the alert buzzer blatted in her ear. She blinked, looked around, remembered where she was, and wished she hadn't. But what had set off the alert? Had something else given out on this old tub? She checked her boards, and her eyes lit on the chronometer. Good. No malfunction. The alert was from the plain old alarm-clock function. Time to wake up and get ready for reentry. She pushed a button and shifted in the pilot's seat and stretched as best she could in a vain attempt to work the kinks out.

Now would come the time for some real piloting. Flying a freighter in on a manual, unpowered reentry was no easy job in the best of times. Coming in at night, over hostile territory, with no guidance, in a badly damaged ship was going to take everything she had—and maybe more.

Hold on. No sense going into this thing with such a negative attitude. Think good thoughts, about how the freighter was a solid old ship to hold together as long as it already had. About all her training, and her painstaking memorization of every map of Corellia. About how it was very unlikely that anyone was looking for her, and how she would be damned hard to find even so.

Yes, that was the tone to take. Good thoughts. Good thoughts. She checked over all her systems one last time, and wished that they were looking better, even as she gave thanks that they were not looking worse. She looked out the port to the huge bulk of Corellia, looming lovely and dark, so close she thought she could reach out and touch it. She was square over the night side of the planet, but by no means was Corellia in absolute blackness. The lights of cities shone here and there, and starlight gleamed off gray cloud tops and dark blue sky and black land, making it all seem to glow as if from within, knots and whorls and points of light shining out from the sleeping world below.

A lovely world, and one full of danger. She would have to be careful down there. If she lived. She checked her countdown clock. It was almost time to cut the engine.

The normal procedure, of course, was for a powered descent, going in with the engines throttled up, decelerating from orbital speed to flying speed with the brute force of the ship's engines. But her freighter's sole remaining engine did not have anything like the power to manage that. She would have to do it the old-fashioned way, bashing her way through the atmosphere, using air friction instead of engine power to slow her craft. In theory, her freighter was built to survive just that sort of emergency entry, but she would have been just as happy not to test the theory. Not that she had any choice in the matter. The countdown clock clicked off the seconds to engine stop, arriving at zero far too quickly. Her one surviving main engine cut off, and Kalenda reoriented the ship, pointing it in the right direction for an aero-braking reentry.

Any moment now she would start to feel the first slight stirrings of atmosphere on the freighter's hull—

Almost before she had finished the thought, the freighter bucked and quivered, and the controls tried to leap out of her hands. Kalenda grabbed the flight stick in a death grip and forced the ship back to an even keel. She had flown plenty of reentries, and on nearly all of them initial contact with the atmosphere had been smooth and subtle. This was more like hitting a brick wall. The exterior of the freighter must have gotten more torn up than she thought. This was going to be interesting.

There was another series of shudders and thuds, and then, with a long-drawn-out shrieking noise, something tore off the aft end of the ship and broke clear. The freighter tried to flip itself over, and it was all Kalenda could do to force it back to a level flight path. On the bright side, it seemed as if the ship were flying a bit more steadily with the whatever-it-was gone.

She checked her actual flight path against her planned course. She found she was running a bit fast, and a bit high. She made what adjustments she could, and started watching her hull temperatures climb steadily upward. The freighter began to shudder again, with a new, deeper noise, a sort of rhythmic banging, thrown into the mix as well. Something else back there wanted to tear itself off, and no mistake.

The freighter plunged deeper and deeper into Corellia's atmosphere, bucking and swaying and banging and shrieking its way down. The nose of the ship started to glow a cherry red, something Kalenda had never seen before. She was used to gentle, fully powered descents, not this sort of primitive aero-braking approach.

The g forces were starting to build up, and Kalenda felt as if she were being shaken to death and crushed to death at the same time. A new alarm went off, barely audible in the cacophony that filled the ship's cockpit. Kalenda was being shaken around so badly that she could focus her eyes only clearly enough to see what the visual displays were telling her. A temperature alarm. It had to be a temp alarm.

Well, that was just too bad. She didn't dare take either hand off the flight stick long enough to make any adjustments, and besides, there was precious little she could do to cool things off. She couldn't even abort the landing attempt anymore. At one-eighth power, her one remaining engine didn't have anything like enough thrust to push her back into orbit.

Not that orbit was a good place to be on a ship that was probably losing air, on a ship with no accessible food or water.

Wham! The noise was loud and sudden enough to make Kalenda jump clear out of her seat if she hadn't been belted in. Something had just broken loose back in the ship's interior. A second, smaller crash announced that whatever-it-was had just slammed into the opposite bulkhead.

The vibration reached a crescendo, and just when it seemed that it would tear the freighter apart, it began to taper off, fading away more quickly than it had come on.

Now Kalenda had some faint hope that she was through the worst of it. The freighter was still jouncing around quite impressively, but it had at least survived the reentry phase proper. It had become a badly damaged aircraft, not a half-wrecked spacecraft. Not that it was handling any better, or that she would be any less dead if she lost control of it and the freighter succumbed to its obvious desire to crash.

Kalenda heard a loud whistling from behind the cockpit door. It began at a high pitch and gradually worked its way down through the scale to a low rumble. It was the sound of air leaking back *into* the aft compartments of the ship. Kalenda did not dare take her eyes off the viewport and the main displays for even a moment to check the environment display, but air in the aft compartment had to be good news. She would be able to get back there and grab the survival gear.

She checked her rates, forward and down. Still a bit fast and high, but now it was a question of energy management, of controlling her descent, trading altitude and speed for distance, rather than any question of burning up in the atmosphere. She set the freighter into a series of wide, gentle S-turns to shed a bit more speed.

Well, at least they were *meant* to be wide and gentle. If the freighter had handled like a live bantha in convulsion during reentry, in normal aerodynamic flight it handled like a dead one. The ship barely responded to the controls at all, and she had to fight it through every moment of every turn. Something in the control system started hammering and banging, protesting the strain. She gave it up and got back on her ground-track course, and never mind if she was a bit fast and high.

The ship glided downward into the velvet darkness of Corellia's night sky, biting into thicker air now—and suddenly all of Kalenda's concerns about being fast and high vanished. The ship's performance in the lower atmosphere was atrocious. She should have expected that, with half the aerodynamic surfaces shot to glory, but she had been concentrating so hard on staying alive long enough to get into deep air that she had never thought of how the ship would fly once she got there.

Suddenly it was not a question of overshooting her target point by a few kilometers, but a question of not undershooting by several hundred kilometers. She had planned to put down just offshore, not in the middle of deep ocean. She had no choice but to relight her main engine and try to stretch out her glide as much as she could. She had hoped to avoid doing so. She didn't trust that engine, and she wasn't sure about the ship holding together while it was taking stress from both the aerodynamic surfaces and the engines. With the stress on the stabilizers and the off-center thrust of one engine, things could go very wrong very fast. However, it was not as if she had a choice at this point. It was relight the engine or drown.

Kalenda looked out the port. It was a lovely view, and even in the midst of her struggle for survival, she felt privileged to see it. She granted herself a second, two seconds, to drink it all in, so that she might die with some recent memory of beauty, if die she must. The clear and cloudless sky was blue black, pocked with jewel-bright stars, white, red, blue; diamonds and rubies and sapphires shining down on the blue-black sea and its gray whitecaps far below.

Lovely. Lovely. But if she was going to live to deserve further such privileges, she was going to have to tear her eyes away and get back to the job at hand. As gently, as delicately as possible, she powered up her single engine and brought it up to one-sixteenth power. The freighter slewed over a bit to port, but she managed to compensate without too much trouble. There was a low groan from the hull as the stresses on the ship rearranged themselves, but that was to be expected.

She checked her displays again, and saw that she was still losing more speed and altitude than she could afford, even if the loss rate had decreased. She was still going to fall short of her intended landing zone, and that was not good. If need be, she could swim three kilometers to reach the shore—but she could not swim fifty.

She bit her lower lip and throttled up toward one-eighth power, as slowly as she could. The hull began to groan again, but this time the sound did not fade out but grew louder. The damaged ship was not likely to take much more strain. The freighter's nose started to drift to port, and she pulled it back to starboard—and then had to heel back over to port as it started to heel over to starboard. Almost before she knew it, the ship was in a dangerous oscillation, its nose wobbling back and forth, unable to hold a stable attitude. If that oscillation got much worse at all, the freighter would heel over all the way and go spiraling into the drink.

Kalenda throttled down until the oscillation faded out again, and the groaning of the hull members receded. She checked her displays and swore. Not enough. Not enough. She was still going to land short of her intended ditch point.

One last card to play. She brought the nose of the ship up just a bit, in hopes of tempting just a bit more lift out of the wings. For a wonder, it seemed to work. Her rate of loss of altitude faded away, and she actually achieved level flight.

But Kalenda knew better than to relax her guard. Something else was bound to go wrong.

It started as a low hum, almost below the range of hearing, but it did not stay hard to hear for long. Bi-bi-bi-be-bee-bee-bee-bang-bang-bang-Bang-Bang-BANG BANG BANG BANG! BANG! BANG! It grew louder and louder, and shook the ship harder and harder. Some bit of the stabilizer, or a torn-up piece of rudder, was slamming itself against the hull with incredible violence. Kalenda set her teeth and hung on. As best she could see with the ship bucking and bouncing like a mad thing, she was still flying level, and every second she did that was another few hundred meters toward shore. So long as it got her in toward shore, the freighter could tear itself to pieces as much as it liked.

Getting closer now. Kalenda scanned the horizon, watching for land. There! A strip of motionless, darker darkness off in the distance. Stars and sky, she was going to make it.

BANG! BANG! *BANG! BANG!* Long past the time when it seemed impossible, the banging was getting worse. What in the name of space was trying to tear itself loose back there? *BANG! BANG! BANG! BAN*—

There was a sudden silence, and then, a heartbeat later, the gut-wrenching shriek of metal on metal and a final shudder that spasmed through the whole ship. Kalenda felt the freighter's tail pull up and heel over to starboard. Well, whatever it was that had just pulled itself loose must have been part of the horizontal stabilizers. She corrected back toward port, but not too far. Let the ship hang at an odd angle of attack, as long as it was flying straight, more or less.

How far to shore now? She checked her navigation displays. Not more than twenty kilometers to go. If she could just hold this thing together that much longer—

Ping-PING! Ping-PING! Ping-PING! Kalenda hit the alarm reset and checked her displays. Damn! The engine overheat alarm. The thing was going to hit meltdown if she kept pushing it, and no mistake. She knew what she had to do, but she didn't like it. What good was it in getting this far if the engine blew up and she crashed into the sea here and now? With infinite reluctance, she throttled the engine back down to one-sixteenth power, and grimaced as the freighter promptly set back to work losing speed and altitude.

Ping-PING! Ping-PING! Ping-PING! She hit the alarm reset and swore under her breath with a fair amount of creativity. The engine was *still* overheating. Some last cooling connection must have failed altogether. With all cooling systems out completely, the engine would explode in short order, no matter *how* little power she ran through it.

For one mad moment she toyed with the idea of letting it blow, taking the explosion in trade for whatever last driblets of thrust she could get from the engine. But if there was one thing this ship was not going to take, it was yet another explosion.

She braced herself, and then cut all power to the engine. The freighter lurched violently, and tried to pull its nose up into a stall, but she forced it back into something like a level glide.

And that was that. No power left, no tricks left to try, all options explored. She was left with a deadstick glide into a nighttime open-ocean ditch. It didn't get much worse than that. Kalenda tried not to tell herself that at least she had the blessing of fair weather, for fear of the universe conjuring up a storm for her out of sheer perversity.

Flying is divided into two sorts of time—the steady, careful stretches where the idea is to keep things more or less as they are, and the sudden, rushing, fast-moving moments where the idea is to get from one state to another as quickly as possible while not getting killed. Pilots should not be rushed or hurried during cruise operations, but they *must* move fast for the takeoffs and landings.

As Kalenda was in the process of learning, all that was true in spades for a deadstick water landing. That water down below was coming up on her awfully fast. Best to get ready. She was going to have to get out of here in a hurry, once she put down. Keeping one hand on the flying stick, she reached up with the other and pulled down on the safety cover for the overhead escape hatch. She risked a glance up to spot the safety releases, then got her eyes forward again. Getting closer. Much closer. She reached up without looking and flipped the releases, then yanked down hard on the hatch eject lever.

Blam! The bolts blew and the hatch flew clear. Suddenly the wind was roaring past, and the stale, burned-insulation-flavored atmosphere of the cockpit was swept away by the cool, tangy salt air of the Corellian ocean by night.

Much, much closer. Kalenda struggled to flatten out her glide angle and braced herself for impact. Water might seem softer than land, but it still packed a hell of a wallop if you hit it at speed.

And here it came. Kalenda resisted the temptation to shut her eyes, and got both hands back on the flight stick, hanging on for dear life.

Coming in closer, lower, faster—faster—faster! The water so close now it was a blur, all the nice neat waves she could see so clearly from higher up nothing more than a smear of blue gray she could not focus on. The wind roared through the hatchway, and her hair got loose and blew wildly into her face. She ignored it. Better to go in half-blind than to take her hands off the stick. Closer faster can't get closer must be there but we're not closer faster faster—

With a shuddering, roaring crash the ruined freighter slammed into the waves, bounced clear, and slammed down again with renewed vigor. Kalenda held on for dear life as the ship slammed head-on into wave after wave after wave, the water splashing up over the viewports, then clearing away before the next wave blinded her again. The shuddering, terrifying ride seemed to go on forever, with always the next wave lunging into view just as the last one washed away.

But at last the freighter slowed, rode lower in the water, eased itself to a halt, and the stupefying, crashing roar of the landing was quite suddenly replaced by the absurdly prosaic, hollow, echoing sounds of water sloshing about under a hull, of waves crashing on a nearby shore. She had made it. At least, made it this far.

Kalenda allowed herself a moment to resume breathing.

She peeled her hands off the flight stick, released her crash belts, and stood up, more than a little weak in the knees. She wanted to give herself time to recover, but there was no time. The nose was already creeping up into the sky as the freighter's aft end took on water.

She went to the cockpit hatch and pulled open the manual release panel. She pulled down the lever and felt the latch disengage. She leaned into the hatch and shoved it open. There. The pressure suit she'd never had the chance to get to—and the standard-issue survival packs. She grabbed both ration packs and the gear case, and noticed her feet were wet. Water. Water already coming in. Hurry. Move. The ration packs had carry straps, and she threw one over each shoulder while carrying the gear case by its handle. She heaved the case out the overhead escape hatch and then scrambled through it herself as fast as she could, for fear of the case sliding off the hull without her. She managed to snatch at it just as it was threatening to slip off into the water.

In theory, there was a life raft in the case, along with all the other hardware. Kalenda had planned to open the case, get the raft and its paddles, close the case, inflate the raft, load it up with the gear case and the ration packs, climb in herself, and then paddle sedately away. She might as well have planned to compose a few Selonian sonnets as well, for all the good it would do her. The freighter was sinking beneath her feet, and it was, after all, the dead of night, and far too dark for rummaging around in a gear case looking for a life raft.

Well, if the survival gear designers had had any sense— she heaved the gear case into the water. Sure enough, praise be, it floated, and fairly high in the water at that. She readjusted the straps on the ration packs—which seemed likely to act in the stead of flotation devices in their own right—and stepped sloshingly off into the cool salt water.

After an anxious moment or two when it seemed the gear case wanted to escape from her altogether, she managed to grab it by the handle, and sort of pull herself on top of·it, so that she was lying on her stomach on the case, her feet dangling off the end. She discovered the case had a handle on either side, and took one in each hand. She started paddle-kicking vigorously without worrying too much about which direction she was going. She was eager to get some distance between herself and the sinking ship. A ship, even a small one, produces quite a bit of suction as it goes down, and she had no desire to be pulled under as the freighter went to the bottom.

Judging that she was far enough away, she turned herself around with a kick or two of her feet and watched as her poor old freighter commenced its final voyage, toward its last resting place, on the bottom of the Corellian sea.

The nose of the ship continued to angle up out of the water. There was a flash, and a shower of sparks illuminated the cockpit from the inside as some power system or other shorted out. The ship's interior lights flared, guttered down, flared again, and then died altogether. There was a dull thud and a mass of dirty bubbles belched out of the water from the aft end of the ship. The nose of the ship swung clear over to the vertical. There were a few creaking sounds, and the sound of water rushing in, and the nose of the ship sank straight down, moving with an odd sort of dignity. A final slosh, a gurgle, and the nose of her ill-starred freighter vanished beneath the waves.

Kalenda stared at the spot where it had been, more emotions than she could rightly name running through her as she watched what might well have been her own watery grave close over itself, as if there had never been any such thing as a freighter that ditched in the sea. It had vanished altogether.

She looked up at the gleaming stars overhead. Possibly someone had seen the glowing trail of her reentry across the sky, but Corellia's skies were just as full of junk as most places these days. That was one grim legacy of the Republic-Imperial War: Most star systems were cluttered up with shot-up spacecraft of one sort or another. No one even bothered to report the most spectacular of fireballs anymore. She had come in at night over water precisely to avoid being seen, but if there were any witnesses on the planet, her arrival would have looked just like the entry of dozens of derelict fighters and tenders and space-probe spacecraft that had crashed into the planet these last few years.

The odds were very good that she had made it, and that the Corellians didn't know she was here, and would have no way of finding her if they did.

The question became—what good was that going to do?

A wave lifted her up a bit, and she levered herself up a bit over the gear case to try to get her bearings. Good. Good. She was already pointed toward land, which looked to be only a few kilometers away.

She started kicking her feet, propelling herself toward the shore.

CHAPTER SIX

Farewell and Hail

L uke threw his black cloak back over one shoulder and stepped out of the shadows, toward where the *Millennium Falcon* was sitting on her hard stand, ready for liftoff. It was a scene of organized chaos—or more accurately, *two* such scenes mixed up with each other.

On the starboard side of the ship, Han was arguing with one of the spaceport safety inspection services, apparently about some sort of clearance regulation, while at the same time shouting at Chewbacca, who was crouched down over an access panel on the starboard wing of the hull. Well, Han and Chewie had been arguing over how to keep the *Falcon* patched up ever since Luke had known them. No reason to expect they'd stop now.

On the port side of the ship, Leia was surrounded by a little knot of governmental types of all sorts and descriptions. Luke looked over the crowd. Clerks, civil-service droids, cabinet officials, senators, and a sprinkling of military officers. No surprises there, either. Even in as democratic and informal a government as Leia was trying to build, it wasn't possible to let the Chief of State escape for her vacation without at least a few stray details—and egos— to sort out at the last minute.

A line of household service droids were rolling through, straight between the two groups and up the ship's ramp, delivering the last of the luggage aboard the *Falcon*.

Han and Leia's three kids were racing around like wild

things, beside themselves with excitement at the start of the big adventure—and, no doubt, well aware of the fact that they were about to get out from under Threepio's nagging and fussing. Luke smiled at that thought. No wonder they had wanted to make their own droid, the way that old bucket of bolts worried and niggled over everything.

As Leia was attempting to deal with the Bimm ambassador, Han was, by default, on child duty, doing his best to control them. Understandably under the circumstances, his best was none too good. Seeing things might be moving toward a crisis, Luke decided to step in. "Jacen! Jaina! Slow down a minute!" he called out. "Take it easy! Anakin! That landing leg isn't for climbing on! Come down from there."

"But *Chewie* climbs on the ship," Anakin protested. He came down off the landing leg, but not willingly.

"But he's not *playing* on the ship," Luke said, reflecting, not for the first time, on the futility of attempting to reason with a child Anakin's age. "He's working on it, trying to make it go better."

"*I* could make it go better," Anakin said, poking himself in the chest with a very confident thumb. "Lots of ways."

"I'll bet you could," Luke said, with a laugh. Anakin *did* seem to have a remarkably precocious way with machinery, but somehow Luke doubted Chewbacca would be eager to take too much help from him. "But why don't we let your father and Chewie worry about all that?" While Anakin was considering that, Luke took advantage of the moment to change the subject. "Are you all set to go on the trip?" he asked.

"Uh-huh. I got all my stuff."

"Good. You ought to have lots of fun." Luke looked up and spotted Jaina trying to get into the luggage the droids were carrying about the *Falcon*. "Come on, Jaina," he said. "Leave that stuff alone."

"But I wanted to get my book chips," Jaina protested. "I think they're in this bag."

"You're not going to have any chance to read until after

takeoff anyway,'' Luke said, hoping that Jaina was in as—
relatively—cooperative and reasonable a mood as Anakin.
He shooed the droid on its way. ''What good is it going to
do to get all your stuff dumped out on the landing pad?''

''But I want the chips now!''

So much for being reasonable. ''Well, you should have
thought of that before you packed.''

''I *didn't* pack. I would have kept the chips out if I had.
The droids packed for me.''

''I *told* you that you were letting them do too much for
you,'' Luke said. ''This is the sort of thing that happens.
Do things for yourself, and they'll turn out right. Let others
do them, and you've got no right to complain. So no sulking,
and remember this for next time. All right?''

''All right,'' she replied, quite reluctantly.

''Good,'' Luke said. Maybe, just maybe, the punishment
she and Jacen had gotten for the previous droid accident
had left some sort of impression. ''Now take Anakin with
you and find a place to sit quietly until it's time to go.''
Luke looked up and spotted Jacen at his father's side. He
was about to call him over, tell him to quit bothering his
father. Then Han put his arm around the boy in an absent-
minded sort of way, while still arguing with the ground
crew. Jacen seemed most interested in the argument. Leave
it be.

Keeping half an eye on Jaina and Anakin, who were, for
a miracle, indeed sitting quietly on an overturned shipping
container, Luke went over to see if he could help Leia
extricate herself from the crowd of people who seemed
intent on keeping her on the landing pad, asking ''just one
last question,'' until night had fallen.

But he should have listened when Mon Mothma reminded
him that he was not the only one of the two siblings with
skills the other had not developed. The crowd around her
was already melting away, each dignitary and hanger-on
leaving with a smile on his, her, or its face, clearly pleased
with the results of the conference, each of them plainly
feeling that the Chief of State had paid special attention to

his, her, or its concerns. Luke had never been that good with people, and he felt the slightest pang of envy to see the apparent effortlessness with which she handled them all. It was the same old story, of course—everything was easy if you practiced the skills required for years on end. He *had* sold Leia short. He could not make it up to her all at once, with a single gesture—but at least he could make a start.

She was bidding her farewells to the last of her visitors as he came up. She turned to him and gave him the starburst-bright smile that always melted his heart. There was no contrivance, nothing but the deepest and sincerest feelings behind that smile. Maybe that was the secret. She always did feel the emotions she was expressing. "Hello, Luke," she said. "An exciting day."

"That it is," he agreed. "You're finally going to get a look at where he came from," he said, nodding toward Han, who was still shouting at the Wookiee and the ground staff even as he kept an affectionate arm around his son. "Must be hard being married to a mystery man," Luke said, only half joking. "I bet you're looking forward to seeing where he got his start."

"Oh, Han's no mystery man," Leia said. "What you see is absolutely what you get. His *past* is a mystery, yes. He's never said much and I doubt he ever will. Anyway, I don't think a family tourist trip is going to do much to shed a dazzling light on the hidden corners of his personal history."

"And that doesn't bother you?" Luke asked.

Leia shrugged. "It used to. Not anymore. Han is Han. How much more do I need to know?"

"I suppose," Luke said. "Still, take a look at Corellia, and tell me all about it."

"That I'll do," she said. "It will be good to get away as a family, too, without all *that* crowd"—she gestured in the direction of the last of the departing dignitaries—"chasing after me every two minutes."

"Well, speaking of family," Luke said, "I have a gift I wanted to give you, brother to sister." He pulled a package out of his satchel. It was wrapped in the finest black velvet. It was thin and heavy, about as long as Leia's forearm. He handed it to her.

"What is it, Luke?" she asked.

"Open it and find out."

There was a silver ribbon tied around the velvet. Leia undid the ribbon, unfolded the velvet—and let out a little gasp of surprise. "But—but—"

"I know you already have a lightsaber," he said, "but I never see you carry it."

"It's been a long time since I felt I had the *right* to carry one," Leia said as she lifted the weapon out of the wrapping. "A long time since I felt as if I were getting remotely close to being a Jedi."

"And that's why I'm giving you one," Luke said. "I couldn't think of a clearer way to say *I* think you're a Jedi."

"But I should make my weapon for myself," Leia said. "That's one of the tests."

Luke shook his head. "It *can* be a test. It doesn't have to be. Yes, all the traditions say a Jedi is supposed to make his or her own lightsaber, as part of the progress toward knighthood. But tradition is all it is, after all. Nothing more. There's no hard and fast law. And remember Obi-Wan Kenobi gave me my first lightsaber, after all. *I* didn't build it. So take this one. I made it for you."

Leia looked at the lightsaber for a long moment and hefted it once or twice.

"How does it feel?" Luke asked.

"Like it belongs there," Leia said. "As if it's supposed to be there, in my hand. It's perfect. But—but I haven't completed the training," she said. "I never built my own lightsaber because I never felt I was ready to do so."

Luke shook his head. "No," he said, "that's where you're wrong. If there is anyone in this galaxy with the right to wear a Jedi's lightsaber, it is Leia Organa Solo, Chief of State of the New Republic. You *are* Jedi. Your training is complete. Different from mine, but complete."

"But that's not true!" Leia protested. "There is so much I don't know. There is so much you still need to teach me."

"But Mon Mothma reminded me that the reverse is also true," Luke replied. "There is much you have to teach that *I* must learn. None of us ever learn all that we should know. If it happens that you don't know a few mind tricks or haven't gotten every move with a lightsaber down cold, that has not prevented you from fighting for justice, or knowing right from wrong and acting on it. Take the lightsaber. You have earned it—and you might have need of it."

Leia tried the heft of the lightsaber again and then stepped back from Luke a pace or two. She pressed the power stud and the saber flared into life with a low-throated hum of power. A shaft of glowing ruby red leaped from the handle. With a flick of her wrist, she whirled the blade through the air, and the hum was suddenly louder for a moment as the saber's lightblade sliced through the air. "Try me," she said to Luke, stepping back another pace or two as she brought the saber to bear.

Luke hesitated a moment. There was something detached, distracted, about her voice and expression. By the way her eyes were locked on the saber's blade, Luke had no trouble understanding why.

Luke stepped back himself and shrugged off his black cloak, letting it fall to the ground. He drew his own lightsaber, keeping his eyes fixed on Leia. He switched the saber on and heard the familiar low throb of power as the blade came to life. Trained to watch his opponent and not himself, he did not see his own blade at all as he held it low, close to his body. Leia took a two-handed grip on her blade and raised it to the classic guard position. Luke raised his own weapon to hers, touched his blade to hers, and was rewarded with a crackling hiss of power as the lightblades met.

Leia's face was a study in concentration and suppressed excitement as she drew her blade back. Luke could understand her reaction. His blood, their father's blood, coursed through her veins as well. Luke knew deep in his heart that he dearly loved the thrill of danger, of challenge, of battle.

Whether that was some aspect of the dark side of the Force, or merely a perfectly normal competitive drive, he did not pretend to know. But for all of that, he knew the feeling in himself—and right now, he could recognize it in his sister as well.

No doubt she had fought many battles of the mind during her recent years of government service. She had won great victories for the New Republic—often by outmaneuvering the enemy so tidily, winning so completely at the conference table, that there was no need for fighting. But it had been a long while since she had been given a chance to fight with her *hands*, her speed, her agility, rather than just her mind. No wonder there was a gleam in her eye as she raised her lightsaber and swung it down toward Luke's blade.

He deflected her first thrust down and to the left and went back to guard just in time to parry another thrust that came close to getting under his guard. Leia let her blade slide down Luke's and then pivoted under his guard, freeing her blade to face him from the right. Luke stepped back and swung around as he adjusted his stance to meet her attack. He had intended to go easy on her, but it seemed that he was not going to get the chance. She was too fast, too good.

Luke decided to move to the attack. He dropped his left hand from the saber's grip and extended his blade in a one-handed thrust to give himself more reach as he advanced toward Leia. But she would have none of that. She brought her lightsaber crashing down on the tip of his blade, striking with maximum violence at precisely the angle required to knock his blade downward. The strike forced Luke into an awkward backhanded stance while weakening his grasp on the saber's handle. His blade slammed down into the perma-crete of the landing pad, gouging a hole in it, forcing him to concentrate, if only for a moment, on freeing his blade, rather than on his opponent.

He almost had the blade clear, but it was already too late. Leia reversed her stroke and swung hard at his blade from the opposite direction, slamming it clear of the permacrete—and knocking Luke's lightsaber completely out of his hand. The lightblade cut off automatically when Luke's hand was off the grip. The weapon went sailing through the air, landing fifteen meters away on the hard stand.

Luke looked up at his sister in stunned surprise, and caught the wide grin on her face. She raised her blade in salute, and then shut off the lightsaber. The ruby-red blade vanished with a final whir of power, and she clipped her lightsaber to her belt.

Luke walked over to his own lightsaber and picked it up. He clipped it to his belt. He stood there and regarded his sister from a new angle. She was a *fighter*. She might not beat him the next time, but she had beaten him this time, and even a fluke victory over Luke Skywalker was impressive. She lacked the polish that could only come from endless years of practice, but she had an inborn talent that needed little urging to come out. He walked back toward her, shaking his head in amazement. "You're good," he said. "Very good."

Leia grinned and patted him on the shoulder. "You'll get me next time," she said.

"Maybe," he said. "If I do, it'll be because I'll know what to watch out for." He glanced over toward the ship, and saw that the three children had seen their mother take a Jedi Master apart. Well, if it made them treat Leia with a bit more respect, maybe getting beaten was no bad thing.

"I've been practicing when I can, on the quiet," she said, her voice a bit more serious. "Even Han doesn't know about it."

"Practicing how?" Luke asked.

Leia shrugged. "With the lightsaber I already have— which is nothing like as good as this one, by the way. Against a series of drone opponents. Mostly I've been working in the courtyard behind my office. I haven't been able to do *much* practice, but I guess it's done some good."

"I'll say," Luke said, massaging his wrist. It still stung a bit from having the lightsaber knocked out of his hand.

"I don't think you realize just how much good. Come on, let's see how Han is getting on with the safety people."

"I'm afraid to look," Leia said. "I could have gotten us waived through all the port formalities, of course. But this is a private trip. It didn't seem right to pull rank just to let us go on vacation. Han told me not to worry about it. He said to file it all as a private trip, and that he would handle all the formalities in his way."

Luke couldn't help but smile at that. Han's way of doing things was rarely the quiet way.

* * *

Han was getting on about as well as could be expected, which was to say not well at all. By now there was a small crowd of spaceport bureaucrats around him, all of them pointing at this regulation or that in their datapacks, each of them engaged in loud argument with Han. It was probably lucky for all concerned that Han was not wearing a blaster. Luke would not have put it past him to quiet them all down with a few shots into the air—and the stars only knew how many safety regulations *that* would have violated.

In the old days, there had been none of this sort of fuss over a takeoff. You just sealed up your ship, got departure clearance, and off you went. But in the old days, there had been something like a tenth of the traffic in and out of Coruscant.

In recent years, there had been one or two crashes too many caused by hot-wired piles of junk that should have been grounded. Elsewhere, flight regs were still pretty free and easy, but Coruscant just had too many ships coming and going to let things slide. There was really no choice but to follow the regulations to the letter, and never mind that no one had paid attention to the regs in generations. The trouble was that the regs required ships as old as the *Falcon* to have a thorough inspection once every standard year. Somehow, the *Falcon* had just happened to miss every inspection for the last umpteen years, but now the bureau-crats had finally caught up with her.

\Well, you really couldn't blame the pencil pushers for wanting the Chief of State to fly in a spacecraft that was at least within hailing distance of the safety regs. No doubt the aforementioned Chief of State could have smoothed everything over with a quiet word or two, or an official signature on the right sort of waiver, but Leia made no move to wade into the fracas, and Luke felt no urge to get involved if she didn't. After all, in some strange way, Han enjoyed this sort of thing. Let him have his fun. Leia and Luke stood by and watched the show.

"Hold it!" Han shouted at last. "One at a time! One at a time, or I call the Wookiee down off the ship and let you shout at *him*." *That* quieted them down. "All right, then. You," Han said, stabbing a finger in the direction of the fussiest-looking official. "Go."

"It's your hyperdrive regulators, Captain Solo. The radiation shields failed their inspection last week—"

Han held up his hand, signaling the inspector to stop talking. "A slight misunderstanding." He reached into one of the pockets of his vest and pulled out a sheet of paper. He unfolded it to show the profusion of stamps and seals and official initials that obscured half the text of the underlying form. "This ought to clear that up, and a lot of the other problems as well," he said. "This certifies that the hyperdrive regulators, the navicomputer, the repulsor sub-systems, and all the other systems have been reinspected and cleared."

"But if you had this form all along, why have you been arguing with us?" the inspector demanded.

"Maybe I just don't like paperwork," Han said.

Or maybe he was waiting until Leia, his wife and your boss, was standing next to him, Luke thought. It had to be a lot harder to kick up a fuss over incomplete paperwork with the Chief of State tapping her foot and waiting to be on her way.

"Here. Take it. Hope it makes you real happy." He handed the form to the chief inspector, and the rest of the inspection team clustered around the paper, studying it carefully, pointing to the various stamps and signatures and approvals, and discussing them quite animatedly. Luke couldn't hear what they were saying, but by the tone of their voices, it was clear they weren't entirely convinced.

However, there were three or four other officials who didn't seem the least bit interested in the document. "Let's see," Han said, addressing the one he had been shouting at the hardest, "you're from immigration, right? Okay, like I told you, my wife here has all the departure forms and passports and stuff for the family. Leia?"

Leia stepped forward and produced the documents, doing a very bad job of hiding her amusement. All the officials knew perfectly well that Leia was the Chief of State and, ultimately, was the boss. But they all likewise knew perfectly well that Leia was traveling with her family as a private citizen, to be treated just like everyone else.

And if *that* wasn't a pile of nonsense, Luke didn't know what was. The idea that some lowly passport clerk was going to dare find anything wrong with the Chief of State's papers was laughable. And while the ship inspectors might have had the nerve to challenge *Han's* paperwork, they certainly weren't willing to do so in front of Leia Organa Solo. Luke didn't need the Force to sense the doubt, the uncertainty, in their minds even as they stamped the final-departure approvals on the form.

Luke heard quiet footsteps behind him, and turned to see Lando Calrissian coming out onto the landing stage. Lando was, if anything, looking more dapper than ever, in a turquoise cape over a gleaming white tunic and trousers the same shade as the cape. But for all of that, he did not, for once, seem much interested in being noticed. His movements were quiet, almost subdued. Luke did not need his Force sense to know that Lando was here to see, not to be seen. Something was up, even if Luke could not quite tell what.

Lando came up beside him and nodded absently. "Hello, Luke," he muttered as he watched Han and Leia dealing with the bureaucrats. Luke looked closely at Lando, but could read nothing from his face. His expression was utterly blank, deadpan, determined to give nothing away.

Luke was tempted to use his powers in the Force to reach into Lando's mind and see what he had to do with this, but his own momentary curiosity was no excuse for such a huge invasion of privacy. Let it be.

"Well, uh, hmm," said the chief inspector. "Everything, uh, *seems* to be in order here," he said, the doubt plain in his voice. "It would appear that we have nothing more to do than wish you a safe and pleasant journey."

Han gave the inspector a roguish, lopsided grin and a clap on the shoulder that the inspector clearly did not appreciate. "Thanks," Han said, grabbing the official's right hand in his own and pumping it vigorously. The inspector nodded and gave a sort of gulp, then backed away, turned, and hurried away as quickly as he could while maintaining a modicum of dignity. His underlings scuttled away after him, and the immigration officers and the other officials seemed no less eager to be on their way.

Han grinned wolfishly at the man's back. "Come on, kids," he called to his children. "Go ahead and get aboard. Chewie, you can shut that inspection panel and stop looking intimidating. Get aboard and start the preflight sequence. I'll be there in a minute."

Chewie gave a short, growled bark and nodded agreement. He pulled his tools out of the service compartment—it would seem he hadn't actually been *doing* anything with them in there—and slammed the panel shut.

Luke turned toward Lando, intending to ask him what was going on, but before he could, Lando shook his head and let out a low chuckle. "You did it, you old pirate," he said as he stepped forward and shook Han's hand. "I guess that means you lose our little bet."

"Han! You and Lando haven't been betting on the *Falcon* again," Leia said.

"Nah, nothing that exciting," Han said. "I just bet Lando dinner that we wouldn't get past the safety inspectors."

"Well, that's all right, then." Leia smiled and patted her husband on the arm. "I'd better go ride herd on the children before they try rewiring the weapons panel." She turned and followed the children into the ship.

Leia was certainly taking things rather casually, Luke thought, feeling more and more confused. Han was dodging a safety inspection and she didn't care? "Why isn't Leia upset?" he asked. "And what's Lando got to do with your ship getting clearance?"

"Who do you think arranged for all the clearance documents to be forged?" Lando asked, grinning more broadly still. "So when do I collect on that dinner?" He turned to Han.

Han frowned. "I'd say here and now, onboard ship with the family, before we take off, except we're in a bit of a hurry to get away. Your people might have forged the paper and sliced into the data banks to show we passed all the safety checks, but I don't think we should push our luck. Something might go wrong."

Lando laughed again. "The man who plans to fly a museum piece across the galaxy is worried about pushing his luck with the safety inspectors! That's a good one. Let's just say I'll pick my own time and place to collect," Lando said. "Good enough for now?"

"Good enough," Han said.

But it wasn't good enough, Luke told himself. Not by half. "Han—wait a second," he said. "It's one thing to risk your own neck in a dicey ship. But you can't take your wife and children along in a ship that the safety people won't pass."

"Take it easy, kid," Han said. "You think I'd take chances on my children? Or that Leia would let me even if I wanted to try? I promise you all the safety systems they were worried about are at spec or above. That wasn't the problem.''

"I don't get it,'' Luke said.

"Real simple,'' Lando said. "According to the official records on file with Coruscant control, the *Falcon* is now a nice, normal light stock freighter. All of the illegal weapon systems and smuggling hardware removed. Except Han never *did* get around to removing all the handy little modifications and add-ons and military-specification sensors and weapons, and it wouldn't be a good thing if the inspectors happened to notice all the things Han forgot to remove.''

"I've had other things on my mind,'' Han said, with a deadpan voice and expression that didn't fool anyone—and was not meant to. "Besides, that sort of gear could come in awfully handy out there. Peacetime or no peacetime, the Corellian Sector can be a tricky piece of space. Safety regs are all very well, but I want a little extra firepower on hand in case the pirates decide it's time to go shopping.''

"Well, I certainly can't blame you for that,'' Luke said. He didn't need his Jedi abilities to sense Han was worried about more than the remote possibility of tangling with half-mythical pirates. But whatever had Han worried, Luke was not going to make things better by pressing him on the subject. "You take care of your family, and never mind about the rest of it.''

"That's the plan, kid,'' Han said. "Anyway, come on aboard you two, and say your good-byes.''

Han led the way up the *Falcon*'s ramp with Lando and Luke following behind. Inside, they found Leia and the children in the lounge. It felt good to be aboard the old *Falcon* again, Luke thought. So many of the key events in his life revolved around the *Falcon* in one way or another. He looked around, letting the flood of memories wash over him. It was here, in the lounge compartment, that Obi-Wan Kenobi had given him his first practice with a lightsaber. It was this ship that had saved his life at Cloud City, that had given him the covering fire he needed to take out the first Death Star.

But all that was in the past. Just now the ship seemed too full of bustle and life for such things to matter. Han had already wandered over to the cockpit to check Chewie's preflight settings. The twins were in their seats, their seat belts fastened, but were bouncing with so much excitement that the belts did not seem likely to hold them down for very long. Leia was just getting an equally bouncy Anakin strapped in for takeoff.

"All right, everybody," Han said, coming back from the cockpit, Chewie right behind him. "Time to say good-bye to Lando and Uncle Luke."

After a deafening chorus of shouted good-byes, Luke gave each child a kiss and a hug. He stood up, hugged his sister, slapped Han on the shoulder, and made a formal bow of farewell to Chewbacca. It was not wise to get too emotional or demonstrative with a Wookiee. If the Wookiee got demonstrative and hugged back, you'd be lucky to escape with crushed ribs.

Lando was making his own farewells, further complicating the choreography in the tight spaces of the ship. But at last all the good-byes were complete, and it was time to head down the ramp, offer one last wave good-bye to Han as he raised the ramp and sealed the ship, and move back to a safe distance for the takeoff.

No ship takes off without a few moments of delay that seem inexplicable from the outside—least of all the *Falcon*. Luke and Lando could see Han and Chewie settling into the *Falcon*'s cockpit, checking switches, setting up the controls.

But at last the moment came, and the *Falcon*'s repulsor lifts came to life, glowing with power. Moving with a smooth and perfect grace that seemed out of character for the cantankerous old freighter, the *Falcon* rose smoothly into the air, did a ninety-degree turn to port, and lit her main sublight engines to move off into the dusky sky.

"There they go," Lando said, his voice betraying a low, quiet excitement. Luke could understand. Maybe they were only a family off on a vacation, a quick trip sandwiched in before Leia got caught up in the Corellian trade talks, but that didn't matter. They were on a *ship*, and the ship was already heading out between the stars. It could have been any ship, going anywhere. To Luke, and to Lando, too, for that matter, there could be no more powerful symbol of adventure, of possibility, of hope and freedom, than a ship heading out into space.

Mon Mothma had told Luke that he craved adventure, and he had denied it. It hadn't taken much to show him the error of his ways. He wanted to be out there, in the thick of things.

"Come on, Luke," said Lando. "You and I have things to talk about."

*　　*　　*

Luke and Lando were not the only ones to watch the departure of the *Millennium Falcon*. Pharnis Gleasry, agent of the Human League, watched as well, albeit from a discreet distance. He was several kilometers away, on an observation platform on another of Coruscant's massive towers. The platform was crowded with tourists who took him for one of their own and paid him no mind. It was far enough away that he was obliged to use macrobinoculars to see much of anything. The constant jostling he suffered from the tourists did not make it any easier to keep the macrobinoculars steady.

But he could see the ship take off for all of that. And he could see two tiny figures, still on the hard stand. He could see them watch the *Falcon* vanish, see them turn away and head back inside. Pharnis was all but certain that the one on the left was Skywalker. The other was definitely Lando Calrissian. Good. Good. Pharnis was pleased to get visual confirmation that his target was on-planet. With Organa Solo safely on her way, it was time for Skywalker. But Pharnis had done his homework. He knew that the *Millennium Falcon* was not the most reliable of craft. Best to give her time to get out of the system. If the *Falcon* broke down and Organa Solo returned to Coruscant, after Pharnis had done the Skywalker job, it could prove most embarrassing.

No. Give them time to get well away. Tomorrow. He would do the job tomorrow.

CHAPTER SEVEN

Proposal Accepted

So what is this project you want my help with, Lando?" Luke asked as they made their way back from the landing bay.

Lando Calrissian smiled at Luke as they walked, and there was more than a bit of mischief in his expression. "A whole new approach to the way I do business," he said. "Or it might be more accurate to call it an investment opportunity. Anyway, I want your help to get it off the ground."

Investment opportunity? Luke thought. He glanced at his companion. Lando had always been one to go after high-stakes, large-scale projects, but he had never been one to invite his friends to join the wild schemes. Even Lando knew there were limits—or at least he had, up until now.

Not that it mattered, of course. Lando could hit up Luke for money all day long, but it wouldn't do any good. You needed to *have* money before you could give it to someone—and Lando ought to have known that a Jedi Master was not the sort of person likely to have a stack of spare credits lying around. To put it rather crudely, saving the universe didn't pay very well.

But Lando had to know Luke was not rich. Was it something worse still? Was he hoping to trade on Luke's good name, get him to endorse the scheme so Lando could get *others* to invest? "Ah, Lando, I don't think I can help you. I really don't have the sort of big-stakes money you're after.

And I don't think I'd be much good trying to sell it to others—"

Lando burst out laughing. "Is *that* what you thought I was after? Calrissian's Fly-by-Night Investments, as endorsed by Luke Skywalker, Hero of the Galaxy? No, no, that's not it. That kind of gall would be beyond even *me*."

"Well, that's a relief," Luke said. "I was scared you were about to ask me to go on some sort of promotional tour."

Lando gave him a funny look and smiled. "In a sense," he said, "I am. But not for the sort of product you've got in mind."

"Lando, so far you're not making sense."

"No, I suppose not." Lando stopped walking for a moment, and Luke did as well. Lando turned toward Luke, took him by the arm, and seemed about to say more. But then he glanced around, as if he were trying to judge the likelihood of unwelcome eavesdroppers. "Look," he said at last. "There's something I've been meaning to show you. A new project of mine. Let's head there. We can sit down quietly, in private, and I can explain the whole thing."

"All right, I suppose," Luke said, more than a little doubtful. "What sort of project?" he asked.

"My new home," Lando said. "Something kind of special."

"Special in what way?" Luke asked.

"You'll see," said Lando, slapping Luke on the shoulder. "Come on. We'll take the scenic route."

Luke had thought he knew Coruscant fairly well, but Lando led him through a labyrinth of passages and tunnels and lifts and moving walkways Luke had never seen or heard of before. All of the passageways seemed to lead off in every direction at once, but it soon became clear that they were going deeper and deeper into the bowels of the city.

By the time Lando had gotten to the level he wanted, Luke guessed they were at least one or two hundred meters below ground level—if Coruscant could be said to have a ground level. The planet-wide city of towers and monolithic structures had been built and rebuilt and overbuilt and dug up and reburied so many times that no one really knew where the original surface was anymore. Virtually all of the land surface had been built over. Here and there were hummocks of dirt where scruffy plant life had managed to secure a foothold. But hardly any of these were truly at "ground" level. They were just sheltered spots where the winds and rains had been able to deposit enough dust and dirt and detritus to form a soil of sorts, places where a stray seed or two from one of the lush indoor gardens had found its way.

But for all of that, Luke knew they were unquestionably underground. Half the tunnels were just bare, raw rock, solid granite. In places the tunnel walls were bone-dry. In others, they were clammy and wet, with riverlets of moisture oozing down the walls and pooling here and there.

If this was where Lando lived now, Luke could not help thinking that Lando had, quite literally, gone down in the world. An underground address was considered a mark of very low status on Coruscant.

That worried Luke. He had always known Lando to be very concerned with appearances. There had been times he had seen Lando quite literally threadbare—but even in the worst of times, Lando had made a determined and successful effort to seem prosperous. Part of it was vanity and ego. Lando had plenty of those in stock. But there was a more practical side to it as well. Lando was, among other things, a salesman, and a salesman who didn't look prosperous was not going to get far.

Except that Lando *did* look prosperous—if anything, better than he had in years. But if he was doing so well, why was he living underground?

For that matter, why was he taking Luke to where he lived by such a round-about route? There had to be a more direct way to get where they were going. Probably that was nothing more than force of habit. Back in the bad old days,

Lando had often felt the need to be rather secretive about the location of his living quarters.

While he had never had half the galaxy's bounty hunters after him, the way Han had at one point, Lando Calrissian had managed to develop a pretty fair number of enemies over the years. There had been times when not even his most trusted friends knew where he lived. Even the most trusted person could be tailed, or be tricked into wearing a tracer tab, or tortured or drugged. Nowadays, there wasn't any real need for such precautions, but old habits died hard in ex-smugglers who didn't die young—and Lando was still very much alive. And it could very well be that Lando still had a few old associates he didn't want to meet unexpectedly. Maybe it wasn't so foolish to take the long way around.

Lando kept up a steady monologue as they walked, nattering on cheerfully about every subject under the stars, from the best odds to be found in the various small-stakes gambling houses—legal and otherwise—in the bowels of Coruscant, to the enormous profits to be realized by anyone in the right place at the right time, should the Corellian Trade Summit prove successful. That much about Lando had stayed the same, Luke thought. As interested in the five-credit bet as he was in the fifty-million-credit investment. And given his usual luck on the fifty-million side of things, he probably was wise to pay attention to those five credits.

Lando Calrissian was famous for developing a huge project, living high off the proceeds—and then, through no fault of his own, having the whole thing crash down around his ears. He had done a splendid job of running Cloud City on Bespin—and gotten out with not much more than the clothes he was standing up in. It was more or less the same story for his mole-mining operation at Nkllon. And then there was that mining on Kessel . . . If he hadn't had a fair bit of skill at the gaming tables, Lando would never have been able to recover from those disasters.

And now, it appeared, he was gearing up to start all over again. But if he didn't want Luke's money, and didn't want to trade on Luke's name, then how in the galaxy did it have anything to do with Luke?

On they walked, through increasingly squalid and dirty passages. The occasional pools of water grew more frequent, and more filthy. There were a number of unpleasant odors, some of which Luke could identify, and a number that he was just as glad he could not.

At last the walkway they were on came to a halt before a huge blastproof door. Lando punched a combination into a keypad, and the door slid back into the wall with a ponderous rumbling of machinery.

They stepped onto a terrace overlooking a huge subterranean cavern, a hollow dome, easily a kilometer across. Luke, quite astonished, found himself on a platform that looked down into a complete pocket city of low stone buildings and cool green parks. The dome was brightly lit, the air sweet and pure, the walkways and byways clean and tidy. The buildings were widely spaced, their stone walls brightly painted. Pathways snaked through neatly kept lawns, and the roof of the dome was painted a royal blue.

"Welcome to Dometown," Lando said.

"Very nice, Lando," Luke said as he leaned over the low wall of the terrace and admired the view. "Very nice indeed. Not at all what I expected."

"Well, our developers kept it quiet," Lando said. "Didn't want just anyone knowing about it. We found this underground chamber. It'd been built for space knows what reason, and who knows how old it is. Back then it was full of ruined machines, and old junk, and a whole herd of mutant hive rats and practically everything else you'd ever want to find. We got it cleaned up, refurbed the air and water and security system, and built some decent housing. It's not exactly in the poshest neighborhood, but who cares? You can rent a nice big place here for a tenth of what it would cost to get a high-status broom closet on the surface."

"I supposed you were one of the investors in this little project?" Luke said.

Lando laughed, clapped him on the shoulder, and led him down a low, wide ramp into the dome. "Suppose away," he said. "I decided, just for once, to put my money into something small and local. Just this once, why not be one of many partners, instead of being the whole show myself? Why not think small, and build a nice neighborhood? I've run a whole city by myself, and take it from me, this is easier."

"So you're no longer thinking about the grand-scale projects?" Luke asked.

Lando looked at him as they walked along, clearly surprised and maybe a little bit hurt. "I'll *never* quit doing that, Luke. If you don't think big, what's the point of thinking at all? I just got tired of having nothing at all to fall back on. It might not be in a high-status neighborhood, but status isn't everything—and no one has to know where I live, anyway. Now I've got a little bit of income from this place, enough to live on and just a bit more, and I have a place to live that's *mine*, that no one can take away from me. And it's all in the most bombproof and secure depths of the capital planet."

"A safe, secure investment," Luke said, grinning at his friend.

"I know, I know," Lando said. "Don't let it get around, or I'll ruin my reputation. Come on, my house is just up this way. Let's go in."

*   *   *

Five minutes later they were relaxing in the elegant, if somewhat spartan, confines of Lando's house. Luke had to admit that Lando had a point about space. Only the richest of beings, or the most exalted of government officials, could have afforded anything this size anywhere near the surface. The house was built of stone—a highly cheap and available building material when one is building underground—and the walls and floors were smooth-polished granite. It was cool and quiet, and the rooms were comfortably expansive.

Lando sat Luke down on a low, luxurious couch and brought him something cool to drink before sitting down on a matching chair next to the couch. Then Lando began to talk—and talk about everything but the matter at hand. Most uncharacteristically, he seemed reluctant to come to the point. He fussed about, worrying that the room was too hot or too cold, that Luke was not comfortable, and that his drink needed freshening up.

At last Luke decided he was going to have to push a bit. "Lando, you didn't bring me down here to find out how much ice I like in my drinks. Why am I here?"

"All right," Lando said. He paused for a long moment, and shifted in his seat. Even if he *was* coming to the point, he seemed to feel the need to do so gradually. He set down his own drink on the side table and leaned forward, an earnest expression on his face. "I told a bit of a fib back there as we were walking up this way, when I was talking about building this place," he said. "The truth is I *did* stop thinking big, for a little while there. I didn't even realize it at first. I got all involved in getting Dometown put together. It was a safe, secure job, and they needed someone with my skills, and I liked the work. Heck, after putting Nkllon together, getting this place built was more like a hobby than a job—and I *liked* the way it was easy. I'd been shot down and kicked out and blown up and wiped out so many times I just didn't want to deal with that kind of big-time struggle anymore. So I put all my energy into getting Dometown put back together and cleaned up and families moved in."

"Nothing at all wrong with that," Luke said. "You've really accomplished something here."

"Yes, I have," Lando said, a touch of pride in his voice. He looked around his parlor, obviously seeing beyond the walls to the town he had made. "That is to say, I *did* a good job here. But then, after a while, it dawned on me I was still doing the job, even though the job was done."

"I don't understand," Luke said. "How could you be doing the job if it was finished?"

Lando shook his head sadly. "That's easy, Luke. Billions of beings do it every day. They get up in the morning, push some pieces of paper around on a desk, make some com calls, decide on the blue-gray paint for the corridor over the gray blue, have a meeting, and feel like they've accomplished enough for one day. They go home, and then they come back the next day and do it all again. That might be all right for some, but not for me, and when I caught myself doing it I realized it was time to move on."

"Move on to what?"

"I don't know," Lando said, making a rather abrupt gesture of dismissal. "That's not even really that important just now. The main question is move on *with* what? My father used to say, 'You can't think deeper than your pockets,' and there's a lot of truth to that. I started thinking back on all my schemes that had crashed and burned one way or the other. It seemed to me that I could have stuck it out if my pockets had been deeper, if they had been filled with more credits.

"If I had the reserves, the resources, I could have ridden out the bad times and gotten Bespin or Nkllon back on a paying basis. Deep pockets give you staying power, let you hang in and lose money until you're earning it again. I realized that the question was: How to get money? *Serious* money. How could I get those deep pockets?"

"And now you've figured out how, and you want my help to do it," Luke said, more than a little amused.

"Right," Lando said. "Exactly right. I've figured out how to get deep pockets full of money, and I need your help to do it."

"Well, then," Luke said. "How do you get deep pockets?"

"Simplest thing in the universe," said Lando. "You marry them."

There was a moment of dead silence as Luke stared straight at Lando. It wasn't easy to surprise a Jedi Master, but Lando had done it. "You're getting married?" Luke asked at last. "To whom?"

Lando shrugged his shoulders and laughed. "I haven't the faintest idea," he said. "Well, that's not *strictly* true. I do have a short list of candidates, but it could be anyone on the list, or maybe even someone I haven't thought of yet."

"But—but—how can you marry someone you don't know?"

"I'm not marrying a *who*," Lando said. "I'm marrying a *what*. I'm marrying money. What's so strange about that? People have done it since the beginning of time. A rich wife could do me a lot of good—and I could do *her* a lot of good, too. Make her richer, for one thing."

Luke looked at his old friend, and asked a careful question. "Where do I come into all this?" Luke asked.

"Ah, now *that's* the tricky part," Lando said. "I'm not altogether unknown in the galaxy. People have heard of me. Unfortunately, sometimes they haven't liked what they've heard. Stories get started. Some of the stories aren't even true. But they're out there just the same. That's why I want you to come with me while I'm searching for my wife—"

"What? *That's* the reason for the trip you want me to go on?"

Lando looked surprised. "Yes. I thought I had explained that part. I want you to come with me while I go wife hunting."

"And do what?" Luke asked. "Convince them that the true stories *aren't* true? I can't go around bending the facts just to suit you, Lando."

"No, of course not," Lando said. "But I've *changed*, Luke. I'm not going to say I'm a whole new person or any nonsense like that. I couldn't get you to believe it anyway. But I'm not the way I was in the old days. I'm more solid, more steady. Could the old me have gotten this place built?" he asked.

Yes, Luke thought. *Built it and then lost it all on one*

hand of sabacc. But fortunately for Luke, his sense of tact was not called upon to battle with his need to tell the truth. Lando was talking on, without waiting for an answer.

"I'm not going to deny my past," Lando said. "There's no point in even trying. Anyone who wanted to find out about me could do so very easily. I have nothing to hide." He caught the look in Luke's eyes and shrugged. "Well, nothing *much*. Besides, most of the women I want to get a look at know who I am already. Some women even *like* my reputation. They think it's exciting, or romantic or something. Besides, look at where I started, and look at where I am and all the places I've been on the way. I'm *proud* of what I've done." Lando looked at Luke again and put his hands up in a mock gesture of surrender before Luke even had a chance to object. "All right, I'm not proud of *all* of it, maybe, but at least some."

"And you ought to be proud," Luke said, trying to be reassuring. "You've done great things. The New Republic might not even *be* here today if not for you."

"Thanks," Lando said. "I appreciate that, especially coming from you."

"Is *that* what you want me for?" Luke asked. "To go and say that to all your prospective brides?"

"Noooo, not exactly," Lando said. "I just want you to *be* there with me. I figure if I show up with you, that's going to make me more respectable even if you never say a word. They'll know my intentions are honorable if I show up with a Jedi escort. There won't be any hanky-panky while you're around."

Luke fought hard to suppress a smile. "Wait a second," he said. "Just let me understand this. You want me to be your *chaperon?*"

Lando rewarded Luke with one of his most dazzling smiles. "Exactly. Couldn't have put it better myself. With you around, I'll be respectable. They'll know I'm sincere."

"*Are* you sincere?" Luke asked.

Lando looked surprised again. "About money? Never anything but."

"No," Luke said. "About *marrying*. What about the woman in question?"

Lando looked puzzled. "How do you mean, what about her?"

"Well, you can't just walk up to a woman and say, 'Hello, I heard about your large bank account, let's get married.' Why should she want to marry *you?* And what about love, and romance, and commitment, and children and so on? She'll want to know where you stand on all that sort of thing."

Lando seemed a bit taken aback. Perhaps it had never entered his head that there was a woman alive who *wouldn't* want to marry him. "You've got some good points there," he said, in the tone of voice of a man tripped up by an unexpected question. "I must admit that I haven't thought them all through. But don't *you* forget that marriages are more than just love and flowers. They're business relationships, even political relationships.

"Besides, even if you leave romance out of it, I really am not at all a bad catch." He made a wide sweeping gesture with one hand. "I have this place—not just the house, but Dometown—providing me with a nice little income. I won't need my wife's money to live on. I'd just use it to invest. I could take money that's just lying around and make it *work*, make it *grow*. I have a lot of experience in managing large projects and dealing with people, I have a pretty fair war record, and let's face it, I *do* have some connections with the powers-that-be on Coruscant."

"And bringing me along would remind them of all that," Luke said.

"Absolutely," Lando said, completely unabashed. "You'd make a great sales tool even if you never said a single word."

"I see. Well, who's on your list?" Luke asked, no longer even trying to suppress a smile.

"Quite a number of people," Lando said, his voice earnest and thoughtful, like a salesman who wanted to be sure you knew just how impressive his stock was. "I've been working the data banks hard, of course, doing all sorts of searches. But not everything gets into the computers. In fact, most things don't. So I've been working the rumor mills, reading off-planet news, talking to ship captains, that sort of thing."

"All the things you do when you're looking for a business opportunity," Luke said.

But Lando missed the joke. "Exactly," he said. "I've been doing it all. And I've come up with about two hundred and fifty candidates."

"Two hundred and fifty!" Luke half shouted.

"That's right," Lando said. He pulled a portable data reader out of the pocket of his blouse. "I've got 'em all right here."

"Lando, I can't go around with you to visit two hundred and fifty women!" Even as he said the words Luke knew he was trapped. Lando, galaxy-class salesman and con man, had pulled him in. Luke had just let Lando know there was *some* lower number of women that Luke was willing to go and see. Luke hadn't really wanted to agree, but it was already too late. Now it was merely a question of haggling over the price, the number of women Luke *would* be willing to visit.

"Oh, I don't expect *that* much of you," Lando went on in the same earnest, slightly anxious tone. "For that matter, I certainly don't plan to visit anywhere near that many myself. I've ranked the list, and I sincerely hope I don't have to go past the five or ten most desirable candidates."

"Five or ten most desirable, eh?"

"That's right. Of course, when I find what I'm after, I'll stop looking. Maybe we'll—I'll—get lucky at the first stop."

Luke reached for his drink. "So who's that first stop?" he asked, making ready to take a sip. "Who's your number-one prospect?"

"A young lady by the name of Tendra Risant. Ever heard of her?"

"No," Luke said. "Any particular reason that I should have?"

"Not really. She's a minor functionary on Sacorria, one of the Outlier worlds in the Corellian Sector. She's not the richest on my list, but she's wealthy enough, and her family is the real draw. They have strong contacts throughout the Corellian Sector. And those connections could be worth a lot more than cash to the right sort of fellow."

"To a fellow sort of like you?" Luke asked.

Lando smiled wolfishly. "A fellow sort of like me," he agreed.

"Who else?" Luke asked.

"Let's see," he said, consulting the data reader. "There's Condren Foreck on Azbrian. She's a little on the young side, but her father's getting on in years."

"What's that got to do with it?" Luke asked.

"Come on, Luke, think it through. If I'm going to marry an heiress for the money, I've got to consider how long it will take me to collect." He took a moment to read over the notes on the data reader again. "Still," he said thoughtfully, "her father has *quite* a stack of the stuff. It'd be worth waiting for, and besides, she gets a pretty fair income off the trust funds in the meantime. Not a bad prospect at all. Hmmm. I assume she's healthy enough. It says here she's a famous athlete on her world. Of course, that could just be Daddy buying her way to the trophies. You never know."

Luke did not pretend to follow the last portion of what Lando had said. Maybe Lando wanted a wife who would die early and leave him in sole possession of the proceeds. Or else maybe he *wanted* a young, healthy wife who was likely to outlive her father in the long run and keep the trust funds coming in the meantime.

"All right," he said. "Who's next on your list?"

"Actually, the first one I plan to visit," Lando said. "Sort of a long shot, but she's on the way to the Corellian

Sector, and that's where I want to end up, so I can attend the last half of the trade summit and see what deals are being made.''

"So who is your choice number three?"

Lando looked at his notes again. "Karia Ver Seryan," he said. "Lives on the planet Leria Kerlsil. Getting on toward middle years, or perhaps a bit past. Widow of one Chantu Solk, a rather sharp fellow I knew pretty well in the old days. He was a ship broker who made his money knowing which side to bet on in the war against the Empire—and kept his money by knowing when to change his bets. She married him about eight years ago and he died about five years ago. Left everything to his wife. She sold the business. I don't have much information on her, but according to my accounts, she doesn't seem to do much now that she has her money. I guess she's better at spending the money than earning it.''

It didn't take much for Luke to develop a mental image of Karia Ver Seryan that was, to put it mildly, not alluring. "And that's someone you'd be willing to marry?" he asked.

"For the right money, absolutely. I'd leave her alone and put her money to work making more money, and she'd leave me alone and still have money to spend. *More* money to spend, for that matter," Lando glanced at the data reader again. "Then, rounding out the top five, we have Dera Jynsol on Ord Pardron, and uh—oh yeah, one Lady Lapema Phonstom on Kabal. And so on down the list. But I'm not going to worry much about *them* until I've dealt with the first three names.''

"Lando, you're making my blood run cold."

"Come on, Luke. How long have you been out in the real world? Money is what makes the galaxy go round. People have treated marriage as the business deal it is since the beginning of time. The only difference here is that I'm not dressing it up in pretty words, or pretending that I'm going to seek out my one true love, and she'll just happen to be the richest woman who'll have me.''

"But this is all so ruthless. You're just looking for the woman you can make the best use of, as if you were shopping for a good deal on a landspeeder."

"That's the way it is in lots of cultures. They don't have much interest in true love—just marriages that can stand the test of time. Besides, the lady in question is going to be shopping for the best deal *she* can get. The best kind of business deal is the one where both sides get what they want. That's all I'm after. A nice, honest business deal."

"And do you seriously think that any of these women might consider you as a husband?"

"Why not?" Lando said. "Besides, I'm not really expecting to settle a final deal on this run. It's a scouting trip." He held up the data reader. "I know some of this information is dated or incomplete, maybe even inaccurate. I need to gather some more intelligence. I want to get a look at a few possibilities and let them get a look at me."

"So these women know you are coming?" Luke asked.

"Of course," Lando said. "Not that I've done intense negotiations. Just that I am shopping, I'm interested, and I'd like to come get acquainted."

"And they've said yes?" Luke asked.

Lando shrugged. "A lot didn't." He gestured with the data reader. "These did." He dropped the data reader down on the couch and looked Luke straight in the eye. "So what do you say?" he asked. "Want to come along? I need *someone* to keep me out of trouble. It'd do you some good to get off this overgrown apartment house of a planet. Get out in the galaxy and spread your wings a bit."

Luke hesitated. He hated to admit it, but he was tempted. He had been kind of cooped up on Coruscant for a while. And he had to confess to a certain curiosity. How the devil would Lando handle himself? It would require more gall than Luke could imagine to wander the galaxy brazenly shopping for a wife. And Mon Mothma *had* urged Luke to join Lando on his journey. "How many of them do I have to help you see?" Luke asked, trying to retain the last scraps of his caution.

"The first ten on the list," Lando said, just a bit too eagerly. "That would be enough. That would get the word around that the great Jedi Knight was traveling with me. Even if you didn't stay with me longer, the fact that you had been with me would help improve my credentials."

"Three," Luke said, knowing full well that that was not what he was going to get.

"Eight," said Lando.

"Four," Luke said.

"Come on, Luke. For old times' sake. Six."

"Well—five," Luke said.

Lando's face split into a wide grin. "Great! Great. That's perfect," he said. He stuck out his hand, and Luke took it, more than a little reluctantly. Lando had not wanted or hoped for Luke to go along on any more than five of these absurd visits. Yet he had managed to make five visits seem like a grand compromise, a great concession on his part— while it was Luke who was doing him the favor.

"So," Lando said. "When can you be ready to go?"

Luke stood up and shrugged vaguely. "Tomorrow morning, I guess," he said. Mon Mothma had hit close to the mark when she had suggested that there wasn't much holding him to Coruscant. Maybe she was right. Maybe it would do some good for him to get back out into space. Into action. If you could call chaperoning Lando much in the way of action.

"Great, great," Lando said. He pulled a piece of paper out of his pocket. "This is where the *Lady Luck* is berthed. It's just south of the Windward docks. Know where that is?"

"Of course," Luke said, taking the paper. "I've flown in and out of Coruscant enough times."

"Good. See you there after breakfast?"

Luke was almost tempted to haggle over the departure time as well, just on general principle, but there wasn't much point. Lando had him, had his word as a Jedi Knight that he would go along. Lando wouldn't care about departure time. Tomorrow or the next day or the next week would suit him just as well as tonight. No doubt Lando had the *Lady Luck* being held ready to go right now, just in case Luke had been willing to leave at once. No, Lando had rolled over him already. No purpose would be served by any further game playing. "See you then," Luke said, and offered his hand again.

Lando grinned and shook hands with even greater vigor. "You've got yourself a deal," he said.

*   *   *

Lando gave Luke detailed instructions on how to get back to the higher levels of the city, and of course Luke had them memorized on first hearing, but he didn't bother to follow them. He chose instead to wander the city on his own, moving now through the sordid byways of the undercity, built by long-forgotten workers in days lost to memory, now through the magnificent upper city, with its mighty castles and grand promenades and gleaming towers. Even in the darkest ways of the city, Luke Skywalker had nothing to fear. There were few on Coruscant with so little sense as to disturb a Jedi Master, and fewer still that Luke could not sense long before they could attack. He could walk where he would without fear of molestation.

But Luke paid little attention to his route. Fetid tunnel and grand esplanade were all the same to him that night. His mind was elsewhere. He walked for hours, thinking of Mon Mothma's advice, of his sister and her family off on their holiday, of Lando's amazing gall, of the hugeness of the city, and of the galaxy beyond.

But his thoughts kept returning to Lando. He was a piece of work, that was for certain. Lando had had absolutely nothing that Luke needed, and yet he had managed to convince Luke to do exactly what he wanted.

Amazing, really. Luke had the power to look into the minds of others, to manipulate their thoughts. He could lift a whole spacecraft with the power of his mind. And yet Lando had managed to play him like a windblower.

Luke smiled to himself as he reached his front door. No two ways around it. Some people managed just fine without the least little bit of help from the Force.

CHAPTER EIGHT

Homeward Bound

Peace and quiet were rare commodities in Han Solo's family, and they should have been rarer still when the family was cooped up in a small ship. And yet, two days out from Coruscant, things seemed to be going remarkably well. Oh, there had been one or two minor scuffles, and a bit more fussing than normal at bedtime the first night, but all in all, there was far less trouble than Leia had expected from her husband's children.

She smiled to herself. No doubt she had that habit in common with every mother in history. When they were good, they were her children. When they were bad, or when she feared they *might* be bad, they were Han's.

Well, just at the moment she was more than happy to admit to mothering this brood. It would be hard to imagine any children behaving better than Jacen, Jaina, and Anakin were right now.

It was just after dinner on the first night out from Coruscant, with the *Falcon* due at Corellia in two days. The *Falcon* could have made the trip in far less time, of course, but just this once blind speed was not the only consideration. Leia had urged Han not to try to set any records. Better they got there a day or two later rather than not getting there at all because they had run the hyperdrive at max and blown out a coil or something. For once, Han had been easy to persuade. Maybe he felt it would be no bad thing to baby his ship, just this once.

Things seemed so calm that Leia wondered if she was with the right family. The remains of dinner had been cleared up, Chewie was sitting at the table with his tools spread out, tinkering with some broken bit of machinery. Anakin was watching Chewie with rapt attention, offering his own advice now and again, speaking in a low voice, and pointing here and there at the gizmo's interior. Chewie was either taking the advice seriously, which seemed unlikely, or else displaying a degree of patience that seemed more unlikely still.

The twins were sprawled out on the floor—except, Leia reminded herself, she ought to call it a deck now that they were on a ship—both of them reading. Han was at the auxiliary control station at the aft end of the lounge, doing some sort of check or another on the *Falcon*'s systems. Probably it was something that didn't really need doing, just some bit of fiddling with part of the biggest, best toy in the universe—a starship. Han looked happy, at ease, in a way that Leia had not seen in quite a while.

Leia was seated at the far end of the table from Chewbacca and Anakin. In theory, she, too, was reading, giving herself the rare treat of curling up with a good book instead of slogging through some bureaucratic report. She had been looking forward to this for a long time. Instead she found herself doing little more than sit there in a maternal glow. She was basking in the moment of family, with her children and her husband around her, all safe, all well, and all happy to be together.

"What's it like, Daddy?" Jaina asked, looking up from her book. There hadn't been much in the way of conversation for a while, but it would seem that Jaina had something on her mind.

"What's what like, Princess?" Han asked, turning around in his swivel seat.

"Corellia. What's it like? I keep hearing everyone being so excited that we're going there, but no one ever says much about the place." Jaina stood up and walked over to her father.

Han seemed flustered for a moment, and Leia looked at him intently. Han had hardly spoken about his homeworld, and had said even less about his life in the Corellian Sector. For years, she had forced herself to restrain her curiosity. But now. Now he would surely have to say *something*.

"Well," Han said thoughtfully, "it's a very interesting place."

"And you lived there when you were a kid?" Jaina asked as she climbed up into her father's lap. Jacen stayed where he was, sitting crossed-legged on the floor, but Anakin took his cue from Jaina. He hopped down from where he was sitting next to Chewie, went around the table, and climbed up into his mother's lap. *He* could tell when it was story time.

"That's right, I lived there," Han said, putting on his best storytelling voice. "And it's a beautiful place. The only trouble with it is that a lot of the names sound the same, so that sometimes outsiders get a little confused by them. Corellians never do. And if I'm a Corellian, and you're my children, that makes *you* Corellians. So listen very carefully, and don't make any mistakes, or you'll make me look bad. All right?"

Jaina giggled, and Jacen smiled. Anakin nodded solemnly.

"Well, the Corellian Sector is made up of a couple of dozen star systems, but the most *important* star system in the sector is the Corellian star system. And the most important *planet* in the Corellian star *system* in the Corellian *Sector* is Corellia, and the capital city is Coronet. The star that the planet Corellia goes around is called *Corell*, and that's where all the other things with the word 'Corell' in them get their name. But no one ever calls the star 'Corell.' Everyone does what everyone does everywhere else and just calls it 'the sun.' Everyone always does that."

"Uh-huh," Jaina said.

"Good. Now, I'll tell you all about the planet Corellia in a minute, but one of the most interesting things about the Corellian star system is that it has so many inhabited planets. It's rare for a star to have even one planet that people can live on, but it's even rarer for a star to have more than one. That's one of the things that makes the Corellian system so special. It has five habitable planets. The Five Brothers, we call them. The five of them have had so much to do with each other over the generations that we never really thought of them as five different places. They were together, the way you and Jacen and Anakin are. But Corellia has the most people and the biggest cities, and so they call it the Elder Brother, or sometimes just the Eldest.''

"But why are there five habitable planets?" Jacen asked. "Does anyone know how that happened?"

"Good question," Han said. "The scientists are very confused by the Corellian system. The planets' orbits are so close to each other, and are so strange, that some of the scientists think the whole star system is artificial. They think somebody *built* it, a long, long time ago.''

"Wow," said Jacen. "Someone *built* a whole star system?"

"Well, that's one idea. Other scientists say that's crazy. They've worked out a way that it all *could* have happened by itself. But one thing is for sure. If the Five Brothers *were* put in their current orbits on purpose, it must have happened in the dimmest mists of time, even before the dawn of the Old Republic, more than a thousand generations ago.

"But the next thing you need to know is that there are more than just humans in the Corellian Sector. There are the Selonians and the Drall, lots of them, and a few of all sorts of other kinds of beings. At least there used to be. We don't really know what things are like now.''

"Why not?" Jaina asked.

"Well, it's tricky," Leia said. "We have a lot of *general* information about what's going on in Corellia, but it's very hard to get solid details on a lot of things. It makes a big difference. It's like if someone who knew you twins loved each other, and that's all they knew. They wouldn't understand if they saw you fighting with each other—and then saw you playing nicely together two minutes later. We sort of know the broad outlines of what's been going on in the Corellian Sector, but we don't really know the background to it all. And we don't know what details are really important and which don't matter.''

"Even in the old days, you had to do a lot of guessing if you were studying Corellia," said Han. "It's always been sort of inward looking, not much worried about the outside. And don't forget that half the galaxy is still recovering from the Imperial-Alliance war. Corellia has probably taken its lumps along with everyone else. But Corellians don't like to show their dirty laundry in public. So we might find out it's the beautiful, well-run planet we hear about, the kind of place it was when I lived there. Or we might discover it's a hardscrabble sort of place, with lots of problems and lots of things not working very well."

"I don't want to go to any place that's all crummy," Jacen said.

"But it might do you some good if you did," Han said. "Your mother and I both feel it'll be good for you to see something of life besides the cushy deal you have on Coruscant. You should see how the other half lives. After all, it's how your parents lived, not all that long ago."

"Were you guys poor and stuff?"

"Well, I always was," Han said. "And your mother—well, she lost everything she ever had in the war."

That was an understatement, Leia thought. The Empire had destroyed her entire planet, for no better reason than to terrify the rest of the galaxy.

"Anyway," Han went on, "let me tell you about the Drall and the Selonians. An adult Drall is about as tall as you are, Jacen, but a lot heavier set. They have two short legs and two short arms in the usual places. They have short brown or black or gray fur—or sometimes red. Their bodies look a little like taller, thinner Ewoks with shorter fur, but their heads are completely different. Rounder, more, ah, intelligent looking to human eyes, with a bit more pronounced muzzle, and with their ears flat to the head instead of sticking up. They are *very* dignified, *very* sensible beings, and they expect to be treated with respect. Is that clear?" Han looked around and made sure he got a nod out of all three kids.

"Good," he went on. "I won't have to warn you to take the Selonians seriously, because you'll know to do that five seconds after you see one. They are big and strong and quick, the average adult a bit taller than me. Most humans think they are a very refined-looking species. They're bipeds like humans and Drall, but they have long, slender bodies, and they can go on all fours if they want to. They probably evolved from some sort of active, nimble, swimming mammals. They have sleek, short fur and long, pointed faces with bristly whiskers. And *very* sharp teeth, and long tails just right for whapping you if you don't behave. They live underground mostly, and they are very good swimmers. But there's one other thing you should know about them. Chances are the only ones you'll ever see are going to be sterile females, and it's always a sterile female who's the boss. All their males, and all the females who can have children, have to stay at home, in the dens, all the time."

"That doesn't sound very fair," Jaina said.

"No, it doesn't—to a human," Han said. "Maybe it doesn't even sound that fair to some of the Selonians. But that's the way their society works. Lots of humans have tried to barge in and tell them to change their ways, but it just doesn't work."

"Why not?" Jacen asked.

Han laughed. "Oh no, you don't. Some other time. Ask me in about ten years or so—"

"When I'm old enough to understand," Jacen said, rolling his eyes.

"Exactly. Anyway, there are the three main Corellian species. Every now and then a group from one world decides to move to one of the other worlds. So they pack up and off they go. Then, the next day, or a thousand years later, *another* group on *another* of the Brothers will decide to move, and off *they* go.

"Now all that's been going on for thousands of years. Nowadays, all of the worlds are all scrambled up, with all the species on all of them. Sometimes, it's just one kind of people—humans or Selonians or Drall—in one town. Other places, like in Coronet, all three of the species live there. Not only them, but species from a hundred other star systems besides. They all came to Coronet to buy and sell and trade." Han hesitated a moment, and a look of sadness came over his face. "At least there *used* to be that many traders from the outside," he said. "Things have changed, because of the war, and a lot of the traders left Coronet a long time ago."

"How did the *war* make it change?" Anakin asked.

Han thought for a moment before he answered. "It was sort of like those games where you set up a whole line of little tiles and then knock over the first one in line. The first one knocks over the second, and the second knocks over the third, and so on, until they all fall over, one after another. Even before the war really got started, the navy found it harder and harder to keep enough patrol craft out in the space lanes. They kept getting called away to chase this bunch of Rebel raiders, or to show the flag in that outpost, or to deal with those crises. The more the navy wasn't there, the more the raiders and pirates showed up. The more the pirates chased the traders, the less worthwhile it was for the traders to do business. And when the traders went away, the trading went away, too, and lots of people in the Corellian Sector got poorer and poorer."

"And then the war itself came," Leia said. "And the whole Corellian Sector might as well have built a wall around itself. The Emperor's Corellian government got scared," she said at last. "Not just scared of the Rebellion, but scared of everyone. They decided the safest thing to do was not to trust anyone at all. They decided they didn't want the traders. In fact, they didn't want *any* outsiders. The sector's government stayed more and more to themselves. They didn't trust anyone else. The government started making up all sorts of rules to keep more and more things hidden and private. It got harder and harder to get the most ordinary sort of information, harder and harder for outsiders to send messages or visit any of the Corellian planets. And the Corellian leaders stopped trusting their own people, and put more and more of the same sort of restrictions on them. And with the Imperial government propping up the Corellian Diktat—that's what they called their chief of state—the Diktat could do whatever he wanted without any fear of the people protesting.''

"But you guys won the war a long time ago," Jacen said. "Without the Empire, didn't the Diktat guy have to quit?"

Leia smiled at that. If only the universe were that tidy, that sensible, so that the losers knew when it was time to quit, and gave up once it was over.

"The Diktat never did quit," Leia said. "Not in the way you mean. There wasn't a day when the Diktat got up in front of the cameras and announced his resignation. But once there was no more Empire to provide outside support, people started to be less and less afraid. They started doing what they wanted, instead of what the rules said they should do. The more people got away with breaking the rules, the braver they got, and the more rules they broke. The security forces didn't feel brave enough to stop it all—and they didn't want to go on shooting their own people. It all just sort of collapsed. The Diktat was still there in his palace giving out orders and demanding that people be executed, but no one listened anymore, and no one obeyed his orders.''

"But what happened to him?" Jacen asked.

"Nothing much, really," Leia said. "The New Republic didn't want to arrest him. After all, the Diktat was the legal head of government. Even if we had thrown him in jail, we would have angered a lot of the old loyalists we were trying

to win over. We were still trying to decide what to do with
him when he disappeared. We think he was taken off to
one of the Outlier systems."

"What are Outliers?" Anakin asked.

"That's just the name for the star systems in the Corellian
Sector that are sort of small and far away from Corell itself,"
Leia said. "The Outlier systems are so secretive they make
Corellia look wide open. Lots of people from the sector's
Imperial government ran off to them and just dropped out
of sight. The Republic installed a new sector governor-
general," Leia said, "a Frozian by the name of Micamberlecto, but when the Corellians held local elections, a lot of
the old Imperial types got back into office."

"But can't you just kick the bad guys out?" Jacen asked.

"No," Leia said, "we can't, because, even if we don't
like them, they followed the rules. The people elected
them."

"So this Governor-General Micamberlecto is a good guy
who has a lot of bad guys working for him, and he can't
do anything about it," Jacen said.

Leia smiled. "That's about the size of it," she said.

"So how are you and Dad planning to fix it all?" Jaina
asked.

That question threw Leia for a loop. It would seem that
her daughter simply assumed that Leia was in charge of
stomping out all wrongdoing. "Nothing directly," she said.
"If we went in and threw out all the elected officials we
didn't like, we'd be just as bad as the Empire. Sometimes
you just have to hold your nose and accept the situation.
But part of the idea of the trade summit is to make things
tough for the bad guys in the future. They're the sort that
do well when things are bad. They stir people up about their
troubles. When things are going well, no one wants to elect
that sort of rabble-rouser. We're hoping that if we can get
trade going again, people won't have so many troubles for
the wrong sort of candidate to exploit."

Jacen made a face and shrugged. "I *guess* I see," he

said. "But won't the guys you want to throw out figure this stuff out, too, and try to stop you?"

"They sure will," Leia said. "So we'll just have to know more than they do, and think faster than they do."

"Anyway, getting back to Corellia," Han said, speaking just a little too loud so as to fill up the slightly awkward pause that had suddenly appeared in the conversation. "It's a strange and wonderful place. Like nothing you've ever seen before. Nothing at all like Coruscant."

And then he proceeded to tell the children all about the worlds of Corellia. He told them about the glittering, wide-open city of Coronet, so unlike the oversized, overstuffed, covered-over city-planet of Coruscant. "On Coruscant, we're indoors all the time, practically," he said. "It's the capital of the galaxy, but you could live your whole life there without ever going outside to see the sky! Now, Coronet is different. It's lots of little buildings, with plenty of room in between. You can go outside all the time. The city is full of parks and plazas and palaces. And there's Treasure Ship Row, with all the vendors selling good things to eat, and the shops full of things to buy from all over the galaxy—at least they used to be. Well, who knows, maybe they still are. . . ."

Leia listened to Han, every bit as swept up by his words as the children. A city full of parkland and wide-open spaces sounded good to her. *She* had had enough of the troglodytic life of Coruscant for a while, whether or not the children had. And if Han didn't say much about the casinos and saloons and nightclubs and less reputable establishments that clustered around Coronet's spaceport, she knew they were there as well. Even if she would never go into them herself, they were part of the legend of the place, part of Corellia's rough-and-tumble heritage of smugglers and pirates.

There *was* a certain romance to such places. Maybe she *would* go into one or two of them, one night. She could get the children tucked into bed, get Chewie to watch them for the evening, dress in something the Chief of State would never wear, and then slip out with her husband, get him to show her some of the more grown-up playgrounds of Coronet. There could be no harm in taking in a show or two, or even trying her own hand at sabacc. But it seemed that Han had moved past Coronet while she was distracted, and was telling them about the other worlds.

"Will we get to see Selonia and Drall?" Jacen was asking.

"We sure will," Han promised. "Selonia and Drall and the Double Worlds, Talus and Tralus—maybe we can even get a look at Centerpoint Station."

"What's Centerpoint Station?" Jaina asked.

"Well, Talus and Tralus are called the Double Worlds because they are just the same size as each other. They orbit around each other. Centerpoint Station is in the balance point, the barycenter, between Talus and Tralus. You get quite a view from there."

"I'll bet," Jacen said.

"And then there's the Boiling Sea and Drall, and the Cloudland Peaks on Selonia, and the Gold Beaches on Corellia. You kids have never been swimming in a real, honest ocean, have you? We can all go to the beach and build sand castles and go swimming in the great big ocean!"

"What about sea monsters?" Anakin asked, clearly a bit dubious about the swimming part.

"Well, that's why we'll go swimming on Corellia," Han said. He gave Jaina a little push and she hopped off his lap. Han stood up, went over to Anakin, and scooped him up in his arms. "There aren't any sea monsters there. They keep all of *them* on Selonia, because the oceans are much bigger there."

"Honest?" Anakin asked.

"Honest," Han said, quite solemn and sincere. "But I think it's time for certain little land monsters to get ready for bed, don't you?"

That was enough to elicit a round of good-natured groans from the children, but for once, getting them ready for bed and down for the night was hardly a struggle at all. All three of them were suddenly yawning, struggling to keep awake long enough to get faces washed and teeth brushed, clothes off and pajamas on.

All three of them climbed willingly into their bunks, and snuggled happily into their pillows. Jacen and Jaina were already fast asleep, their breathing low and regular, by the time Han knelt down by Anakin's little bed, helped pull the cover up over him, and gave him a gentle kiss on the forehead.

But sleepy as he was, Anakin was not quite ready to sleep yet.

"Daddy?" he asked.

"Yes, Anakin? What is it?"

"Daddy—when are we going to get there?"

CHAPTER NINE

Courting Disaster

Gone. There could be no further doubt. Luke Skywalker was gone. Pharnis Gleasry, agent of the Human League, could no longer deceive himself. The Jedi Master had not been home for at least a full day. A check of Calrissian's not-all-that-well-hidden home in Dometown showed that it, too, was empty, and his ship, the *Lady Luck*, was no longer in its usual berth. Given that he had seen the two of them together the night before both had vanished from Coruscant, it seemed most likely that they had gone off together.

Pharnis knew there was nothing for it but to follow the backup plan, as dicey as it might be. He would have to use the message probe and hope against hope the *Jade's Fire* stayed to its shipping schedule. Otherwise—

Otherwise, the Hidden Leader was not going to be pleased. And that was not a pleasant thought. In fact, it might be best to get the probe sent, and then follow Skywalker's lead.

Given the Hidden Leader's temper, it might be wise to vanish.

* * *

"Did you have to bring *them* along?" Lando asked, not for the first time. The objects of his complaint, the droids R2-D2 and C-3PO, were on the opposite side of the *Lady*

Luck's wardroom, and neither of them seemed to be any happier to be with Lando than Lando was to be with them. Luke and Lando were sitting at the *Lady Luck*'s wardroom table, relaxing after their meal. At least they were supposed to be relaxing. Clearly the droids were getting on Lando's nerves.

Luke smiled to himself. There were other, legitimate reasons for bringing the droids along, but truth to tell, he had wanted them on this trip to twit Lando just a little, pay him back in the subtlest way possible for dragging him off on this lunatic scheme. He could never admit that to anyone but himself, of course, but still it was so.

But Threepio answered before Luke even had a chance. "I assure you, Captain Calrissian, that my counterpart and I have demonstrated the highest degree of utility on any number of occasions. I might add that I in particular will doubtless be of the greatest possible use on a mission of romance. In addition to being familiar with over six million forms of communication, I have provided myself with additional programming. I have done extensive searches of data sources on Coruscant not generally available to the public. I am now well versed in the courtship rituals of two thousand and forty seven human cultures, as well as five hundred and sixteen nonhuman cultures."

"Put a lid on it," Lando said to the droid. "The day I ask *your* advice on how to treat a lady is the day I take a vow of chastity."

This remark not only clearly took Threepio aback, it also inspired a whole series of rather rude-sounding beeps and bloops from Artoo. "That's scarcely accurate, Artoo, and I doubt it's the sort of advice that Captain Calrissian had in mind in any event."

Artoo made an even ruder noise and backed away from Threepio just a bit as he swiveled his visual sensor toward Luke.

"Take it easy, Artoo," Luke said. "No need to be quite *that* insulting."

"Come on, Luke. Do we really have to put up with all

this backchatter the whole trip? Can't we shut them down, or ship them home from the first port, or something?''

Luke smiled and shook his head no. "Every time I've brought the two of them along, I've been glad I did, Lando. Trust me, they'll come in handy."

"Well, they'd better do it fast," Lando growled. "Otherwise they're going to keep an appointment with the spare-parts bin."

"Come on, take it easy. Besides, you've got another appointment to keep first," Luke reminded him. "We should be breaking out of hyperspace into the Leria Kerlsil system any time now."

Lando glanced at the chronometer. "Another fifteen minutes or so," he said as he stood up. "We ought to go forward to the cockpit." Threepio took a step forward, as if to follow, but Lando held up his hand. "Hold it right there, golden boy," he said. "You two stay safely locked up and out of the way here in the wardroom while we're flying the ship and while we're planetside. Is that clear?"

"Perfectly, sir," Threepio replied, "but might I suggest that—"

"Good," Lando said, cutting him off. He turned toward the hatch. "You ever been to Leria Kerlsil?" he asked.

Luke shook his head as he got up to follow Lando. "No," he said. "Not too much about it in the data banks I searched either."

"Well," said Lando, "we're about to find out more."

The hatch slid open and they headed for the cockpit.

*   *   *

Threepio watched as the hatch slid shut behind the two humans—and was astonished to hear the click of a bolt sliding to. Captain Calrissian had locked them in. "Well!" he said. "This is not at all the refined sort of treatment I expected from Captain Calrissian, considering the circumstances. Rough-and-ready manners might be all right at a mining colony, but they certainly aren't the proper sort of thing for a gentleman searching for a wife. At least Master Luke was kind enough to come to our defense.''

Artoo let out a long, questioning series of bloops.

"What?'' asked Threepio. "No, I didn't catch the name of the place we're going to. No one ever tells me anything.''

Artoo let out a low moan and then repeated his query a bit more slowly, with an extra flourish on the end.

"Well, if you noticed them saying we're going to Leria Kerlsil, why did you bother asking me?''

Artoo replied with a series of staccato bursts.

"That is not true!'' Threepio said. "I don't just brag about what I know. I do indeed make use of it. What point in my searching out all those obscure mating rituals in out-of-the-way data sources if I didn't even think to examine the information and see—''

Artoo beeped and blooped vigorously, and rocked back and forth on his roller legs.

"Oh! You mean I could look up what I have concerning *Leria Kerlsil*. Well, why didn't you say so?'' Threepio paused for a moment, and accessed his data memory. "Oh dear!'' he said. "Oh my!'' he said. "Artoo! Whatever are we going to do?''

* * *

Lando Calrissian was more than a little used to dealing with places he was not at all used to. He had long ago lost count of the planets on which he had done business of one sort or another. Now, as he set foot on Leria Kerlsil for the first time, he knew almost nothing about it—and yet he knew more about it than he knew about most worlds he had visited.

He had learned long ago how to improvise, how to watch the local customs and ways of doing things, how to spot which were the trivial differences, and which differences were vital.

But he had also learned about more than differences. He had learned how much all backwater worlds were the same.

Or at least how much the same were all the backwater worlds a trader might be interested in.

There had to be a spaceport, and that automatically meant all the things that went along with a spaceport. Lodgings for crewmen, almost always a bar or tavern of some sort, cargo facilities, someplace to change credits in and out of the local currency, and so on. In plain point of fact, Lando had seen little more than the spaceport on most of the planets he had visited.

He would land, meet with the local reps for whatever he was buying or selling, keep an eye on the cargo going on and off his ship, make and receive whatever payments were required, get a bite to eat and something to drink in the bar, perhaps catch a night's sleep in the hostelry if his bankroll was up to it and the beds looked comfortable enough, and then he'd be on his way in the morning. All the spaceport bars and cargo facilities and customs clerks seemed to blur together after a while. It didn't help that so many of them looked alike. He had "been" to dozens of worlds wherein he had seen nothing of the local culture beyond the customs clerk.

It wasn't always that way, of course. There had been plenty of times when he had stepped outside that imaginary bubble around the spaceport into the real life and culture of the world. Lando was determined this would be one of those times he got out and saw the world he was on. After all, if things broke the right way, he was going to end up living on this planet—at least part of the time—for years to come. It would behoove him to get a look at as much of it as he could before he agreed to anything rash.

At first glance, at least, it seemed like a rather pleasant place. The sky was a crystal blue, with fluffy white clouds scudding along, riding a freshening breeze. The air smelled pure and clean. The spaceport itself was small but well maintained, with every surface well polished and gleaming, all the staff cheerful and helpful.

As on so many small worlds, the spaceport had been built far outside the city limits, and then the city had grown up around it. A five-minute ride in a hovercar brought them into the center of town, and a handsome-looking center of town it was. Waist-high trees with pale blue bark and small round purple leaves lined the neatly kept avenues. Wheeled vehicles moved quietly and sedately over the well-paved roads. The houses and shops were of modest size, but clearly it was a city of house-proud folk. Everything was tidy and clean, everything handsome and well made.

"Not bad," Lando said as the two of them walked along. "Not bad at all. I could see this as a very nice little base of operations."

Luke laughed. "You're getting a bit ahead of yourself," he said. "Wouldn't it be better to wait until you've met the lady in question?"

"We will, we will," Lando said. "The appointment's not for another half an hour. I don't want to get there too early and seem eager."

"What will you do if *she* seems eager?" Luke asked.

Lando looked over at his friend and winked. "Then I'll raise the ante, of course. That's how the game is played."

At that, both of them laughed, and turned a corner to get a look at another street in the pleasant capital city of Leria Kerlsil.

* * *

"Hurry! Hurry! Burn it open if you have to, you miserable bucket of bolts," Threepio shouted at Artoo. The little astromech unit was struggling to get the wardroom hatch open. His datalink probe was plugged into a wall socket, and he was trying to find a circuit link that would allow him to operate the lock from inside. "Captain Calrissian could be in great danger. Hurry! Don't bother with all your fancy data slicing! It's not going to work."

Artoo replied with a testy-sounding series of buzzes and clicks—and then the door slid halfway open, just far enough for the two of them to get out of the wardroom. "Oh, good work, Artoo," Threepio cried. "I knew that you could do it. Oh, why couldn't Captain Calrissian or Master Luke be carrying a comlink so we could warn them. It could be too late already. We *must* get to a city dataport and find out if my information is correct. Hurry! Hurry!''

*   *   *

Luke Skywalker walked along beside his friend, enjoying the pleasant morning—but also starting to realize that something was not quite right. His Jedi senses were trying to tell him something, but he was not quite sure what.

Luke glanced up and down the quiet street. There were fewer houses out this way, and they were larger and grander than the ones in the center of town. There were only a few passersby on the sidewalk, and they merely glanced over at the pair of strangers with the mildest of curiosity. No threat from that quarter, clearly enough.

And yet there was something. Luke realized that his hand had drifted toward the handle of his lightsaber. He was more spooked than he realized. He glanced over at Lando, but it was obvious that his friend was quite unconcerned. Plainly there was nothing on his mind more stressful than his usual cheerfully larcenous schemes. So what *was* it? For a half a moment he considered the possibility of grabbing Lando by the arm and urging him to turn back. But no. Even a Jedi Master needed more than a vague notion of something not quite right.

*   *   *

The two droids finally found a public city dataport in an obscure corner of the main terminal building of the spaceport. ''Plug in! Plug in!'' Threepio cried, urging on Artoo. ''Everything, *everything* you can find on Karia Ver Seryan. I only hope I'm wrong—''

Artoo beeped and blurped rapidly in a high register.

''What do you mean, why should this time be different?'' he demanded, swatting Artoo on the dome. ''Plug into the dataport and don't give me any more nonsense. As I was about to say, if I am right—which is not so rare an occurrence, thank you very much—we might well need all the evidence we can find to convince Captain Calrissian of the situation. Hurry! Hurry!"

* * *

Lando and Luke managed to time their walk rather well, getting to Karia Ver Seryan's house just a minute or two before the appointed time.

Her house was hard to miss in that quiet, tree-lined street. It was, by far, the largest in the neighborhood. Nearly all the other homes were made out of a sort of dark yellow brick, with here or there one built from bluish-gray wood. But Ver Seryan's house was built of well-mortared dark gray stone. It was five stories tall, although all the other nearby buildings were two or three stories at most. It stood on a piece of land at least four times as large as any of the other houses. The grounds were surrounded by a high fence made up of elaborately decorated black iron bars, set into the ground, twelve centimeters apart. It looked more like a fortress than a home.

Luke noticed that the houses on either side of Ver Seryan's house were empty and abandoned, their grounds overgrown with brambles, in stark contrast to the elaborate gardens and private menageries on display everywhere else.

At first glance, the gardens surrounding Ver Seryan's house seemed a tribute to ostentation for its own sake. There were paths and stone seats, and exotic plants from a dozen foreign worlds. A decorative artificial stream completely circled the house, no doubt set in motion by some sort of pumping system. A path led from the front gate over a diminutive footbridge to the front door.

There was a widening in the brook on the right side of the house, and in the middle of it stood a complicated three-tiered fountain. Its jets of water played high into the air in an intricate and ever-shifting pattern. However, despite the distraction of the fountain, it did not escape Luke's attention that, if the bridge were raised, as it seemed it could be, the decorative circular brook would stand in good service as a moat.

And there, in the middle of all the elaborate landscaping, was the house itself, and the house seemed to have nothing in common with its own grounds. There was nothing pretty or ornamental about it. It was built to be big and strong, and that was that. Despite the attempt to disguise the fact with fancy plants and whimsical fountains, it was plain to see Ver Seryan's house *was* a fortress, designed to keep people out.

Luke looked up at the place, feeling even less happy about the circumstances. What sort of woman needed a home that could protect her against a mob? It was plainly a mob that the owner of this house was worried about. Moats and iron fences were not the sort of precautions that would hold back a determined burglar, or an organized assault with modern weapons. No. It was the sort of setup designed to slow down and discourage a crowd in an ugly mood, and hold a disorganized, emotional mob at bay.

Nor was there any way Luke could tell himself that it was all decorative, some sort of holdover from an architectural tradition. The proof was there, in front of his eyes, on the wall of the house, just to the right of the door. There was some sort of creeping plant growing up over them, but it would take more than a few leaves and tendrils to hide blaster burns that big.

"Looks like she's pretty well-off," Lando said.

Luke was about to say something, but thought better of it. There was just too much of a difference between his viewpoint and Lando's. Where Luke saw a defense system, Lando saw evidence of cash flow. Who was to say which of them was right? Maybe everything Luke had noticed involved the previous owner, or some spot of bother brought on by the war against the Empire.

But he could not convince himself. Something was not right. Luke reached out with the Force and tried to get a sense of the place, a feel for the mood of the people. Now the feeling that had bothered him before came back, clearer and more intensely. Luke could feel the way it centered around this point, this house.

Now that he knew what to look for, he sought out the minds of whatever people his Force sense could locate in the general vicinity of Ver Seryan's house.

Every mind he could find held at least some trace of the feeling. It was not uppermost in their thoughts, but it was there, and it got stronger the closer people were to the house. Not hatred, or anger. It was a muted, subtle kind of fear, something closer to the state of mind of someone trying to avoid touching a plant with thorns, someone aware they were sitting a trifle too close to a campfire, someone wary of getting any closer to a potentially dangerous animal. In the back of every mind there was the sense that it was unwise to get too close to the house of Karia Ver Seryan.

Luke refocused his Force sense in a new direction, and got another surprise. He could sense only one sentient living mind in the house. It had to be Ver Seryan. But it was abundantly clear from the first brush with her mind that there was nothing malevolent there. She did not regard herself as dangerous but as quite the opposite. In her he sensed an almost cloying benevolence, someone almost overeager to do good for anyone and everyone, whether they liked it or not. There was more than a whisper of greed in her mind as well, but nothing that could account for the cautious, careful fear that surrounded her. If that degree of greed was all it took to inspire fear, Lando should have caused a worldwide panic the moment he set foot on the planet.

Still, it was a truism that no person ever regards himself or herself as evil. Even the emperor believed himself to be in the right, even as he crushed the Old Republic and established his tyranny throughout the galaxy. Just because Ver Seryan regarded herself as good, it did not mean she was. But even so, something here did not fit.

"Come on, Luke," said Lando, breaking into his

thoughts. "You going to spend the whole day staring at her house? I don't want to keep the lady waiting."

Luke put his hand on his friend's arm. "Lando," he said. "Be careful, all right?"

"In a negotiation? What else have I ever been? Come on."

Lando pushed on the gate and it swung open. He led the way into the grounds of the house, and Luke followed a step or two behind and more than a little reluctantly.

The two of them went up the path, crossed the little bridge, and went up the stairs to the solid-looking steel doors of the house. Lando waited for Luke to catch up and pressed the annunciator disk as soon as Luke joined him.

After a delay brief enough that Luke assumed they had been watched from inside the house, the door swung open to reveal a strikingly lovely young woman. Luke was about to ask if Ver Seryan was at home when he recalled that he had only sensed one human being in the house. This had to be her—though this woman was nothing like he'd expected.

"Welcome to you both," the woman said. "I am Karia Ver Seryan. Welcome to you, Lando Calrissian. I received your communication and am eager to speak further with you. We may well be able to come to an arrangement of mutual interest." She turned to Luke. "And of course, welcome to you, most high Jedi Master. Your exploits are legend, and it is the greatest of honors to welcome you into my humble abode. Please, gentles both, do come in."

Lando winked at Luke when Ver Seryan was not looking. Obviously, it was Luke's reputation that had opened this door. Lando lost no further time in stepping through it, with Luke following behind.

Luke was not quite sure what he had expected of the interior, but it was certainly not what he saw. The dark solidity of the exterior was nowhere in evidence. Inside, all was softness and light. The interior walls were white stone, and they were decorated with elaborate and costly hangings and paintings from across the galaxy. The ground floor seemed to be one vast room. A grand staircase led up the back wall from left to right, the line of stairs broken by landings a third and two thirds of the way up. Doorways led out of each landing, presumably to living quarters.

Folding screens and freestanding shelves and display cases broke the space up into a number of cozy-looking sitting areas. Comfortable-looking couches and chairs and luxurious carpets were arranged invitingly. It looked to be the sort of room made for a splendid party, not for sheltering one lone woman.

But if the room was unexpected, it was far less so than their hostess. Working from the scanty information Lando had been able to gather, Luke had been imagining Karia Ver Seryan as a frumpy, indolent sort of woman who had married for money, and then let herself go completely once her husband was safely dead. From the way Lando had spoken, it was clear that he had expected much the same.

But the reality of Karia Ver Seryan could not have been further from that image. She was tall, slender, and dark-skinned, with eyes of the most startling deep violet. Her hair was the color of late sunset, and she moved with a remarkably artless grace. She was dressed in a simple, elegant, black dress of modest cut that did more to accentuate her figure than any more revealing dress could have possibly done, and a single large diamond hung around her neck on a platinum chain. One look at Lando, and it was obvious that the size of the bankroll it would take to get him to marry her had just shrunk rather precipitously.

"Your home is lovely," he said, "but not remotely as lovely as its owner."

Ver Seryan smiled prettily and gave a very slight bow of acknowledgment. "Thank you, kind sir. It is difficult for me to hire servants, as you might imagine. I will not disguise from you the problems of maintaining my home with nothing but droid labor. I do freely admit that I would be most happy to have a man about the place—to serve as a handyman, if nothing else."

"I can assure you that I would be most interested in the position," said Lando, in a tone of voice that left no doubt of his sincerity.

"Come," she said. "Do sit yourselves down, and make yourselves as you would be at home."

Lando grinned so broadly it seemed as if he was about to sprain a few muscles. He stepped forward, took Ver Seryan's hand in his, and bent low to kiss it. "I will gladly come and sit," he said, "but I assure you that I could not make myself any more at home than I am at this moment."

*   *   *

"Oh, my!" Threepio cried out as they swerved to avoid a slower-moving ground car. "Friend driver, please do be careful!"

"Careful or fast, take your choice," the driver growled without looking back, and pressed his foot down harder on the accelerator

Artoo and Threepio sat in the back of a speeding hovercar, rushing for Ver Seryan's home. Artoo seemed to be taking it all in stride, perhaps even enjoying the ride, but Threepio had found the whole affair most upsetting already. He felt certain that his circuits were already overheating from the stress.

There are some spaceports where it is merely difficult for a droid to hire a hovercar, and others where it is all but impossible. Leria Kersil's spaceport, unfortunately, fell into the second category. The automated cabs flatly refused them, their programming refusing to take orders from mere machines. That had left the droids with no other option but to try their luck with the human-operated cabs.

Even that would have been absolutely out of the question if Artoo had not been carrying a modest supply of Coruscant credits in one of his concealed compartments. Master Luke had put the money there some years ago, against just the sort of emergency they now faced.

But even with ready cash in hand, it had been difficult

to find a driver willing to drive droids around the city. The only one they did find, the disreputable-looking fellow who was now breaking every traffic law in the city, had seemed to make some sort of mental estimate of the market value of their desperation, and then demanded an astronomical price.

Threepio, well versed in the art of haggling, had attempted to talk the man's price down, but Artoo had spoiled everything, as usual. He had deliberately rammed himself into Threepio's leg in order to silence him. Then Artoo had simply offered all of the cash they had to the driver.

Granted, it had worked, and they were in a hurry, but even so, there were times when Artoo's overbearing ways were most provoking.

The cab veered hard to the left as the driver took a corner at speed. Threepio just managed to hold on for dear life. Artoo, propped up next to him on the backseat, toppled over again, and immediately bleeped and blooped for Threepio to help him up. "I should let you stay down there this time," Threepio said, rather petulantly, even as he helped Artoo up. "You've been even more insufferable than usual this time out."

The driver took another curve rather violently, but this time Artoo kept his balance. He let out a triumphant burble and extended a work clamp to brace himself into one corner of the seat.

"Oh dear!" said Threepio. "I only hope we're in time after all this. According to my information, the process is quite irrevocable."

*   *   *

Lando Calrissian could not have been happier. He should have thought of this getting-married business years ago. Here he was, first try out of the box and, as best as he could tell, well on his way to a very satisfactory arrangement. Even after only a few minutes of small talk he was sure of that. Karia and he were getting along wonderfully. She was not only rich, she was young, charming, and beautiful. Clearly, there had been some errors in his information, but expecting an old battle-ax and discovering a young goddess was the sort of mistake he could deal with.

Luke was the only fly in the ointment. He was being polite enough, but not exactly charming. He seemed distracted, distant. If they had been sitting around a table, he would have kicked Luke in the shin and tried to snap him out of it. As it was, Lando, Karia, and Luke were seated facing each other in three extremely comfortable armchairs, the fantastically luxuriant rug under their feet would be enough to buy and sell Dometown three times over, and Karia was giving him a smile that would have melted the door of any bank vault. Some bit of Lando's hindbrain was delivering a line of charming small talk on automatic pilot, letting Lando relax and admire Karia without having to worry too much. All else was right with the world. He could tolerate Luke being a bit out of it.

But, it would seem, Karia had something on her mind. She smiled appreciatively at whatever charming compliment had just come out of his mouth, but then she leaned forward on the arm of her chair, and her face took on a more earnest expression. "I am glad of all this pleasant talk," she said, "but the folk who come to me ofttimes have but little time to spare. I find that I prefer coming to the point most quickly. Would that be suitable to you?"

Lando smiled, just a trifle uncertainly, and nodded. "Absolutely."

"That is good," said Karia. "It is plain that you have made inquiries concerning me, else you would not have come. Is there anything that you must know now that you do not? Have you any questions?"

Lando spoke again, a bit more puzzled this time, but still determined to play the gallant suitor. "There is, ah, much about you that I *would* know, and hope I will come to know, but nothing that I *must* know immediately."

"Excellent," she said. "I shall conceal nothing. When I received the first communication from yourself, I made inquiries of my own. I must needs confess that, in normal times, I would not consider your suit. But times are not as they often are. Although my time of rest is over, my life with my previous husband was—taxing. I am not as refreshed as I might wish. Though your wealth is not as great as it might be, nonetheless it is substantial, and growing. I am impressed by your work on Dometown. I believe that given sufficient backing, you could accomplish much in a short space of years. On your honor, do you think likewise?''

"I do indeed," Lando said, as fervently as he could.

"Yes," said Karia. "I see that you do. You are young still, and energetic. One thing I have not been able to learn from my investigations—it would seem that you are in quite good health. Is this the case?''

"Why, yes—yes, of course," Lando said, clearly taken aback. "Lots of good years left in me."

Karia leaned back in her chair. "And yet you are here. Most interesting. Not unheard of, and yet most interesting. There is the saying that the candle that burns shortest burns brightest. There are those who would disapprove, but none come here except by free choice. You realize that the process, the marriage, is quite irrevocable? It is quite impossible to turn back?''

Lando was very definitely starting to feel that he was in over his head. "I, ah, wasn't contemplating the idea of marrying you and then divorcing in hopes of a settlement, if that is what you mean. When I marry, I intend to stay married."

Karia grinned and laughed. "There would be no hope of a settlement in any event, of course, so that is to the good."

Apparently she had a great deal of confidence in her lawyers. That was definitely a point to bear in mind. "No, no," Lando said. "Until death do us part, and all that."

Karia's face became serious once again. "And all that," she echoed. She looked Lando hard in the face for a long moment, clearly trying to reach a decision. "I like you," she said. "Even if you are young, and healthy, I like you.

Life is for taking risks, and I am for life. Your wealth is not great now, but it may well become so. I will have you, if you will have me."

Luke sat forward in his chair, and looked from Lando to Karia. "That's awfully quick," he said. "Do you truly wish to make such a decision so quickly?"

"As I have said, those who come to me rarely have much time to spend in hesitation." She smiled, and spoke again. "Perhaps, just this once, I would wish for myself the luxury of setting the pace myself." She turned back to Lando. "What say you, gentle sir? Will you? Or will you not?"

"Well, I, ah—any man would be honored to accept you, my dear Lady Karia. But surely we must agree to *terms* before we complete the—ah—marriage agreement."

"Well and wisely put, gentle sir," she said. "I spoke too quickly. Let me present the offer I would give you. Marry me, and live with me. I will fully Support you in all ways for five years, longer than is normal."

"You'll Support me?" Lando asked. He could hear the capital "S" in "Support." "Support me in what way?"

Karia smiled, as if it were a silly question. "In all ways. I will care for your health, provide for you financially, clothe you, feed you, and shelter you."

"And in return?" Lando asked.

"And in return you will live well. It is the law on our world that by marrying me, I will become your sole heir."

"And I will become yours?" he asked.

Karia smiled again. "Yes, that is so."

"I'm not quite clear here. What will happen after five years?" Lando asked. "You will cease to support me? Will we then no longer be married?"

"As you said, we shall be married until death do us part."

"But I'll have to fend for myself, eh? Well, that certainly seems fair enough," Lando said. "But let me make something clear. I don't want or intend just to live off you. I want to *work*. I want to make things, build things, run things. I want to find grand projects that deserve to happen and make them happen.''

"Yes, of course. That is your gift. You must pursue it. You are pursuing it, and are willing to sacrifice all for it. You seek a source of investment capital, and that I shall be for you. I will not be so imprudent as to give you all of what I have, but I assure you that this''—she gestured to indicate the incredibly opulent house and grounds—"is but the least of what is mine. You will have the finances to do what you seek to do. Will that be satisfactory?''

"Yes! Of course! Absolutely," Lando said. No one had ever offered him terms like these before. He would have to be insane to turn them down, or give her a chance to change her mind.

Karia stood up. "Then let us perform the ceremony," she said.

Lando and Luke both got up as well, guided half by reflex and surprise. "What, *now?*" Lando asked.

"Certainly," Karia said. "What point could there be in waiting longer? We both know what we want, and each of us knows the other can provide it. Life is short, and delay is death."

"Lando, wait a second!" Luke said. "There's something wrong here. I don't know what it is, but there is something wrong."

Karia's mood changed abruptly. "Does the great Jedi Master question my veracity?" she asked, with steel in her voice. "Come, look into my soul, and see if deception lurks there. I have nothing to fear."

"There is no need," Luke said. "I do not doubt your intentions are all they should be. I do not think you intend to deceive. But even so, there is something wrong. I beg that you give my friend time—if only an hour—to pause and reflect."

Karia's eyes flashed with anger. "In another hour, another suitor may come. In another hour, I might not like your friend so much as I do now. No. He knows all he needs to know, and he knows why he came here. It is now or never.''

Lando grabbed Luke by the arm and pulled him close. ''Luke, back off,'' he whispered. ''She's right. This is what I was after. Don't mess this up for me.''

Luke looked Lando straight in the eye. ''Lando,'' he said in a low voice. ''I tell you that something's missing here. Are you *sure* you know what you're doing?''

Lando felt a knot at the pit of his stomach, and suddenly he realized he was scared. Very scared. Of what, he did not know. But if he were a man who ran away from what scared him, the second Death Star might still be in the sky. Courage was for when you were scared. ''No, I'm not sure,'' he whispered back. ''But as the lady said, life is risk. If here and now is my one chance, then I take my chance now.'' He turned back toward their hostess, smoothed his hair down, and straightened his tunic. ''This ceremony,'' he said in as steady a voice as he could manage. ''Exactly what does it involve?''

Karia gestured toward a five-sided red canopy that stood at the south side of the great room. ''There,'' she said. ''We stand under the canopy, activate a recording device, repeat a brief oath in front of a witness, perform the blood kiss, and the deed is done.''

''Blood kiss?'' Lando asked, a bit anxiously.

Karia smiled. ''A most lurid name for a most gentle ritual. It is nothing. A pinprick on your right forefinger. A spot of blood. I kiss it. You do the same to me, and that is all. We will be wed.''

''And that's legally binding?'' Lando said. ''We'll be married in the eyes of the law, and of society?''

Karia laughed again. ''Oh yes, indeed. It is most certainly a binding ceremony. We shall be well and truly wedded, one to the other.''

Lando took a deep breath and stepped forward. He extended his left hand toward his bride, and she put her hand on his. ''Then here is our witness, and now is the time.''

"Lando! No!" Luke protested, and made as if to step toward him.

Lando held up his right hand toward Luke, palm out. "This is what I want, Luke," he said. "This is what you promised to help me get, on the oath of a Jedi Master. I say to you that now is the time for you to honor that oath. You shall be our witness."

Lando could see the conflict in his friend's face, the fear for him struggling with the promise Luke had made. "Very well," Luke said at last. "On the oath of a Jedi Master, let us perform the ritual."

⚹   ⚹   ⚹

The cab driver had made one wrong turn, and corrected it with a U-turn of remarkable violence. Now, at last, they were in front of the Ver Seryan house. Threepio suddenly realized that Artoo could not get out of the hovercar without assistance, and yet was blocking the door.

"Driver!" Threepio cried out, tapping on the scuffed clear plastic barrier that divided the front seat from the back. "I'm afraid I must ask your help again to get my counterpart back out of the cruiser."

The driver turned around and glared at Threepio most unpleasantly. "Come on, you crazy tin box. It was tough enough getting him *into* the cab back at the spaceport."

"True enough," Threepio said. "But the sooner my counterpart is out of your vehicle, the sooner you can be on your way." It had not escaped Threepio's notice that their driver clearly did not like the idea of getting this close to the Ver Seryan place. In any event, the argument convinced the driver. He popped open the door to the driving compartment, got out, opened the rear door, slapped one meaty hand on either side of Artoo, and pulled him out of the cab with a single mighty heave. He dumped Artoo unceremoniously on the grass by the side of the road. Threepio was barely able to get out of the cab before the driver was back behind the controls and driving off at high speed, using the acceleration of his start to slam the passenger door shut.

"Well!" said Threepio. "I can't say that I am sorry to see the last of *him!* Come along, Artoo, we must hurry."

Artoo managed to right himself, but it was plain to see that he was going to have some difficulty navigating his way up to the house. Artoo swiveled his visual sensor toward Threepio and whistled frantically.

"Oh! My goodness, Artoo, you are quite right. Under the circumstances, I certainly should *not* wait for you." Threepio turned toward the house, and made his ungainly way toward it, moving as fast as his somewhat ill-coordinated locomotion system would carry him.

It would be most vexing if they were too late, after all the trouble they had been through. No doubt Master Luke might well be upset. It would be a great inconvenience to everyone if it turned out Captain Calrissian was doomed to mortal peril.

*   *   *

They stood under the red five-sided canopy near the south wall, and low, haunting music played from some hidden source. A single red candle stood on a low five-sided table at the exact center of the canopy, and burned with a strange blue flame. Lando stood on the east side of the low table, and Karia on the west.

Luke stood, watching, just outside the canopy, on its north side, with the length of the great room at his back. He did not like this. He did not like it one little bit. But he had sworn an oath, and he saw no way out. He watched as the wedding ceremony began.

Karia lifted her hands, and offered them, palm down, to Lando, one hand on either side of the candle. Lando placed his hands over hers, close enough to the candle that the blue flame cast its light on his skin.

"Left hand in right, right hand in left," she began. "East

to west, west to east. Sunrise facing sunset as dusk faces dawn,'' Karia said. "Life, shorter than a moment. Life, longer than memory. Each side touching each. Two shall be one, and one shall be all.'' She nodded to him, indicating that he should repeat the words.

"Left hand in right, right hand in left,'' Lando said. "East to west, west to east,'' he said, speaking the words slowly and carefully. "Sunrise facing sunset, as dusk faces dawn. Life, shorter than a moment. Life, longer than memory. Each side touching each. Two shall be one, and one shall be all.''

She nodded, and moved her left hand away from his right. She reached down onto the table, and picked up an instrument with an elaborately carved handle, resembling a ceremonial dagger. But this dagger had no blade. Instead, it had a ten-centimeter needle, its point so sharp it was hard to see. She stuck the needle's point into the candle's flame, which flared from bright blue to glowing, ruddy red.

Her right hand was still under Lando's left. Now she turned Lando's left hand over so that it was palm up. She held Lando's forefinger between her thumb and forefinger, raised the needle dagger and—

There was a sudden, violent pounding at the door, so loud that both Karia and Lando jerked back in surprise. The door annunciator bonged loudly, over and over, and the pounding on the door redoubled.

"Hold it!'' Luke said, his hand suddenly close to his lightsaber. Whatever that was at the door might provide a way to stall. He reached out with his Force power and found that he could not sense a living mind there. A droid then, of some sort.

Whatever. It didn't matter. It might be nothing more than the grocer's droid demanding that Karia pay her bill, but Luke didn't care. It bought him time, and he was going to use it. "The ceremony stops!'' he said. "I don't know who or what that is at the door, but the ceremony stops until we find out. Neither of you move.''

Karia seemed about to protest, but Luke could see her

eyes move toward his lightsaber. She nodded agreement and kept silent. Lando nodded as well. "Go," he said.

Luke turned around and hurried toward the door. He unclipped his lightsaber, just to be on the safe side. He threw back the bolt and pulled the door open—and was astonished to find Threepio rushing into the house.

"Threepio! What in space are you—"

"Stop! Stop! Stop!" Threepio cried out as he burst into the room. He stepped inside, paused a moment as he looked around, and then spotted Lando and Karia under the canopy. He hurried toward them, gesticulating frantically. Luke followed behind the droid, utterly baffled.

"Go no further, Captain Calrissian!" Threepio shouted. "Stop! Stop!"

"What are you talking about?" Lando said. "Threepio, this is no time for you to barge in. When you made that racket at the door, I thought you were going to be someone important. Now get out of here."

"But you must stop, I tell you!" Threepio turned toward Luke. "Master Luke, please tell me. Have they gotten to the ceremony of the blood kiss yet?"

"No. They were just about to do it," Luke said.

"Then thank heavens I am in time. You *must* stop, Captain Calrissian. The woman is a life-witch!"

"She's a *what*?" Lando asked.

"A life-witch!" Threepio said, pointed at Karia. "The honorific 'Ver' before her last name signifies that she is a life-witch."

"That is a term that I do not like to hear," said Karia. "We call ourselves life-bearers, for that is truly what we do." She looked at Lando. "But did you not know? Were you not aware? How could you seek me out and *not* know?"

"What's a life-witch?" Lando asked. "And are you one?"

"I am a life-bearer," Karia said.

"Call it by whatever name you wish," said the droid, in tones that were even more frantic than usual. "But it is true. True! We checked the records before we came over here, Artoo and I. He'd be in here showing them to you, but he's having trouble getting up the steps." Threepio turned toward Karia. "Go ahead," he said. "Tell them. We have the records. *Tell* them how many times you have been married."

"It is my gift, the gift of the life-bearers," Karia said, ignoring Threepio and addressing Lando with an unnerving calm. "We are found only here, on this world, born now and again by random chance. Even here we are rare. Ours is a special gift and skill. By linking close, we can keep the old, the sick, the dying, alive for a time. The blood kiss bonds my body chemistry to my husband's. I can link to his life essence, and so sustain him. The sick and the dying are relieved of pain, and can live, for a time, in vigor and health. That is the Support I spoke of. But we cannot provide Support forever. We can hold back pain, and forestall death, but only for a time. Then we must withdraw Support, or die ourselves. And a life force that has come to rely on Support cannot long survive on its own. It dies."

"You mean after five years of Supporting me—"

"I would withdraw Support and you would die," Karia said. "I thought that you knew this." She shrugged. "You would not be the first young and healthy man to exchange a long and uncertain life for a short one of comfort and security. And no, before you can ask, no, I could not marry without providing Support. We must have a time of recovery between husbands, but our life forces are likewise shaped by what we do. A life-bearer who does not provide Support for a time will soon sicken and die."

Lando opened his mouth and shut it again.

"Your friend Chantu Solk was a more typical case. When he came to me, he had but a few months to live, months of pain and failing health. I gave him three years of health and comfort and companionship, and in return I became his heir, taking on his wealth only when he had no further use for it. Does that not seem a fair exchange?"

Lando looked back and forth from Karia to Threepio and back to Karia before he found his voice again and managed to gasp out a single, strangled question. *"How many husbands?"* he asked.

She drew herself up to her full height, folded her arms, and spoke with a calm, low dignity. "I shall conceal nothing," she said. "The life-bearer can bear no children of her own. We are sterile. But our compensation is long life, and time enough to do our work. I have had the honor to survive forty-nine husbands thus far."

"Forty-nine husbands?" Lando repeated in horrified astonishment.

Luke looked at Karia, amazed. How old was this woman? *Was* she a woman, a human, at all?

Karia Ver Seryan turned to Lando and smiled. "But all this I thought you knew. In my eyes, and heart, nothing has changed. I shall have you if you shall have me. All that remains is the kiss of joining, the touch of my blood mingled with yours. Yes, there have been forty-nine. But should you still wish to undergo the ceremony, and the marriage, it shall be your happy death, five years from today, that will bring it to an even fifty."

CHAPTER TEN

Showtime

S omething was happening to Star Number TD-10036-EM-1271, something that went against all experience, all patterns of stellar mechanics. Strange forces reached out for it, huge and unseen hands manipulated its interior, forcing the internal heat and pressure up to levels that such a star never experienced.

The surface of TD-10036-EM-1271 began to roil more and more violently. Powerful seismic waves started to pulse through the supercompressed matter at the star's core. Its outer layers began to expand as a result of the increased heat and pressure. It changed in color from yellow to white to blue-white to pulsating blue-white glaring up into the ultraviolet—

And then, quite impossibly, TD-10036-EM-1271 exploded.

The shockwave shell of energy rushed out into space in all directions, an incredible blast of light and heat that would be plainly visible to the naked eye from a half-dozen inhabited systems—once the light from the explosion reached those stars, years or decades later.

But the event did not go unobserved. By something more than chance, an automated probe droid was on hand to witness the explosion. It carefully recorded every detail of the supernova, noting the time, the place, and making a scan of the background stars to confirm the coordinates. Then it powered down its detection systems and switched on its navicomputer. It headed out of the TD-10036-EM-1271 system, out toward where it could safely drop into hyperspace. It dropped out of normal space, and rushed into the dark between the stars. It had an appointment to keep.

An appointment on Corellia.

*   *   *

Han Solo had gone to sleep happy indeed. After tucking the children in, he had gone to be by himself and shut his own eyes, thinking nostalgic thoughts about his old homeworld. He had felt full of love and pride in his children, felt glad that everyone was safe and secure aboard the good old *Millennium Falcon*.

But all that good feeling vanished as he slept. Han was tormented by dreams that night, fearsome dreams of all the most nightmarish moments of his old adventures, the monsters that had tried to kill him or eat him, the crash landing he should not have survived, the deadly traps he had been caught in and, by all rights, should not have escaped. Han was not the sort of person who had nightmares very often, but when he did have them, they struck hard, and deep—and the dangers he had faced in real life were ample fodder for a lifetime of bad dreams.

But the real dangers he had faced in the past paled in comparison with the imaginary terror Han faced in his dreams that night. Again and again, he found himself trapped in the same few horrifying moments. A something, a faceless, secret, hidden, deadly *something* was stalking Han and his family, tracking them across a lurid, distorted jungle landscape full of the shrieks and cries of the hunter and the hunted, the air pungent with the stench of dead things putrefying in the steambath heat. But even as the heat and the stench and the sound hit Han smack in the face, he would find himself suddenly running, running for his life, his family just ahead of him, Chewie just behind. The children were screaming in terror as they fled, and Leia was in the lead, slashing a path through the vegetation with her lightsaber.

Han knew he shouldn't waste time or energy trying to see the *something*, but he could not help himself. He turned, looked back over his shoulder, and tripped over a vine in the path. He went sprawling, and landed faceup, looking straight up at—

His eyes snapped open, and Han realized that he was awake, safe in his bed, on his ship, with Leia by his side and all safe, all well. He sat up and swung his feet out of bed and sat there for a moment, trying to steady himself. He realized that he was covered in a cold sweat. He took a deep breath and forced himself to relax.

He got up, moving carefully in the darkness of the tiny cabin, and made his way out to the passageway, out to the refresher stall. He turned on the light, squinted in the sudden brightness, ran some water, and splashed it on his face. Why had the dream frightened him so much?

It didn't take much reflection for him to come up with an answer. His family. The dream was not about Han being in danger, but about his *family* being in danger. Here he was, about to bring his wife and children to Corellia, where New Republic Intelligence thought there was enough danger that their agents disappeared, but not so much that it would be any problem to have Han and his family serve as decoys. Corellia, where even in the good times, pirates had been part of everyday life. What in the universe had he been thinking of, bringing Leia and the kids to such a place?

"Ah, give it up," Han said to the face in the mirror. Leia would have gone anyway, to attend the trade summit, and Han knew full well just how determined she was to keep her family with her. There had been too many separations over the years for Leia—or Han—to put up with yet another. Even Chewbacca would have insisted on going— especially if he felt the kids were in any danger.

In short, there really hadn't been anything he could have done to stop them all from going. Not without convincing everyone that the danger was a lot greater than it seemed to be.

And yet. And yet. That NRI agent had known more than she was telling—or perhaps telling more than she knew. *Something* wasn't right. Han was certain of that.

He checked the time and sighed. He was supposed to be getting up in an hour anyway. No real sense in going back to sleep. Might as well head up to the cockpit and start getting ready for their arrival in the Corellian System, a few hours from now.

He headed back to the cabin, and dressed as quietly as he could. Leia muttered in her sleep and rolled over, but did not awaken. Good. Han stepped back into the corridor and made his way forward to the cockpit.

He was not particularly surprised to see Chewbacca there already, in the copilot's chair, doing systems checkouts.

"Hey, Chewie," Han said, slapping his old friend on the shoulder. "You couldn't sleep either, huh?"

Chewie let out a low growl and got on with his work. Han sat down in the pilot's chair. He flicked on a few of the control systems, glanced at a readout or two, but then he dropped his hands away from the control panels, leaned back in his chair, folded one leg over the other, and proceeded to get lost in thought.

His knowledge of Corellian politics was at least twenty years out of date, but it might be enough to make some educated guesses. Who was stirring up the trouble? Humans? The Drall? The Selonians? And of course it could not be laid out that simply. All three of the races had their own factions, and the three races were, after all, on all five planets, making for a dizzying number of potential alliances and enemies for any given faction. And who could tell what groups had faded away or sprung to life in that time?

But Han realized that he didn't need to worry about any of that. He knew better. The Drall were too careful, too sensible, to start trouble they could not finish, and the Selonians would see it all as beneath their notice, to say nothing of unrefined, to go knocking off NRI agents. Besides, the NRI had a well-deserved reputation for keeping hands off any group that might have been oppressed under the Empire. The NRI wouldn't have gone nosing around in Drallish or Selonian matters in the first place. Even if they had wanted to give it a try, they would have found it all but impossible to infiltrate native agents. It was not much of an exaggeration to say the number of Drall or Selonians outside Corellian space could be counted on the fingers of one hand. Even if the NRI had found a few, what were the odds of their finding one ready to play spy for them against their own kind?

No, the NRI couldn't go up against the Drall or Selonians very well, and it probably wouldn't if it could, and the Drall and Selonians were not likely to give the NRI a reason to try. Which, of course, left humans. And, if there were various external reasons that made it unlikely for the nonhuman species to be the source of the trouble, then there were lots of external reasons why it made a great deal of sense for humans to be the most likely suspects.

For starters, the Empire had been notoriously prohuman. It had treated the members of nearly all other species as second-class citizens, at best. Han glanced over to where Chewbacca was working. Some species, like Wookiees, were made slaves. Few nonhumans would have much reason to grieve at the Empire's demise, but there were plenty of humans for whom the Imperial era had been the best of times. There were no doubt quite a few humans in the Corellian Sector who mourned the Empire's passing, and had little reason to love the New Republic.

But the sheer fact that the NRI was involved made it likely that the opposition was human. The NRI had lots of human agents. That made it possible for the NRI to infiltrate a human opposition—and vice versa.

Han sat upright. Wait a second. That was the part that had been bothering him. Kalenda had told him that the opposition had managed to capture or kill at least six NRI agents. No one was that good. Not unless they had help.

In short, it was all but certain that the bad guys had infiltrated NRI. Han checked his instruments. They had another hour and a half before the drop out of light speed. All right then, they would just have to make the best use of that time. "Chewie," Han said, "I'm a little worried about this one."

Chewie answered with a complicated hoot and a display of his fangs.

"I know," Han said. "I've been thinking about what Kalenda said myself. It's possible that they're waiting for us with something besides a marching band."

Chewie made an interrogatory sort of noise and gestured toward the navicomputer.

"No, that'd be worse," Han said. "What with the pirates and all, the Corellians have always been very particular about people coming out of hyperspace in just the right place and just the right time. If we shifted our arrival coordinates, they'd blow us out of the sky first and ask questions later. We'll just have to come in at the designated time and coordinates and be ready for any surprises they might have waiting for us. I want you to check all the systems and then double-check the weapons and defense systems. Even if you find a failure in a minor system, don't fix it until you know we can fight if we have to. I'd rather have the plumbing go out than find out the hard way that the turbo-lasers aren't working. I'll be back soon to give you a hand, but first I'm going to go aft and get everyone ready."

Chewie shook his head mournfully and gave a sort of openmouthed snort.

"Hey, relax, will you? I'm just going to have a quiet word with Leia. I'm not going to act nervous and scare the kids, all right?"

Chewbacca hooted quietly, clearly unconvinced.

Han climbed up out of the low seat and went back to the rear of the *Falcon*, to find that the kids were already up and, needless to say, had gotten their mother up as well. They were all bustling about the lounge area, getting breakfast together. "How is everyone this morning?" Han asked.

"Hi, Dad! Fine," Jacen said as he opened up a meal pack. "We gonna get to Corellia today?"

"We sure are," Han said, smiling as cheerfully as he could. "But we have to drop back out of light speed first, in about an hour and a half."

"Wow!" Jacen said. "That must be neat to see. Can we ride up in the cockpit and watch?"

"Not this time, sport." If things got dicey once they were in-system, the last thing Han would need would be frightened children in the backseat. "Maybe some other time. Right now I want you three kids to get everything stowed, do what your mother says, and be strapped in for the jump out of hyperspace—or we turn around and go back home. Got it?"

"Yes, Dad," Jaina and Jacen replied in unison as Anakin nodded, wide-eyed and solemn.

"Good," Han said. "Now, I want to borrow your mother for just a second, and then I have to go back to the cockpit, so I won't see you again until after we're in Corellian space. So behave yourselves until then. Okay?"

Han was rewarded with a ragged chorus of "okays" and nodded. He led Leia out into the corridor and shut the hatch to the lounge behind them.

"What is it, Han?" she asked, before he even had a chance to speak.

"What's what?" he asked, a little baffled by her rather clipped tone of voice.

"What is it that has had you worried since before we left?"

Out of reflex more than anything else, Han threw a big, lopsided grin on his face, and got all set to deny it all. But then he stopped, and let the smile fade away. This was his wife. This was the mother of his children. More to the point, this was Leia Organa Solo, Chief of State of the New Republic, war hero, strong in the Force, and capable of being every bit as ruthless as a Noghri assassin. He couldn't play the fool with her and have the slightest hope of getting away with it.

Besides, it would be wrong to try. It was his duty to play it straight, and there was nothing more to be gained

by his pretending things were fine. Not when it was plainly
obvious he wasn't fooling her.

"I don't know what's wrong," he said, "but something
is. I didn't see any point in worrying you when I didn't
know anything in the first place. An NRI agent approached
me a few days ago and said their agents in the Corellian
Sector weren't checking in. That was the one piece of hard
information I got out of her. I don't think she knew much
more herself."

"So why come and tell you that?" Leia asked.

"They wanted me to draw attention to Corellia, act suspiciously. Make whoever it is look in my direction so maybe
the heat wouldn't be on their people."

"I don't see any need to ask you that either," Leia said.
"I can't remember the last time you *didn't* draw attention
or act suspiciously."

Han smiled, but knew she had a point. "I know. No
Corellian local bad guy would ever believe I was just a
tourist. They'd have to watch me."

"So what's the point of NRI asking you to do what
you'd do anyway so the opposition will do what *they'd* do
anyway?"

"I've been thinking on that," Han said. "I think it was
a warning. Looking back on it, I'm not so sure this agent
was authorized to tell me what was up."

"A warning of what?"

"That we might just be about to walk into a bad situation.
I don't know. A half-dozen times since then, I've almost
canceled the whole trip. But if the NRI felt the chief of
state's family shouldn't go somewhere, they'd say so. I
think the agent was trying to tell me to be careful. I *don't*
think she was trying to say we were in danger."

Leia sighed and leaned back against the bulkhead.
"That's it?" she asked. "Nothing beyond that to get you
worried?"

"Well, one other thing. Five minutes after she left,
Chewie spotted a probe droid snooping around. We made
a try for it, but this particular probe droid shot back instead

of self-destructing. Chewie nailed it just before it nailed me. I don't think it had a chance to report in before it died, and I don't think we said all that much of interest in the first place.''

Leia raised an eyebrow. "I thought I noticed something burned smelling when you came home that night."

"I don't know why I bother trying to fool you," Han said.

"Well, don't try. Was there anything else? Nearly getting killed by a probe droid is bad enough, but is there more that's got you worried?"

"Nothing besides the fact that it's Corellia," Han said. "But that's enough to make me want to find reasons to bail out. The place has the politics of a snakepit."

"That's why I'm headed there in the first place," Leia said. Leia had managed to avoid most of the demands for her to appear at this planet's coronation or give a speech at that planet's university commencement, or rush out and settle this diplomatic tiff or stomp out that minor political brushfire. It had taken a lot of time and determination on her part to get things running so that she wasn't being hauled off to every ribbon-cutting and every jurisdictional fuss throughout the New Republic.

The very fact that she had agreed to go to Corellia showed how important the place was—and how difficult it was going to be to straighten things out. But if they could open Corellia back up to trade and normal relations with the rest of the Core Sectors, it would be an incredible breakthrough. It would resolve half the New Republic's diplomatic problems at a stroke. Leia's very presence sent a signal, telling everyone just how much importance the New Republic attached to resolving the Corellian situation.

However, it also raised the trip's visibility level that much more. It meant the stakes, which had been high, were suddenly that much higher. The dangers were too hypothetical, too unclear, to allow them to interfere. Besides, the dangers might not even exist outside the fertile imagination of a junior NRI agent.

"We have to go in, don't we?" Han asked.

"But we don't have to like it," Leia said. "It's almost time," she said. "You'd better get back forward and start getting ready."

Han let out a sigh. "Right," he said. He gave her a kiss and headed back to the cockpit, but hesitated just outside the sealed hatch. He felt a strange sort of relief now that he had told her. The danger—if there *was* danger—hadn't decreased at all, but at least the secret was out. He didn't like keeping things from Leia.

But enough of that. Han wasn't much interested in introspection in general, and right now he had other things to worry about. He slapped at the button, the hatch slid open, and Han dropped, rather heavily, back into the pilot's chair.

It was time to go to work.

* * *

Han checked the navicomputer's countdown clock again. They were getting close. Only a few more minutes until the drop out of hyperspace. Chewie had checked over all the crucial systems twice, paying special attention to defense and weapons. Short of pulling into a spacedock and doing visual checks, they were as ready as they were going to be.

And so, presumably, were their friends in Corellia. No doubt they knew the *Falcon*'s arrival coordinates every bit as well as the *Falcon*'s own navicomputer. Maybe better, given the computer's somewhat checkered history in the reliability department. If there were any surprises—to put it more baldly, if there was someone interested in assassinating the chief of state—they would almost certainly make their moves moments after the ship dropped out of hyperspace.

So why let them? Why take the chance? What point in following Corellian Traffic Control regulations if it meant getting jumped? Han made a decision. "Chewie—scratch everything I said before. Touchy traffic control or not, we're going to drop out of hyperspace twenty seconds early."

That earned Han the expected roar of complaint. "I don't care how far it takes us out of the arrival zone. We can blame it on the navicomputer, and let the New Republic pay the fines. I'm still not happy about the situation, and I'd rather be off course than pop into normal space lined up in some pirate's crosshairs."

Chewbacca nodded his agreement and asked a question in a slightly lower-pitched growl.

"Yeah, I *thought* about staying in hyperspace longer and arriving closer to the planet," Han said. "But I figure it's smarter to come in behind our arrival point, rather than ahead of it. Besides, the sooner we're in-system and can report our arrival and position, the sooner we can call for help if we need it."

Chewbacca thought it over for a moment, then nodded his assent.

"All right, then," Han said. He reached over and switched on the intercom. "Everyone all right back there?" he asked.

There was a raucous chorus of yeses from the younger set, and then Leia spoke. "We're fine, Han. Almost time?"

"Just about," he said. "I'm going to drop us in twenty seconds early, just to be on the safe side." Han kept his voice casual, knowing that the kids could hear and not wishing to alarm them. He wanted it to sound like some routine matter, rather than a major change in plans.

"That sounds fine," Leia said, her voice every bit as relaxed as his own. "I was about to suggest that myself."

"Glad to hear it," he said. "See you on the other side." He flicked the intercom back to the off position, and double-checked the switch setting. This would be the perfect time to leave it on by accident. If things did get hot, he didn't want the kids back there listening in.

Han spread out his right hand, flexed his fingers twice, and grasped the lightspeed control levers. He reached out with his left hand and cut off the automatics on the navicomputer, but left the countdown display running. "Okay, Chewie, I'm dropping us out of light speed at minus-twenty seconds. Stay on top of it.'' The numbers clicked downward, and the seconds melted away.

Han watched the countdown clock, and pushed the lightspeed control levers forward just as the clock hit the twenty-second mark. The universe reappeared as the viewport filled with starlines that rapidly downshifted into the familiar points of light, the stars of Corellia. The stars of home.

For a moment, and only for a moment, Han allowed himself the luxury of glorying in the stars he had known and loved as a child. He picked out two of the constellations that had been there in the sky when he was growing up. Memories of his youth burst, unbidden, into his mind. The warm summer nights, staring up at a sky full of inviting stars that seemed to be pulling at him, calling to him—

A warning growl from Chewie brought Han back to himself. He blinked, and found that his hands were already on the proper controls. He made ready to get under way.

But before he could act, the com system lit up. ''Unknown vehicle, you are in a restricted area. This is Corellia Traffic Control. Identify immediately,'' a rather brusque voice demanded.

Han responded with the little white lie he had at the ready. ''Corellia Traffic Control, this is *Millennium Falcon*. We had a slight navigational error. Now preparing to proceed to designated entry coordinates.''

There was a slight pause before they got an answer. ''Very well, *Millennium Falcon*. Proceed at standard transit velocity to designated rendezvous coordinates and hold there for further instructions.''

Rendezvous coordinates? They weren't supposed to rendezvous with anyone. Did someone on Corellia have a surprise waiting for them? ''Will comply, Corellia Traffic Control,'' Han said, looking at Chewie. By the expression on his face, it was clear that the Wookiee had caught the slip as well. ''Looks like they're telling us more than they intended,'' said Han. He confirmed the *Falcon*'s fix on the planet Corellia, a gleaming blue-and-white marble in the sky, did an offset calculation to the rendezvous coordinates, and lit the sublight engines. "There we go, Chewie. On course for target point. Let's see if there's a reception committee."

But Chewie already had the long-range passive scanners doing a sweep—and the sweep didn't have to work very hard to find something. There. Centered exactly on the *Falcon*'s designated entry coordinates. No fewer than six faint blips, in a spherical formation. If the *Falcon* had come in where she had been supposed to, she would have been surrounded.

Han whistled softly. "That's some rendezvous," he said. "Small military craft of some sort. It's hard for us to see them now, and if we didn't have the mil-spec sensors, we couldn't see them at all. But is that an honor guard for the chief of state, or did someone get the bright idea of *arresting* Leia?"

Chewie made a slightly derisive snort with a sort of interrogative noise at the end.

"Well, yeah, it *could* be me they want to arrest," Han said. "But those warrants should have expired years ago. Believe me, I checked on it. But it doesn't matter. With six escorts waiting for us, we can't make a run for it anyway. There's bound to be other patrol craft ready to cut off our escape."

Chewie let out a low moan of agreement.

"All right, then. They have military-quality sensors, and they're getting data from Corellia Traffic Control. But I bet they think we have the standard commercial grid we're registered as having. And if they don't know how good our detectors are, they'll think *we* can't see *them* from way out here. So what do they do when they can see us and think we can't see them?" He watched for a moment, and got his answer.

"They move," Han announced to Chewie, even though the Wookiee was watching the same image on his own screen. "They move right *toward* us. And that doesn't tell us a thing. Honor guard or bandits would do the same thing."

Chewie burbled a protest.

"Yeah, you're right," Han said. "They got off the mark awfully fast. They *couldn't* have chosen a course and timed a synchronized maneuver like that in just a few seconds." Han thought for a moment. "Preprogrammed," he said at last. "They just performed a preprogrammed maneuver, heading straight for us. Except we're a million kilometers back of where we ought to be. Chewie—cut main engines and give me rear detectors, fast!"

Most ships had blind spots in the stern, where the thrust from the sublight engines effectively jammed any and all detection and visual frequencies. The *Falcon* had a much smaller blind spot than most, but she still had one. But by shutting down the sublight engines, she could bring her rear detector to bear.

Like most pilots, Han didn't like the maneuver because he was likely to need it at exactly the moment when he could least afford to have his engines off. Normally Han would have simply spun the ship around to bring the forward detector array to bear—but with a fleet of six armed and possibly trigger-happy ships of questionable motive bearing down on him, it did not seem to be the time for violent maneuvers.

The sublight engines died with a low groan, which was normal, and a sudden thud, which was not. Chewie and Han exchanged glances, but then Han shrugged. "This old crate comes up with new noises all the time," he said, trying to sound optimistic. "Probably nothing at all."

Chewie was about to reply, but just then the rear detector came on-line, and suddenly a possible problem with the sublight engines wasn't on the top of the list anymore. There was company coming to visit, and it was coming at high speed, straight for the *Falcon*.

There were three of them, bearing down straight for the

Falcon, close enough that Han could get a visual on them. "Three Uglies," he shouted, "dead astern! I *hate* Uglies."

Han had reason to hate them. "Uglies" were an unpleasant little specialty of the less reputable of the Corellian shipyards—patch-up jobs cobbled together from whatever wrecks happened to find their way into the scrap heap. By the looks of them, two of the things—Han could not bring himself to call them "fighters" or "ships"—had started out life as X-wings. Now, however, the wings themselves had been stripped off, and the side shields from a pair of early-model TIE fighters were welded on.

The third Ugly wasn't even that recognizable. It had a cockpit section from a Corellian stock light freighter—one of the *Falcon*'s sister ships—bolted onto the fuselage of a badly damaged B-wing, with a turbo-laser cannon slung under the ship's belly. By the look of it, the laser had started life as a ground-based unit. It would have to be all but impossible for the gunner to aim with great accuracy, but with a cannon that size, the gunner would only have to get lucky once.

The problem with Uglies was that it was impossible to know their specs at all. The X-TIE fighters might have no shields at all, or double-powered ones. Or one might have completely different armament from the next. None of the three of them was likely to be all that spaceworthy, which meant that the pilots onboard had to be either stupid or suicidal, if not both. In any event, Ugly pilots weren't likely to be very good—and in a close-quarters dogfight, a bad and desperate pilot in an unreliable ship could be more dangerous than a skilled pilot who valued his own skin and knew what his ship could and could not do. Perhaps worst of all, however, was the fact that only the real dregs of Corellian space flew Uglies. Down-on-their-luck pirates, mercenaries who would change sides in the middle of a battle if the price was right, losers who had nothing left to lose. And people who did not wish to be identified.

All of this flashed through Han's mind in something less

than a heartbeat. He turned toward Chewie, about to order him to get the main shields up and the forward lasers on-line, but Chewie was already on it. Han skipped to the next item on the agenda. "Chewie, you're gonna have to fly her. I'll take the upper quad-laser turret."

Chewie nodded and gestured violently, urging Han to be on his way. Han hit the hatch-open button and was on the other side of the hatchway before the thing was half-open. He scrambled through the accessway to the upper laser turret and into the control chair. He jammed the headset on and powered up the turret.

"Chewie!" he cried out. "I've got 'em on visual. Not quite in range yet, and I want it to stay that way." With the kids onboard, he was more interested in running than duking it out with a bunch of Uglies, and maybe the honor guard, too, if they turned out to be less than honorable. "Relight the sublight engines and get us out of here," Han said. He swung the turret gun around and got a tracking lock on the first X-TIE fighter. He was about to fire when the *Falcon* suddenly pitched around, a hard ninety-degree rotation. Chewie was lining up the ship on a trajectory that would get them out from between these ships. Good. He'd settle for losing the shot if it got them out of here. He waited for the sublight engines to kick in and throw them clear of this mess.

But then nothing happened. Han, who had learned from bitter experience what nothing happening meant at such times, already knew what the story was before Chewie even roared his frustration. That unexpected thump when Chewie shut down the sublight engines had meant something after all. Han looked up the accessway panel just in time to see Chewie rushing past the base of the passage, headed for the sublight engine access panels.

Han muttered a silent and profane prayer to whatever powers might be looking in, asking that, for once, it would be a simple problem. Then he thrust the question from his mind and concentrated on the incoming Uglies. He checked his tactical display. They would be within range in another 2.5

seconds. The tactical display was preparing an automated firing run, but Han slapped it over to manual. He didn't trust a computer to do his fighting for him. Take the B-wing chop job with the laser cannon first. It posed the biggest threat. After all, he was just guessing that the B-wing's laser was hard to aim. Line it up. Pray that Chewie had set all the shields on max before he dove at the engines.

The B-wing was getting closer. Han held his fire for just a fraction of a second longer than he wanted, letting the B-wing get fully into range. Then he pulled at the trigger, let it have a long volley of fire. He caught it with a nice series of hits amidships as it swept past, swinging the quad-laser turret around to pound another volley into its sublight engines. One of the portside engines flared suddenly and then went dark. Good. That was not just a definite hit, but one that had done some damage. Han swung the turret back around to take a crack at the X-TIE fighters, and suddenly realized they had flown past with the B-wing, flying outboard to it.

Then it struck him. *They had all flown right past him.* They had ignored him altogether. None of them had fired at all.

"Oh, no," Han muttered to himself. Had he just fired on three heavily armed ships that had no quarrel with him, that just happened to be flying on the same vector as his own ship? There had been an old saying in the Corellian Sector Fleet of the old Imperial Navy, back when Han was a junior officer there. "Never get an Ugly angry." As best he recalled, there were very good reasons for that advice.

Then, with a sudden lurch that made itself felt, artificial grav system or no, the sublight engines came back on-line— and then shut down again just as fast. At a guess, Chewie had gotten them working again by doing whatever he had done aft, and then was forced to shut them down again until he could get back forward to the cockpit and light them up from there. Han judged how much time it usually took Chewie to perform this sort of maneuver, figured in half a step's worth of delay to account for Chewie being out of practice, then took another quick peek down the accessway. Sure enough, there was Chewie, hotfooting it back to the cockpit.

Han allowed himself a half moment's regret that he hadn't put Leia on the quad lasers. That way he could have stayed in the cockpit while Chewie ran back and forth on repair duty. Too late for that idea now, and besides, someone had to watch the children. Poor kids must be in a full panic by now. Not that there was anything he could do about it but man the quad-laser turret.

A half moan, half growl coming through the headset told Han that Chewbacca was back at the flight controls. There was another hard jerk as the Wookiee slammed the sublight engines back on at full power, and Han struggled to keep a track on the Uglies as they headed straight for the honor-guard ships. The *Millennium Falcon* took off at right angles to the line between the Uglies and the honor guard. But something was wrong. Very wrong. Neither the Uglies nor the honor guard was paying the *Falcon* the slightest attention. "Chewie!" Han shouted. "Full stop! Cut the engines, do a one-hundred-and-eighty-degree turn, reverse thrust, and hold us here." Chewbacca replied with a wholly predictable roar of protest, but Han shouted right back at him. "Do it!" he said. "Something's not right. That chop-job B-wing could have vaporized us on the first shot from its range, and it didn't even try."

Chewbacca's voice hooted again, a bit softer, in Han's ear. "So if they were pirates, they would have tried to disable us, not fry us. So what? They didn't try *that* either. And they should have. They had us dead to rights. A blind shot to our rear as we were coming out of hyperspace, and we'd be lunch."

Leia's voice came on from the ship's lounge. "Han, this is Leia on a headset link." She was telling him the children couldn't hear. "What's going on?"

"Later, Leia. Don't joggle my elbow just now." Han reached up and cut the lounge out of his com circuit. Not the most respectful way to treat his wife, but on the other hand, one distraction too many could be fatal just now. He could apologize later, if they lived. "Chewie," he said again. "Full stop, *now*. Reverse course and hold this position, then adjust ship attitude to give both of us a good field of view of—of whatever's going on out there." The ship lurched again as Chewie finally obeyed his orders, and the *Falcon* came about to its new heading. Han checked to make sure the tactical display was being recorded, then zoomed the view to get a good close look at the Uglies.

They were nearly on top of the honor guard now—but instead of engaging them, they came about, and—

"Chewie—all power to forward and starboard shields! Now!"

Now the Uglies were opening fire on the *Falcon*, from a much poorer firing angle, with twenty times the distance of their closest approach, with the element of surprise gone and with the honor-guard ships—if they *were* an honor guard—just about to jump on them. But why? Why? A volley of near misses from the B-wing's ground laser blazed past the *Falcon*, bouncing off the shields and rattling the ship. It was close, but it should have been much closer.

Chewie's voice growled again in the headphones, but Han cut him off. "No! Do *not* maneuver!" he said. "They're shooting to miss. Even a bunch of Uglies couldn't miss *that* completely from that range unless they were trying. If you move the ship, we might fly into a shot that was intended as a near miss. Hold position. I'm not sure, but I think I know what's going on."

Han watched as the honor-guard ships jumped the three Uglies, none of which did a very credible job of responding to the threat. The B-wing ignored their attack altogether, and concentrated on firing near misses and the occasional glancing hit at the *Falcon*. The X-TIE fighters turned on the interlopers and blasted away, to very little effect. To Han's experienced eye, it was clear that either the X-TIEs' weapons were extremely underpowered, or the PPBs of the honor guard were packing some implausibly powerful shielding—far better shielding than Han could credit in a vehicle that size. And if they did have shields that good, they certainly couldn't have laser cannon of any size. And yet it took only five or six desultory shots from the lead PPB to disable one of the X-TIEs. Its engines and weapons died and it drifted off, derelict. Three of the PPBs took off on a needlessly complex synchronized maneuver and came up under the other X-TIE, blasting away. The X-TIE came about, managed to land a few shots on the lead PPB, and then its left wing blew off.

Its fighter cover gone, the B-wing Ugly finally broke its ineffectual attack on the *Falcon* and came about in rather lumbering fashion. It leveled its cannon at the one PPB that hadn't managed to do much besides fly straight, and the little fighter exploded on the first shot. The five remaining PPBs converged on the B-wing from all sides and concentrated their fire on it. The B-wing took several hard hits from multiple directions and a small explosion amidships sent it into a hard tumble. The PPBs poured the fire on from every point of the compass. Another explosion in the B-wing's aft section sent it tumbling even harder. Then a whole series of blasts ripped through the ship's interior, merging into one huge firestorm that lit up the sky, blinding Han for a moment or two before it guttered down to nothing. The chop-job B-wing Ugly wasn't there anymore.

Han watched as the surviving PPBs did a graceful joint victory roll. "Very nice," he said. "Very nice. Almost makes me want to believe it. But will they have the nerve to play it out to the end?"

"*Millennium Falcon*, this is Captain Talpron, leading Squadron Two, Corellian Space Defense Forces Space Service. Are you all right?"

"Ah, yes," Han said, trying to sound convincingly grateful. "Just fine, thanks. Thanks for the rescue."

"Our pleasure, *Millennium Falcon*." It had been agreed long before that all Corellian craft would address the ship, and not mention the name of anyone onboard, to provide at least a mote of security for the chief of state's private visit. Apparently, Talpron was determined to honor that arrangement, even if it was spectacularly obvious that security was shot full of holes.

Well, if Talpron wanted to pretend everything was fine, Han had his own reasons for playing along. "Whose ships were those?" he asked in a conversational tone of voice, as if he didn't already know.

"Unknown group, *Millennium Falcon*," Talpron replied. "Could be any of the Corellian pirate groups out to score big. They might be from one of the Outlier systems," he said.

"That'll make 'em hard to trace," Han said sympathetically.

"So it will, *Millennium Falcon*," Talpron said, in a world-weary sort of voice. "So it will."

"Well, even if you can't track them down, we can't tell you how grateful we are for your assistance," Han went on. "We're very sorry that you lost one of your craft. We would like to express our condolences to you and to the family of the crew you lost."

"What?" Talpron asked. "Oh, yes. Of course. We'll make the arrangements."

"Yeah, I bet you will," Han said under his breath, low enough so the mike wouldn't catch it. He spoke again, louder, into the microphone. "Captain Talpron, thanks once again for assistance. However, I've got to get my ship secured from general quarters and run some systems checks. Will you excuse me?"

"Of course, sir. We'll stand by until you are ready to proceed. Signal us when you are ready to start the flight to Corellia."

"That we will do, Captain. *Millennium Falcon* out."

Han shut off the com system, hung up his headset, unstrapped himself from the gunner's chair—and then just sat there for a moment, thinking.

In the game of sabacc, the rules could change in the middle of a hand, and all the cards that were going to do you good could suddenly be the worst kind of bad news. But the opposite was also true. A disaster of a hand could turn around just as quickly, and win you the pot. The trick was in *knowing* exactly when, and exactly how fast, and exactly by what means the change could come. Then you could be ready for it; know exactly how to deal with the new situation.

Every now and again your opponent made a mistake, showed a card he should not, and you knew more than you were supposed to. The most honest sabacc players were good enough sports to tell their opponents when it happened. But sabacc players who wanted to win were never *that* honest.

The opposition, whoever that was, had just showed Han some of their cards. Han was not about to let them know he had seen anything at all.

But neither was he the least bit sure what rules he was now playing by.

*　　*　　*

Han stepped into the cockpit, and was not overly surprised to see Leia in the pilot's seat, watching the main viewport. He hadn't really expected her to sit by quietly while the ship was under attack. He was glad she hadn't. Assuming she had the kids squared away, getting a second pilot into the cockpit was the best thing she could have done. She turned to face Han. "Did you have a nice chat with our new friends?" she asked. She clearly wasn't too happy about being cut out of the comlink.

"Oh, yeah," he said. "Great bunch of folks. Are the kids still okay?"

Leia nodded toward a small repeater screen that was showing a view of the lounge. Han could see three small figures, their expressions very serious, very solemn. "I told them that if they moved out of view, there would be no dinner for a week," she said. "For once it seems like they knew when I needed them to obey. But what the burning skies is going *on*, Han?"

"Sorry I cut you off from the com back there," he said, answering the hurt in her voice rather than the words of her question. "I just needed to concentrate. If things had gone the wrong way, we could have been in trouble." Han wasn't really paying attention to what he was saying. His mind was on the problem at hand, not on being polite to his wife. "Look, lemme into the pilot's station, will ya? I've got to try something."

Leia got out of the seat, but she clearly was not yet placated. "*Could* have been in trouble?" she repeated. "*Could* have been? What do you call pirates shooting at us?"

"There weren't any pirates, and no one was shooting at us," Han said, his voice flat and tired. "That's why I ordered Chewie not to maneuver. I was worried we might fly into one of the intentional near misses." Han settled into the pilot's chair. "Chewie, punch up the tactical playback and run it, will you? Main screen."

Chewie gave Han a strange look, but obeyed. The tactical display popped up on the screen, and showed a schematic diagram of the encounter just past. "Watch the Uglies come in," he said. "Remember we came in out of hyperspace, well short of where we were supposed to be, but on a straight-line course for our intended arrival point. The Uglies were coming in on that same course in normal space— but they were expecting us to show up twenty seconds later and a million kilometers away. Then they throw away perfect firing position and fly right past us. They don't even shoot back when I take a shot at them. For a second there, I thought I had just gotten us all killed by opening fire on a nonhostile ship, but then I figured out what was going on. Instead, they flew past us, then waited until they were almost on top of the honor-guard ships before they turned and opened fire on us. And they kept missing. Threepio couldn't miss us at that range."

Chewbacca growled and burbled.

"Exactly," Han said. "The Uglies were robot ships,

and not very well-programmed ones. No one was onboard those ships. They were programmed to fly to a designated point in space, then open fire with near misses at a ship meeting the *Falcon*'s description. They were expecting the *Falcon* to arrive roughly in the center of the honor guard's spherical formation,'' he said. ''If we had shown up there, it would have worked great. It would have made perfect sense to open fire where they did. Perfectly sound tactics. Except we came in from a million kilometers away, and they flew past us at point-blank range, took up an absolutely lousy firing position, and started blasting. As I said, somebody didn't program their robots so well.

''Chewie, modify the display to show the encounter if we had arrived as per the flight plan.'' The screen cleared and then displayed the image of a miniature *Falcon* popping out of subspace in the center of the honor-guard sphere. ''If we had arrived *there*, in the middle of the PPB's spherical formation, and had gotten there twenty seconds *later*, the act would have worked. The bad guys would have shown up coming straight for us, gotten off a shot or two, and then been blasted by the heroic pilots of the honor guard, firing their popgun lasers at the attacking ships.''

''But the PPBs lost one of their own ships,'' Leia objected.

''Another robot-drone ship,'' Han said. ''The one that ended up getting shot was the one that was at the back of the formation and flew the simplest maneuvers.''

''That doesn't prove it's a robot,'' Leia objected. ''Maybe it was just that the least skilled and experienced pilot was the one who got hit.''

''Except that the squad leader didn't seem to care about his own pilot getting killed. He didn't seem to know what I was talking about when I offered my condolences. He'll never win any awards for acting.''

''But if they were running a deception, they would have thought about that sort of detail ahead of time.''

''If *you* were running the deception, you would have thought of it,'' Han replied. ''Maybe these guys aren't so good at this sort of thing. Or maybe they didn't have time to set things up just the way they wanted. Maybe they're improvising." He looked at the display for a moment longer and then spoke again. "That might explain the B-wing. I can't see how we were supposed to believe that those little PPBs could take on that chop-job B-wing. Maybe they didn't have time to put together a more plausible matchup."

"All right. Assume you're right. The next question is—who are 'they'? This was a pretty big operation. You can't just order some PPBs to go out and play shoot-'em-up. There would have to be a huge conspiracy with a cover-up all set and ready to go. Greasing a few palms I can see, but how can you bribe the whole armed forces?"

"With a larger bag of money," Han said. "This is Corellia. Everything is for sale here. And cover-ups aren't that hard when everything is a secret. It could be that the highest level of command ordered this, or that they know nothing about it."

"So it's either an official mission, or it isn't, and the military and government might be behind it, or they might not," Leia said. "That's very helpful."

"Well, look on the bright side," Han said. "For the moment at least, we have at least one advantage. *We* know someone's playing games, but *they* don't know *we* know."

Chewie had been unusually quiet for a long time. Now he let out a low edgy-sounding bellow.

"I don't *know* why," Han replied in an irritable voice. "I can make *guesses* why they did it. Someone in the Corellian Defense Forces wanted to throw a scare into us—and make us trust the CDF."

"If they think we fell for it," Leia said.

"Well, it's good to have things nice and clear," Han said. "But just for the moment I don't think there's much we can do besides follow these guys in and keep our eyes open."

"Wide open," Leia said. "Take us in, Han."

Han set to work laying in a course, but then looked up at the PPBs still holding formation. Well, it wouldn't be the first time he had tangled with the heavy hitters in this part of the sky. "Just like old times," he said to Chewie, who replied with a noncommittal yawp. Han nodded. "You've got that right," he said as he went back to his work. "Welcome to Corellia."

CHAPTER ELEVEN

Message Intercepted

Mara Jade stared at the message cube, wishing she could send it to someone else, or make it cease to exist altogether. Or discard it, ignore it, pretend it had never arrived. But she couldn't. Not under the circumstances.

Well, no sense staring at the miserable thing. She wouldn't learn anything further by looking at it. In fact, that was the whole point. She sighed, stood up, crossed her cabin, put the cube back in the safe, and sealed the safe's door. She stepped out into the corridor of her ship, the *Jade's Fire*, turned, and headed toward the sloop's bridge. Might as well give the orders in person.

Once she had decided what orders to give.

Long years ago, so long ago that it seemed another lifetime, back when there had still been an Empire and an Emperor, Mara Jade had been the Emperor's Hand, doing his bidding on a hundred missions, carrying out his will in secret. She had been his courier, his courtier, his envoy, his assassin, on more occasions than she could count. The Emperor had sensed her power in the Force and made use of it. He had commanded her, ruled her, owned her, body and soul.

And then, out of nowhere, had come crashing, headlong, sudden destruction. The Rebellion, the Alliance, had defeated the Empire and killed the Emperor.

Mara had landed on her feet, more or less, working for

the smuggler and trader Talon Karrde, and keeping her past life as secret as she could. She had never developed any deep or abiding love for the New Republic, to put it mildly, but being able to recognize and accept the reality of a situation was a survival skill. And if there was one thing Mara was good at, it was surviving.

For that matter, she was no slacker when it came to prospering, if current evidence was any sign. She had made a—reasonably—amicable split with Karrde some time ago, and set up in business for herself. It was a different universe out there, one that didn't have quite so much use for smugglers anymore. She established herself as a trader in her own right, running a small, quiet, but highly profitable trading company. Like a number of others who had been active in the wars, she had found the return to civilian life more than a little difficult. It was hard to find much excitement in getting a good price on habbis-root after fighting for the future of the galaxy. Still, she was out in space, the master of her own fate, able to go where she wanted and do what she wanted.

She paused at the sealed hatch leading to the bridge, smoothed her tunic, and set her face into its usual stern expression.

There might be other captains who tried to set their crews at ease, strove for a relaxed atmosphere on the bridge. Not on Mara Jade's ship, thank you very much. Her style of ship management carried over directly from her personal style, which was to say it was more than a little severe. Mara Jade was a strikingly lovely woman, her pale skin accentuating her high cheekbones. Her red-gold hair ran down her back in a thick, heavy, luxuriant braid. Her body and her graceful movements were more in keeping with those of a professional dancer than a captain.

On the rare occasion when a formal reception or other social event required her to dress in something less utilitarian than her customary one-piece jumpsuit, the effect could be startling. People would take one look at her and instantly assume her to be some carefully bred member of the aristocracy. They expected her to behave with demure refinement. However, Mara had never been one to let the expectations of others get in her way, and she had never been one for honeyed words either. She could play that part when it suited her, but it rarely did.

What she did best was crack the whip, enforce discipline, command—and earn—respect. Nor would she employ anyone who could not earn *her* respect. That was the way she handled her ship, and more or less everything else in her life as well. It behooved her, therefore, to appear in front of her crew in a cool, calm, and collected state. Never mind that she was actually more agitated than she had been in a long time.

An Imperial code. The courier had used an Imperial code. One that had been obsolete years before the first Death Star had become operational, but an Imperial code nonetheless.

What could it mean?

Never mind. One step at a time. Take it one step at a time.

Mara hit the switch and the hatch slid open. She stepped into the bridge of the ship and took her accustomed place at the command station. The navigator, a goggle-eyed Mon Calamari, swiveled one eye toward his captain and then back to his console, but did not otherwise acknowledge her. The pilot, a human male, looked over at her and gave a solemn nod. Good. That was the way she liked it. Discipline Mara insisted upon, but she had no use for people jumping around saluting everything that moved.

To be opened in the presence of Leia Organa Solo, self-styled Chief of State of the so-called New Republic, Han Solo, and the de facto governor-general of the Corellian Sector, Code Rogue Angel Seven.

The message had been there, in old-style Imperial code, written in neat lettering on the side of the message cube. Mara had unbuttoned the code almost without thinking, but knowing what the words said told her precious little about what the cube meant. Clearly the cube was from someone who had no great love for the New Republic, but beyond that it was difficult to comprehend. There was another label on the cube, but the writing on it was in a script Mara did not recognize. By the look of it, the Imperial-code label had been slapped on the package quickly, and one edge of it overlapped a corner of the unreadable one. Either the Imperial one had been put on second, in some haste, or else it was meant to look as if it had.

The cube had been aboard a message drone that had intercepted the *Jade's Fire* a day or two after she arrived in the Talfaglio System, in the hinterlands of the Corellian Sector. Not that the intercept location told her much. The drone had been equipped with lightspeed engines, and could have come from absolutely anywhere.

But no matter where it had come from, Mara could not understand why in space it should follow her. And follow her it had. There was no chance of the *Jade's Fire* finding the drone by chance. The drone had homed in on the *Fire*'s ID beacon, and the message cube itself had been wrapped up in a package with Mara's name scrawled on it.

But who had sent it? And why? And why had they sent it to Mara? Presumably the reference to "Code Rogue Angel Seven" would mean something to Organa Solo or one of the others, and let them know how to open the cube without destroying its contents. But if it was to be opened in their presence, why send it care of Mara Jade?

And why use the Imperial code? It certainly wasn't there to hide information. Surely the New Republic's people could read it, given a very little bit of time. Was it there to inspire Mara's Imperial sympathies? Certainly the wording of the coded message was not meant to make anyone in the New Republic happy. Could there actually be some Imperial remnant still remaining? It seemed utterly implausible. Or was the whole affair some elaborate attempt of her business rivals to tag her as pro-Imperial and ruin her business?

But that was absurd as well. The Empire was as dead as an embalmed corpse. There were no remnants left. There was nothing left to be pro-Imperial *about*. Besides, even if she had managed to keep the *details* of who and what she had been in the old days secret, everyone in the business knew that she had worked for the Empire. There were times when that didn't make business any easier, but it was no grand secret. There wasn't much point in trying to wreck her reputation by telling people what they already knew.

So what was it about? Mara knew enough about message cubes to know that she would not be able to find out by any amount of computer slicing. The message on the outside might have been in an easy-to-read code, but she knew that make of message cube, and knew that it would take years of work to slice it—and even then it might go wrong, erasing the contents just as she finally got it open.

No. There was only one way to find out what it was all about. And that decided her. Mara had a lot of personality traits that had stood her in good stead over the years, but plain old-fashioned curiosity was the one she had been least able to indulge. Smugglers and Imperial agents couldn't afford to stick their noses wherever they wanted.

But well-to-do traders could, if they had what others wanted. And Mara had the cube. She could trade physical possession of the cube for knowledge of its contents. And there was always profit in knowledge.

"Mr. Tralkpha," she said to her Mon Calamari naviga tor. "Turn us around, if you please. Provide Mr. Nesdin with a direct course for the Corellian System, and let's put speed ahead of fuel economy just this once."

"Very good, Captain," said the taciturn Tralkpha.

"Mr. Nesdin," she said, addressing the pilot. "While Mr. Tralkpha is so engaged please contact our next scheduled stop and advise that we will be delayed by a priority courier mission." If whoever had sent the drone had the sense to monitor transmissions from the *Jade's Fire*, that would tell them she was taking the bait, delivering the cube. "Then get us moving to Corellia."

"Yes, ma'am," said Nesdin. No questions, no raised eyebrows, no reminders that they had a schedule to keep. Just calm, competent obedience to orders. That was the sort of crew she liked.

But something else, a turn of phrase she had just used in her thoughts, was trying to tell her something. What was it? Ah! Of course. *Taking the bait.* Bait was what you put in traps. Was *that* the plan here? Was someone planning to draw her into an ambush?

Mara Jade smiled to herself, and knew it was not a pleasant expression. Those who wished to entrap Mara Jade were welcome to try. She doubted they would wish to repeat the experiment.

"I'll be in my cabin," she said, standing up. It would be completely useless, of course. But she *had* to take another look at that cube.

*   *   *

Lieutenant Belindi Kalenda, long-term operative of New Republic Intelligence and recent shoot-down and shipwreck victim, lay on her stomach on a low hill and watched the sky. She was doing her best to be inconspicuous as she hunkered down on a piece of land just to the east of Coronet Spaceport.

The gleaming towers and graceful domes of the city were plainly visible in the middle distance, a splendid sight on a clear morning. But Kalenda paid them no mind. The waters of the eastern ocean were there at her back, the whitecaps almost painfully bright against the deep blue of the sea. The sun danced on the water, a shimmering, endlessly changing constellation that flashed and glimmered across the face of the deep. The surf was an endless low roar, and the air was flavored with the salty scent of sunbaked sand and clean ocean.

But Kalenda had no interest in any such things. She pulled herself in lower against the short rise of land, and wished she could have found something more substantial to hide under than a threadbare clump of razor grass that drooped down two or three feet over her head. If it had been a more robust sample of the species, it would have sliced her clothes to ribbons if it so much as brushed against her, but she would have gladly traded that for better cover.

She was wearing a nondescript coverall, taken from a landspeeder garage on the other side of the continent. The landspeeder she had obtained at the same time and by the same means she had abandoned in a ditch just outside Bela Vistal, a midsize town two hundred kilometers from Coronet. With any luck, if anyone had managed to trace her that far, they would think she was headed for Bela Vistal and not the capital.

It had taken all of her skills as a pickpocket to obtain a sufficient supply of credits to finance her trip the rest of the way, and even then she had been forced to economize.

Fortunately, she had been waylaid by a gang of rather incompetent bandits shortly after she got off the monorail from Bela Vistal. The results of that encounter were doubly satisfying. Not only did she gain the use of their landspeeder and guns and other gear—none of which they were likely to have much use for in the hereafter—but all of it was quite untraceable.

Kalenda readjusted the macrobinoculars she had inherited from the bandits for the hundredth time. The contrast enhancers just wouldn't stay aligned. Well, you couldn't expect the likes of those thugs to keep their equipment up properly. Not that it mattered. The macrobinoculars were working quite well enough for her present needs. She didn't need to see well when there was nothing to see. She took another scan of the patch of sky they should have come through already and let out a sigh. There was no need to worry. Not really. They were still only a few hours late.

A thousand things could have delayed the *Millennium Falcon*. She could have suffered a mechanical problem—not for the first time, if the stories about that ship were true. Some political dustup could have forced the Chief of State to delay her departure. They could have arrived in the Corellian System exactly on time, but then made a spur-of-the-moment decision to visit Drall or Selonia, or Talus and Tralus

before flying to Corellia itself. Or her given schedule could
have changed since Kalenda left Coruscant.

Or the ship carrying the New Republic's Chief of State
could have been violently converted into an expanding cloud
of disassociated atomic particles. No matter *how* much Organa Solo had insisted, they should never have let her go
wandering off in a windup toy like the *Millennium Falcon*.
Private family trip or not, the chief of state shouldn't have
flown on anything smaller than a corvette.

Too late to worry about that. But if the *Falcon* turned
up missing, there was going to be a galaxy's worth of trouble
to pay, and no mistake. The fact that Corellia would almost
certainly be the focal point of the aforementioned trouble
was not lost on Kalenda. She was not looking forward to
being in the middle of it all. But no sense borrowing trouble
from the future when there was so much immediately available. The Corellian Defense Force's Public Security Service
tended to take an understandably dim view of people who
staked out spaceports. But since she had to assume that the
PSS had been on her tail from the moment she swam ashore,
it might simply be a question of who got her first—PSS
spaceport perimeter guards, or a PSS counterintelligence
team.

Or maybe, just maybe, things were actually as they
seemed, Kalenda told herself. Maybe she had gotten this
far completely undetected, and faced no immediate danger
worse than getting cut by the razor grass. Well, she could
hope for it, but she did not dare let herself believe it. Not
in her line of work.

Come *on*. Where *were* they? Kalenda did not know exactly what she would do if they turned up and were all right,
or what she would—or could—do if they never turned up
at all. She would have to play that part of it by ear. What
she did know was that the Chief of State and her family
were about to walk into a planet on the verge of chaos. On
the surface, all still seemed calm and controlled on Corellia.
But Belindi Kalenda had spent the last handful of days
hunkered down, struggling to stay out of sight in the dark

corners of a foreign culture. She was not the sort of person who could do that without noticing that things were very, very wrong. The proliferation of competing security forces was not a good sign, to put it mildly. The CDF and its offspring, the PSS, seemed to be at loggerheads as often as they cooperated with each other.

But there were at least three other official security forces stepping on each other's jurisdictional toes, to say nothing of the various private militias that seemed to be popping up everywhere. The Human League was the biggest, but by no means the only such group. And of course none of the private militias, not even the League, could have survived ten minutes without some sort of sponsorship or support from someone in power somewhere. Kalenda had no doubt whatsoever that the League's Hidden Leader had lots of friends in high—and low—places. But, more importantly, things were not going well when so many of the higher-ups wanted their own private armies.

Governor-General Micamberlecto's Republic-installed government might as well have been in another sector of the galaxy for all the control it had over events. It was quite obvious that it was all but completely disconnected from the day-to-day management of the planet. Graft, corruption, hidebound tradition, and sheer cussedness on the part of the bureaucracy seemed set to prevent any chance of reform.

And if the capital planet was in this sort of shape, what was the rest of the sector likely to be?

Worse, the economic situation made the political climate look promising. The cities of Corellia were falling apart. There was no work anywhere, and no prospect of work—hardly helpful for a trade-based economy that had cut itself off from most of the outside universe for half a generation or more. And it was, of course, the economic misery that made the place such a fertile breeding ground for discontent.

But none of that mattered just now. There was something else. Nothing that Kalenda could put her finger on just yet, but something was about to happen. Something big. She could sense it, feel it, almost taste it. She had never been wrong when she had had such feelings in the past. Who knows, maybe she had some small ability in the Force that let her know when something was up. Whatever it was didn't matter just now.

What mattered was that the Chief of State—if she was still alive—was about to wander into the middle of chaos—and Kalenda had to assume that she was the only surviving NRI agent, the only New Republic security force of any kind on the planet. Kalenda knew that the NRI had been planning to insert any number of agents into Corellia. Maybe all of them had gotten through, or maybe none. It was, for obvious reasons, best that she know nothing. That way, there was nothing she could tell either.

It had crossed her mind that there weren't really any other NRI coming in, but that her higher-ups had told her there were in order to provide a headache for the opposition in the event that she, Kalenda, was captured. Best not to worry too hard about such things. Life in her line of work was enough of a wilderness of mirrors without her erecting new ones on her own. It was safest to assume she was the only one who had made it. That left her with the question of what she should do, and that question was easy.

She had been sent here to gather intelligence, but Kalenda had decided she knew more than enough already. She had to concentrate on keeping the Chief of State alive until the trade summit, when her official entourage—and security team—would arrive.

But to keep Leia Organa Solo alive, Kalenda would have to keep herself alive as well. *That* was the tricky part. She had to assume that the CDF or PSS were smart enough not to assume that she had died in the crash, and were on the lookout for her specifically, and for NRI agents generally. Presumably, they would also have the sense to be keeping a watch on Organa Solo's family, in order to monitor their activities, if nothing else. Whether or not they would interfere if someone else took a potshot at the Chief of State—or whether they would make a try for her themselves—was impossible to say.

In any event, they would not be likely to welcome an NRI agent popping up in their midst. They might even decide she was a good excuse for a provocation, and grant themselves the license to stir up trouble. All of which meant that Kalenda did not dare make an approach to Organa Solo's party.

So all she could do was watch from a distance, try not to get caught herself, and hope that some way to contact them would present itself. Maybe, just maybe, she could even do some good from a distance, though she could not imagine what, just at the moment.

But for now, all she could do was wait. Wait and watch, and hope they showed up soon.

* * *

Long hours later Kalenda was starting to worry in earnest. Night was coming on, and no matter how good infrared systems got, they were never as good as visible light. And the IR system on her purloined macrobinoculars wasn't that good to start with.

Over and over again, she would spot spacecraft on approach, feel her heart start to race, zoom in with the macrobinoculars—and spot a craft that looked nothing like the *Falcon*. She was starting to wonder exactly how she was going to manage overnight surveillance, when one more ship came into view. Kalenda lifted her macrobinoculars to her eyes one more time, expecting to be disappointed again—and suddenly her heart was racing.

It was not one ship, it was six. There was the *Millennium Falcon*, quite unmistakable, in the center of the formation, with five Pocket Patrol Boats flying in a standard *six*-boat escort formation. The aft portside boat wasn't there. Or maybe it was just hidden from view by the *Falcon*. Kalenda fumbled a bit with the controls to get a better view. She belatedly thought to hit the record button on the macrobinoculars. She might well want to review this imagery later on. No, the sixth boat was definitely not there.

Kalenda instantly jumped to a dozen conclusions, and then forced herself to stay focused on what she was seeing. There would be plenty of time for guessing later.

The *Falcon* and her escorts swept past the public landing bays, lit their repulsors, and came to a stop in midair over the military part of the field—by chance, the part Kalenda was closest to. Three of the escorts broke formation and landed, each boat at the point of a tidy isosceles triangle, while the two other PPBs remained on station in midair. The *Falcon* eased downward on her repulsors, coming to a smooth landing at the exact center of the triangle formed by the grounded boats. *That* was not the way a ceremonial escort acted. Something had happened. But what?

Kalenda shifted herself about a bit to get a better look at the *Falcon*, and was rewarded with a rather nasty cut on her forearm from a bit of razor grass she hadn't noticed before. She cursed absentmindedly and zoomed in as tight as she could on the *Falcon*. She seemed undamaged, as best Kalenda could tell from rather extreme range. She could see no sign that the modified freighter had been in a recent fight. But she could not know for sure. Maybe she would be able to tell more when they all disembarked. She focused her attention on the ship's gangway.

At last it swung down, and she could see the tiny figure of Han Solo and the rather less tiny figure, even at this distance, of Chewbacca the Wookiee, coming down the gangway, each carrying a fair-sized piece of luggage. There was something cautious, even edgy, about their body language, as if they had had one nasty surprise already and were expecting another. Kalenda chided herself anew for reading too much into the situation. Maybe the only thing worrying them was the astronomical fees the spaceport charged.

Almost before the two of them reached the ground, the three children hurtled down the gangway and onto the surface of Corellia. It was plain to see *they* were glad not to be cooped up anymore. Then, last of all, came the Chief of State of the New Republic, Leia Organa Solo, carrying a medium-sized bag. Kalenda let out a sigh of relief, feeling tension ebb away that she hadn't even been aware of. Organa Solo was alive and well. That was the main thing. Now if only Kalenda could make sure Organa Solo stayed that way. She kept watching.

Han Solo waited until his wife was off the ship, and then punched in the lock controls. The gangway swung shut, and the *Falcon* switched herself into standby mode. Kalenda watched as an open ground car rolled up.

Organa Solo stepped away from the ship—and then hesitated a moment. She stopped walking, and frowned, a bit uncertainly. She looked around, apparently scanning the horizon—and then stopped, staring straight at Kalenda. For a terrible moment Kalenda was certain that Organa Solo had spotted her, decided she was a sniper or a terrorist, was going to shout a warning to her family, alert the local security forces. Kalenda wanted to dive for cover, run for it, but she knew better. Staying absolutely still was much more likely to keep her alive. And besides, what were the odds that even a Jedi adept would be able to see—or sense—a single watcher from that sort of range?

Especially since all that Organa Solo did next was shrug, frown again, and head for the ground car. Kalenda let out a sigh of relief.

The rest of the party started following Organa Solo toward the groundcar. They all seemed calm enough. Kalenda began to decide that she was wrong, that she had been imagining signs of trouble.

But then she noticed Solo talking with the Wookiee.

Or, more accurately, the *way* he was talking with the Wookiee.

Kalenda was a pretty fair lip-reader, but she knew better than to trust her skills at this extreme range. Besides, even if she could manage to catch what Solo was saying, there was not the slightest hope of understanding the Wookiee. But it is a truism that throughout history, no pilot has ever talked flying to a colleague without using his hands. There was something very close to a conventional nomenclature and grammar of hand movements used to describe flight and encounters with other craft.

And Han Solo was, beyond question, using his hands to help describe a spaceside dogfight. He might not be sending Kalenda a message, but she was certainly intercepting one. A most important one.

Kalenda watched in fascination as Solo's hands bobbed and weaved through the air, following each other, then breaking off to show two craft—or two sets of craft—on a collision course with each other. He pointed up into the sky, at the PPBs still hovering overhead on point guard, then put his hands together in a ball before pulling them apart with his fingers spread. So. A PPB *had* blown up. The Wookiee was shaking his head no, disagreeing on some point, making his own gestures.

Then Organa Solo managed to round up the last of the children. Solo and the Wookiee stopped their conversation, plainly not wishing the children to hear. Organa Solo got the kids onto the ground car, and signaled the driver to start moving.

The ground car pulled away, and Kalenda scrambled to her feet, nearly beheading herself on the stand of razor grass before she remembered and ducked. If she was to have any chance of following them, she was going to have to get back to her own landspeeder on the double and position herself on the road leading out of the spaceport, where she could pick them up as they headed into town. It would be a hell of a note if she had managed to spot them there and then lost them. She scrambled back toward her landspeeder, feeling more worried than ever.

Someone had already made a try for the Chief of State. She was in no doubt about that. Things were going to blow. Things were going to blow on this planet, and the Chief of State of the New Republic was going to be standing right at ground zero when they did.

And there was not a bloody thing Belindi Kalenda could do about it.

CHAPTER TWELVE

Learning Curve

L ando Calrissian stepped out of the hatch of the *Lady Luck* onto the surface of the planet Azbrian feeling a lot less cocky than he had back on Leria Kerlsil. The encounter with the life-witch had done a first-rate job of focusing his attention on the number of things that could go wrong with his marriage scheme. Luke was right behind him, and this time both of them were carrying comlinks, and the droids were not locked up on the ship. Lando knew how lucky he had been on Leria Kerlsil. He had no desire to push his luck a second time.

He stepped out of the ship and looked around. The *Lady Luck* sat in the middle of a gently sloping pasture of some sort. There was a herd of placid-looking black-and-white, eight-legged beasts a few hundred meters away. They were munching on the low, bushy green plants that filled the field, and every now and then one of them would raise its head and make a long, low thrumming noise for no apparent reason. A fence separated them from the field in which the *Lady* stood, and though they did not look like the sort of creatures made for jumping or attacking, none of that fooled Lando. The way his luck was going, they would all leap over the fence and savagely attack Luke and him in the next moment.

Hold it, Lando told himself as he picked his way through the bushy ankle-high plants. *Get a grip*. It wasn't that bad. It couldn't be.

"Hey, Lando, snap out of it!"

Lando turned and looked back toward Luke. "What is it?" he asked.

Luke nodded in the direction of the farmhouse at the bottom of the gentle hillside. "Here comes the reception committee."

"Oh, boy," Lando said, forcing a smile onto his face. "All right, here we go." He waved toward the two white-clad figures coming toward them, and headed downhill toward them. A young man and a young woman. "Hello!" he called out.

"Hello!" the young woman called out. "Is there something we can do for you?"

"Great," Lando said under his breath to Luke. "Wrong landing coordinates. We've just landed on the wrong farm." He raised his voice and shouted back, "We're looking for the Condren Foreck place."

The man and woman looked at each other in some puzzlement as the two parties drew near to each other. "I'm Condren Foreck," the woman said in her regular speaking voice, which turned out to be a bit high and squeaky. "But I'm afraid we're not expecting any visitors."

"Who might you be?" the young man asked, in a tone of voice not all that far from belligerent.

"I'm Lando Calrissian," Lando said. "This is my friend, the Jedi Master Luke Skywalker." Lando took a good look at Condren and her companion. She was a pale, reedy-looking sort of woman, small and slight, with shoulder-length frizzy blond hair that didn't seem much interested in staying under control. She was wearing a loose-fitting white ankle-length skirt and a plain white blouse. Her companion was a big, beefy-looking sort of fellow, sallow-faced, with his eyes perhaps just a trifle too close together. He was dressed in dirt-smeared white work clothes, and the frown on his face seemed to be permanent. Lando put him down as some sort of hired hand and forgot about him.

"Lando Calrissian? Oh," said Condren, in a distracted sort of voice. "Oh, dear. And you've come all this way. I knew I should have contacted you again when, when, ah, things changed. But I never really thought you'd come, and things happened so fast, and well, um, I forgot. I'm sorry.''

"I don't understand," Lando said. "You should have contacted me when *what* changed?"

"Things," Condren said, not very helpfully, looking vaguely toward her companion. "This is *really* awkward," she said, and then hesitated for a long moment that did not make things any less awkward. "Oh, dear," she said at last, and took the young man's hand. "Mr. Calrissian, this is Frang Colgter. My husband. We just got back from our honeymoon last week."

* * *

"I can't *believe* my information is this bad," Lando said as he watched the planet Azbrian slide under the *Lady Luck*'s portside wing. They were leaving, and good riddance. The ship was on autopilot, and he and Luke were sitting in the cockpit, in the pilot and copilot's station, and watching the universe roll past. "I mean, what's next? A potential bride who has been dead five years? One that's male? A Wookiee?"

"I understand that some Wookiee females are extremely romantic if you approach them the right way," Luke said, smiling.

"Ah, you can afford to laugh," Lando said. "It's not *your* reputation that's going to pile it in if this stuff gets out."

"Hey, my lips are sealed," Luke said.

"Yeah, but those droids wouldn't mind spilling the beans," Lando said, hooking his thumb toward the wardroom, where Threepio and Artoo were. "And for that matter, I might not be able to resist telling the life-witch story myself," he admitted, shaking his head ruefully.

"That was as close a call as I've ever seen," Luke said, still smiling. "Still and all, maybe you ought to think it over again. After all, she was beautiful, young—and single."

"Oh yeah," Lando growled. "Beautiful, young—if you

don't think of three hundred years old as old—rich, kind, gentle. But by the time you really get to know her, you're dead and she's on to the next lucky victim. No, the life-witch was bad enough. But *this* business with Condren Foreck on top of it—I grant it's not as bad, but it *is* embarrassing.''

"Come on," Luke said. "How were you to know? It could happen to anyone. She's the one who failed to re-contact you when that Frang Colgter character popped the question. Not your fault."

Lando rolled his eyes. "Sure. Anyone could land on the planet, meet with a rich young heiress to discuss the prospect of matrimony, and then find out she's just back from her honeymoon. Right. No way. *I'm* the only one with that kind of luck."

Luke laughed. "Well, you might have a point at that," he said. "But you're not giving up, are you?"

"Of course not," Lando replied, trying to achieve just the note of wounded pride. "It'd take a lot more than this to make me quit." He thought for a moment and then shrugged philosophically. "On the bright side, I'm not exactly sure how much of a prize Condren would be. I'm not sure I could have lived with that squeaky voice. Anyway, we've got to press on. We're expected."

"On Sacorria, right?"

"Sacorria it is," Lando said. "We pay a call on the Outlier planet Sacorria in the Corellian Sector, and visit a young lady by the name of Tendra Risant. Assuming she doesn't turn out to have six kids, three husbands, and a beard down to here."

"*That* doesn't sound like a likely combination," Luke said with a smile.

"Give it a chance," Lando growled. "In *this* universe, absurdity tends to a maximum. Especially when I'm around."

"You know, there *is* a way you could avoid a lot of these problems, if you don't mind spending a bit of time and money," Luke said.

"What way?" Lando asked.

"You *could* try calling ahead. People don't expect each other to call ahead from interstellar range because it's so expensive, but think about it. You've come in cold twice, and it's turned out wrong twice because your information was bad or out-of-date. You could try calling this Tendra Risant via holocom. It'd cost you, yes—but it might save you a lot of time and embarrassment in the long run."

Lando frowned thoughtfully.

"And besides," Luke said mischievously, "think of how much it will impress the lady to get such expensive holocom calls."

That was all it took to convince Lando. He reached for his data reader and started hunting for Tendra Risant's call code.

* * *

Lieutenant Belindi Kalenda knew she had done the best she could. She had taken advantage of the fact that times were bad, and found an unused villa a few hundred meters up the road from the villa where the Chief of State was lodged. It had been a simple enough matter to break into the villa and conceal her stolen landspeeder and other equipment, and the upper bedroom of the empty villa made for an ideal observation post.

Almost too good a post. It was no good thing that the CDF security team, the uniformed officers she could see so busily marching about on patrol around the Chief of State's villa, had not thought to check out her watch post. Either they weren't good at their job, or someone was telling them not to be very good.

In any event, she would be able to watch everything from here, so long as she didn't bother with eating or sleeping or other such trifles.

But that was absurd, of course. It was time to accept the limits on what she could do, and they were extreme. She could not protect the Chief of State or her family if the CDF decided to move in. She could not tail every member of the

entire party. Nor could she be in more than one place if
they decided to split up. And if they traveled by hovercar,
she was out of luck as well. There was no way she could
stay unnoticed flying along behind them—assuming she
could get her hands on a hovercar that could stay in the air
for more than five minutes at a time.

But there was one thing that gave her comfort. Outfits
like the CDF rarely used their own uniformed agents and
officers to do the dirty work. If they decided to make a try
for the Chief of State, they would send in covert operatives
of one sort or another, quite possibly without the knowledge
of the uniformed officers. In fact, if the uniforms actually
were trying to protect Organa Solo, or maybe even died in
the attempt, that would be all to the good, from the conspiracy's point of view. It would give them deniability.

It was that sort of attack she could be at least some
defense against. From her vantage point, Kalenda could
watch all the approaches to the house. If the security detail
changed its routine, for example in some way that would
open a hole in the patrol pattern, that would be a sign to
Kalenda to go on the alert. The most likely attack scenario
would be for an assault team to come through just such a
hole in the security, kill a few uniformed guards for the
sake of verisimilitude, and then wipe out the family.

She could be ready for that, ready to shoot up the assault
force, or at least fire a few rounds that would attract the
attention of the uniformed guards.

Such a hit was most likely to come at night, in bad
weather if possible. She could catch quick naps during the
middle of the day, if she put the macrobinoculars on a
tripod, pointed them out the window, and set them to go
off if they detected abrupt motion. She would get roused
out of bed every time one of the kids ran across the yard,
or a sea skimmer flew past the window, but at least she
would be able to get *some* rest.

*   *   *

"No one said anything about a tutor," Jaina said, staring up at the darkened ceiling of the room the children were sharing. "Why do we have to have a tutor?"

"So we can learn stuff, dummy," her brother Jacen replied, his voice coming from the bed next to her. "Why else would they be picking one out for us?"

Jaina shrugged, although she knew her brother could not see her in the dark. "I guess. But it's supposed to be our vacation."

"So what?" Jacen said. "We're the leaders of tomorrow, or something, whether we like it or not. You think Mom and Dad would give up a chance this big to teach us stuff we might need to help run the galaxy?"

Jaina giggled. She liked it when Jacen talked that way, making fun of how seriously the grown-ups seemed to take everything.

She sighed contentedly and rolled over in her nice big bed. Those bunks onboard ship had been awfully small. It was nice to be planet-side again. It was the end of their first day on Corellia, but they had barely seen anything of the planet yet. The whole day had been given over to getting through the spaceport, getting to the villa on the edge of town, unpacking, and getting organized. That didn't matter. Jaina was glad to have arrived, even if they hadn't done much yet. The trip on the *Falcon* had been fun, of course, but it had been getting a bit cramped onboard. Besides, there had been that strange trouble at the end of the trip that neither of their parents was willing to talk about. Jacen insisted that some other ship had been shooting at them, but that didn't make sense to Jaina. Mom was the Chief of State. Why would anyone want to shoot at *her*?

There was a quiet murmur from Anakin, sound asleep in his bed on the other side of the room. It was good to have them all sharing a proper room again, the way they did at home. Yes, indeed, it was good to be off the ship. "So what do you think the tutor's going to teach us?" she asked. "I mean, besides how to run the universe."

Jacen laughed. "Well, that right there will probably take most of the first day. I guess we'll just have to wait and find out about everything else."

*   *   *

The villa they had rented had a fine view of the city from the one side, and an even better view of the eastern ocean from the other. It sat on a low bluff, with a pathway affording easy access to the white sandy beach below.

Han was on the patio to the rear of the villa, leaning on the railing and staring out to sea. The skies were clear, the air was clean, and a gentle breeze was blowing. He was on his homeworld on a beautiful morning. The three kids were down on the beach, under Chewbacca's watchful eye. Good of him to do it, Han told himself. No one with that much fur could enjoy getting sandy—to say nothing of getting wet.

Everything should have been fine. All the folklore of the spaceways said you were never more comfortable than on your own homeworld, where the gravity, the air-pressure-and-atmospheric-gas mix, and language and accent and cuisine and everything else were precisely the ones that your body had been born into.

But it just wasn't true for Han. Not this morning. And it was more than the incident with the PPBs and the Uglies. That was worrisome, but not as much as it might have seemed at first. After all, they plainly *could* have killed them all, and yet did not. That meant that some powerful someone definitely wanted them alive, at least for the moment. It wasn't much of a comfort, but it sure beat knowing with absolute certainty that someone wanted you *dead*.

But there was more. Much more. Leia had told Han that she had the very clear sense of being *watched* at the spaceport, by someone outside the official security net. When a Force adept, even a half-trained one, told you something like that, it was probably smart if you believed it.

It was the way the countryside and the city had looked as they had driven through them. Han had expected a certain amount of change, and even a certain amount of decline. He had followed the news from Corellia as well as anyone outside the sector could.

But the unkempt fields, the unpainted houses, the lines of boarded-up stores a half kilometer long, the worn look of the people. It was bad, worse than he had thought. Han felt a strange, irrational guilt for not having been here, with his people, to experience the suffering with them.

And suddenly he was taken with an impulse to do exactly that. Be with them. Standing in a villa at the edge of the city was no way to see what was going on here on his home planet, in the capital city. He turned and went inside, and found Leia still at the breakfast table. "Listen," he said. "Do you think you can handle this tutor thing on your own?"

Leia looked up at him in mild surprise. "I suppose so," she said. "Why? What's up?"

"I don't know, exactly," Han said. "I just feel like I have to get out of here, go and see what it's really like in town. Walk around on my own two feet, instead of driving around in a nice armored CDF landcruiser. I can catch the airlifter shuttle at the village station."

Leia nodded, her expression a bit sad and serious. "I was half expecting you'd want to go in," she said. "Go on and get a look. I can find a tutor by myself. The first of the candidates is due in an hour."

Han leaned over and gave his wife a gentle kiss on the cheek. "Thanks," he said. "It really is something I need to do."

"Don't forget we have dinner with the Governor-General tonight at Corona House," Leia reminded him. "The hovercar is supposed to come for us at eight o'clock."

"I'll be back in plenty of time to get ready," Han assured her. "But I really have to go see the city. I've been away too long."

*   *   *

By the time the third candidate for the tutor's position had come through, Leia was already regretting her willingness to take the job on by herself. The Governor-General's office had sent over a list of candidates who had undergone intensive security clearances—and she had her own abilities in the Force. She could read any attempt at deceit or fraud. She did not have to worry about unknowingly hiring some covert operative to educate her children.

However, it seemed that she *would* have to worry about hiring an absolute incompetent. Of the first three—a human woman, a female Selonian, and a human man—all were pleasant, but none of them seemed reliable enough to be trusted watching a kettle boil, never mind dealing with three rambunctious children. Nor did it help that each seemed to undo the others in concocting elaborate compliments for Leia. She had never had much patience for such nonsense, and just at the moment she had even less.

Leia, sitting in the rather formal confines of the villa's study, braced herself for the next onslaught, and pressed the button on the desk that would signal the next candidate to come in.

An elderly male Drall entered, followed closely, much to Leia's surprise, by a jet-black droid. The Drall was fairly tall for his species, about one and a quarter meters. His thick, short fur was a deep gray, but shot through with a hint of light gray here and there on his face and at his throat. He wore no clothing or decoration.

The Drall were fairly conventional bipeds, short, dark-furred, solemn-faced, dignified-looking creatures. They were short-limbed, with clawed, fur-covered feet and hands. And this one here was living up to the species' reputation for self-confidence.

The droid rolled in behind the Drall, and Leia took a good hard look at it. The droid more or less resembled a taller, thinner version of R2-D2—a cylinder with wheels on extendable legs. It appeared to be a highly modified astromech unit. However, unlike Artoo, this droid could move, not just on wheels, but on repulsor lifts, as best Leia could tell. At least those *looked* like repulsor pads on the bottom of its cylindrical body. Leia had never seen a droid quite like it. However, Corellian etiquette followed the general pattern in regards to droids: unless the droid was actually in use, you were supposed to ignore it.

The elderly male was as rotund as most of the Drall Leia had seen, and even if he did not move fast as he came in, there was nothing clumsy or awkward in his gait. He moved with an impressive bearing, his jet-black eyes calm as he gazed steadily at the Chief of State of the New Republic. "I am Ebrihim," he said in a low, growly voice.

Leia found herself standing and coming around the desk to welcome him, something she had not done for any of the other guests. This Ebrihim was the sort who commanded respect, even from a Chief of State. "I am Leia Organa Solo," she said, following his lead in leaving off all honorifics and titles. According to the information she had, Ebrihim had quite a list of accomplishments himself.

"You are looking for a tutor for your children," he said, moving toward the visitor's chair. "You wish the same person to act as guide for your entire party, arranging trips to interesting places. Is all that correct?"

"Yes," Leia said. Somehow it suddenly felt as if she were the one being interviewed.

"Good," the Drall said. "Please, do be seated." He pulled himself up into the human-height chair. Leia obediently returned to her chair and sat down, not at all unaware of how much self-confidence it took to tell the leader of the New Republic how to behave in her own office.

"I am looking for a tutor," she said. This fellow seemed to prefer blunt talk. Very well, she would try it his way. "Why should I give the job to you?"

"A fair question. Because the job intrigues me. I know the history of this sector. Because I have experience in the field of tutelage to well-to-do humans. If I may make an educated guess or two, judging from your background, you wish your children to have a nonhuman tutor in order to expose them to an alien viewpoint. You want that nonhuman to be one of the species native to this system, and thus provide insights that no outsider could. I am about the same height as your children, and they will not be intimidated by me—unless I *wish* to intimidate them. Are those reasons sufficient, or do you wish more?''

"That list of reasons is quite adequate,'' Leia said with a smile.

"Good. You have my qualifications listed on that data pad in front of you, I imagine. Do you know enough to make a decision, or do you wish to examine with those ridiculous Force powers of yours and probe the depths of my soul?''

"You do not believe in the Force?'' Leia asked.

"I believe in it, the way that I believe in gravity or sunshine. I have observed it, and therefore know it to be. But I do not take it seriously. There is not a confidence artist or sabacc shark on this planet—or, I would expect, any other—who does not claim to have vast skill in the Force.''

"There is something in what you say. But how can the lies of a confidence artist have any bearing on the importance of the Force?''

"Because, in everyday life for the vast majority of beings, the Force has no real meaning. *You* live in a world of Jedi powers, where wondrous things are commonplace. *I* live in a world where I cannot leap five times my height no matter how much I try. I must get a ladder, or have Q9-X2 lift me up. The galaxy that you lead, that your children may well help to lead, has far more of my sort of folk than yours. Your children are strong in the Force, yes?''

"Very much so.''

"Then don't let them rely on it too much,'' Ebrihim said. "It can become a crutch, a shortcut, an easy way out. Let them learn the everyday way of doing things. Let them

do as ordinary folk do. Let them build from there toward
the Force, rather than letting them trust to the Force to start
with.''

"I see," said Leia. It dawned on her that she should
have been mortally offended by a number of the things
Ebrihim had said. But maybe she had been around the court-
iers and flatterers too much. She found his bluntness re-
freshing. And it was distinctly pleasant to deal with someone
who was not falling all over himself, treating her like some
sort of mythical being. He sounded more like a school-
teacher giving advice from a lifetime of experience, telling
a parent who was trying too hard how to back off just a bit.

And, she realized, that was exactly the sort of person
she wanted schooling her children. He had a point about
the Force. It might well be good for her children to be
exposed to a viewpoint that did not see the Force as the be-
all and end-all, the starting point and ending point of all
things. After all, her children *were* going to live their lives
in a universe where the vast majority of sentient beings
never have the least thing to do with the Force. "You have
the job," she said. "Will the advertised salary be adequate?''

"I would be a fool to turn down more if you should offer
it, but yes, it is 'adequate.' And if you have no objection,
I will set to work at once.''

"No objection at all," Leia said.

Ebrihim got down from his chair, and turned toward his
droid. "Come along, Q9," he said. "We have work to
do.''

Now that Ebrihim had brought attention to his droid,
Leia could remark upon it. "Might I say that is a most
unusual model," she said. "I don't believe I have seen one
like it. Might I ask what use a tutor has for an astromech
droid?''

"A great deal of use indeed," Ebrihim replied. "His
skills at data access alone are beyond value. But his abilities
extend far beyond that. He has—''

"I *am* capable of speaking for myself, Master Ebrihim," the droid announced. "You needn't talk about me as if I were not here."

Leia raised an eyebrow in mild surprise. "I don't think I have ever seen an astromech droid capable of speaking Basic before," she said, addressing Ebrihim. "Did you modify him or does this model come that way?"

But the droid turned toward Leia. "Your pardon, ma'am, but as I said, I *can* speak for myself. And I might add that I modified myself for speech as well."

"Q9, that is no way to talk to the leader of the New Republic," Ebrihim said.

"Why not?" the droid asked, in a tone of voice that made it clear that it was asking out of genuine curiosity.

"Because she could order you taken apart for spares, among other reasons."

"You would not permit her to do so," Q9 replied. "*That* particular empty threat no longer impresses me."

"One of these days you will be insulting to the wrong person, and I will not be able to prevent your being punished."

Leia could not help but smile. "While I would suggest you try to be more polite, I for one won't order you taken apart."

Q9 turned toward his owner. "You see?" he said.

"No, I don't," Ebrihim replied in mild tones. "Being forgiven is far from the same as being right."

"Perhaps so," Q9 replied. "But thus far I have found it is far *easier* to be forgiven than it is to be right."

"*That* is why people talk to you as if you aren't here," Ebrihim said. "They find out very quickly that you are not worth talking to."

Q9 looked from Leia to Ebrihim, but plainly could not think of any sufficient rejoinder. Instead of speaking, he simply turned toward the door and rolled himself out.

"He *must* be tremendously useful if it's worth putting up with that much backtalk," Leia said.

"Sometimes it's a difficult call," Ebrihim replied. "But

I must admit that I find him an interesting case. I have never encountered a droid with quite his viewpoint. I find it most stimulating. He has very definite ideas about droids, and tries to live up to them. I think that is part of why he tinkers with himself constantly."

"Then the voice upgrade isn't the only thing?"

"Oh no, not at all. Whatever the latest and greatest commercially available upgrade is, he has to have it. I'd estimate that something less than half of him is original factory equipment at this point. Beyond that, of course, he designs his own improvements. He built those repulsors himself, for example. I keep hoping that the next addition will be a courtesy module, but no luck as yet." Either because he enjoyed talking about his droid, or because he had the job, Ebrihim was relaxing a bit.

"Come," Leia said. "I think it's time you met the children."

"I am looking forward to it," Ebrihim said, making a slight bow, inviting Leia to lead the way.

*   *   *

Not far from Coronet City Spaceport, Han Solo turned off Meteor Way and walked into Treasure Ship Row, and could not believe it. Not at first. Not when he remembered how it used to be. How had it come to this? Was he even in the right place?

Treasure Ship Row had been the market, the bazaar, the entertainment center, the legend you had to pass through—or, if you had no imagination or spirit of adventure at all, go around—on your way from the spaceport into the central city.

He remembered the hundreds of stalls that had crowded the center of the broad road, selling everything imaginable, from every corner of the galaxy. He remembered the vendors, the beings of every kind, from star systems Han had never even heard of, thronging here, in this place, to hawk their wares. Every day new ships landed, and every day something new, something unexpected, would appear on the sales tables.

Once Treasure Ship Row had been packed with buyers and sellers from across the galaxy. Once the very sound of the place had been overwhelming, all by itself. The songs of the street players, the banging and crashing and tootling and oompahing of the strolling musicians, the sound of a thousand languages being shouted at once as the vendors urged every person walking past to sample the finest, the most lovely, the rarest, all going for the most absurdly low prices—and any buyer who did not haggle the price down by at least half deserved whatever happened to him next.

Once the air had been full of the pungent odors of roast meats and strong drink and fresh breads, and of less pleasant scents as well. Your nose was enchanted in one moment by the most exquisite of perfumes, and assaulted in the next by a whiff of what was either the offal from the bottom of a rotted-out animal cage or some other species' idea of a good meal.

Once Treasure Ship Row had been a riot of color— brightly hued tents, and signboards that flashed and strobed and throbbed their messages. The shop fronts had been painted in every color of the rainbow, and a few were painted in colors that no human could see. But you knew that the storefront that looked slate gray or dingy white was probably shriekingly bright in the ultraviolet or infrared, and the stores with the strangely textured exteriors of intricately patterned sound-reflective baffles were full of merchandise that would appeal to the species that navigated by echo-location.

The same sort of rule applied to the small lamps that hung discreetly outside certain otherwise unmarked doors. It took little guessing to know what sort of business was transacted behind those doors, and the lamps that appeared to be burned out were bright in infrared or ultraviolet, signaling the same sort of services to those species who quite literally saw the world a little differently than humans. A famous bit of schoolboy folklore had it that there was an intricate and subtle color-coding system at work even among the lamps visible to human eyes, though no one Han ever met could actually explain how it worked, or what a given color meant. But it was a good story.

Once the nights of Treasure Ship Row had been just the same as the days, only more so. At dusk, half the vendors would pack up their stalls and then reopen them again as carnival games, sabacc salons, tattoo parlors, betting shops. The others would never close at all. The singers and dancers and street players would come out in greater force, and crowds from the bars and restaurants would overflow out into the balmy evening air. You never wanted to stop in one place for long, for fear of missing what was going on behind the next line of stalls.

Once all that had been. Now the sounds, the smells, the colors were vanished, the exciting days and magical, mysterious nights were gone. The vendors' stalls were no more, leaving a broad and empty boulevard behind. The stores were boarded up as well, all except those with their windows smashed, and those that showed the scars of fire damage. All was silent, except for the blowing of the wind, and the scuttlings of small scavenging creatures that hurried into deeper hiding as Han walked down the abandoned street. The only scents on the air were the faint hints of mildew and dry rot, of moldering wood and stagnant, dirty water.

Sickly-looking trees and tall weeds sprouted here and there in the street—and from the broken windows of several of the shops. Some scraps of ancient, weather-beaten canvas, and a few heaps of abandoned poles and broken-up folding tables scattered about were all that were left, besides Han's memories of halcyon days and nights.

All gone. All gone and lost forever. Back in another life that seemed so distant that it might have happened to someone else, Treasure Ship Row had been a place of mystery, of magic and excitement, of promise and danger for a much younger Han. But now the magic was over, and Treasure Ship Row was empty and forlorn.

Han remembered a famous actor he had met once. He had first seen the man from the fourth row of the theater. The actor had portrayed a dashing young lieutenant, and Han had never seen a man as vital, as alive, as energetic as that imaginary officer. Later he had talked his way backstage, and walked boldly into the actor's dressing room. He saw the costume on its rack, the wig and the sword and even the nose of the character, each neatly taken off and put away. And sitting in their midst was a tired, gray-faced old man with nothing in his eyes.

It had taken a conscious act of will on Han's part before he could even believe that the old man had been the dashing young officer moments before, that the old man fretting that it was closing night, and he had no other part to play, had just moments before been onstage defying the universe.

Everything special and exciting and thrilling, all the illusions, had been stripped away from Treasure Ship Row, until now there was nothing left at all but the harsh reality of a grimy street.

Han walked the length of the place, and then turned down Starline Avenue and headed for the center of town. He had to see more, even if he did not want to.

*   *   *

It was not all ruined, Han told himself. Just *nearly* all. Here and there, as he walked along, there were still well-kept houses, businesses that were still open, and even one or two that looked prosperous. But Han knew he was grasping at straws. Coronet City was Treasure Ship Row writ large.

The only difference was that Treasure Ship Row was completely dead—and the city was not. The streets were only half-empty, not wholly so. There were vehicles on the road, even if a fair number of them were broken-down, still sitting where they had been abandoned months or years before. Idlers and loiterers gathered on nearly every street corner.

And nearly everyone he saw was human. Scarcely a Drall

or a Selonian in sight. Each of the species had always had its own enclave in the city of Coronet, but in the old days, it had never seemed to matter that much. Selonians would buy groceries in the Drall shops, humans would go visit Selonian friends at home, Dralls would come and see a show in one of the human neighborhoods.

Not now. Not when there was no money, and no work, and everybody had to look out for themselves—and look over their shoulders as well.

He should not have been surprised. He knew that now. Nearly all of Corellia's chief industries had revolved around trade in one way or another. Entertainment for the ship crews, financial services for the shipping companies, droid manufacture and repair, shipbuilding and repair. Even the criminal offshoots of those industries had been based on trade. Con games, money laundering, smuggling, droid hacking, and illegal ship upgrades all required customers from out-system.

In the good old days, beings had come to this world to have a good time, to sell their cargoes, to get their droids and their ships looked after. All too often people had gotten more than they bargained for—but that, too, had been part of Corellia. Now, thanks to the war, thanks to a paranoid fear of foreigners, thanks to government antialien policies that amounted to financial suicide, no one came to Corellia anymore. There was no one to sell to, and nothing to buy, and no credits to buy and sell with anyway.

As Han walked toward the center of the city, it seemed as if things improved, at least a little. More shops were open, and those standing in line outside them seemed bored and resigned, not brimming with anger.

Han passed through a still-prosperous neighborhood he had known in the old days, full of grand old houses, and was pleased to see that it, at least, was much as it had been—until he noticed all the guard droids on patrol, the discreetly placed static force-field generators, the surveillance cameras, the guard posts. A guard droid hovered down out of the sky to float beside him as he walked along. Han took the hint and left the area. Some folks still had money, but they were plainly afraid of those who did not.

It was getting on toward the middle of the day as Han's wandering took him toward the business district. He was just on the verge of looking for a place to grab a bite to eat when he heard shouting and chanting coming toward him. He realized that he had been hearing the sound for a few minutes, growing louder in the distance.

Han looked around, and it suddenly dawned on him that the street was emptying out. People were moving quickly, quietly, off the street as the sound of the march got close. Han heard the slamming of doors, the rattle of window guards dropping into place. The manager burst out of the store Han was in front of, looked down the street, then reached for a hand crank set into the front wall. He turned the crank and a plasteel shutter started rolling down into place.

Across the street, a woman scooped up her child, turned back, and ran inside. A man ducked into a small tavern just before the manager slammed the door and started rolling down the shutter.

The street was suddenly empty except for Han and the sounds of doors being slammed and locks being set, and the sound of marching feet and harsh singing. The tinkle of glass breaking floated up, followed by heavy laughter.

Han started to run in what he judged was the opposite direction from the shouting, but the sound echoed off the buildings and the vacant streets, making direction hard to judge. He decided to turn at the next corner—

And ran headlong into them, blundering into the front ranks of the march before he could stop himself. But the press of bodies was so tight, and the crowd so boisterous, that for the first few moments at least, he was merely caught up in the crowd, swept along by the tidal wave of bodies.

They were singing at the top of their lungs, so loud it was impossible to understand the words. They wore cheaply made dark brown uniforms of severe cut. Their feet were shod in metal-toed black boots. They wore black armbands, and on the armbands was the stylized image of a grinning human skull with a dagger clenched in its teeth, and the words HUMAN LEAGUE below.

The marchers were all men, and they were making a halfhearted effort to march in rhythm with their song, but they were not well organized—or sober—enough for that. The smell of cheap liquor was on every man's breath, mingled with the hot odor of sweaty flesh.

Han untangled himself from the front ranks of marchers, and found himself more or less in step with the third or fourth rank. He tried to work himself toward the end of the rank, trying to escape the march—and the marchers.

He had almost made it when a meaty paw wrapped itself around his collar. It yanked him off his feet, and another paw pulled him on the shoulder and spun him around. Han stumbled and recovered and found himself face-to-face with a huge, greasy-looking man with bloodshot eyes, a flabby, grimy face, bad teeth, and worse breath. The man had simply stopped dead in the middle of the street. He let the march flow around him, ignoring the buffeting he was taking as the marchers squeezed past. He regarded Han closely, then looked up again at the marchers. He reached and grabbed another marcher. "Hey! Flautis!"

"Barnley! Watch out the way you grab me."

"Flautis, get a *look* at this guy," Barnley said, ignoring his friend's protest.

Flautis was a somewhat smaller and greasier version of Barnley. He looked at Han and his eyes widened in surprise. "What do ya think of *that?*" he asked of no one in particular.

Han was used to people recognizing him, even this long after the adventures that had made him famous, but these guys didn't seem to *recognize* him, exactly. "Ah, fellows, is there a problem?" he asked, shouting in his friendliest voice over the din of the march.

Flautis and Barnley exchanged looks, and then each of them grabbed an arm. They dragged him to the side of the street, shoving the marchers out of the way. They got to the sidewalk and Barnley threw Han up against the side of the wall. "Okay, buddy, what's the game? Who are you?"

"No game. No game," Han said. "I was just walking along and got tangled up in your march by accident. I was trying to get back out when I bumped into you," he said, trying to put the best possible face on things. "Sorry I did that, really. Honest. And thanks for rescuing me," he said.

Barnley grabbed Han by the front of his shirt and pulled Han so close he could feel Barnley's hot breath on his face. "Your name, buddy. Your name right now."

"Han," he said in as friendly a voice as he could manage. "Han Solo."

Barnley looked at Han in greasy astonishment. "*Solo?* Yeah, sure," he said. He turned to his companion. "We *gotta* pull him in."

"Absolutely," Flautis agreed. "We have *got* to check this out."

"But—wait a second!" Han protested. "I didn't—"

But then he felt a blow on the back of his skull, and the universe went black.

*   *   *

"Now then, children. We shall begin at the beginning," Ebrihim said. The three children—Jacen, Jaina, and Anakin—were sitting on one side of the low table in the playroom. Ebrihim was seated on the other side, in the same sort of children's chair as his three charges, and more or less at eye level with them. Q9 stood next to him, taller than his seated master.

"*What* beginning?" the boy, Jacen, demanded, a scowl on his face. His sister Jaina's expression was no less unpleasant, and the little one, Anakin, seemed to be trying to take his cue from his elders. At least he tried to sulk, but somehow it was not a very convincing performance. He seemed to be distracted by Q9.

Ebrihim sighed. It was plain to see that his charges were not very happy to be dragged in from the beach on a beautiful day and plopped down in front of a tutor. "The beginning of your education concerning the Corellian Sector," he said. He paused long enough for the groans to subside before going on. "After all," he said, "I can scarcely take you exploring if you don't know where we are going."

"Exploring?" Jaina asked.

That got their interest, as he intended that it would. "Of course," Ebrihim said. "There are five worlds to get a look at. Drall, Selonia, Tralus and Talus, Corellia—and Centerpoint Station, for that matter. I am to be the guide for you and your families as you tour those places."

"Well, all right, then," Jacen said. "Where are we going first?" he asked.

"If we are to learn about the history of this system, I thought it best if you got a look at its past. There is a large archaeological dig not far from the city of Coronet. Your mother has agreed that we should all go and take a look at it tomorrow."

"What kind of archaeology?" Jaina asked.

"The site in question is actually underground. It appears to be some sort of large industrial site from long ago. We still don't know exactly what sort of place it is—but humans and Drall and Selonians were clearly using it for something—and something big—at least two thousand standard years ago, and possibly long before that."

"Wow," said Jacen. "Will we see skeletons?"

Ebrihim nodded. "In all probability," he said. "Quite a number have been excavated."

"Is *he* like Artoo?" Anakin suddenly demanded, pointing a pudgy finger at Q9-X2.

Q9 rolled back a few centimeters and swiveled his camera eye around to look at Anakin. "I beg your pardon?" he said, clearly a bit startled.

"R2-D2," Jacen explained. "It's the droid our uncle Luke has back home. I think he wants to know if you're the same kind of droid."

"I am not," Q9 said, rolling back toward the table. "I will thank you not to make such a suggestion again."

"But you *look* like Artoo," Anakin insisted. "Kinda. But he's shorter, and you can talk regular."

"I am a Q9, a highly modified and experimental type based on the R7 version, itself a far more advanced version of the R2 series. I might add that I am highly self-modified above and beyond my initial specifications. I have nothing to do with the R2 series."

"What's wrong with Artoo?" Anakin insisted.

Ebrihim chuckled to himself. "I'm afraid Q9-X2 has a rather low opinion of the R2 series."

"Artoo is a good droid!" Anakin protested.

"That is as may be," said Q9. "But the designers of the R2 made them effectively voiceless and equipped them only with wheels."

"So what?" Jacen demanded.

"The result is that the R2s cannot do their work as well as they should. I find the very idea of an android that cannot do its work properly most upsetting. It is not just your R2 unit, and not just a question of design. Here on Corellia, for example, many, many androids are in a state of disrepair, and no one can afford to repair them. It is a massive waste of potential. I find it shocking."

Anakin glared fiercely at Q9. "You shouldn't say mean things about Artoo," he said, then hopped down off his chair and stalked out of the room. "Nice going, Q9;" Jacen said. "I'll go bring him back." Jacen got up and went after his little brother.

"I am pleased that young Master Jacen thinks I expressed myself well."

Ebrihim turned toward his assistant. "I suspect," he said, "that you have not quite mastered the concept of sarcasm."

*   *   *

The lights were dim when Han woke up in the cell. There

was a dull, throbbing pain at the base of his skull and a foul taste in his mouth.

Why in the world had this Human League crowd snatched him up off the street? The only thing he could think of was that a hero of the Rebel Alliance might not be the most popular sort of person in a group that probably had Imperial sympathies. But even that idea didn't hold water. He was missing something.

Han looked around, and saw that there was nothing in the cell but the dank cot he was sitting on and a bucket in the corner. Somehow it didn't look like the room was being used as originally intended. Rather, he was in what looked to be a converted basement storeroom. Well, purpose-built or not, the cell was impossible for him to get out of all the same.

Han had been in enough cells enough times that he was not particularly terrified by being thrown in yet another one. He was safe in the cell. It was when they *came* for him that the trouble would start.

It was at the precise moment that he had that happy thought that the lights came on, blindingly bright, and the door swung open. Han stumbled to his feet, struggling to force his eyes to adjust. By the time he could see clearly, Barnley, Flautis, and a third man, whose insignia appeared to show him to be of higher rank, were in the cell, peering at him intently. "Well, boys," the third man said. "I can see why you did it, and you were right to do it. It could have been a trick, but it turns out it wasn't. Turn him loose."

"But—" Flautis protested.

"Orders," the third man interrupted. "From *way* up, if you know what I mean."

"From the Hidden Leader?" Barnley asked, something like awe in his voice.

The third man merely nodded, as if his meaning were obvious.

"Well," Flautis said, immediately chastened. "Okay then."

Han turned toward the third man to ask what was going on, but he never got the chance. It was only as he was about to speak that he realized that he had put his back to Barnley again.

The blow on the back of his head didn't feel any better this time. The universe went dark again.

*   *   *

It was evening, getting on toward night, and Leia could not decide whether to be angry or worried. Either Han was off having such a good time with some old cronies that he had forgotten to call home, or else he was in trouble. The Governor-General's hovercar was supposed to be calling for them in a half hour.

It was then that she heard the sound of a hovercar coming in. Could the Governor-General's car be early? She went to the window and looked up into the sky—and knew instantly, by the way that hovercar was coming in, hard, fast, without running lights, that it was not the Governor-General or anyone else come to pay a social call. The CDF security teams had installed panic buttons throughout the house. A tap on any of them would call the guards to red-alert status. There was one by the window, and Leia reached to slap it down.

*   *   *

It was a quiet evening, Kalenda told herself, but things were most likely to happen when it was quiet. And then she heard it, the low whirring sound of a hovercar coming in on its repulsor lifts.

Suddenly the night was full of the sound of blaring alarms, and the grounds of the Chief of State's villa were flooded with light. Guards scrambled for position. Kalenda ignored it all and scanned the sky for the intruder.

There it was! The hovercar dropped out of the evening sky three hundred meters shy of the villa, the bluish glow of its repulsors throwing strange and shifting shadows on the narrow country road. The hovercar bumped once, hard, as it landed. A rear door popped open, and a large, indistinct shape was dumped out. Almost before it came to a halt, the hovercar had bounced back up into the sky and away.

Guards rushed forward from the villa and surrounded the new arrival. Kalenda grabbed her macrobinoculars and zoomed in close.

The figure lurched to its feet, and she saw that it was Han Solo, looking very much the worse for wear.

Kalenda swore to herself. This was not good. Not good at all. Someone was sending another message, and even if she could not read it, it clearly was not meant to be friendly.

Things were beginning to go sour.

CHAPTER THIRTEEN

Conversation by Torchlight

Dinner was done, and it had not been a cheerful affair. Getting Han patched up from his injuries had put them behind schedule, but they had turned what was meant to be a social occasion into something closer to a council of war.

Nor had the noise from outside helped matters. Despite being six floors up, despite the soundproofing in Corona House, the Governor-General's official residence, the shouting and the singing of the demonstrators were too loud to ignore. Now they had retired to the Governor-General's private study, and from here the sound was even louder. They had given up all pretense of not hearing it. Instead they watched the proceedings from the study's window, the lights in the room low both to make it easier to see, and harder to be seen. The windows were supposed to be blasterproof, but there was no sense taking chances. The flames of the flickering torches lit their faces as they watched the march of the thugs.

Governor-General Micamberlecto stared through the window, looking mournfully down at the spectacle below. "There they are," he said. "Again tonight. And I dare not, dare not, call in the Corellia Defense Forces or the Public Safety Service. I am not even sure they are on my side anymore. Indeed, I am nearly sure they are no longer with me. If I called them, they might just join in."

He sighed and leaned his spindly shoulder against the

edge of the window frame as he watched the rowdy demonstration below. To Leia, the sound of his sigh was the
saddest part of it all. It was such a *tired* sound, so full of
resignation and frustrated hopes that were no longer even
worth recalling. That one little sigh told her there was no
real hope at all.

Leia and Han stood next to Micamberlecto, watching as
well. Gray wisps of smoke still hung in the air, and the
effigy of Micamberlecto was still smoldering, though by
now it was so trodden upon as to be scarcely recognizable.

The demonstrators, all of them humans, nearly all of
them men, were carrying torches as they marched in a circle
around Corona House. The torches let off their own smoke
as well, and it hung heavy in the windless air, draining the
color from everything, making the night seem darker than
it truly was. Those who did not have torches had placards
and signs with anti-Drall and anti-Selonian slogans.

The singing—if you could call it singing—started up
again, louder this time. The lyrics were coarse, obscene,
and quite distinctly not supportive of the New Republic.
The song reached its climax, the demonstrators bellowed
out the last and most graphically offensive line, and then
cheered for themselves.

"They'll go on, go on that way for quite a while yet,"
said Micamberlecto. He spoke Basic with hardly a trace of
accent, but with one or two patterns of Frozian grammar
and word order—most noticeably the tendency to repeat a
phrase for emphasis. "They will march for a bit longer, a
bit longer," the Governor-General went on, "but for all
intents and purposes, I expect that's the end of the show.
Not much more to see that you have not seen already.
They'll sing and shout slogans, and get drunk and start some
fights and break some windows, and drift off to wherever
they come from—until the next time. The next time. But I
doubt the streets will be safe tonight." Micamberlecto shook
his head mournfully. "I am afraid you did not pick, did not
pick, the ideal spot for your vacation."

Micamberlecto was a Frozian, and the Frozians were not

known for their cheerful outlook. No one could doubt their probity, honesty, or diligence, but they were a somewhat melancholy species. Still, there did not seem to be much to be optimistic about at the moment. "It doesn't look good," Leia said.

"No, it does not," Micamberlecto agreed as he turned away from the window and sat back down at his oversized desk. He was a typical Frozian—tall, gangly, a scarecrow of a figure, a third again as tall as Han. Frozians were a fairly standard hominid species, if a rather elongated one. The extra joint in their arms and legs made their movements a bit offputting at first. To human eyes, the Frozians looked to have had all their arms and legs broken. To see Micamberlecto folded up in a chair, with his arms crossed—and recrossed through the second elbows—was a strange sight indeed.

Micamberlecto had short, golden-brown fur over his entire body. He had no noticeable external ears, and his deep brown eyes were set wide apart. His nose was on the end of his prominent muzzle. His mouth was small and lipless, as if it decided there was no sense even attempting to compete with that magnificent nose. Long, black whiskers grew from either side of his muzzle, forming a sort of enormous spiky mustache that grew past the sides of his head. He wiggled his nose thoughtfully, and the whiskers bounced up and down vigorously.

"Is it always this bad?" Han asked.

"Yes and no," Micamberlecto said. "Mind you, even now, tonight, no doubt ninety-five percent of the city of Coronet is quiet and calm. Four blocks from here, perhaps no one knows that there has been another demonstration. But it used to be that I would assure visitors that ninety-*nine* percent of the city was calm. Things are getting worse, coming to a head. I wish to Froz we could cancel the trade summit. But too late. Too late. Delegates are already on their way, and we in the New Republic cannot, cannot afford any further loss of face here in Corellia Sector. No, we cannot."

"I'm afraid I agree with you, friend Micamberlecto,"

Leia said, talking over her shoulder as she watched the torchlight procession wend its way around the building. "We did not know it was like this. We should cancel, but we can't."

"But what's it all about?" Han asked as he turned his back on the window. He winced as he turned his head, and he was moving stiffly. Obviously he was still in some pain. "No one seems to be able to answer me that. This should be a rich planet, a rich sector. It has all the resources and talent and investment capital it needs. It *used* to be rich, and peaceful. What went wrong?"

Micamberlecto shrugged elaborately and impressively. "On Froz we have a saying. 'Things are bad when there are more questions than answers, but worse, but worse, when there are more answers than questions.' You ask me one question, but I could give you a dozen, a hundred answers." He extended a long arm toward the window and the demonstrators beyond. "I wonder if any of our friends out there could give one, give one. As for myself, I *could* tell you the economy was bad, or that people are frustrated, or angry, or that there is much intolerance, if you like."

"Those are all true," Leia said, "but those are symptoms, not the cause."

"Quite right, quite right. Yes, economic dislocation caused by the upheaval of the last war is the proximate, proximate cause of unrest, but the root goes much deeper, deeper. Without a strong external government to keep the peace, malcontents and rabble-rousers of all sorts are coming out of the woodwork. And it is not just our friends out there. It is the other species as well. The Drall, the Selonians, and the humans have all produced their demagogues. And they have set to work demonizing each other. But all those, all those answers tell us nothing. Your question asks after the symptoms, not the disease. I think the real answer is that you ask the wrong question. I think you have to ask—*why didn't it happen before*, before now?"

Han frowned as he sat down in a chair facing Micamberlecto's desk. "Go on," he said.

"It's a simple question," Micamberlecto said. "I ask—what has changed that makes this chaos possible? And the answer is simple—the collapse of empire. There is no power from above *forcing* all of them to behave. There was a gun to Corellia's head for a long time. 'Pretend you love your neighbor or we'll kill you,' said the Empire. No dissent, no dissent allowed, those on top supported, those below held down. No movement possible. Except the economy decayed, decayed during the trade disruptions, and everyone sank lower. That aggravated the crisis, but it did not cause it."

Leia looked out the window, down into the darkening night, and the gloom of a torchlit parade seen from a distance. She turned her back on the view, crossed, and sat next to Han. "I'm not sure I like where you're going with this, but say on," she said.

"For millennia, all the species of the Corellian Sector lived under the monolithic government of the Old Republic, and then under the Empire. But then the war came, war came, and the Empire collapsed. There was some fighting here, but not much. Here, the Imperial system simply fell in on itself. It collapsed, like a balloon with a slow leak.

"Since the Empire ceased to govern here, the sector has been left, left to its own devices. Our very fine New Republic sent me in as a Governor-General, but what is there for me to govern? Where are my tools to govern with? These last years, the Corellians have learned to pay me no mind. I have a huge, a huge shortage of skilled, politically reliable people. There are not enough actively pro-Republic people to fill all the needed governmental positions, or to staff the internal security forces. I must hire ex-Imperial bureaucrats and soldiers. Worse, nearly every one of these breakaway groups employs some sort of mercenaries. Mostly ex-Imperial soldiers, but there are a few, a few retired from the Republic's armed forces. But scarcely any of them are truly loyal to me, to the New Republic. And so the people know my soldiers and bureaucrats fail to follow my orders.

"Under the Empire, the generals and bureaucrats gobbled up other jobs with power. They were factory managers, business directors, on the controlling board of this and that and the other thing. Now, even with their Imperial positions and commissions gone, they still have the power of those *other* jobs.

"We say the Empire is dead, but here in Corellia the body lives on after the head has been lopped off. The little bosses are still there, doing what they have always done. But now these police officials and Imperial bureaucrats answer to no one, no one. There is no higher authority that can punish them for going too far. And they are discovering that they like it that way. They can have the revenge, revenge, for the harm done to them five, ten, twenty, a hundred standard years ago, safe in the knowledge that no Imperial stormtroopers will break down their door and take them away. And *that* is the core of the problem.

"For endless years, endless years, it was the strong central government that kept the different species from having at each other. The Empire didn't much like nonhumans, but it liked antialien riots even less. They were bad, bad for business. People learned that if they caused trouble, they would be punished. So they didn't cause trouble. The three Corellian species lived in harmony because they were forced, forced to do so. Now no one is forcing them. Times are bad. They need someone to blame. They blame each other.

"During the war, Corellians were asked to choose between alliance to the Republic and fealty to the Empire. Now members of all the species of the Corellian system are asking, asking themselves—why any exterior authority at all?" Micamberlecto gestured out the window. "They are starting to ask—why be in the New Republic if it cannot promise order? Why not one planet, one government? Or one landmass, or one race, one government?"

Han shook his head mournfully. "I can't believe it. I can look out the window. I can see it. I know it's happening. But I don't believe it. I was born and raised in a united Corellian Sector—"

"Except that you weren't," Leia said. "What Micamber-lecto is saying is that the Empire forced the Corellians to *pretend* they were united and at peace."

"And now they—we—don't have to pretend anymore. Incredible."

"Incredible, only perhaps, but true, certainly. The Five Brothers, the inhabited worlds of the Corellian System, are on the brink of anarchy. Generations of enforced peace between the three leading species—human, Selonian, and Drall—have come to an end."

Leia looked at her husband, and she needed no ability in the Force to understand his pain, his numbness, his shock. The sights they had seen were bad enough for her. She could imagine what they had been like for Han. But for Leia, what Micamberlecto was saying was far more disturbing than a mob of street brawlers. Her whole life had been centered around the choice between Republic or Empire. The question had always been *which* was to be the central authority, never whether there was to *be* a central authority. Now, here, that was no longer so. The idea of going it alone was starting to take hold. It took little imagination to see how quickly that might spread.

"Micamberlecto, we cannot allow this to happen," she said. "If the Corellian Sector is allowed to disintegrate, the idea of separatism could spread—and lead to chaos."

"It has begun to spread already," said Micamberlecto in a still more morose tone of voice. "Groups of all three species—and of other Corellian Sector species—are starting to set up independent states in the Outlier systems that surround us. Already a number of them have broken away, broken away from the sector, rejecting my authority—and thus, by extension, the authority of the New Republic as a whole. The sector is threatening to degenerate into a crazy quilt of mini-empires and rump states."

"Is that such a bad thing?" Han asked. "I mean I can see the problems, but what does it matter if all these little planets are independent, as long as they're peaceful and don't hurt anyone?"

Micamberlecto shook his head sadly. "But they *do* hurt each other," he said. "You saw the sort calling for independence tonight. They are rabble-rousers, and rabble-rousers need enemies. People like your friends in the Human League need someone to blame. No, there will be no peaceful, amicable separation. There will be war and riot and vengeance that will go on and on. If the old enemy was the Empire, the new enemy is fragmentation and chaos, chaos."

"How serious a threat is the Human League?" Han asked. "And who's this Hidden Leader character?"

Micamberlecto shook his head sadly. "If I could answer those questions, I would be a most happy, happy Froz. There seem to be Human League thugs everywhere one moment, and none at all the next. They are good at vanishing when they need to do so. And the Hidden Leader is just that. Hidden. Some inside the organization know who he is, but no one, no one outside. I simply don't have the police and intelligence facilities to do a proper investigation of them. And of course the NRI seems to have its own troubles, own troubles in Corellia. We don't get much information from them."

Leia frowned. "If the situation gets much worse, the New Republic is not going to have much choice but to start acting like the Empire. We'll have to bring in peace enforcement troops to stop the fighting. We'll have to impose our will on the Corellian Sector, the same way the Empire did."

"But we fought the war *against* the Empire to put an end to that sort of thing," Han said.

"I know," Leia said. "And just think what it will be like to get that sort of policy approved, and how expensive it would be. But the alternative is to stand back and let a bloodbath happen."

"I am not even sure, even sure, we *can* impose a peace," Micamberlecto said. "We have no heavy ships to speak of in the sector."

"Can't we bring in ships and troops from elsewhere?" Han asked.

"That would cost a tremendous amount of money that we just don't have," Leia said. "Besides which, there's not much call for warships or armies at the moment, thank the stars. Most of the forces have been disbanded. We've got lots of New Republic and captured ex-Imperial ships, but most of them are mothballed, or being broken up for scrap. And a lot of the supposedly active-duty ships are in drydock getting upgrades. What few ships are effective are on duty in other sectors."

"There must be *some* sort of forces in reserve," Han said.

Leia shrugged helplessly. "There are, but there aren't many. And what reserves we do have will take time to activate. We're stretched awfully thin. Readiness is at its lowest ebb in years."

"Then let us hope there is nothing we need be, need be ready for," said Micamberlecto. "I suspect it is a forlorn hope, but there it is."

"But what are we to do?" Leia asked.

Micamberlecto shrugged again. "There is nothing we can do," he said. "However, there is another point, another point. Although it sounds as if Captain Solo's capture was almost at random, it could have been a deliberate threat directed at all of you. A warning. A warning."

"You're saying they might be trying to chase us off," suggested Han.

"Possibly," Micamberlecto said. "The staged attack certainly makes it seem that way."

"Well, we're not going to let them win," said Han. "I don't cut and run. I say we stay—that we stay and do exactly what we would have done otherwise."

"Excellent," said the Governor-General. "However, I would suggest taking one or two precautions. I know that your ship is under guard at the spaceport, but it is not the most secure of locations. Someone could place a tracer— or, ah, other device—aboard it."

" 'Other device,' " Leia said. "You mean a bomb."

Micamberlecto nodded. "Well, yes, I do. In any event, it might be best to place the *Falcon* elsewhere."

"I've been thinking on that point myself," said Han. "But there's no place out by the villa that would be any better."

"I was about to suggest that there is a small, a small landing pad and hangar complex here, on the roof of Corona House," said Micamberlecto. "You could store the ship there, and I could have my own personal technical staff examine it to make sure that no one has played any games with it already."

"Can they be trusted?" Leia asked. "You've made it clear that you can't rely on most of your staff."

"My technical staff, and my personal bodyguards, are all decorated veterans of the war against the Empire," he replied. "They are all handpicked, handpicked, and all of them have been vetted. I am quite comfortable with my life in their hands. It is the locally recruited people working in other departments I suspect."

"Okay, then," Han said. "I'll have Chewbacca fly the ship over tomorrow morning, first thing. It'll give him something to do. More to do than we'll have, in any event."

Leia smiled, with at least some hint of real humor in the expression. "Oh, we have a lot to do, Han, if we're going to keep up appearances."

"Like what?" he asked.

"We have to play tourist."

Han let out a low moan. "I don't know," he said. "That's what I was doing today, and look how it turned out."

* * *

The next morning was not a pleasant one. The weather had shifted, and rain was lashing down on the villa. That meant the kids were trapped inside, and that meant they were restless, and that meant noise. Despite the best efforts of the CDF medical droids, Han's head was still throbbing from the beating he had taken, and that did not help either.

Han sat in the living room and watched the children set to work once again, attempting to build another impossibly tall and spindly tower out of the blocks. Blocks. All the super-duper high-tech toys in the universe, and they were playing with blocks.

At least Chewbacca had managed to escape. He got to fly the *Falcon* from the spaceport to the top of Corona House. Han reflected that things had to be pretty bad if the idea of flying a spacecraft in a rainstorm through congested airspace to a rooftop landing sounded like fun by comparison. On the other hand, Leia had retreated to her office with Ebrihim to plan their itinerary, and *that* didn't appeal to Han at all.

The tower of blocks collapsed in a totally predictable roar of noise, and the kids all laughed just a bit too loud.

Han decided to beat a retreat. He went upstairs to the library, in hopes of being alone. He needed to think things through for a while—and maybe a bit of calm and quiet would keep his head from throbbing.

He went into the library and sat down in one of the infinitely comfortable reading chairs. Some part of the back of his mind, trained back when he had been a smuggler, warned him that he had made the double mistake of leaving the door open and sitting with his back to it.

But Han pushed that foolish worry aside. It was just that he was nervous and edgy, and his old reflexes were coming back. Besides, he had other worries. He thought back to the incident—no, use the real name—the *kidnapping* yesterday. Why had they grabbed him? Why had they held him? And why on Corellia had they let him go? The only thing he could think of was that, somehow—

"Master Solo, if I might have a word?"

Han jumped, startled, and turned around in his chair to find Q9-X2, that weird droid of Ebrihim's, floating behind him. So much for the idea of peace and quiet. "Don't *do* that," he said.

"Do what, sir?"

"Come up behind me so quietly. Make a little noise. Use your wheels instead of floating around like that."

"But I would not have been able to get upstairs using my wheel system," Q9 said.

"And wouldn't that have been a shame," Han muttered. "Look, I came up here after some peace and quiet. Could you please just roll away, or float away, or something?"

"But there is something of importance that I must tell you," the droid said as it floated around to face the front of the chair. "Something that I thought that we should discuss in private."

"Yeah?" Han asked tiredly as he leaned back in the chair. "What might that be?" It had been his experience that what droids thought of as important rarely matched his ideas on the subject.

"First, when I learned that Master Ebrihim and myself were to serve in the household of such important persons as yourselves, in a situation as unsettled as that currently obtaining on Corellia, I elected to make whatever contribution I could to your security, and I therefore made a number of purpose-built modifications to myself."

"Huh? What?" Han asked. "What are you talking about?"

"Excuse me for taking so long to get to the point, but you must understand that I have installed quite a bit of sophisticated detection and observation equipment. I now carry a wide range of highly capable scanners and comparators, and I have performed repeated sweeps of the vicinity, whenever possible, in between the execution of my other duties."

"Good for you," Han said, still not really paying attention. Why did every droid feel the need to buttonhole him and yammer on about its specs and capabilities?

"And good for you, too, Master Solo," Q9 said. "I do think you would be well advised to take what I am saying more seriously."

"And why is that?" Han said.

"Because you are being watched."

That got his attention. "If you mean the CDF agents—"

"Please, Master Solo. I am no addlebrained protocol unit. Give me *some* credit. No. In fact, judging by her behavior, I believe the watcher in question is doing her best to stay out of *their* sight, more than she is worried about hiding from you or your family."

"She?" Han asked.

"Yes, sir. There is just one, a human female, and she appears to be on her own. At least I have spotted no one else working with her. She has stationed herself in the empty villa a short distance from here. She watches from an upstairs window, doing her best to conceal herself. I might add that she is probably all but invisible to normal human vision. The window transparency is thick, the room she is in is dark, and she has been quite skillful in keeping a low profile. However, I managed to record a few low-resolution flat-image shots of her in polarized infrared before the rains blew in earlier this morning."

"Let's see."

Han had expected Q9 to project a fuzzy holographic image on the wall or something. Instead, there was a quiet whirring noise, and a flat-image photo rolled out of the printout slot in Q9's chest. Maybe there was something to be said for a droid that upgraded itself. "Most of the time, of course, the macrobinoculars conceal her," Q9 went on. "This is the highest-resolution image of her face that I have secured. The quality is still quite low, although I have run it through all the appropriate enhancement routines."

Han took the photo from the slot and looked at it. It was rather grainy and extremely contrasty, and the image itself was a bit blurred. But there could be no mistake. It was Kalenda, the NRI agent, caught in the act of lifting the macrobinoculars to her face. Somehow, Han was not at all surprised. She was just the sort of person who would pop up out of nowhere, light-years from where he thought she was.

She had a worried look on her face, and she looked gaunt

and worn. But it was her, all right. There could be no mistaking those disconcertingly wide-set eyes. He thought back to what Leia had said, about her sense of being watched at the spaceport. Yes. It all fit.

But what did it all *mean*? What the devil was Kalenda doing here, and if she was here, why hadn't she tried to contact Han? The only answer he could come up with was that she didn't trust the CDF either.

"Have you told anyone else about this?" Han asked.

"No, sir. It seemed to me that I should come to you first."

Han thought for a moment. "You have done very well, Q9," he said. "This is vital information—but I must order you to tell no one—*no one* else about it. Not your master, not my wife, not anyone. It will be bad enough having *me* wandering around pretending not to know I am being watched. If the whole house had to pretend, someone would make a slip."

"Then this watcher is an enemy, sir?"

"No, no. A friend. I don't exactly know what she intends, but she is on our side. The problem is that we are not at all sure the CDF is friendly. It might be that she is there trying to protect us *against* the CDF in some way. If their agents discovered her, we could lose a very useful asset."

"Useful for what?"

Han shook his head. "I don't know yet. Before I could tell you what we'll need her for, I'll have to figure out what game we're playing. But she's there, and the people we don't trust don't know it. That might be useful."

"Shall I attempt to signal her in some way?" Q9 asked. "By some means that the CDF agents could not detect?"

"No," Han said. "Not yet. Not until I know more. The situation is complicated enough without introducing a new variable. And the CDF might have a few tricks up their sleeve we don't know about."

"Very well, sir," Q9 said. "The situation is rather serious, is it not?"

"More so than any of us thinks, if you want my opinion," Han said. He handed the photo back to Q9. "Destroy
this," he said. "Keep a very low-key eye on our friend.
And do not discuss this situation with *anyone*. Not even
with me, unless I bring up the subject, or unless the situation
changes. Is that understood?"

"Quite well, sir."

"Thank you, Q9. You may well have just done the most
important work in your life."

Q9 backed away, and dipped down on his repulsors a
bit, doing a pretty fair simulation of a bow. "So far, at
least," he said, without a trace of humor. "So far."

Han watched the droid leave, and swore under his breath.
Something was going to blow. Something. Things could
not hold together under all this pressure for long.

And meanwhile, all they could do was play tourist and
pretend they knew nothing and that everything was fine.

Han hated politics.

Outside, the rain thundered down.

CHAPTER FOURTEEN

Sightseer

T he rain continued into the next day, but by that time, everyone had had quite enough of being cooped up in the house. Rain or no rain, they piled into a hovercar the Governor-General had loaned them, and took off, with Han at the controls. He reached for altitude as quickly as possible, punching through the gray misery of the driving rainstorm, bouncing and bucking the hovercar's way through the storm clouds themselves, and then up into the clear blue gleaming skies above.

It was remarkable what a change the sight of blue skies made. Everyone's mood lifted, even Chewbacca's, shoehorned though he was into a copilot's seat not nearly large enough for him. The bickering children suddenly went quiet, and forgot the sulky arguments about who was crowding whose seat. All at once they were pointing out the cloud tops below to each other, and telling each other what monsters and aliens the clouds looked like.

Han felt better, too. Getting out from under the rain was part of it, of course, but it was also the idea of getting away—far away—from Coronet, if only for a while. There was something to be said for playing tourist if it kept you out of town.

*　　*　　*

Kalenda watched the family hovercar with feelings of relief and fear. It was impossible for her to follow them. She could rest, at least for a while. However, it didn't seem as if they had taken a great deal of luggage. Probably they were only heading off on a day trip. But that would be enough for her to wash up a bit, get a decent meal, and catch some sleep. Of course, there was always the chance that the opposition would take advantage of their absence for some sort of skulduggery. But she could set the macro-binoculars on time-lapse record while she slept, and play the recording back later. If there was any hanky-panky, she could still catch it on the recording and take action in time.

The situation was no better, and she knew that she was not likely to do anyone any good anytime soon. But she could think of no activity more worthwhile than staying close to the Chief of State's family.

She would figure out what to do next later.

In the meantime, she could get some sleep.

*   *   *

They flew past the clouds, and down below them, the rolling landscape of Corellia came into view. Low tree-covered hills and steep valleys broke up the steady march of tidy fields, and here and there, a small town slid past the left or right of the hovercar's line of flight.

Han looked down, and it felt good to see it all. This was the Corellia he remembered, or at least he could pretend it was. Perhaps all those tidy little farms, all those handsome little towns, were as destitute as Coronet. But at least he could *imagine* they were happy and prosperous.

The autopilot alert beeped, and an indicator light came on. They were getting close to the archaeology dig. Han looked ahead, and saw a huge pit, a dark blot on the land-scape. "Ebrihim!" he called out.

Ebrihim undid his seat belt, hopped out of his seat, and came forward. "Yes, Captain Solo. What is it?"

"Is that where we are going?" he asked.

"Yes, sir. At least that looks like what I have heard described."

Han looked at the Drall in surprise. "You've never been here before?" he asked. "I thought you were going to be our guide."

"And so I shall be," Ebrihim said smoothly. "I have studied this site from afar for some time. I have read all the published papers concerning it, and talked with many of the principal investigators. It is the first major archaeology site ever studied on this planet, and thus of considerable interest. It is just that I have never before been able to get clearance to get to it."

"So you're using the Chief of State of the New Republic as your personal ticket into this place?" Han asked, his tone somewhere between annoyance and amusement.

"Absolutely," said Ebrihim. "How could I pass up the opportunity?"

"This is the *first ever* archaeological dig on the whole planet?" Leia asked from the second row of seats. "How could that be?"

"Yeah. No one was interested in that kind of stuff when I lived here," Han said. "Why are they interested now?"

Ebrihim turned the palms of his hands upward and shook his head. "It's hard to explain," he said. "I believe it comes from the sudden strong species-ist feelings on Corellia and the other worlds in this system."

"I don't see the connection," Leia said.

"Well, the past has become an issue of pride. Who was here first? Who has the strongest claim to this or that spot of land, or this or that planet? Even among those not particularly interested in that sort of politics, antiquities have become all the rage on all five worlds. I'm told there are teams of human, Selonian, and Drall researchers on all the Five Brothers, performing digs, doing research, vying against each other to prove their species was the first to arise, or had the highest achievements earliest, and so on."

"Political archaeology," Han said. "That's a new one on me. What are we going to see down there, anyway?"

"That is the interesting question," Ebrihim said. "No one quite knows what it is. It is an extremely ancient system of artificial underground chambers, many of them collapsed or filled in by sediment or what-have-you. Some of the chambers are in quite good condition, however. They are full of machinery of one sort or another, and no one knows what the machines are for, or who built them, or why."

Han frowned. "Isn't archaeology usually mud huts and pottery shards?" he asked.

"That's the way we usually think of it," Ebrihim admitted. "But civilization has been around a long, long time in one way or another. We talk of the thousand generations of the Old Republic, as if that was all that came before. But that is only, what, twenty thousand standard years or so? Perhaps twenty-five thousand at most?"

"That's a long time," Jacen said.

"Is it?" Ebrihim asked. "How long have the stars been shining? How long has there been life on the planets?"

"A *really* long time?" Jacen asked.

Ebrihim laughed, a sort of *er-er-er* noise. "It certainly has been a long time," he said. "A thousand times, three or four thousand times as long as those thousand generations. More than enough time for all sorts of things to happen that we don't know about anymore."

"So sometime before the Old Republic even got started, someone built the whatever-it-is down there?" Han asked.

"The *belief* is that it is that old," Ebrihim said. "No one really knows for sure. There are dating techniques we could probably use, but no one in the Corellian Sector knows how to use them. Perhaps, in better days to come, that sort of expert will come in and visit us again."

Han checked his controls. "Maybe they will," he said, "but just now we've got to come in for a landing. Back to your seat, Ebrihim, and the rest of you, check your seat belts and here we go."

*   *   *

The surface level of the dig resembled a colony of social insects that someone had stepped on, with the insects now frantically racing to repair the damage.

Workers—all of them human—were rushing in all directions, moving piles of dirt and debris out of the excavation in big roller cars. Droids of all sorts and descriptions were carrying various sorts of hardware in and out of the huge pit.

It was organized chaos, and Han and his family stepped from the hovercar a bit uncertain about where to go or what to do. But there was more than uncertainty in Han's mind. "Leia," he said under his breath. "Look at the uniforms on the workers."

"What about them?" she asked.

"They're the same as on the fun boys who roughed me up. The only thing missing is the Human League armbands. The marchers around Corona House had them on, too."

"You're right," she said. "But we can't talk about it now. Here comes our guide, I think."

A man of middle age, looking rather on the portly and well-fed side, was coming toward them. He was dark skinned with short-cropped dark hair and a broad, toothy smile. He wore the same uniform as the rest of his team, and his uniform had the same sweat stains as everyone else's, but there was an elaborate insignia pinned on the shoulder boards of his tunic, and no one else had that. His hat was a bit more elaborate as well, and he wore it at a jaunty angle. "Greetings to you all," he said in a surprisingly soft and mellow voice, with the slightly slurred accents of the northern reaches of the main Corellian landmass. "I am General Brimon Yarar," he said. "Welcome to our little project." He bowed respectfully to Leia. "Madame Organa Solo. It is an honor to have you here." He stuck his hand out to Han. "Captain Solo, an honor as well."

Han could not help but notice that their host was giving him a good hard look, as if Han were some particular curiosity he had been eager to see for some time. It was not a pleasant sensation. "Thanks," he said slowly as he accepted the proffered hand. "We're glad to be here. General of what, if I might ask? Were you in the war?" *And on which side?* he wanted to ask, but did not.

"Hmmm? What? Oh, that," the general said, clearly a bit nonplussed. "An honorific only, I am afraid. An informal title in a private organization."

"The Human League, perhaps?" Han asked. "Are you with them?"

Yarar's smile dimmed, if just for a moment. "Why, yes," he said. "They provide the bulk of our financing. But we try not to advertise that *too* broadly. Some people might get the wrong idea. But the workers today are from a Human League Heritage Squad, working to reveal our species' glorious past here on Corellia. Are you familiar with our work, Captain Solo?"

"I'm becoming so," Han said.

"And these must be your children," Yarar said, sweeping on past the awkward moment. He squatted down and gave Jacen a friendly wink. "I'm surely glad to meet you all," he said.

"Yeah, great," Jacen said, sidling back a bit. "Glad to meet you, too."

Jaina gave a forced little smile, and left it at that. Anakin didn't move a muscle, but simply stared at Yarar.

Yarar stood up again, smiling as if he had completely charmed all of the children. "Shall we head in?" he asked.

"Sure," Han said. He noticed that Yarar had completely ignored both Chewbacca and Ebrihim. Han exchanged glances with Chewbacca, and Chewie responded with a slight shake of his head indicating no. He looked at Ebrihim and got the same response. Han agreed. No sense in forcing the introduction and making an incident out of it. That would distract from—

Distract from what? Looking at a cave full of rusting machines? No. No, there were hidden currents here. Currents that needed to be explored. What was an outfit like the Human League doing digging up old machines?

Yarar had to know he wasn't fooling anyone. It was

armies that had generals, not archaeology clubs. And it was armies that could enlist and finance the amount of manpower on display here.

So what was a private army doing, not so secretly digging up an ancient civilization? Ebrihim might have suggested they were out to prove some ideological point, and maybe Yarar would tell them the same thing, but Han was not ready to believe it. These boys were out here *looking* for something, and Han wanted to find out what. *That* was what he did not want to be distracted from.

"We're glad to be here," Han said. "We're all very interested to see what you're doing out here."

Yarar laughed, and grinned hugely. "We're not doing much at all out *here*, but come and take a look at what we're up to underground."

* * *

Maybe the grown-ups found all this stuff interesting, but Jacen most assuredly was finding his attention starting to wander. At first it had been kind of fun to be underground in the strange old tunnels. According to what Ebrihim had said, they had found the tunnels all full of dirt that drifted in from the entrance, and water that had leaked in, and some of them had just plain fallen in on themselves. The tunnels they had cleaned up so far felt *weird*, somehow. Maybe it was just that he was not used to being underground. Maybe it was just the strange musty smell of the tunnels. It was hard to say.

That General Yarar guy was all full of excitement and enthusiasm about all the mysterious old machines they had found, but Jacen didn't see why. There were a lot of big rooms where you could see the floors and walls and ceilings had been smooth and white and perfect about a zillion years ago, but now they were cracked and half caved in, and even where they had been cleaned and fixed up some, they were still broken up and dirty.

And most of the machines they were finding looked as

if they were a million times worse off than the rooms themselves. Most of them were just piles of rust and rotted-out
plastic and moldered-away synthetics. Jacen couldn't see
any way you could possibly tell much about any of them.
The lettering—if it was lettering—on some of the machines
was so faint as to be hard to make out, and General Yarar
told them it wasn't in any alphabet or other writing system
anyone had ever found. Even Ebrihim seemed a bit disappointed by the tour.

They didn't even get to see much of the guys doing the
work. Understandably enough, they didn't want a bunch of
tourists wandering around the active work sites. The general
let them see one room where they were going at it with all
sorts of complicated digging machines, but after that, he
just took them down a bunch of side tunnels where no one
was doing anything anymore.

But something else seemed odd to Jacen. He had read
some books about archaeology, and about how you always
had to be careful about leaving everything just as you found
it, and being sure to go through all the crud you dig out,
to make sure that you didn't miss some incredibly vital clue
that was hidden there.

They weren't doing that here, and they weren't, as best
Jacen could tell, doing much to investigate the things they
did find. They weren't even digging them out all the way.
They went through room after room after room that was
only half dug out. It was like they were only digging far
enough to make sure that they hadn't found the one thing
they were looking for, and then moved on. They had even
left a few skeletons half dug out—Selonian and human,
mostly, and one Drall—and some of the bones looked as
if they had been damaged in the process. If there was one
thing Jacen's books had told him, it was how important it
was to be careful digging out bones, and how much a set
of remains could tell you. But these guys acted as if they
didn't care about the bones.

At least it was kind of exciting to look at the skeletons

and enjoy a creepy little thrill of fear from looking at the grinning skulls and the empty eye sockets.

But Jacen didn't even get a chance to do much of that. General Yarar was always determined to trot them off to the next room, ready to boast about how fast his men had dug out so much dirt and rock, and how much it all cost, and how it was the equivalent of digging a hole straight down, this big around, and this far down.

Now he was turning a corner, leading them all into yet another tunnel, just like all the others. At first Jacen and his brother and sister had been leading the pack, scooting ahead, eager to see the next room. By now, however, all three children were hanging back, bored by it all. Jacen was following behind the adults, with Jaina and Anakin behind him.

But then Jacen turned around and noticed they weren't following anymore. He went back around the corner to see what was up.

Anakin was staring fixedly at a spot on the floor of the tunnel, muttering to himself. Jaina was watching her little brother. "What's he doing?" Jacen asked.

Jaina shook her head. "I don't know, exactly. He just walked over to that spot and stopped dead, and started talking to the floor."

"Has it answered?" Jacen asked, almost but not quite kidding. With Anakin around, stranger things could happen.

"Not yet," Jaina replied.

The twins watched their little brother intently, wondering what he would do next. Whatever it was, it was bound to be more interesting than General Yarar blabbing on again about how much dirt they had dug up.

"There!" Anakin suddenly announced, and pointed in the opposite direction of the side tunnel the grown-ups had gone down. He turned and started trotting down it, still staring intently at the tunnel floor. Jacen and Jaina looked at each other, shrugged in perfect synchronization, and followed along behind him.

"Anakin!" Jaina called out. "What is it? What is it you're following?"

"There!" he said. "Under."

"Under the tunnel floor?" Jacen asked, puffing a bit with the effort of talking while he jogged along. "Is it a cable or something?"

"Under there!" Anakin said. "Big strong power running!"

He trotted along, following the whatever-it-was. The tunnel came to another intersection, and turned the corner so abruptly that his brother and sister almost ran straight past him. By the time they caught up with him, he was already headed down a ramp that led down into a lower level.

"What is he after?" Jaina asked.

Jacen shook his head. "I don't know," he said. "But I know I'm glad Anakin's not doing this with that general guy around. I think his guys have been looking for something in particular—and I've got a hunch that Anakin's just found it."

*   *   *

Q9-X2 floated along on his repulsors, following behind the tour group, not feeling at his most useful. He was strongly of the opinion that droids should be useful at all times and in all places. He regarded it as a moral affront that the incredibly sophisticated technology that was a droid should go to waste in a universe so obviously full of work to be done.

But tagging along behind the rest of a group that was being told useless information had to be about as useless as it got. And their host was pretending that Master Ebrihim was not even here. Q9 never enjoyed being ignored, as droids generally were, but somehow it was even worse being the ignored droid of an ignored person. Clearly this General Yarar was one of those humans with an utterly irrational belief in the inferiority of all other species, and he was not going to pay any attention to Master Ebrihim if he could possibly help it. That Wookiee fellow was in the same situation.

But for all the use Q9 was being, he might as well be one of the children.

The children.

Suddenly it registered with Q9 that the children were no longer with the group. For a full tenth of a millisecond, he toyed with the idea of sounding the alarm, but then rejected the idea. Master Solo had made it clear that nothing was very clear at all. There might be some reason for the children to be missing. Perhaps their parents had instructed them to find something out. Perhaps their hosts would take it ill if they found out the children had been wandering off where they should not have been.

No. After all, he had installed all that sophisticated detection and sensing equipment. It was time that he put it to use.

Q9-X2 slowed to a halt and allowed the tour group to get ahead of him. He turned around and headed off in the opposite direction, extruding sensor probes as he went. He already had powered up his molecular backtrack sniffer, his residual heat trend directionalizer, and was starting to absorb data from them, when it dawned on him to look down. Footprints. Footprints in the grimy floor of the excavated tunnel. It was with a sense of mild frustration that he pulled the sensors back into their recesses. What was the point in having the best equipment available if there was never any need to use it?

He headed off down the tunnel.

*   *   *

Anakin was moving faster now, running full tilt down the gloomy passages of the lower level. If anything, it was a bit danker, a bit darker, than it had been above. Jacen tried to peer into the dim tunnel. Whoever had installed the lights down here had been working on a tight budget, that was for sure. It was *dark*. But that didn't seem to bother Anakin.

He was moving straight ahead, still staring at the tunnel floor. Jaina and Jacen were hard-pressed to keep up.

Suddenly Anakin stopped dead in his tracks, and the twins nearly bowled him over before they could stop. As best either of the twins could see, he was standing in front of a stretch of corridor that looked exactly like every other stretch they had seen. But that did not seem to bother Anakin. He was literally hopping with excitement. "Here!" he muttered under his breath. "Here! Here! I need to . . ." His voice faded out, and he stopped moving. Then he squatted down on the floor of the tunnel, stuck his right index finger out, and pointed it at the tunnel floor. "There," he whispered. "And it goes up. . . ." Holding his finger about ten centimeters away from the floor, he moved his hand toward the wall, and then, slowly, up it.

"He's tracing something," Jaina said in a whisper. "Following it back."

"Yeah, but what's he tracing?" Jacen whispered back. "And what's he tracing it *to?*"

By now, Anakin was pointing to a spot on the wall a good fifteen centimeters beyond his reach. He jumped up and tried to reach it, but he could not. He turned toward the twins, and it seemed to Jacen at least that he was only just at that moment aware of them at all. "Up!" he said. "I need to go up. Let me up on your shoulders."

Jaina knelt down next to her brother and he scrambled up on her shoulders. She stood up carefully, Anakin swaying back and forth just a little bit as she overbalanced a trifle. "Forward!" he said. "More, more. Stop. Good. Now go left—no, right. No, no, not so far. Back . . . back—stop! Good, good. Hold it."

"Jacen, what's he doing?" Jaina asked. "I can't see."

"He's got his hand flat out against the wall," Jacen said. "He's pushing against the wall, real hard. Oh, wow!"

There was a slight shower of pebbles and dust. "Great, I just got a face full of gravel," Jaina spluttered. "What happened?"

"It's a panel," Jacen said. "Like a keypad panel, but

way different. It's a five-by-five grid of little green buttons. A little door popped open in the tunnel wall, and there was this little panel behind it. It lit up kind of all purple and green as soon as the little door swung open."

"It lit up?" Jaina asked. "You mean there's still a live power supply down here?"

"I guess. Probably that was what Anakin was tracing."

"*Now* what is he doing?" Jaina demanded. "Anakin, hurry up, whatever you're doing. You're getting heavy."

"Just a sec," Anakin said. "Almost got it."

"I think he's trying to figure out what button to push," Jacen said. "This is getting weird."

Anakin stared hard at the purple keypad, whispering to himself and pointing at the green buttons. "Okay," he said at last. "Here goes." He started pushing buttons, one after the other. Every time he pressed a button, another green light would wink out.

"Here goes *what*?" Jaina demanded. "Jacen, what is he doing?"

"The thing he does best," Jacen said. "He's pushing buttons."

"Done," said Anakin. "Let me down."

Jaina complied eagerly. "But now what?" she asked. "What happens now?"

And then, with the dull rumble of heavy machinery, a ten-meter-wide section of the tunnel wall in front of them slid out of the way, dropping down into the floor. There was a clattering of pebbles, and a feeble cloud of dampish dust shook loose from the wall.

Behind the false wall was a huge, seamless panel of faultless, gleaming silver. Suddenly a seam line appeared in the silver wall, and a huge section of it swung back, like the door of a huge bank vault swinging open. The children hurried to one side to get out of its way.

A gleaming light poured out into the tunnel as the vault door opened, and the children had to shield their eyes for a moment before they could see clearly.

Inside the door was a long corridor, made of the same

silver stuff as the vault door. The corridor seemed to be open at the other end, but they could not make out clearly what was there. There did not seem to be any sort of place for the light to come from, but it came just the same. The three children stared down that corridor for a long moment. They knew what to do next, but there was a universe of courage between *knowing* and *doing*.

"What is it, Anakin?" Jaina asked her little brother.

He shrugged. "Don't know. I just felt it there, and I followed it. Don't know what it *is*."

"Well," said Jacen with far more confidence than he felt, "we'll never find out here. Come on."

The three children took each other by the hand, with Anakin in the middle, and stepped up onto the gleaming corridor.

The corridor was a good hundred meters long, and they moved down it at a slow, careful pace. At last they reached its other end, and stood looking down at—at something that Jacen had never seen before. He had never even seen anything *like* it before.

The floor went past the end of the corridor, and ended in a view platform about five meters across. The platform hung out in empty space, with no guardrails or any other sort of protection around the edge.

And it was the sort of platform you wished *did* have guardrails. It stood at the apex of an impossibly deep artificial cavern, made of the same silver-colored material, a half kilometer deep at least. The cavern was in the shape of a sharply angled cone, with the platform at the point, and the base of the cone on the floor of the cavern, far below.

Jacen let go of his brother's hand, got down on his hands and knees, and crept out toward the edge of the platform. He stuck his head out over the edge, and swallowed hard.

The first thing he noticed was that there seemed to be no support of any kind for the platform they were on, other than the bit of walkway that stuck out of the tunnel they had come down.

Far below, he could make out other conical shapes, much smaller than the cavern itself, yet still extremely large. There were seven of the cones, with six in a circle around the central seventh. All of them seemed to have the same height-to-width proportions as the cavern itself.

"What in the name of *space* have you children gotten yourselves into now?" a querulous droid voice demanded.

Jacen's reflexes tried to jump him out of his skin, nearly sending him right off the platform. He had to shut his eyes for a second when he thought about how he could have gone right off the edge. He found he had the shakes, and he had to lie still for a moment before he settled down. "Hello, Q9," he said. "Thanks for almost scaring me to death," he said, scooting back in toward the center of the platform before sitting himself up and getting to his feet.

"Were those thanks sincere, or was that more of this sarcasm business?" Q9 asked.

"Oh, sarcasm," Jacen said. "Very definitely sarcasm. Did you come looking for us? Are the others looking, too, or just you?"

"Yes, I came looking for you," he said. "And no, none of the others are looking for you. At least they weren't when I left them."

"Good," said Jacen. "Jaina, Anakin, we've got to get out of here."

"But we just *got* here," protested Anakin.

"I know, I know. I want to explore it, too. But the longer we're missing, the more likely they'll come looking for us—and find this place. Do you want that General What'shisname—"

"Yarar," Q9 interjected.

"Right, Yarar. He's no nice guy, no matter how hard he smiles. Do you want *his* people finding this—this whatever it is? It's *got* to be what they're looking for. And it's got to be very big and important."

Anakin thought for a moment and then shook his head violently *no*. "Uh-uh," he said. "No. *Can't* let that general guy in here."

"Then we have to leave," Jacen said. "Can you make the vault door and the panel hide themselves again?"

"Sure," said Anakin. "That's automatic when we go back out."

"How do you know that?" Jaina demanded.

Anakin looked at her in blank surprise. "I know, that's all. I feel it."

"But—" Jaina began.

Jacen cut her off. "Later, Jaina. Later. Listen, both of you—and Q9, too. We don't say anything about this to *anyone*, okay? Not just yet. There might be spy eyes or snoopers in the hovercar or back at the villa. We wait until all of us can get together someplace safe and talk it over. Then we decide. Okay?"

Jaina nodded her agreement, and Anakin a bit more slowly. The three children turned toward the droid. "Oh, I quite agree," he said. "However, I do think it would be best if you allowed me to take as complete a scan as I can before we depart. We might well want a record of this place for future reference."

"Okay," Jaina said, "do it, but do it quick. Jacen's right. We have to get out of here. Come on, Anakin."

Anakin obediently took his big sister's left hand in his right, and offered his own left hand to his big brother. The three children hurried back down the silver corridor, Q9 hanging back for a few moments as he floated above the view platform and got as good a scan as he could. He could not get much closer to the edge than the human children had dared, for his repulsors were low-powered models that would not work more than a few meters above a surface. If he had floated out over the platform edge, he would have dropped like a stone.

The three children waited for him at the entrance to the silver corridor, and at last he came zipping back down along it at high speed.

He came out into the dingy tunnel and floated back down it a few meters, to make sure he would be well clear of the vault door closing.

Jacen stepped up to the purple keypad. "What do I do, Anakin?" he asked.

"Push the center one in, and hold it for three grimnals."

"What the heck is a grimnal?"

"I don't know," Anakin said, "but that's how long you hold it in."

Jacen sighed and shook his head. Maybe someone out there had a weirder little brother. If so, he wanted to meet the guy. He stabbed his finger down onto the center button of the five-by-five grid. All the buttons instantly lit up green again. He held the button down until the vault door began to swing shut, and then let it go and stepped back a pace or two.

The vault door swung to and latched itself shut. The section of tunnel wall slid back up out of the floor with a rumbling thud, and the cover over the keypad panel swung itself shut. The silver corridor and the huge conical chamber were as well hidden as they had ever been.

"Now all we have to do is get back there before they notice we're gone," Jacen said.

"Wait a second!" Jaina objected. "Q9—how did you find us?"

"Isn't it obvious?" he asked.

"If it was obvious, I wouldn't ask. Tell me."

"Your footprints," he said. "I simply did the obvious thing and followed your footprints."

"Oh, great," Jaina said, looking down. "Yarar's guys will follow them straight here and they'll know right where to look."

"Maybe not," said Jacen. "All of you go back down the tunnel a bit. I want to try something." The others obediently got out of the way, and Jacen turned his attention to the much-trampled dust of the corridor. Uncle Luke could have smoothed it all down without even breaking a sweat.

He reached out with the Force and *willed* the dust to

smooth itself out in front of the vault entrance. Nothing happened for a moment, but then the dust began to stir just a bit—and then, quite suddenly, all the footprints vanished, the dirt floor of the tunnel smoothing itself out.

Now that he had the hang of it, Jacen jogged back a bit farther and tried it on another section of tunnel, with equally satisfactory results. His sister saw what he was doing and joined in. Working with the sort of unspoken coordination that was part of being twins, they took turns smoothing out the tunnel floors behind them as they retraced their steps.

The three children and the droid had made it back up to the upper level, and were well on their way back to where they had snuck away from the grown-ups when their mother came hurtling around a corner and spotted them. "There you are," she said, the relief in her voice obvious. "I could sense you with the Force, but I couldn't find you. Where have you been?"

"Oh, we just sort of wandered off with Anakin," Jacen said, hoping that he was managing to sound casual. "Q9 found us and brought us back."

Leia looked to the droid. "Good work, Q9. I'm glad we have you along. Now let's go find the others before our host decides to turn the dig site upside down looking for you. Come on."

Jacen and Jaina exchanged a knowing look as their mother turned away from them and headed back the way she had come. Good. They had gotten away with it.

At least for the moment.

Leia turned and gestured impatiently. "Come on," she said. "Can't keep them waiting."

Jacen thought of the huge and hidden machines that had clearly been waiting for a very long time indeed, and smiled. He had a feeling they wouldn't have to wait very much longer.

"Coming, Mother," he said, and hurried along to catch up.

CHAPTER FIFTEEN

In Transit

L uke stuck his head into Lando's cabin and caught him staring at the holocom unit again. "Haven't you worked up the nerve *yet?*" he asked.

Lando turned in his seat and gave Luke a reproachful look. "It's not that easy, you know, just calling a woman out of the blue."

"But you do that sort of thing all the time," Luke said, coming into the cabin and sitting down on the bed. "You certainly managed to do all right charming Karia Ver Seryan."

"Yeah. I charmed her so much I nearly got killed. But that was different. That was in person. I was there, in front of her. I knew I was welcome, and I could see by the way she stood, the way she held her head, a million little things, that she was receptive. An uninvited holocom call is much more of an intrusion. I don't know anything about this Tendra Risant woman. What am I going to say to her?"

"You might start with hello and see how it goes from there," Luke suggested.

"Big advice from Luke Skywalker, noted ladies' man," Lando said.

"Okay, maybe I'm not a galaxy-class smooth-talker. I don't claim to be. But you do. Make that call." Luke stood up and slapped his friend on the shoulder. "Now." He turned and left the room.

"Easy for you to say," Lando muttered. But Luke had

a point. If he was going to do it, he might as well do it now. For about the hundredth time, he started punching in Tendra's call code. But this time, for the first time, he actually got all the way through the call code and sat still long enough for the connection to go through.

The holocom came to life, and the face of a young woman appeared in it. She was fair-skinned, with high cheekbones and a slender, expressive face. "Hello?" she said.

"Yes, hello," Lando said, his heart pounding so hard the holocom's microphone should have picked it up. "My name is Lando Calrissian. I'm trying to reach Tendra Risant?"

The woman smiled warmly. "Captain Calrissian! How kind of you to call ahead. I am Tendra Risant."

Lando smiled in relief. She hadn't cut the call connection, and she didn't have horns growing out of her head. A good start. "I'm delighted to make your acquaintance, Lady Tendra."

"And I yours. Are you coming to Sacorria soon?" she asked.

"I'm on my way even as we speak, Lady Tendra."

"Please, just call me Tendra," she said. "I can't tell you how much I'm looking forward to meeting you, Captain Calrissian."

"My friends call me Lando," he replied, "and I hope you're going to be one of them."

She smiled. "I have very little doubt of that—Lando."

Lando smiled back, and wondered why he had thought this was going to be tough. "I'm very glad to hear that, Tendra," he said. "Very glad indeed."

*   *   *

The universe exploded into being around the *Jade's Fire*, and Mara Jade watched placidly as the starlines became stars, and the Corellian System appeared around them.

"On course and en route," the pilot reported. "Corellian

Traffic Control has acknowledged, and we are moving toward Corellia in the center of our traffic lane."

"Excellent, Mr. Nesdin," said Mara. "Mr. Tralkpha," she said, addressing her Mon Calamari navigator, "while you are not otherwise engaged, give us a deep scan of the system, if you please." No doubt he had already started the scan—indeed she would have been irritated if he had not shown that much initiative—but for form's sake at least, the order had to be given.

"Yes, ma'am," Tralkpha replied. "I'm getting some interesting results from the special equipment." The *Jade's Fire* carried some advanced technology scanners that any captain in the New Republic Navy would give her right arm for. They were able to integrate the information derived from the drop out of hyperspace into an instant snapshot of the entire arrival star system. The system worked at an astonishing degree of detail—sometimes. Conditions had to be just right. But today at least, it sounded as if conditions were indeed cooperating.

"What have you got?" Mara asked.

"Nothing, ma'am. Almost no ships at all in space in this system."

"What's so interesting about that?" she asked.

"There's much, much less traffic than there should be, even considering the bad shape the economy's in. No military flights, one or two passenger shuttles here and there, and just two or three cargo vehicles approaching Corellia. The only other ships I can see show as the ones bearing the delegates to the trade summit—and there aren't all that many of them either. I think there are going to be some no-shows."

"I suppose I should be surprised by that," Mara said, "but somehow, I'm not, Mr. Tralkpha. There's a bad storm coming here," she went on, "and no one wants to be out of port when it hits."

*　　*　　*

"Can we stop having fun yet?" Han asked. He squinted a bit as he piloted the hovercar through the dark night of Corellia, toward the bright lights of Coronet, dead ahead. The interior of the hovercar was dark and quiet, with the sounds of sleep coming from the rear seats.

Leia, in the copilot's seat next to him, smiled sleepily. "Just about," she said. "As soon as we get home."

"Wherever that is," Han said.

Leia laughed. "It does seem to move around a lot, doesn't it?" she asked. She stretched out her arms, arched her back, and shifted in her seat before settling back down with a yawn. "Well, even if we have to move out of the villa to do it, I won't mind getting into Corona House. I won't feel so *exposed*."

"I don't know," Han said, his voice more serious. "Even if Corona House *seems* safer, I'm not so sure it is. But I guess we do have to be there for the big show. It'd be a real chore commuting from the villa—and having to fly back and forth over the city wouldn't exactly give us first-class security either. But I've got to admit I'm glad we don't have to see any more sights for a while."

A deafening, thunderous roar came from the back of the hovercar, and then a sort of thud and a whimper. Chewbacca, along with everyone else, was asleep in the rear seats, with Anakin curled up in his lap. Anytime Chewbacca started to snore, Anakin would wake up just enough to slug him in the chest and make him stop. Jacen and Jaina were asleep in the rear row of seats, and Ebrihim was out as well, curled up at Jacen's feet, breathing with a funny sort of relaxed wheezing noise. Even Q9-X2 had powered down. He was in the rear driver's-side corner of the car, all power indicators off except for one tiny amber point of light that blinked on and off.

They had been playing tourist all across the main continent of Corellia for more days than Han could count at this point. He had lost track of the sights they had seen. All of Ebrihim's careful explanations of what they were seeing—along with Q9's fussy interruptions and corrections whenever his master skimmed over a trifling detail—had blurred together in Han's mind.

Even ignoring the whole question of sight-seeing burnout, it had not been easy keeping up the pose of carefree tourist family. Especially not after the twins had told them what Anakin had found in General Yarar's little excavation, and they had seen the playback of Q9's scans. There could be no doubt that Yarar's people were there looking for whatever that thing was—assuming they had not found it by now. None of them—not Chewbacca, not Q9, not even Ebrihim—had the slightest idea what the massive installation was, but no one could doubt that it was important. Otherwise, Yarar's people would not be spending so much time and effort looking for it.

The only thing anyone knew for sure was that there was bound to be trouble, sooner or later—and probably sooner. All they knew for certain was that someone wanted them to leave, to be scared. And for that reason, if no other, it was important that they remain where they were, and make it as clear as possible that they had no worries.

And so they had determinedly not noticed the CDF and PPB hovercars that were forever cruising above and behind them, providing escort. They had ignored the discreet guards that had appeared magically around them in every museum, every historic old building and amusement park. It had not been easy, pretending not to see the wall around them.

If there was one positive thing that had come of it all, it was that Han and his family had come to trust in the CDF ground forces. The CDF Space Service was quite another matter, but Han for one no longer had any doubt concerning the agents protecting his family. Perhaps he had seen more professional security teams, but none that tried harder. They had been too cautious, too careful, for him to believe it could all be an act.

In any event, he would not be dealing with them much longer. Tonight marked the last day of their vacation, and Han had a hunch he was not the first father in history to look forward to getting back to the regular working day.

Tomorrow was the first day of the trade summit, and the handoff to Leia's official security detail.

Tonight also marked the family's move out of the beachside villa. They would fly straight to Corona House, where the conference would take place, and sleep in the apartments waiting for them there.

Actually, everyone but Han would sleep there tonight. It had taken some finagling on his part, but he had managed to convince Leia that he should drop everyone off at Corona House, and then fly on to the villa, sleep there, and clear out the last of the family's belongings in the morning. Leia seemed to think that Han wanted to get a night of peace and quiet before diving into the grueling social whirl of a diplomatic meeting, and Han was quite willing to leave her with that impression. He had his own private agenda to take care of overnight, and he could not do what he had to do with company around.

*   *   *

Fifteen minutes later the hovercar settled down onto the roof of Corona House. Chewbacca and Ebrihim woke up, and Q9 switched himself back on, but all of the children were obviously out cold and they were going to stay that way. Han scooped up Jacen, Leia took Anakin, and Chewbacca took Jaina. They carried the children out of the car, down the turbolift to the apartment they had been assigned on the fifteenth floor of the twenty-story building, and got the children roused enough to peel their clothes off, at least go through the motions of getting teeth brushed and faces washed, and get into their sleep shirts.

All three of the children were sound asleep again before their heads hit their pillows. Chewbacca nodded to himself in satisfaction, and yawned hugely, displaying a terrifying collection of teeth. Then he went out of the room, leaving Han and Leia to look down on their children.

"They are beautiful, aren't they?" Leia asked, sliding her arm around her husband's back as they looked down on the three little people, innocent and asleep, all the cares of the galaxy quite out of their minds.

"Oh, yeah," Han said. "*That*, they get from your side of the family. Wonderful children. Beautiful children."

Leia nestled her head on Han's shoulder. "You'll be careful tonight, won't you? I want these guys to have a father in the morning."

Han sighed and patted her on the shoulder. "I don't know why I even bother trying to keep you from worrying," he said. "It's not that big a deal tonight. No real danger. I just need to do something without being seen."

"And I shouldn't know about it?" Leia asked.

"Probably best if you don't. For one thing, we don't really know who might be listening in right now. But you might say I'm going to take out a little insurance policy, and the less anyone knows about it, the more likely it is to work. Besides, I don't know if it's the sort of thing we can really count on."

"All right," Leia said, but the tone of her voice was not altogether happy. "I love you. I trust you. Do what you have to do to take care of us."

"Hey, Your Worshipfulness," he said, calling her by the old teasing nickname, "that's all I *ever* do."

Leia laughed, and looked up at him. "You always were a good liar," she said, and kissed him.

* * *

Han said his goodnights to Leia and then went to Chewbacca's quarters, just down the hall from his own apartment. He did not use the door annunciator, but instead knocked softly. The door came open immediately. Chewie had guessed his next move as well. Han decided he was going to give up trying to fool anyone. He slipped into the Wookiee's apartment.

"Chewie," Han said as soon as the door was shut, "you've got to promise me something."

The Wookiee cocked his head to one side and let out a cautious little hoot.

"Yes, I'll tell you what it is first. I'm going out now, and probably I'll see you in the morning and everything will be fine. But just in case it doesn't go fine, or just in case we don't get a chance, I want you to promise me something *now*. Promise me you'll take care of the kids."

Chewie bared his fangs, took a step toward Han, and let out a terrifying roar as he grabbed Han by both shoulders and lifted him straight into the air.

"Hey, take it easy, will you?" Han protested, his feet dangling in midair. "Want to wake up everyone in Corona House? I wasn't forgetting your life debt, much as I might like to." Han had freed Chewbacca from slavers, long ago, and Chewie had sworn to protect Han's life in return— though he had not consulted Han about the idea first. There had been plenty of times it had been less than convenient for Han to have a self-appointed Wookiee bodyguard. But a Wookiee life debt was irrevocable—and it extended to the children. At least this one did. Han didn't pretend to know everything about the Wookiee ethical code.

Just at the moment, however, Chewbacca was threatening to tear Han's head off because the Wookiee had taken Han's request to protect them as some sort of suggestion that the Wookiee life debt was not assurance enough—a mortal insult if ever there was one.

Han decided to try again, and hope that this time he could express himself clearly enough not to get himself killed. "All I meant was focus on *them*. Don't worry about Leia or me. If things get tricky—and I think they're going to—it might be that Leia or I have to take some risks. If we do, and you have to choose between us and the kids— don't even think about us, okay? And don't think about sailing into glorious battle or Wookiee blood lust or any of that other nonsense. Get yourself killed and the kids might be in big trouble. If things get bad enough, it might be that you'll have just a split second to decide what to do. And you've got to decide to get the kids out of danger. Don't think about anything else. Okay?"

Chewie thought for a moment, then nodded, and let go of Han, setting him back down on the floor. "All right, then," Han said, straightening his shirt. "And next time, don't be so touchy."

*   *   *

Han took the turbolift back up to the roof of Corona House, and smiled politely to the CDF guard on duty there. "Hi," he said. "I'm just going to get something out of the *Millennium Falcon* before I fly the hovercar back over to the villa. Okay?"

The guard shrugged in a friendly sort of way. "Sure, it's your ship," she said. "Do what you want."

"Just thought I'd tell you first," Han said. "Things are a little jumpy, and I don't want to cause any problems by accident." *I prefer to cause them deliberately*, he thought, but he kept that idea to himself.

"Probably smart," the guard said. "You take care of yourself."

"Oh, I intend to," said Han. "You have a good night, and I'll see you later."

*   *   *

There were certain advantages to being a nobody from nowhere. The security types might worry about the Chief of State, but no one was much worried about what happened to a retired smuggler. Once clear of Leia, Han had good hopes of being able to move around without a herd of Corellian Defense Force baby-sitters for company.

And the same went for the villa. As Leia Organa Solo was not going to be there any longer, and as the CDF security teams would have their plate quite full enough dealing with the trade summit, the CDF was packing up and moving out. Han guided the hovercar down toward the villa, and was rewarded with the sight of the CDF security team in the process of pulling out. He just hoped that his timing was good enough. If Kalenda had pulled out as well, that was going to be too bad.

He landed the hovercar and looked up the beach toward the "empty" villa. Was she still there? Even if she was, would it do any good?

Well, no sense worrying about it. Not when he'd find out in a few hours. Better give the last of the CDF team time to clear out first, though.

Then he'd make the try.

* * *

Belindi Kalenda had been all but despondent when she had seen the CDF team getting ready to move out. If they left, that meant Organa Solo was gone, and she wasn't coming back. And that meant all of Kalenda's watching, all her waiting, all her worrying, all of the risks she had taken had been for nothing. She had not done the Chief of State a particle of good. She could have counted the number of army shoes produced by the Corona Footwear Company, divided by two to estimate the size of the army, and done more good for the New Republic.

There was nothing left for her but to wait out the CDF, and make her own retreat once the coast was clear. She had no idea what she would do next. It was tough enough knowing all this had been for nothing.

But then. Then she had seen Han Solo come back. And, somehow, *she knew*. Maybe it was that niggling little nubbin of Force potential she thought she might have. Maybe it was something in the way he seemed to look toward the villa where she was hiding. Maybe it was lack of sleep and she was hallucinating. But she was suddenly possessed of the absolute conviction that *he knew* that she was here, and that he had come back in order to make contact.

Her heart pounded with excitement as she watched him get out of the hovercar, chat with the CDF guards, and shake a hand or two and say his thanks as he made his way into the house. Why else would he come back one more time? It had to be that he was here for her. It *had* to be.

Kalenda settled herself in for one final vigil, the one that would pay for all. She watched as the last of the CDF agents packed up their gear, got into their ground cars and hovercars, and headed off into the darkness. She watched, her eyes glued to the macrobinoculars, for five minutes, ten minutes, fifteen minutes, giving the CDF agents plenty of time to remember something they had left behind and come back for it.

At precisely the moment that she herself judged that enough time had passed, that the coast was clear and they weren't coming back, a dot of ruby-red light appeared in an upper-story window of Solo's villa. It flashed three times long, then there was a pause, three more long flashes, another pause, and another three longs.

Mon Calamari blink code, carried by a very old-fashioned laser beam. Something utterly simple, incredibly crude. Something that every midshipman learned, something they bashed into your head at the NRI Academy. And something the CDF forces, with all their high-tech com gear and snooper systems, would be unlikely to detect at all, even if they did come back at exactly the wrong moment. And more to the point, something they would be unlikely to be able to read.

BEET ME AT YR FRONT DR MUDNIGHZ, the sign read.

Okay, so he was a little out of practice. But the intent was clear.

And maybe her vigil had been worth it after all.

* * *

Kalenda saw him coming up the road, moving quietly, slowly, at just the pace of a fellow out for a late-evening stroll.

She saw him pause, just a moment, at the path leading to her door. He looked around, making one last check for whoever else might have stayed behind to watch out there, and then he walked straight up the path to her door. She pulled it open just as he reached the porch, and he came in without breaking stride. She shut the door behind him, and gestured for him to follow her into the basement of the villa. He nodded and followed without speaking. In the unlikely event that someone was still watching, it would be that much tougher for a sound snooper or a spy beam to penetrate into underground, and besides, they could risk a light once the door to the upstairs was shut. She ushered him down the darkened stairs, closed the door, and hit the wall switch.

A warm yellow light flooded the basement storeroom, and Kalenda gasped in surprise. She hadn't dared use an artificial light for longer than she liked to think.

"I brought you stuff," Han said without preamble, emptying a small carry bag out onto the old table that the owners of the house had abandoned to the cellar sometime in the years gone by. "Some cash, a change or two of clothes— Leia's jumpsuit—some fresh food and water rations in case you're sick of what you've got or you're running out. Glow rod, a pocket blaster—and a comlink."

Kalenda nodded, unable to speak at first. Someone talking to her. Someone here she could trust, who trusted her. Someone doing something for her. She felt a tear run down her face, but she forced herself to calmness, or at least to something close, and spoke. "Thank, thank you," she said. She grabbed for one of the ration packs and tore it open. Food had been getting tight, and anything, anything—even just another brand of shipboard survival rations—would taste better than another meal of the identical mealpacks she had been living on. She took a big bite and chewed vigorously.

"You've been watching the house the whole time," Han said, and it was not a question. "Just in case we were in trouble, just in case the locals tried anything. Hardly any sleep, nothing decent to eat."

She swallowed so she could answer. "Yes—yes," she said, and realized that her voice was creaky from lack of use. She hadn't had anyone to speak with for longer than she cared to think.

"I'm impressed," Han said. "I don't think I could have stuck it out."

"What—what do you want me to do?" Kalenda asked.

"Rest," Han said. "Find some nice quiet hotel or doss-house in Coronet City where you can pay cash and keep a low profile, and get some rest. Do whatever you like. Take in a show, go for a walk. Just keep that comlink on you, and answer when I call you. I want you watching over us still, but now we can call for help if we need it."

"Call for what kind of help?" Kalenda asked.

Han shook his head. "I won't know that until we know what kind of trouble we've got. But I've got a hunch that you might be a very handy hole card to have, just in case."

"What do you think is going to happen?" Kalenda asked.

"War," Han said, making the word sound like the obscenity it was. "Whose war against what, I don't know. Maybe just a little one, not much more than an oversized riot. But a war all the same. Too many people around here are spoiling for a fight. Too many people are playing rough."

Kalenda nodded her agreement. "I think you're right," she said. "But you be careful, more careful than you think you need to be. Someone has penetrated deep into the NRI somehow. I came in-system in a totally covert setup, top-grade cover story, the best the NRI could do—and they were waiting for me the second I came out of hyperspace. Shot me down. I barely got out of it alive. I don't know who it is, or how, but they *know* what we're doing."

Han Solo frowned. "That's worse than I thought," he said. "If they know all that, they know just how little we have in the way of troops and ships just now."

"What do you mean?" Kalenda asked.

"I mean," said Han, "that if I were a Corellian who wanted to break free of the Republic, and I had access to

NRI information, then I think I'd figure that *right now* was the perfect moment to make my move.''

Han leaned back against the wall of the basement and folded his arms. ''Which leaves the question—what is their move going to be?''

CHAPTER SIXTEEN

Hail and Farewell

Lando Calrissian stepped off the *Lady Luck* and had the very distinct impression that his luck was changing. There she was, Tendra Risant. She was a hundred meters or so away, just outside the safety barrier, waiting for him to come down off the ship, and waving vigorously. That *had* to mean something.

He paused a minute and breathed in the fresh, clean air of Sacorria. Not a bad place. Not a bad place at all, even if it was one of the Outlier worlds. The Outliers had a reputation for trouble, but Lando hadn't seen any such signs so far.

Lando turned to watch Luke come off the ship. "Feel nervous about this one?" he asked.

Luke laughed and shook his head no. "Not at all," he said. "I feel just fine."

"Good, good," Lando said as they walked along toward their hostess. "She *looks* just fine, too, I might add," he said as he cast an appraising eye over Tendra.

Tendra Risant was about thirty standard years, tall, strong, and healthy, and obviously well-off. Her complexion was rather fair, and her high cheekbones and slender face set her dark brown eyes off quite dramatically. She had a nice, if not spectacular, figure, though she was perhaps just a trifle heavier set than was fashionable. She was dressed in a pretty, sensible-looking high-collared blue dress of conservative cut, the hem modestly long without seeming prudish. Her hair was a somewhat nondescript brownish blond, and she wore it in a short, dignified cut. Everything about her seemed open, relaxed, friendly.

In short, she was not one little bit like the predatory sirens, the dangerous-looking sex goddesses with everything cut high and low, the women with smoldering, provocative eyes and pasts full of dark secrets, that were more to Lando's usual taste.

And just at the moment, that suited Lando just fine.

"Hello, Lando," she said as soon as they were close enough, and the warmth in her voice and the smile on her face made Lando feel as if he had known her all his life, that they were old friends being reunited rather than strangers who had never met before. Lando had to hand it to Luke. There were definite advantages to long chats via holocom.

"Hello, Tendra," he said as he crossed the safety barrier. She offered him her hand, and Lando, to his own astonishment, did not bend down to kiss it, or make any sort of sweeping, theatrical gesture at all. He took her hand in his, and shook it, the way regular people did it.

This is getting interesting, he told himself. "Tendra," he said, "I'd like you to meet my very good friend Luke Skywalker." Lando realized that he had not said a word about Luke being a great Jedi Master, or any of that. Tendra knew it, of course—but Lando already knew her well enough to know it wouldn't matter to her at all.

"Hello, Luke," she said. "Welcome to my world. I hope that we can make your stay very pleasant indeed."

"Thank you, Lady Tendra," said Luke, accepting the hand she offered.

"Please, just call me Tendra," she said. "Come along, both of you. There is a great deal we have to talk about."

*   *   *

Lando found himself spending most of the evening being astonished, mostly at himself. He had pursued many women over the years, of course, and his reputation for female conquest was far from exaggerated. But with Tendra, he found himself doing something it seemed to him he had never done before. He found himself *talking* to the woman he was interested in, having an actual conversation with her, about something other than how beautiful she was, or all the lovely things he was going to do for her, or any of the rest of the tired old nonsense.

The three of them had dinner at a public restaurant in a handsome old cobblestone square in the center of town, and they talked politics, of all things. Lando could not remember when he had enjoyed a conversation with a woman—or a conversation with anyone, for that matter—more. By the time the serving droids had cleared away the dessert dishes and poured the after-dinner liqueurs, they had worked through all the political scuttlebutt from Coruscant, and had turned to more local questions.

"Things are definitely getting tense here," Tendra said.

"We know," Luke said. "The local customs people almost didn't let us land."

Tendra nodded. "It was a struggle for me to get any clearance at all for you to land, and I wouldn't be surprised if your transit visa was canceled. Whatever is going on in the Corellian System is definitely stirring up trouble here."

"What *is* going on in the Corellian System?" Luke asked. "I've got family there right now."

"Not to mention that we're supposed to head there next," Lando said. "I'm supposed to meet some people at that trade meeting."

Tendra shook her head sadly. "No one really knows," she said. "There are rumors flying in all directions, and proclamations by this Drall or that Selonian or those humans that they are about to seize power, or chase the oppressors from office, or whatever. They seem to spend most of their time calling each other liars."

"What about here?" Lando asked. "This is part of the Corellian Sector, after all. Surely it's all got some direct effect on you."

Tendra shrugged. "Yes and no. We're ruled by the Triad,

so it's a little hard for the government to play the my-species-first game.''

"Triad?" Lando asked.

"Oh, sorry, of course, you're not from here. How would you know? The Triad is a council of three members—a human, a Selonian, and a Drall. They make all the major decisions about policy and so forth. It used to be the Triad wasn't much more than the mouthpiece for the Diktat back in Coronet, but Coronet hasn't taken much of an interest in us the last few years. We've had to learn to take care of ourselves, and these days the Triad pretty much runs to please itself.''

"And it would seem that it pleases them to clamp down," Lando said, glancing out the plate-glass front of the restaurant. A squad of rather angry-looking Selonians in police uniforms was coming across the square, straight toward the restaurant. Selonians were generally regarded as a rather handsome species, with their long, lithe bodies that were plainly the result of evolution from active, nimble, swimming mammals, and their sleek, short fur. But these Selonians did not seem to have anything much to recommend them. They were big, burly, thuggish-looking specimens, their fur a bit ratty, their bodies thickened by too much food and not enough exercise. They were plainly brawlers, not athletes. "I don't like any kind of cop," Lando said, "but especially ones that look that ticked off.''

"And I've got a feeling they're looking for us," Luke said.

Tendra shook her head. "I was afraid of this," she said. "Some late-working bureaucrat or other just decided the two of you are undesirable for some reason.''

"But how did they find us?" Lando asked.

Tendra raised an eyebrow. "Following people is one of the few growth industries on Sacorria," she said.

"Lando," Luke said. "We only have a few seconds. This is your call. You're the one with a stake in this place. How do you want to play it?''

Lando looked toward Tendra, and then out the window

at the cops. They were definitely headed straight for the restaurant. His first instinct was to raise a ruckus, create a diversion, try to bribe them—anything rather than play along. But it was suddenly quite clear to him that he would want to come back this way again, as soon as possible. He had best be as law-abiding as possible. "We cooperate," he said, most reluctantly. He turned back toward Tendra, and smiled. "I must admit it would be more in line with my image if we pulled out our blasters and shot up half the neighborhood in our heroic attempt to escape, but I have a feeling the restaurant management would object."

"I'm afraid they would," Tendra agreed. She flipped open a little compartment set into the arm of her chair, and punched in a quick sequence of commands. "There," she said, "I just bought you dinner. What do you say we meet our uniformed friends outside instead of causing a scene in here?"

"You clearly have no flair at all for the dramatic," Lando said as he stood up.

Tendra smiled broadly as she got out of her chair. "Try me some other time," she said. "I might change your mind."

Luke got up as well, and the three of them went out into the cool and pleasant night.

The squad of Selonian police came up to them immediately, and did not waste any time in pleasantries. "Calrissian? Skywalker?" the paunchiest of them demanded.

"That's right," Lando said. "What can we do for you officers?"

"You can get off our planet," the head cop said, smiling unpleasantly and displaying her full set of extremely sharp teeth. "Visas canceled. You've got six hours to get off the planet, and eighteen to get clear of the system. Got it?"

"Yes indeed," Lando said, struggling to keep his voice smooth and genteel. These were the sort of cops he hated the worst. "We get it. And we were just going, in any event. Good evening to you, officers," he said.

"You watch that wise-guy polite stuff," the head cop

snapped, and Lando reflected that it truly was a snap when a jaw that size slammed shut suddenly. "Just get back on your ship, pretty boy, and take your friend with you."

"We're going," Lando said, no longer able to keep the edge out of his voice. "We will meet the deadline."

"See that you do, pretty boy, or you'll be spending ten years banging rocks together in Dorthus Tal prison. We'll have cops watching to see that you go. Now beat it." The four cops turned their backs on the three humans, and stalked off, clearly disappointed that there hadn't been a fight.

Luke watched the police go, and then turned to Lando and Tendra. "Well," he said, "I hope I don't put our police friends to any inconvenience by going my own way, but it's my guess that they have enough operatives on duty to watch us even if we split up. You two aren't going to have much time together, and you don't need me tagging along. Lady Tendra—Tendra—it has been a pleasure to meet you, but I think I had best say my good-byes here and now."

Tendra smiled warmly. "Thank you, Luke. It is most generous of you."

"Thanks, Luke," Lando said. "I owe you one."

Luke grinned. "See you back at the ship," he said. "Good evening to you both." He gave a polite little bow to Tendra, and was on his way.

"Quite a guy," Tendra said.

"That's an understatement," Lando said. "Walk me back to my ship? Slowly?"

"Very slowly," she said. "It's been good to meet you, to see you in the flesh, Lando. I don't want to lose touch."

"No reason why we should," he said as they started to walk. "I can still call you over the holonet."

"For the moment, anyway," she said. "But there's a lot of talk going around about restricting access to the interstellar communications grid. Maybe even banning it altogether. To keep us from getting foreign, non-Corellian ideas, or something."

"*That's* bound to work real well," Lando said. "It's not that easy to keep ideas out. But it would mean we'd have no way to keep in touch, assuming I can't get another visa for a while. I'd assume the people here can't get leave to travel very easily."

Tendra shook her head. "It's almost impossible," she said.

"It doesn't seem fair," Lando said. "I just met you, and I don't want to lose touch with you."

"Ah, well, that's life," Tendra said, a sad little note of resignation in her voice. "I suppose you'll just have to move on to the next star system and try your luck there."

"What do you mean, try my luck?" Lando said.

"Your luck at finding a rich wife, of course," she said. "That's what you're here for, isn't it? Object, matrimony?"

"I must admit that I'm starting to rethink the whole idea of marrying for money," Lando said. "Things are a lot more complicated than I thought."

"Well, if it's any help, I'm not as rich as all that, anyway," Tendra said. "It's my father that has all the money."

"Well, I could be patient, I suppose."

"It's not even that simple," Tendra said. "I'm afraid there's a problem or two I haven't told you about."

"Uh-oh," Lando said. He stopped and turned toward her. "Here it comes."

"The first one isn't so bad. Women on this world aren't allowed to marry without their father's consent, no matter how old they are. It's a barbaric law, but there it is. If my father doesn't approve of you, I lose my inheritance."

"And that's not so bad?" Lando asked.

"I think Dad would like you, actually," she said. "I could talk him around." She smiled again. "*If* I decided *I* wanted you."

"Thanks, I think. But what's the bad part?" Lando asked.

"Well, you're shopping for a rich wife. You haven't tried to pretty that up, or treat me like a fool, so I suppose I'd better come clean. I've been shopping for an off-world husband for quite a while now. Someone who could get me off this planet, and away from the Triad and all the rules and regulations. Marrying an off-worlder was just about the only way a woman could get permission to leave. I advertised here and there. That's how I ended up in whatever datalist you were working from.''

Lando nodded. ''I sort of figured that,'' he said. But even so, he was glad to hear it from her, straight and clear. ''So what's the problem?''

''The problem is that xenophobia is getting worse around here. They aren't just kicking all the foreigners off the planet. The Triad announced yesterday morning that effective immediately, it is illegal to marry an off-worlder.''

''What?''

''I should have told you at once,'' Tendra said, ''but by the time I heard the news, your ship was already in its landing pattern.''

Lando did not know what to say, or even where to begin. It was not that either of them was madly in love with the other. Not yet. It was too soon for that. And after his adventures with the life-witch, Lando realized that he wanted to be good and sure he knew his intended bride very well before he did anything irrevocable. No, he told himself again, it was not love—not yet. It might be, given half a chance, given time.

And Lando found that he didn't *want* to try the next star system over and see what rich women were on offer. No. He had found someone here. Now. Tonight. Someone who might, just might, be *right* for him. She was rich, yes, and that didn't hurt. He was even honest enough with himself to wonder what he would be thinking if she'd just told him she was poor. But rich and poor wasn't all of it, any more than his being from off-planet was all of it for her. They could *talk* to each other. They understood each other, in some way that was quite new to Lando. She was someone with whom he would always have to be honest. He knew that, instinctively. That wasn't love, of course—but it was something he had never felt before, and he was not going to let it dry up and blow away just because some fat-headed bureaucrat had decided to invent some new rules.

Suddenly Lando had an idea. "Listen," he said. "I just thought of something. It might be a way around it if they *do* shut down the holocom net. A clumsy way, an awkward way—but a way."

"What?" she asked.

"It's an old gag I learned back in my smuggling days."

"Smuggling?" she asked.

"That's *another* story, for later," he said. "But there's a very old communications system, that doesn't use hyperspace at all. It uses modulation of low-frequency electromagnetic radiation, in the radio band of the spectrum. Radionics, they call it. It's constrained by the speed of light, and it's limited in range, too, unless you beam it or use a lot of power. But no one uses it, so cops and border patrols never bother to listen for it. I have a matched set of senders and receivers tucked away in the hold of the *Lady Luck*."

"But at light speed, if you were in another star system, it would take years for a message to get to you that way—if you got it at all."

"So who says I'm going to be in another star system?" Lando said with a smile. "I have to go to the trade summit. I've promised some people. But then I'll come back here to this system, real quietly and sneakily, the way only an old smuggler would know how to do." He hesitated for a moment, hoping for inspiration. And he spotted his answer, up in the sky. "And I'll park myself *there*," he said, pointing up at a fat crescent hanging high in the sky.

"On our moon?" Tendra asked. "On Sarcophagus? It's nothing but one big burial ground. No one ever goes there, except to inter their relatives."

"Then no one will ever look for me there. But you get your radio out, and point the antenna at Sarcophagus, and I'll be sitting there, waiting to get the message. We'll have time to work out some way to see each other again. Some way for me to slip back down to the planet, or something."

"It sounds crazy," Tendra said, "but I can't see anything wrong with the idea."

"Oh, I can," Lando said. "There's plenty of things that

could go wrong. But it would be even wronger if I let you get away without trying to get to know you.''

Tendra laughed, and smiled, and threw her arms around him.

And for once, Lando Calrissian meant every word of his elaborate compliment from the bottom of his heart.

CHAPTER SEVENTEEN

News Travels Slowly

What if they gave a trade summit," Han muttered, "and nobody came?" That wasn't *exactly* fair, but he had seen longer reception lines. He was in his best formal clothes, standing in the lineup with Leia and Governor-General Micamberlecto and several other local big shots. So far, they hadn't had all that many hands to shake. The unsettled situation had clearly frightened off a lot of would-be delegates to the talks. And Han was willing to bet that some of the alleged delegates were really NRI agents. The trade delegations were just too good a cover to pass up.

"Quiet, Han," Leia said, keeping the smile on her face looking warm and sincere as she chided her husband under her breath. Han had to admit she looked stunning in the flowing, off-the-shoulder royal-blue gown she had chosen. It set off her coloring and her eyes and hair beautifully. "All of these people took big chances coming here for this meeting," she went on, still smiling. "This summit is important to them—and to your planet, in case you forgot. So behave yourself and make everyone feel at home."

"Home, right," Han said. "As if their home was a cocktail party. Now, there's *my* idea of endless torture. Hello, how are you?" he said to the next delegate, interrupting himself to greet a rather regal-looking Selonian female who towered over him by six or seven centimeters.

"I am fine, Captain Solo. It is a pleasure to meet you."

271

"And a pleasure to meet you, too," Han said. He waited until the Selonian was out of earshot and added, "Whoever you are. Head over to the bar, why don't you, the booze is free. Yup, there she goes. Hello there," he said to the goggle-eyed Mon Calamari who had materialized in front of him, and accepted the proffered flipper hand. "Welcome to our little party." The Mon Calamari nodded, gurgled something in a dialect that Han could not understand, and gave him an enthusiastic slap on the back that nearly bowled him over. By the time he had recovered, the Mon Calamari was gone. "Another great moment in the annals of communication," Han said. "Who *are* these people?"

"Traders," Leia said, "as you know full well. Hello, so glad you could come," she said to the next person in line.

"It is a deep honor to meet you both," said the Drall, bowing so low he nearly toppled over. Apparently a few delegates hadn't waited to pass through the reception line before heading for the bar.

"Don't make it too deep," Han said after he helped the Drall to recover his balance and sent him on his way. "I just can't keep this smile pasted on my face much longer."

"Well, how about being completely astonished instead?" Leia asked. "Could you handle that?"

"I suppose," Han said.

"Then look to see who's fourth in line at the moment."

Han looked up, and was sufficiently amazed that he failed to make any snide comments for the next three delegates. In fact, he was not aware of talking to them at all. Mara. Mara Jade. Ex–Emperor's Hand. Ex-smuggler. The woman who had sworn to kill Luke, and then had a change of heart. There she was, in a long black gown that seemed to make her seem even taller, even more slender—and even more threatening. The years had been good to her. She had lost none of her poise, none of her beauty—and she looked as dangerous as ever. He and his family had been on better terms with her in recent times, but there was something in her demeanor tonight that set off alarm bells in his head. It would be best to tread carefully around her.

"Good evening, Captain Jade," Leia said to her, offering her hand.

Mara accepted it, nodding slightly. "Good evening to you, Madame Chief of State. And to you, Captain Solo. I have a message for you." Mara directed her attention to Leia. "For you both, and for the Governor-General."

"A message?" Leia asked.

"A message cube, to be more exact," she said. "I couldn't open it—and I don't mind admitting that I tried. I would suggest that you and the Governor-General find a nice, safe room where we can all meet at once."

Leia thought quickly. "My apartments," she said. "On the fifteenth floor. They're swept for bugs and listening devices every day. Meet us there in twenty minutes. Han, give her a thumb pass for the turbolift."

"Huh? Oh yeah, right," Han said. The turbolift was running in secure mode. You had to put a passcard in a slot and hold your thumb over a print reader before it would let you in. You could provide guests with access by giving them a passcard that scanned their thumbprint and keyed it to your card. Leia would have carried a few of her own, but there weren't any pockets in her long blue gown. He pulled a guest's thumb pass, a small white rectangle of plastic, out of his pocket. He pressed down on one of the two scan areas. The second scan area lit up. "Press your right thumb down there," he said to Mara, and she did so. The glow faded from the second scan area. Han gave her the pass. "This will get you in and out of the lift, and into our apartments," he said. "Wait for us there. We'll be up as soon as the reception line is over."

Mara Jade took the passcard and smiled coldly at Han. "I'll be there," she said as she walked away, "and don't worry, I won't steal the silver."

"Maybe not," Han muttered to Leia, "but remind me to count the spoons later just the same."

*   *   *

The three children were, in theory, fast asleep. In practice, of course, the fact that all the grown-ups were downstairs meant that it was their big chance to stay up late. However, bitter experience had taught them it was safest to stay in their bedroom, with the door shut and lights low. Grown-ups had a nasty habit of coming back unexpectedly.

Even so, none of them were quite prepared to hear the click of the lock or the sound of the door opening. They instantly abandoned their board game and all three of them dove under the covers. It was only after he was in bed, eyes shut, and pretending to be asleep as hard as he could, that Jacen realized they had left a light on. One look at that, and Mom and Dad would know at once they had been up after bedtime. He toyed with the idea of using his ability in the Force, but he knew that his fine control was not that good. He would be just as likely to smash the lamp to bits as hit the switch properly. He decided to risk it. He slipped out of bed, crossed the room to the lamp, and flicked it off. He was just about to dive back to his bed when he noticed something. He listened carefully, to make sure he hadn't made a mistake, then tiptoed over to Jaina's bed.

"Psst, Jaina," he said.

"Quiet!" she hissed. "Do you want to get us caught?"

"Listen!" he said. "That's not Mom and Dad. It's just one person walking around, and that's not Mom's footsteps or Dad's. There's someone in the apartment."

Jaina sat bolt upright in bed and listened for herself. "You're right," she said. "Come on." And with that, she was out of bed and over to the door. Jacen wanted to ask her what she thought she was doing, or what she expected to be able to do against a burglar that could get past all the security in Corona House, but it was too late. He knew he would have to follow after her. Otherwise, he would have to spend the rest of his life being told what a coward he was. He went after his sister, out into the upstairs hallway, and was not in the least surprised to see Anakin hopping out of bed and following after *him*.

The family had been put in a two-level apartment, with the bedrooms upstairs and the living room and dining room down below.

The living-room ceiling went as high as the ceiling of the upper floor, like someone had taken all the rooms that should have been over the living room and turned them into extra ceiling space. The stairs leading from the lower floor came up along the west wall of the high-ceilinged living room, and ended in a landing that ran the width of the north wall. A railing ran along the edge of the landing to keep people from falling off into the living room below. An entryway at the end of the landing opposite the stairs led off into a narrow hallway, where the doors to the bedrooms were. It had taken the children about eighteen seconds after moving into the apartment to realize just how good a place for spying the entryway to the landing was. You could stay in the shadows there, and see practically everything that went on in the living room.

The three children huddled there in the shadows, and looked down into the living room. And what they saw did not look much like a burglary-in-progress. For one thing, burglars rarely turned the lights on.

A tall, pretty lady with red-gold hair, wearing a long black dress, was pacing back and forth. She had a worried expression on her face, and she kept glancing at the door. It was obvious that she was waiting for someone. And that someone had to be Mom and Dad.

Jacen thought for a moment, then plucked on Jaina's sleeve, and gestured for her and Anakin to follow him back to the bedroom. As soon as they were all back inside, he swung the door shut, but did not let it close all the way, for fear of making a noise. "Listen," he said in as low a whisper as he could manage. "Something is going on. It has to be. That lady is there to talk to Mom and Dad. As soon as they come back, the first thing they're going to do is check on us to make sure we're asleep so it's safe to talk.''

"I recognize that lady,'' Jaina said. "It's Mara Jade.''

Jacen's eyes widened. She was right. How could he have missed that?

But Jaina was still talking. "We have to be in bed, and doing the best job we ever have of pretending to be asleep, when Mom and Dad come back. *After* they check on us, we can sneak back out to the landing.''

Anakin and Jacen nodded, and all of them hurried back to their beds and pulled the covers over themselves.

This was going to be interesting.

*   *   *

Leia ushered Han and Micamberlecto into the apartment, and then followed them in, closing the door behind her. "I'll just be a moment,'' she said. "I want to check on the children.'' She crossed to the stairs and hurried up to the children's room. She swung open the door and looked in on three softly breathing small bodies. Anakin's arm had slumped out again. She knelt by his bed, tucked his arm back, and gave him a kiss on the forehead. He muttered something and rolled over on his side. Leia glanced at the twins. Clearly they were fine. Satisfied, she turned and went out of the room, closing the door behind her.

Leia returned downstairs. "All asleep,'' she announced. "Now then, Mara, what is the message?''

Mara was carrying a small satchel, and she opened it up. She looked around the room and nodded toward the far end of it. "Over there,'' she said. "On the couches.''

The room had been designed for holding small, informal meetings. In the center of the living room were three couches, formed in a U-shape, all facing a low table in the center. The open end of the U-shape faced the south wall, so that anyone sitting on the center couch would have his or her back to the upstairs landing—and anyone standing at the south end of the room would be clearly visible to as many people as you could crowd into the place. There was a flat panel display on the south wall. At the moment it was showing a reproduction of some painting of a stirring moment in Corellian history, but it could be set to display more or less any two- or three-dimensional image.

Han, Leia, and the Governor-General found places on the couches, and Mara pulled the message cube out of her handbag and set it on the low table. She stood over the open end of the U-shape, and gestured to the other three with a sweep of her hand. "There it is," she said.

None of the others made a move to touch it. All of them knew it might have been set to activate at the touch of their fingerprints, or body chemistry, or whatever. All three of them leaned in and examined it carefully.

"Any markings on the bottom of it?" Han asked.

"Believe me," Mara said, "I've looked at that thing up, down, and sideways. Nothing on the bottom. The only markings are the ones you see on the top."

"Which look suspiciously like an Imperial code I used to crack now and again for very profitable reasons," said Han. " 'To be opened in the presence of Leia Organa Solo,' " he read, " 'self-styled Chief of State of the so-called New Republic, Han Solo, and the de facto Governor-General of the Corellian Sector. Code Rogue Angel Seven.' Well, they're not going to get high marks for politeness, that's for sure. What's the Rogue Angel Seven business?"

"Oh, nothing very much," Leia said. "Just the key phrase for my private diplomatic cipher. Someone wants us to know they can read my mail."

Micamberlecto let out a low whistle, a sound that somehow seemed wholly incongruous coming from him. He unfolded his long, multijointed legs and leaned in closer to the cube to get a better look. "Someone knows, someone knows very much about us," he said.

"The thing I don't understand," said Mara, "is why

they used me for the courier, whoever they are. They'd have to know that my relations with you people haven't always been of the warmest.''

"I can answer that," Leia said. "You were second choice. Luke. Luke was intended to be the courier for this message." She pointed at the cube, still being careful not to touch it, and pointed at the lettering peeking out from under the label. "I don't read it myself, but that looks like the written form of Jawa.''

"Jawa?" Mara asked.

"The language of a race from Luke's homeworld, Tatooine. He could read it pretty easily, but most other people couldn't make anything of it without a great deal of effort—the same way you could read the Imperial code. I'll bet that's the same message as the code, intended for Luke's eyes.''

"So why didn't Luke carry it?"

Leia shrugged. "I don't know," she said.

"I do," Han said. "Remember he was going to go meet with Lando about some business deal just before we left. Lando told me that he was planning to go off on a trip before he came to the trade summit here. My guess is that Luke decided to go along for the ride, maybe on the spur of the moment.''

"And so he wasn't there to get the message cube," Mara said. "So when they couldn't find him, they threw together a backup plan and came looking for me. It makes sense.''

"Well, now that we all feel better about that, how about reading the message?" Han suggested.

"Right," said Leia. "Han, start the sight-and-sound, will you? I want to have a recording of this, in case this is one of those one-playback-only units.''

Han flipped open a small panel on the corner of the table and pressed in a button. "All set," he said.

"Okay, then," Leia said. "Here goes." She reached out gingerly with one hand and picked up the cube. It immediately let out a low beeping noise, and there was a loud click. The lid of the cube popped up a millimeter or two.

"Cued to my fingerprints, all right," Leia said. She opened the lid and looked inside. "Well, that's a bit anticlimactic. I thought there was going to be a holographic image popping out of the top. But there's nothing but a data chip." She took the small black chip out of the cube. "Han, are the player controls there, too?"

"Yeah," he said, and took the chip from her. He examined it. "Well, it's not a one-shot, anyway. We can play it as often as we like." He dropped it into the slot of the player set into the tabletop. The display screen suddenly stopped being a heroic Corellian scene and went blank. Mara stepped out of the way.

"Everybody ready?" There was a murmur of assent, and Han pressed the play button.

Without any preamble, a screenful of numbers appeared, and stayed on the screen. A male human voice began to speak in Corellian-accented Basic. "This will be your only notification prior to events," the voice said. "Inform no one of this message and await instructions so as to avoid the need for further action. We will be monitoring all communications. Do not attempt to call for help. Any violation of instructions will result in an acceleration of the schedule."

The numbers stayed on the screen, but the voice said nothing more. Han frowned. "That voice almost sounded like *me*," he said. "Why would they want to simulate my voice?"

"If they did want to, they didn't do a very good job," Mara said. "It's close to your voice, but it's not you exactly."

"What are those numbers?" Leia asked, looking up at the screen. "Are they another code? What are they supposed to tell us?"

"Those on the right are static stellar coordinates," Han said. "And with three extra decimal places. The Imperial Navy used to do that, but the only people who have them that accurate is the New Republic Navy. Whoever wrote this got their data from the navy's secret data sets. Must have sliced a computer, or done some good old-fashioned bribery, or else the opposition has friends in high places. And that's recent data, too.'' The stars were in constant motion as they orbited the core of the galaxy. It was therefore necessary to note not only where an object in space was, but when it had been there.

Han looked harder at the numbers. ''If I've got this right,'' he said, ''those are all points in a rough sphere around the Corellia star system—and the last set of coordinates is for the star Corell itself. I recognize it from setting our navicomputer on the way in. At a guess, the other coordinate sets are all star positions, too.''

''The numbers on the left are time notations in astronomical format,'' Mara said. ''Not astrogational notation, but the time format astronomers use. Those are extremely accurate time notations as well. The first one is about sixteen standard days ago. The others are all in the future.''

''In other words,'' Han said, ''something is going to happen at these places at these times, unless we do whatever the guy who sounds like me says in his next message.''

''Burning skies,'' said Micamberlecto as he stood up to his full height. ''Burning, burning skies. Three days ago a probot droid came out of the sky and set off a CDF beacon signal. The CDF picked it up, and found a message for me. An image of a star explosion, with space-and-time coordinates. Nothing else. The time data was sixteen days ago.''

Han shrugged. ''So someone got imagery of a star blowing up. So what? Mara—when did you get this message?''

''Fourteen days ago,'' she said. ''*After* the star blew up.''

''But *Luke* was supposed to get the message,'' Leia said. ''Allowing for time for them to discover he wasn't there, and to find Mara, and get the cube to her, and it would have gotten to him before the star exploded.''

''Unless it's a big-time con,'' Han said. ''The sort of thing Lando might have done in the old days. Suppose somebody spotted the explosion, faked up the message cube to *look* like it was intended for Luke, and just got there late? They could make it look like they had caused it, if they were really sharp.''

''But my scientists tell me the star in the image was of a type that could not possibly undergo a supernova explosion,'' Micamberlecto said. ''They were quite at a loss to explain how it could be. They wanted to dispatch a ship at once to get a look at it. I said we could not afford the mission—''

''But you'd better afford it now,'' Mara said. ''Solo's right, it could be an extremely clever con job—or it could be that someone is better at blowing up stars than sending messages. I don't think you can afford to assume it's a trick.''

''No, we can't,'' Han agreed. He was punching the stellar coordinates into a data pad. ''The first star on that list is in an uninhabited system. All the rest of them have inhabited planets. It looks like they are listed in order of population. The second star just has a small outpost, but the next one on the list—'' Han checked his numbers and shook his head. ''One inhabited planet, population eight million at the last census. And, like I said, the last star on the list is Corell.''

'' 'Do what we say,' '' Leia half whispered. '' 'Do what we say or we'll kill everybody.' ''

At the back of the room, at the top of the stairs, inside the shadows of the entryway, three small scared children listened in horror.

*   *   *

In a secret bunker deep under the city of Coronet, the Hidden Leader of the Human League read over the latest reports with a stern and hard-edged calm. Perhaps his underlings would have expected him to show some sign of jubilation that the moment had finally come, that the last piece of the puzzle was finally in place. But that was why he was the Leader, and they were underlings. Let them show their every reaction and emotion. The Hidden Leader would hide his emotions, as well as his identity.

But for all of that, the time had come. All was in readiness. Everything he had worked for, schemed for, plotted for, was in place. It was time.

The Hidden Leader dropped the report on his desk and leaned back in his chair.

"Begin it," he said.

CHAPTER EIGHTEEN

Uprising

H an! Han! Wake up and come to the window." Leia was shaking him hard.

Han lurched up into a seated position and stumbled out of bed. "What? What is it?" He glanced at the wall clock and confirmed his suspicion that he hadn't gotten much sleep. It had been a very late night indeed, trying to hash out the implications of the threat message, trying to come up with some answer, some plan of action. And none of it had come to anything.

"Look out the window!" Leia said again. "There, to the south of us."

Han went to the window and looked out—and swore to himself. "Devils in space," he said. "It's started. It's started." A thick plume of black smoke was rising up out of the city, about three kilometers away. He pulled open the window and heard, far off but distinct, the sounds of sirens, of shouts, of blasters being fired.

"*What's* started?" Leia asked.

"That's the Selonian Enclave on fire down there," Han said, his voice sad, bitter, tired. "Something has touched it off—and now it will spread from there."

There was a loud, far-off thud, and a second or two later a slight tremor that sent just the tiniest of shakes through the window. "Wide-area concussion grenade," Han said. "About three kilometers away. Probably right in the middle of all that." Even as they watched, another plume of smoke began climbing lazily into the air, followed by another, and another. "This isn't a coincidence," he said. "It can't be. There are people watching. Once they knew Mara had gotten the message to us, they touched this off. Has to be."

"Come on," Leia said. "We have to find the Governor-General."

"What about the kids?" Han asked.

"Chewbacca's with them, and so are Ebrihim and Q9. They're all right. Come on."

*   *   *

Micamberlecto was in his office, where they had watched the torchlight parade. By the time they got there, fire was once again visible from the window, but this time it was the Selonian Enclave burning. Back then the office had been calm, quiet, dark. Now it was the brightly lit center of a madhouse, of aides rushing in and out, assistants shouting into phones, two men in navy uniforms setting up a large-scale wall map of the city. And, not to Han's surprise, several of last night's supposed trade delegates were in the thick of it, helping to work the com system. Well, no point in the NRI agents sticking to their cover stories now.

"It's everywhere, everywhere," the Governor-General said to Han and Leia as they came in. "Not just here in Coronet, but all over the planet. The other planets, other planets, too."

"Where and when did it start?" Han asked.

"It seems as if the first incident was in Bela Vistal's Selonian neighborhood about eight hours ago. Somebody threw a punch, and that began it, began it. But since then, everywhere. Drall attacking Selonians, both attacking humans, and humans attacking, humans attacking everywhere. Here, on Drall and Selonia, and we're getting the first reports of trouble on Tralus and Talus."

"You're right, Han," Leia said. "The timing is too

tight, too perfect. Someone had this all set to go, and sent the go code the minute we met with Mara.''

"Yes, yes," said Micamberlecto. "That is my conclusion also."

"What about the CDF?" Han asked. Yesterday he had decided that he trusted them. But today nothing was for sure.

"Almost all the ground forces are still with us, still with us, loyal to the Republic. But I have not been able to contact anyone in authority in the spaceside, spaceside service."

"And it was the spaceside CDF that set up that phony attack on us," Han said. "Forget them as an asset, Governor. They aren't yours anymore. They never were yours."

A com panel lit on the Governor's desk, and Micamberlecto pressed the answer button. "This is the Governor," he said.

"Sir, this is Captain Boultan, CDF groundside." *Groundside*, Han thought. *The loyalist faction*. It would seem the CDF had already found names for the two sides. "My unit was attempting to get to the CDF barracks in the navy yard to collect our riot equipment. The spaceside service has secured the base. I'm pretty sure that I saw people in New Republic uniforms assisting them."

"The *navy?*" Leia asked. "The *navy* has gone over?"

"No," Han said. "Just the navy yard has, though that's bad enough. Don't forget that used to be the Imperial Navy Yard. Lots of ex–Imperial military enlisted in the Republic Navy are here in Corellia. Now we know why." Han turned toward the Governor-General. "What about the civilian spaceport?" he asked.

Micamberlecto shook his head. "I don't know," he said. "It's hard to know anything. Too little staff. They are all here, working, and all loyal and trusted, but half the com systems are down. We are helpless, helpless to do more than watch."

Han looked at the Governor-General, and knew Micamberlecto was right.

There was nothing he could do but go to the window and watch his planet burn.

*   *   *

Within a few hours, enough information had come in so that it was at least possible to get a clearer picture of the confused situation. It was soon apparent that the human rebels, the Human League, had indeed been waiting for the signal to start a fight. However, their Drall and Selonian enemies had been ready and waiting for them, much to the apparent surprise of the Leaguers.

In the city of Coronet, it looked as if the Selonian and Drallan Enclaves had managed to throw back the League for the moment, but only just. There was no clear information from Bela Vistal or any of the other large cities on Corellia.

There were only scattered reports of fighting on Drall and Selonia as yet, but no hard information.

The situation on the Double Worlds was more complicated. On Talus, a mixed force of Drall and humans seemed to be fighting off a savage Selonian attack, if the broadcasts were to be trusted. A human/Drall coalition was holding Centerpoint Station. But on Tralus, the Selonians and Drall were making common cause against the humans.

The short form was that all three sides—human, Selonian, and Drall—were busily engaged in grabbing as much territory as possible, along with whatever ships and equipment they could.

It was chaos.

*   *   *

Chewbacca roared his frustration and punched another hole in the wall. He picked up a wall lamp and threw it through the hole, and it stuck there, half in and half out of the wall.

"It's okay, Chewbacca," Jaina said. "You don't have to be scared."

Chewbacca bared his teeth and stomped to the other side of the room.

"I don't think he's *scared*, Jaina," Jacen said. "You want to fight, don't you, Chewie?"

The Wookiee nodded vigorously, then threw his hands in the air and roared again.

"I don't know against who, either," Jacen said. "Sure looks like everyone is fighting everyone else out there." Privately, he felt pretty sure that half of Chewbacca's frustration was a direct result of having to play baby-sitter to a bunch of dumb kids, but there didn't seem to be any diplomatic way to say that.

"Do you understand who's fighting who, Ebrihim?" Jaina asked their tutor. Ebrihim and Q9 were both standing at the window, as they had been most of the morning, watching the disaster unfold.

Ebrihim shook his head sadly. "I understand, and I do not understand. It is species against species, but I believe— no, I *know*—that the vast majority of all three species would rather live in peace. It is rabble-rousers, fools who only know how to blame others for their own failures, that have started this fighting. But I fear it can only spread. A human will kill a Selonian, and a Selonian will kill a human in revenge—and kill a Drall he dislikes while he is at it. The Drall will fight back against both, or one or the other. People will get drawn in, against their will, by ties of blood."

"I'm scared," Anakin announced from his seat facing the window.

Jaina came over and sat next to him on the couch. "It's all right," she said, repeating what she had said to Chewbacca. "You don't have to be scared." Anakin threw his arms around his big sister and she rocked him back and forth. Apparently the formula worked better on little brothers than Wookiees.

It was at that moment that the first explosion rocked Corona House. The sound was deafening, so loud that it almost did not seem to be sound at all, and over so suddenly that it was as if they never heard it at all. The whole building shook, and the window blew out. Q9, moving with incredible speed, knocked his master out of the way of the flying glass, and took most of the force of the blast himself. Anakin wailed in terror, and buried his head in Jaina's shoulder.

Jacen was knocked flat by the first blast, and had barely gotten to his feet when—

Blam!

Another explosion, sharper and closer, shook the building. He was about to get to his feet again when a huge, furry arm scooped him up. Jacen looked up to see that Chewbacca already had his brother and sister in his other arm.

The Wookiee roared at Jacen, loud and fast, but he at least managed to get the sense of it.

"Ebrihim!" he shouted across the wind that was suddenly blowing through the room. "Chewbacca's taking us to the *Millennium Falcon* on the roof. Follow if you can."

But Ebrihim had been knocked about by the second blast, and was still too dazed to respond. Q9 extruded a pair of his carry arms, scooped up his master, and levitated on his repulsors. "Lead the way!" he shouted.

Boom! Another explosion, farther off this time, shuddered through the building. Chewie turned and headed for the door, already wrenched halfway out of its frame. He kicked it the rest of the way down and rushed out into the hallway, Q9 right behind him.

The turbolift had been designed to survive a major earthquake and still keep working. Chewbacca slapped at the call button, and the doors of the turbolift car slid open. He half dropped, half threw the children into it, and stood aside as Q9 hustled in.

The door slid shut—and Chewbacca suddenly roared in frustration again and started pounding on it. The controls were dead.

"It's okay, Chewbacca," Jacen said. "I've got my thumbprint card." He pulled it from his pocket, put it in the slot, and pressed his thumb down on the verification plate. The controls came to life, and Jacen punched the *roof* button. The turbolift car started moving up.

* * *

The first explosion had been at ground level, and had shaken the lower floors of Corona House with greater violence. The second had been some sort of rocket fired into the seventh or eighth floor. No one seemed quite sure where the third had hit. Not a piece of furniture was still standing upright in Micamberlecto's sixth-floor office. All the lights and the wired com lines were dead, but the portable com links were still operational. There had been two or three bad injuries from broken glass, but no fatalities, for a miracle.

"Chewie! Chewie! This is Han! Come in!" Han had been frantically trying to raise Chewbacca on his comlink since the moment of the first blast. His children. His children were up there. If anything had happened to them . . . "Chewie! Chewie! Come in, please!"

"Dad! It's me, Jacen. Dad, are you and Mom okay?"

"Jacen! Yes, yes, we're fine. Where are you?" Relief washed over Han, and vanished just as suddenly. They were still alive, but the danger wasn't going away.

"We're on the roof, headed for the *Falcon*. Chewie's too busy to talk."

"I'll bet he is. Did he get all of you out?"

"Yes! He got all three of us kids up here, and Ebrihim and Q9, too. But Chewie says we have to leave without you!"

"He's right, son," Han said. "He's right. Your mother and I have to stay here." No sense telling him that they had to stay here because the lower turbolift shaft had almost certainly been blown to bits along with the stairwell. Han was fairly certain that the explosions had been touched off in order to bottle up the Governor-General in his office. "We'll meet up with you when we can. Right now you have to do what Chewie says, and take care of your sister and brother."

"But, Dad—"

"No time for that now," Han said. "Get in that ship and do what Chewie says. Tell your brother and sister that your mother and I love you very much. Now go. *Go.*"

"O-okay," said the tiny voice coming from the comlink. "We'll do our best. Good—good-bye, Dad."

"Good-bye, son," Han said, wondering just how long a good-bye it might be. There were at least fair odds that it would be forever. He stuffed the comlink in his pocket and went over to where Leia was tending to the Governor-General. It looked as if Micamberlecto was only shaken up, not seriously injured. Not even a broken bone, which was a bit of a miracle considering how long his arm and leg bones were.

"Chewie has the kids," Han said. "They've reached the *Falcon* and should be able to lift off any second now. They're all okay."

"Thank the stars for that," Leia said. "I reached out to them with the Force, and I could feel they were scared but all right, but they were so terrified I couldn't get anything more. Good. Good."

"Well, it's the only thing that is good around here," Han said.

*   *   *

Chewbacca powered up the *Millennium Falcon*'s repulsor engines and slammed them over to maximum from a standard start. He did not want to let anyone get a chance to draw a bead on the ship. The *Falcon* shot straight up in the air, and Chewie cut in the main sublight engines the moment he was clear, not even thinking about a course. The *Falcon* leaped forward and up into the sky, toward space and the safety of the stars. Chewie had no course, and no navigational fixes, but he also had no options. He had to get out of there and far away as soon as possible. Once they were in space, he could worry about where they were going.

Assuming, of course, that the *Falcon* held together that long.

*   *   *

Two hours after the double explosions, the Governor-General's office was back in some sort of order. There didn't seem to be any hope of reaching the upper floors for the time being, but the lower-level explosion had not been as effective at cutting off escape—if that indeed had been its purpose. It might just have been someone raising a rather vigorous objection to New Republic policy. In any event, there seemed to be two or three places where it would be possible to drop to the ground from what was left of the second or third floor.

Of course, it seemed more than a little likely that there were snipers out there. But Han didn't see much chance of living through all this anyway. At this point, everyone still in Corona House was, to all intents and purposes, a political prisoner, and probably a hostage as well. And the people running this show didn't seem like the types who would need much excuse to shoot hostages. No, better to go out his own way. He had a job to do, and he would do it as soon as it was nightfall.

He found a private corner of the office, pulled out his comlink again, and set it to a new frequency. He had to assume that someone out there was listening in—but on the other hand, either the comlink's scramblers were working, or they weren't. It was not a time for playing it safe. If he started talking in vague, cryptic phrases that could easily produce fatal confusion.

"Solo to Kalenda. Come in. Come in. Do you read." No answer. He tried again. "Solo to Kalenda. Come in. Come in. Do you read?"

"This is Kalenda to Solo," said the voice over the comlink's tiny speaker. "I was starting to worry."

"Well, don't stop yet," Han said. "Things are not going

to get better. I have a job for you, and it needs doing. Do you think you could get to the spaceport and steal a ship? One with a hyperdrive?''

"Possibly," Kalenda said. "It won't be easy."

"Then it's time to do something hard. Besides, I should be able to give you some help. I am going to try and get out of here an hour after sunset. Do you have a groundcar or a hovercar at this point?"

"Groundcar, yes."

"Good," he said. "Then meet me in three hours at the corner of Starliner and Volbick." He did not bother to ask her if she knew where that was. If she was the sort of person who couldn't manage to find it on her own, they were all dead anyway. "I have a package—a very small package— for you. You are to deliver it directly and personally either to Mon Mothma, Admiral Ackbar, or Luke Skywalker."

"You sure don't ask for much," she said.

"I try to avoid thinking small," Han said. "See you in three hours."

*   *   *

Chewbacca roared his anger as the two PPBs came back for another pass. The patrol boats had picked him up just after he cleared the atmosphere, and they had been maintaining the pursuit ever since.

Ordinarily, a pair of PPBs would be no match for the *Millennium Falcon*, but Chewie was flying with a droid, a Drall, and three children for a crew. The best he could hope for was that they would all stay strapped in. None of them could be any help in a dogfight. With no one on board capable of handling the quad-laser turrets, the ship was without half of its firepower. He had to fly the ship and fight, all on his own.

He swung the nose of the *Millennium Falcon* about and made ready for another pass. He fired the forward lasers, and took out one of the PPBs, but the second shot passed over the starboard wing, laying down intense fire from close range.

A lucky shot managed to get in through the shields, and the *Falcon* shuddered with the force of the hit. Chewbacca brought the ship around one more time and pumped fired into the PPB. He caught it on the last burst, and its shielding gave out. It flared over and exploded in spectacular fashion. That was good as far as it went, but Chewbacca didn't even need to check the systems board to know that the one lucky shot had blown out part of the hyperdrive.

They were stuck in the Corellian System.

*   *   *

It was an hour short of sunset at Corona House when the next, and biggest, surprise came. The holoscreen and flat-view screens tuned to the standard broadcast channels had been showing nothing but static since dawn. Suddenly the static cleared, and an emblem Han had seen before appeared on the screen, to the sound of trumpets blaring and drums pounding a martial beat.

The emblem of a grinning, stylized human skull with a knife in its teeth, and the words HUMAN LEAGUE underneath. It was suddenly very plain indeed who had the upper hand, at least in the city of Coronet.

The trumpets kept up their fanfare for a few minutes, summoning everyone to come and see, come and hear. Han, Leia, the Governor-General, and his staff gathered around the largest holovid that was still functioning, and waited to see what would happen next.

It was not what any of them expected.

The skull emblem faded out, and a human male face took its place. A face that brought gasps from half the people in the room, and had all of them turning and looking at Han.

It was Han's face.

Han with black-brown hair that was shot through with

gray, Han a few kilos heavier, Han with a beard, Han with a stern expression that did not belong on his face. And yet, even with all the differences between Han and the man in the holovid, the resemblance was close enough to be eerie. Han stared at the screen, and felt his heart pounding hard, his hands growing clammy with sweat. It was impossible. Impossible. But there it was.

"Humans of Corellia!" the man in the holovid said, and that was enough to evoke another gasp from everyone in the office. The man had Han's voice as well. "I am the Hidden Leader of the Human League of Corellia, and I do now hereby reveal myself to you. Many of you may well have known there was a Hidden Leader, even if you did not know who had the honor to hold the post. That person is myself. My name is Thrackan Sal-Solo."

Leia looked at the screen in astonishment. "Han—that man. He's—"

"He's my cousin," Han said, his voice flat, bitter, angry. Suddenly the past that he thought he had escaped had caught up with him again. "My first cousin, my father's sister's son," he went on. "He is not a nice man, to put it mildly. I thought he died years ago, before I left Corellia, back when he dropped completely out of sight." Han looked at the screen, at the face that was so like his own. "Of course," he said thoughtfully, "a few people have thought I was dead myself, now and then."

"At least it explains why that Human League mob grabbed you and then let you go," Leia said. "They must have thought you were someone doing a bad job of pretending to be him. And it was his voice on the recording."

"I should have known then," Han said. "Maybe I did know, and I didn't want to admit it."

But Thrackan Sal-Solo was still speaking. "I was once a high official in the Imperial government of this sector," he said, "and I was the designated successor to the last Diktat under the Empire, before the usurpation by the so-called New Republic. I am, therefore, the legitimate ruler of this sector, and I do here and now declare myself to be the legally appointed Diktat of Corellia.

"My trusted comrades and I have worked long and hard for this day. Now, finally, the day of our liberation from the oppressive all-species policy of the traitorous New Republic is at hand. I hereby further declare the secession of the Corellian Sector from the New Republic. From this time forward, we shall be independent, with no Republican master in power over us.

"For those of you who doubt that my colleagues and I have the power to back up these pronouncements, let me say more. About two weeks ago a supernova explosion occurred on the outskirts of the Corellian Sector. The de facto Governor-General of the New Republic government has recently been provided with convincing proof that it was the Human League who caused that explosion, and the Human League that stands ready to cause further stellar explosions if our just demands are not met."

"Wait a second!" Han protested. "The message last night told us that we weren't to tell anyone. Why is *he* telling everyone?"

"Shhh," Leia said. "We need to hear this."

"We hereby demand that the so-called New Republic commence immediate operations to deport all Drall and Selonians and other nonhumans off the planet of Corellia within thirty standard days," Sal-Solo went on. "Otherwise, we will be forced to proceed with plans for our next stellar detonation."

It was Leia's turn to object. "Is he insane?" she asked. "Even if we brought every transport in the galaxy, there wouldn't be time enough to evacuate them all. And where would we put them?"

Thrackan Sal-Solo smiled at the camera, but his eyes remained hard and flinty. "This is a day we have waited for these many years. It is now at hand. Now we can build toward freedom for all humanity in this sector, unfettered and unsullied by association with lesser species. The current disturbances will soon be under control. Your new government will be issuing new pronouncements within the next few days. The future is full of promise.'' He paused a moment, and the smile fell away from his face, leaving behind only hard-edged steel.

''And the future is ours,'' he said. ''Thank you all, and good night.''

The holovid went blank, and then filled with static—and then, suddenly, was filled with blindingly bright flares of color, while blaring, deafening sound roared from the speakers.

''Jamming!'' Han shouted over the noise. Someone shut off the holovid, and silence returned.

''It's all channels,'' one of the com techs announced. ''Everything is blanketed.''

''So that's why they could tell the people and still tell us not to tell the universe,'' Leia said. ''But if all communications are blanked out, how are we supposed to negotiate, or call in transports, for that matter?''

''I have the feeling we'll find out,'' Han said. ''But I'm not playing by his rules, anyway. I'm going to meet Kalenda in a little over an hour, and hand her a copy of the data chip we got last night, together with whatever other information we can get together. I'm going to create as big a diversion as I can and hope she can steal a ship and go for help.''

''I can't help noticing that you're not asking permission about all this,'' Leia said. ''But at least you're being straight and telling me about it,'' she said.

''Then I'll keep on being straight and say that I doubt I'll be coming back anytime soon,'' he said. ''The guy creating the diversion is usually the one who gets caught, and this time I don't think they'll let me go because I look like the boss.''

''Then we don't have much time,'' Leia said, putting her arms around him and laying her head on his shoulder.

''We never do, Princess,'' he said. ''We never do.''

CHAPTER NINETEEN

Circle Unbroken

That's not going to work," Anakin said, looking over Chewbacca's shoulder. "You'll have to go outside to fix it."

The Wookiee let out an irritated burbling noise as he traced out the burned circuit.

"Am not either," Anakin said. "I don't have to guess." He pointed to a component that Chewbacca hadn't gotten to yet. "See? This toroidal reflector went pow. *Has* to be because the starboard ion regenerator misaligned. Nothing else could do *that*."

Chewbacca moaned as he looked at the reflector. It had indeed burned out.

Q9 hovered in, irritatingly close. Chewbacca resisted the urge to throw him against the compartment. "Interesting," the droid said. "It would appear Anakin is correct. Which means there *is* no hope of reaching hyperspace until we can land and make repairs. As there is not much chance of our returning safely to Corellia, I would suggest we try to reach Drall. My master's people are there, and we have at least some hope of a peaceful reception."

Chewbacca leaned back against the bulkhead and moaned to himself. He had reached precisely the same conclusion ten minutes before. There was nothing worse than a smart-aleck droid—except for a smart-aleck droid who was right.

* * *

Kalenda watched Solo as he drove the groundcar. So far it had all gone well, in fact remarkably well considering the level of chaos in the city. They had passed any number of burning buildings, shot-up vehicles, and dead bodies. But there did not seem to be many people willing to be out after dark, and Solo knew the city well. He could thread them through the back streets, away from the looters and the rioters and the goon squads.

She looked again at the data chip she was to carry back. It contained a copy of the threat message, along with whatever other information the staff of the Governor's office could think of to include. A little blob of black, the size of her thumb. Strange that something so small and unimportant looking could be so vital. If the Human League meant what it said about more supernovas, millions of lives might depend on her getting through. She slipped it back and sealed it into the pocket of her jacket.

"We're almost there," Han said. "You ready?"

"More or less," she said. "As ready as I'm going to be." But there was more she had to say. "Captain Solo, I just wanted to say that—that I'm sorry I got your family into this."

"You didn't," Solo said, his eyes still on the road ahead. "You tried to give us the clearest warning you could, and we didn't listen to it. I think we would have come here no matter what you said. All you did was make us a bit more careful. You did right. And you did well."

"Thank you," she said. "That means more coming from you than you can imagine. I hope—" She stopped, knowing she had said too much.

"You hope what?" he asked.

"I hope that your family comes out of this all right. I'm sorry. That's awfully personal. But I spent so long watching them, keeping an eye on them—"

"It's all right," he said. "Thank you for saying it. I hope they come out of it all right, too."

"Thank you, sir. It's—it's been an honor to serve with you."

Solo took his eyes off the road for the first time and smiled at her, a kindly, gentle expression. "Likewise, Lieutenant. Likewise." He turned his eyes back toward the road. "But we're getting close to the spaceport. Where's this turnoff of yours?"

"Just up ahead," she said. "It's barely a dirt road—there it is!"

The groundcar swerved onto the turnoff and bounced along the washed-out road. "Keep going, keep going—okay, slow down," she said. "Shut off all your lights and stop here for a moment."

Han stopped the engine. Kalenda grabbed her macrobinoculars and got out, gesturing for Han to follow her. She dropped to her knees and crawled up a low rise to her left—and promptly cut her arm on the same old patch of razor grass. "This is the place, all right," she said to Han, who had managed to get to the top of the rise without self-injury. She laughed quietly to herself.

"What?" Han asked. "What is it?"

"Full circle," she said. "This is where I watched to see you come in, and here you are in the same spot to see me go out."

"It's a bigger circle than that," he replied. "We finally get to use the original plan. I draw all the attention by making a lot of noise, and give you a chance to do your job."

"Well, let's hope it works the second time around," Kalenda said, and then turned back to the business at hand. "Anyway, this is the closest you can get to the perimeter fence. See it there, just below us, about a hundred meters forward?"

"Right," he said. "No problem. You picked out a ship yet?" he asked.

"Give me a second." She pulled out her macrobinoculars and put them to her eyes. "These things never were anything much on infrared," she said. "Let's see. No, nothing there but PPBs. No hyperdrive. Wait a second. There. An X-TIE Ugly, about five hundred meters from the fence."

"I hate Uglies," Han said, "but it's your call. You sure it'll have hyperdrive?"

"It ought to," she said. "Besides, there's nothing else out there I'd even have a chance of reaching."

"Guards?"

"One on the X-TIE, none on the PPBs. Maybe they're a little shorthanded."

"Let's hope so," he said. "And if they are, then those PPBs have a very limited future. Off I go. You just be ready to cut that fence when I come over the rise."

Kalenda pulled out her blaster. "All set now," she said.

"Then I'll see you on the other side," said Han. He gave her a jaunty salute, and then crawled backward down the hill to the groundcar.

*   *   *

Han got back into the groundcar, and made sure his own blaster was at the ready and the miniature thermal detonators were within easy reach. He put on the flash goggles, and hoped they worked this time. They were supposed to respond instantaneously to any level of ambient light, but they tended to be a little persnickety. This was going to be interesting. He rechecked his seat belt, switched the lights back on, and gunned the engine hard.

The lumbering old groundcar tore its way over the rise, smashing down the stand of razor grass as it went over the top. A series of fast blaster shots flashed out from the right of the car as Kalenda shot up the section of perimeter fence directly in their path. The blaster shots were right on target, but the fence stayed up. It must have been tougher than it looked. Han floored the accelerator and aimed the groundcar straight for the fence. The car lunged down the other side of the rise, and smashed into the fence head-on. It slammed its way through, and Han fought to keep control as the car bucked and swayed over the uneven ground. Finally its wheels hit the hard tarmac of the landing field, and Han was back in control. He pointed the groundcar at the nearest PPB and floored the engine again.

A blaster shot flared out of the darkness, and struck the pavement just in front of the groundcar. Han jerked the steering wheel sideways, acting on sheer reflex, and then got back on course toward the PPB. He pulled his own blaster out and stuck it out the driver's-side door. He fired wildly in the general direction of the shot, not really expecting to hit anything. But a flare of light exploded in the middle distance as a fuel tank went up, and Han was happy to take the bonus. He was almost at the first PPB. He dropped the blaster, juggled his hands to keep one on the wheel while he reached for a minidetonator with the other. He flicked the safety off the little bomb, slowed long enough to toss it in the general direction of the patrol boat, and then accelerated, having no desire to be too close when that thing went off.

Baroom! The detonator went up with a flash of light that the goggles handled perfectly, darkening down in the blink of an eye. The goggles cleared, and Han risked a glance behind him. Yes indeed, the detonator had taken the PPB with it, and judging by the size of the crater, the ground-car had come close to joining the party as well.

Han looked back toward the fence, and spotted a small figure, dressed in black, running for all she was worth, straight for the X-TIE.

"Go!" he shouted, though she could not possibly hear him. "Go!"

Bits of flaming PPB were starting to drop out of the sky all around him, and he wove back and forth across the tarmac, struggling to avoid them all.

Fwap! Another blaster bolt, but this one hit his ground-car right in the engine. The vehicle instantly burst into flame, and Han decided it was time to be elsewhere. With the groundcar still rolling, he let go of the wheel. He grabbed his blaster in one hand, scooped up the rest of the minidetonators and tossed them in his pocket with the other, then undid his seat belt and popped the door.

He rolled out of the groundcar and landed hard on his pocketful of detonators. He got to his feet, and trotted forward as best he could, using the rolling, burning, smoking groundcar for cover as he headed for the next PPB. He pulled out the next detonator, set it for a longer delay, and rolled it gently toward the patrol boat.

Shorthanded or not, the spaceport guards were starting to respond. Han could see the lights of vehicles heading toward him, and airborne PPBs coming in. More blaster fire struck to his right, and he fired back as he dove.

The second detonator went up, but it must have rolled past the PPB. The explosion merely set this one on fire, rather than destroying it.

Han glanced toward the X-TIE just in time to see a slight figure scrambling into it.

He decided to get rid of the little nasties and stop worrying about causing maximum damage. He pulled out his last three, punched in the timer studs, and threw them as far as he could, one in every direction but that of the X-TIE.

The triple explosion was too much for the flash goggles, and they blacked out altogether and did not clear. Han peeled them off, and watched, with a smile on his face, as the X-TIE Ugly flew directly over his head and headed for the sky. No way the PPBs could catch that thing with a *real* pilot in it.

The spaceport guards were starting to converge. A spotlight from an approaching security hovercar caught Han in its beam. He laughed, threw down his blaster, put his hands over his head, and waited for them to come and get him.

Mission accomplished.

*   *   *

They had found an emergency stairwell that wasn't too full of debris, and managed to clear it far enough for Leia to get up to the fifteenth floor of Corona House.

Early in the day these apartments had been the home to

her family, and her family had all been there, safe and together. Now, now they were all gone, scattered to the four winds, and the apartment was a darkened, ruined shell of a place, with the cold wind coming in through the broken windows.

But from here, she could see the spaceport. With a good strong set of macrobinoculars, she could see the flares of the explosions, the flicker of blaster fire, the duller flame of burning ships. She could even see the X-TIE getting away into the sky.

But she could not see Han.

And she knew she might never see him again.

* * *

The X-TIE shuddered its way up into the sky, the crude crossbreed of a ship threatening to come apart at the seams at any moment. Belindi Kalenda hung on for dear life and forced the wretched thing up into the sky, out of the atmosphere, and out into the depths of space. She could see now why this sort of chop-job ship was called an Ugly.

But at least this particular Ugly had an absolutely standard hyperspace drive and navicomputer. At long last she had the X-TIE up out of the atmosphere. She set it on a course that would keep it flying while she did the jump calculations for the run to Coruscant.

She frowned at the readings the navicomputer was giving her. Something was not quite right. The gravimetric background readings were way too high, and growing stronger even as she watched. Not strong enough to stop her jumping into hyperspace, but they would be soon. She had never seen a reading like that, except around an interdiction ship in training exercises.

And who would have an interdiction ship out here?

Kalenda compensated as best she could for the heightened readings, and made ready for the jump to hyperspace. She turned flight control over to the navicomputer and hung on.

The lightspeed engines kicked in. Starlines formed, and

the X-TIE Ugly bucked and shuddered its way into hyperspace.

* * *

One of *them*, one of the cloud of helpers and assistants who always wanted something of her, was waiting for Leia when she got back downstairs. She could see him, watching her come back in, hoping for the nod from her, the gesture that would allow him to approach. Very young, very earnest, with the inevitable datapad full of vital data in his hands. His office worker's clothes were still neat and clean, as if the whole nightmare day had never happened. Bright, energetic, relentlessly polite.

Ones like him were always waiting for her, wherever she went. The helpful people with the piece of information they wanted to give her, the people who wanted just two minutes of her time, the ones who wanted to give or get just one tiny bit of advice, and never mind that her husband and children had just been swept away from her, perhaps forever. Couldn't they give her any *peace?*

But the answer was, of course, that they could not. There was a galaxy to run, and never enough time to do it. Other people's families were in jeopardy this night, and they were trusting in Leia to put things right. She pushed her sorrow to one side and walked briskly over to the bright young technician who wanted to see her.

"Ah, good evening, ma'am."

Good in what way? she thought. But the words she spoke were at least somewhat more polite. "Good evening," she said, her tone a bit brittle. "You looked as if you wanted to see me."

"Yes, ma'am. There's something I think you need to know. I work in the com section. We're not having much luck getting through the jamming, but while I was working on that, I noticed some very strange readings on the gravimetric sensors."

"Is that supposed to mean something?" Leia asked in

acid tones, and then instantly felt guilty. "I'm sorry," she said, rubbing her forehead. "That was uncalled for. Please tell me what I need to know."

"Ah, yes, ma'am. Thank you. What it boils down to is that something seems to be disrupting realspace in the same way an interdiction ship does."

Suddenly the earnest young technician had her full attention. An interdiction ship did one thing, and one thing only—generate gravitic energy in such a way that hyperspace could not form in its vicinity. Ships inside an interdiction field could not jump to hyperspace, and ships in hyperspace that passed through an interdiction field were abruptly—sometimes violently—decanted out into normal space. "Tell me more," she said.

"Well, right now it's a fairly weak effect, but it's getting stronger by the minute, as if there were a very powerful interdiction generator just warming up very slowly. At the moment it's not enough to force a ship out of hyperspace or keep one from entering it, but it will be soon. But that's not the bad part."

"What *is* the bad part?" Leia asked.

"The size of the interdiction zone, ma'am. If this field keeps growing at the present rate, it's going to blanket the entire Corellian star system."

"The whole *system?*" Leia asked. "That's impossible. No one could generate an interdiction field that big."

"Except someone is, ma'am. And when that field reaches full strength, nothing is going to be able to get within a light-week of this star system in hyperspace. We're going to be cut off from the outside." The young technician put down his datapad, knit his fingers awkwardly together, and he looked away from Leia, down at a corner of the floor. For the first time the fear in his own voice came through. "It means," he said, "that we're not going to get any help."

*   *   *

Leia Organa Solo found a place to be alone in an empty,

windowless conference room across from the Governor-General's office. It was a good place for her, just then, for from there she could not see the sky, or the spaceport, or the stars that were suddenly so much farther away.

Her family was lost to her, lost to the depths of space. The Corellian System, in a single day, had somehow found a way to backslide into the worst sort of irrational species hatred, the sort of thing that should have been left in the slime a thousand generations before. Neighbor was turned against neighbor in a three-way fight that could only grow more vicious as the wounds cut deeper. And the Corellian Sector had seceded from the New Republic in a way that could only tempt others to do the same. She knew how fragile the fabric of the New Republic still was. She knew how easy it would be to tear it to shreds, how impossible it would be to put it back together.

But there were plenty of other worries besides mere politics. Where had Mara Jade gone? She had vanished. How were a bunch of thugs like the Human League capable of stealing the most secret New Republic data? How were they able to blow up stars on command? Were they truly capable of exterminating an entire living star system if they did not get their way? And who was producing this massive new interdiction field?

And they were all *counting* on her. If she made only the slightest effort, used the least of ability in the Force, she could quite literally *feel* their need, there in the Governor-General's office. They needed her, had faith in her, believed that she would find the way out of this for all of them.

And she did not have the least idea what to do next.

Leia reached down, deep into herself, into the power of the Force, and searched for the strength that would let her hang on.

*   *   *

Luke Skywalker made his way back to the control cabin of the *Lady Luck* and sat down in the copilot's seat.

"Almost there," Lando said, glancing up from his seat at the pilot's station.

"Good," Luke said, strapping himself in. "It'll be good to see Han and Leia and the kids again."

Lando looked over and grinned wolfishly. "It'll be even better to cut some nice big deals at that trade summit."

Luke laughed. "If only it were that easy," he said. "Then maybe—"

Suddenly the *Lady Luck* shuddered violently from stem to stern, and went into a violent tumble as half a dozen alarms sounded at once. "Luke!" Lando shouted as he wrestled with the attitude controls. "It's an interdiction field! It's knocked us out of hyperspace. Shut down the hyperdrive motors before they burn out!"

Luke reached out and shut down the hyperdrive, silencing most of the alarms. Lando pulled the ship out of its tumble and hit a series of reset commands, quieting the last of the alerts.

Luke let his friend work. He could sense something, a huge and powerful disturbance in the Force. He closed his eyes and reached out with his Force senses.

"What was *that?*" Lando demanded, when he finally had the ship put to rights. "What maniac would put an interdiction field way out here in the middle of nowhere?"

"Not out here," Luke said as he opened his eyes. "In there." He pointed through the viewscreen toward the still-distant point of light that was the star Corell, at least two months' travel away at sublight speeds. "It's very weak, and very subtle, but I can feel the way it interacts with the Force. We've just hit the fringes of an interdiction field that covers the whole Corellian star system."

"Are you nuts?" Lando asked. "No one could build an interdiction field that big. No one."

"Well someone has," Luke said. "It's here. We've just run into the edge of it."

Luke reached out again, this time trying not to sense the shape of a field in space, but the feel of the minds in the Corellian System. He did not try to reach any one mind, but instead to get some overall sense of emotion. Even at this extreme range, he ought to be able to get something. But the power of what he got back astonished him. Hate, fear, revenge, anger, terror—all the dark emotions were running wild in the minds of the Corellian System.

"Lando," Luke said, "turn this ship around. We're not more than a few hundred kilometers inside the interdiction field. Fly us back out of the interdiction field in normal space, and then set a lightspeed course for Coruscant. We need to go for help. Now."

Lando seemed about to protest, but then he stopped. "You're right," he said. "You're absolutely right." He took up the controls, and began turning the ship around.

"Hurry, Lando," Luke said.

Luke looked out the viewport again, to the gleaming light of Corell. "Hurry," he said again.

"I've got a bad feeling about this."

TO BE CONTINUED

ABOUT THE AUTHOR

Roger MacBride Allen was born in 1957 in Bridgeport, Connecticut. He graduated from Boston University in 1979. The author of a dozen science fiction novels, he lived in Washington, D.C., for many years. In July 1994, he married Eleanore Fox, a member of the U.S. Foreign Service. Her current assignment takes them to Brasilia, Brazil, where they will live for the next two years.

STAR WARS®